I0665579

FORWARD TO CAMELOT:
THE FINAL EDITION

SUSAN SLOATE
KEVIN FINN

COVFEFE PRESS

FORWARD TO CAMELOT: THE FINAL EDITION

Published by Covfefe Press

This novel is a work of fiction. Any resemblance to actual persons, living or dead, is entirely coincidental. The characters, names, plots and incidents are the product of the authors' imagination. References to actual events, public figures, locales or businesses, are included only to give this work of fiction a sense of reality.

Copyright © 2024, by Susan Sloate & Kevin Finn.

All rights reserved; no part of this book may be reproduced, stored in a retrieval system, or transmitted by any means, electronic, mechanical, photocopying, recording, or otherwise, without prior written consent from the authors.

Photo Credit for cover image of John F. Kennedy to Ted Speigel, White House photo circa 1962.

ISBN 979-8-218-31833-8

Content

ONCE AGAIN…
To Colin & Kenny
and
Emily & Nick

You are the future

PART ONE
IN THE WINGS

OCTOBER 2000

"We celebrate the past to awaken the future."
--President John F. Kennedy

Chapter One

October 2000

Six seconds can make such a difference.

I felt no pulse, heard no heartbeat, only the steady whoosh of my own breath as I administered mouth-to-mouth resuscitation. The face of the man on the floor was whitening by the second. His beautiful blue eyes, those eyes which could dance with laughter or light with love, were half-closed, his body limp.

He wasn't responding.

Behind me, his mother cried out, "For God's sake, help him!"

I had done everything I knew how to do. We lived in a small town. The closest hospital was twenty miles away. He would never last out the trip. Yet even with hope lost, I continued CPR in a steady rhythm.

"No pulse," my partner Cole announced, grimly looking up at Peter's parents from his knees. "I'm sorry—"

"No!" I insisted. "Just a little longer!" I wouldn't let Cole say it, wouldn't let myself admit it. I couldn't let Peter die. I loved him.

Cole took my wrist gently, to stop me from ministering further. I shook his hand free and continued my dogged rhythm. "I can't lose him again," I said desperately.

Though Cole loved me himself, he knew I wouldn't stop loving Peter, not even when he had dumped me at the altar and run off with my best friend.

"Sheila," he said in despair. "Sheila, you can't save the entire world."

I ignored him and kept working. Keep it going... just... a little... longer...

I felt it before I saw it. An indefinable something had changed. I was beginning to sense... a faint pulse.

His mother bent over him with that maternal instinct that seems to supersede all other knowledge. "Peter? Peter, baby?"

Then we heard another sound, like a muffled roar. It was coming from the hallway...

"Fire!" Cole shouted, leaping to his feet. Flames climbed up the outside of the windows. Smoke billowed in from beneath the doors. "The whole floor's on fire!"

"The Amantis!" the husband gasped. "They swore revenge for Peter's testimony."

"My God, they're going to kill us all!" Peter's mother screamed.

"Everybody out!" Cole ordered, kicking open the library doors. He herded Peter's mother through them, past the building inferno. "Hurry!"

Flames raced across the carpet, engulfing the heavy drapes at every window.

"Sheila! I said out!" Cole cried. "You can't save him now!"

"I've got a pulse!" I looked up at Cole with new hope. "You've got to take him out," I said urgently.

It was a miracle. After months of estrangement, Peter and I could be together again. Despite what Cole said, I had saved him. Whether through love or skill, he had come back to me.

I wanted to cry tears of joy, but I couldn't. Other women cried. I couldn't seem to loosen the logjam of emotion to shed tears for anything. And, I thought reluctantly, it's impossible to cry when there's no one you can trust to hold you and be stronger than you are. Maybe that was the real root of the problem.

"You get out too!" Cole said. "You've got to get out now!"

Peter's mother had already gotten to safety, but as I turned, my eye caught Michael, Peter's father. Overcome by smoke, he had fallen behind the sofa. If I didn't get him out, in a minute or so, it would be too late.

"I'll get Michael," I told Cole. "You take Peter. Hurry!"

Cole looked at me in anguish. "You can't bring him out alone."

The longer we argued, the longer Peter's escape would be delayed. "Take him, Cole! Now!"

Cole snatched up Peter's limp body and darted through the doorway to safety. I grabbed Michael, hoisted him under the arms and dragged him across the room. The smoke was so thick it was hard to see. Cole reached out for Michael's ankles and yanked him through the doorway. I started to follow, only to be driven back by a wall of flame leaping across the opening. All around me, thick flame and thicker smoke blocked every exit.

Cole cried out my name in horror.

Another voice, high and male, yelled, "Cut! That's a wrap, folks."

In an instant, the smoke and flames vanished in a special-effects haze, and the bright, heavy lights above us were turned off.

It was Friday afternoon at 3:30 on the soundstage, the end of another week of taping *The Wind and the Stars*, the network's most popular daytime drama. I was well into my twelfth year playing Sheila, the smart, resourceful and courageous paramedic who'd fought to save lives in the jungles of Central America and then fought for love in the small town she'd recently returned to. I considered it the best acting job I'd ever had.

Actually, it was the only acting job I'd ever had.

Cole, actually an egomaniacal actor named Phil, walked off without sparing me a glance, as usual. The director stopped me as I stepped off the set. "You okay, Cady?"

"Fine, Mitch. No problem."

"Good girl." He was relieved of his responsibility to me, which consisted mostly of thanking me for doing most of my own stunts and making sure I had no bodily damage afterward. After that, Mitch usually turned his attention to bullying the camera crew. Today, however, he had more important pursuits in mind.

"Let's go, Mets!" he shouted across the set, pumping his fist in the air. A chorus of raucous boos drowned him out. The entire camera crew wore pinstriped Yankees jerseys and midnight blue caps with the interlocking "NY" logo. Mitch and the crew had been taunting each other all week about the Subway Series, the all-New York World Series which started tonight.

I had more on my mind than baseball.

"Cady! Good job!"

I shielded my eyes with my hand to shut out the glare and turned instinctively toward a familiar voice. As the studio lights dimmed, I saw Craig beaming at me, flipping shut his cell phone with one hand, the other hand waving me over impatiently.

I felt cold inside.

I hadn't seen Craig in eight months, since before our divorce became final.

Though still my agent, he had moved to the West Coast, settling in with a high-flying talent agency in Beverly Hills and taking on a whole new level of client since we'd parted. I'd heard he tooled around town in a chocolate Mercedes and only dated up-and-coming actresses on his agency's list.

I hadn't found anyone to date. Worse, I seemed to have no desires at all. I wondered if it was possible I would never want to make love again.

It was a question I tried not to ask myself. When I did, I told myself that Craig and I hadn't yet worked out a new relationship. Until we came to terms with our new status, I didn't believe I would meet anyone.

I didn't want Craig back, but I couldn't yet imagine being with anyone else. Yet he seemed to have made a new life quite easily, a life he clearly loved.

So why was he here?

I should have known.

"Get changed quick," he said, hustling me into the stairwell leading to my dressing room on the second floor. "We've got a meeting with Gail Carroll in twenty minutes."

I felt a familiar exasperation. "Craig, you could have called me!" But I also felt a slight chill: Why was he coming with me to meet the show's newest producer?

"Busy, busy …" Flipping open his ringing cell phone, he became immediately engaged in a new conversation.

"Same old Craig," I said dryly. "You're looking well."

He was. The L.A. sun had bleached his light-brown curls lighter, with just the hint of a sun-kissed glow on his face. He sported a new gold Rolex and when he smiled, it wasn't the tight, humorless grin I remembered but a quick flash of artificially white teeth and a hint of sparkle in the eyes. Life in the fast lane in L.A. clearly agreed with him.

To my surprise, he followed me into my dressing room, motioning me to get dressed while arguing gross and net points on his phone. I sighed. We weren't married anymore, but I couldn't figure out how to tell him to wait outside. He clicked on the radio I kept on my dressing table. Some jerk was sharply criticizing last night's televised debate between Presidential candidates George W. Bush and Al Gore. I twisted the dial sharply, turning it off. This was my territory, not his.

I hung up my paramedic jumpsuit. In the early years, when Sheila had been a Red Cross volunteer in a fictitious South American country, I'd bounced between hideous dark brown overalls and glamorous short shorts and cotton halters. Now, with Sheila back home, I usually wore a simple, professional uniform, which I preferred. Sometimes, I even preferred it to my own clothes.

Friday was not the best day for me to meet new producers. By Friday I had gone through my favorite clothes and was reduced to wearing whatever was clean. Unlike other actresses, I did not keep an extensive personal wardrobe. I knew people around the studio thought I was cheap. One malicious rumor even said I deliberately dressed badly, in order to shame the producers into giving me Sheila's cast-off clothes as a gift.

I saw no reason to tell them the truth.

Today I had thrown on a soft gray sweater and slim gray slacks, which to me enhanced my light-brown, chin-length hair and fair skin and highlighted my gray eyes. I wore the same plain watch I'd worn for five years and the small gold hoop earrings Craig had given me before we were married.

I've been told more than once that I look younger than I am. I'm 36, but can play as young as 23. It had been a boost to my career when I'd been hired at 24 to play the seventeen-year-old Sheila. When meeting producers, though, it helped to look older. More settled, more powerful.

Couldn't be helped.

In twelve years, I'd lived through five producers. I considered myself a team player. I came in on time, knew my lines and didn't cause trouble. The meeting had to be little more than a formality.

Then why was Craig here? In fact, how did he know about the meeting when I hadn't?

He ended his call as I finished hooking my belt. "Cady! I thought we agreed you'd spend more on your clothes."

I shrugged. "Sorry. I'm behind on laundry."

"Good God, Cady, think dry cleaning! Don't wash it yourself, send it out!"

Craig never stopped nagging me to equate my lifestyle with my salary. Perhaps to calm himself, he glanced around the dressing room, trimmed in my favorite peach accents, past the big colorful travel posters of places I'd never visited, to the row of photographs I'd set along a counter. A picture of my mother and me at my college graduation, a rare photo of us smiling at each other; a picture of me posed as Sheila in my very first costume from my very first day. There was a space between the photos, where I used to keep a framed photo of Craig and me on our wedding day, eight endless years ago.

That gap, to me, symbolized many gaps in my life. Blaming Craig was a past reflex, now inappropriate. I said quietly, "Craig, you know where the money goes."

He sighed. "Still?" I nodded. "How is she?"

"The same. She'll always be the same. The latest project is redoing her house to resemble her old house in Dallas. It's costing me a fortune, but as long as she's happy … you know."

He contemplated me for a moment. "I've got a great new shrink in L.A. He says it's not about anyone else's happiness, it's about your own."

"Great. If I could afford it, I might try him myself."

Craig shrugged. He knew I'd never been in therapy and didn't plan to start, and I didn't like the way he was looking at me—as though he actually pitied me.

"Come on," I said. "Let's go see Gail Carroll."

*   *   *

Gail Carroll was slender and severe—a military-cut, fitted black suit; high-heeled designer shoes; a Rolex but no wedding ring, standing ramrod straight behind her desk. Through the window behind her, I saw a lustrous carpet of red and gold leaves spread across the visible treetops of Central Park, heralding fall.

"Catherine Cuyler," she said, in the smoky, sultry voice of a young Lauren Bacall. But I'd have bet my last Emmy nomination that sex wasn't her weapon of choice. She looked at Craig. "And Craig Bronkle, I presume. I'm Gail Carroll." She nodded us to the chairs in front of her. "Well, Catherine, as I told Mr. Bronkle on the phone, we have to make some changes."

This wasn't my idea of a good beginning. In fact, it sounded downright ominous. I'm sure Craig felt the stare I turned on him. Why had he been on the phone with our new producer before I even met her?

Gail Carroll, not noticing my discomfort, shuffled through a stack of papers on her desk. "No wonder the network decided to bring me in. These numbers are frightening."

"Excuse me. I thought our ratings were generally excellent."

Craig elbowed me. I was supposed to let him do the talking, but I was curious: What could Gail Carroll do that our last producer couldn't?

"I'm not talking about ratings." She paused to re-stack the papers into a knife-edged pile. "I'm talking about market research."

"What?"

"We ran some focus groups," she said impatiently. "These are the results." She looked me squarely in the eye. "Apparently the character of Sheila is—threatening—to women."

"Threatening?" My eyebrows rose. "Women find Sheila threatening?"

Gail Carroll read from a sheet on her desk. "She's 'too competent, too attractive, too idealized for real women to relate to. Can look glamorous anywhere while preserving her sense of self, yet still accepted by everyone.' Sheila is also 'hot', 'sexy', and 'everything a woman should be', according to the men we surveyed." She put the sheet down, placing herself directly before me. "Real women find that hard to live up to. They resent her."

I knew I looked as bewildered as I felt. "But she's not real. She's a character on a daytime drama, for heaven's sake."

"Doesn't matter," Gail Carroll said with a freezing smile, "when the audience sees her that way. Unfortunately, only six percent of our viewing audience is male. So the females are the ones we want to keep, anchor and add to. Having a top female character who threatens them is not the way to do it.

"On the other hand," she continued, seeing the look on my face, "just changing Sheila's character won't cut it. It's sweeps next month, and I'm going to make this sweeps our biggest ever. We need a big event to get people interested and talking about us again. And we need to heavily feature those characters our audience can relate to."

She paused and laid it out for me. "So our big event will be Sheila's death."

Sheila was going to die. But I was Sheila! I was so stunned I couldn't think what to say.

Craig jumped in. "We've anticipated this, and frankly I'm relieved my client will be free. We have some serious interest in her services."

I almost groaned aloud. Now was not the time for phony Hollywood hype! I needed Craig to fight for my job, the one I knew, the only one I wanted. I would work for scale, if I could just persuade this ratings witch to go along!

Gail Carroll nodded. "Of course. We wouldn't want to stand in her way." The standard goodbye line in the business. I wanted to weep. "Catherine's made a fine contribution to the show, and we wish her the very best. We'll pay off her contract, of course, and add that bonus we talked about, Mr. Bronkle. I think, given the lack of notice, it's the least we can do."

Craig smiled at her, a genuine phony Hollywood smile, and rose smoothly to his feet. "Thank you, Ms. Carroll. I was sure you would understand how a creative actress like Cady would feel about letting go of a part she'd originated."

More Hollywood garbage. I really had to say something, at this point. "I assume you have a plan to kill Sheila off."

Ms. Carroll looked surprised. "In the fire, of course," she said. "It's dramatic, it's in character—so brave and heroic—besides, we've just shot it."

"And afterwards?" I asked. "Hospital scenes—deathbed— do I get some big last speech?"

Again, Ms. Carroll looked surprised. "Sheila dies in the fire, don't you see? What you shot today are your last scenes." She paused, a flush mounting her face. "I assumed you two had discussed this."

Craig cut in easily, smiling like a barracuda. "I thought it would be better for Cady to hear it from you."

They were both in on it, in collusion. I felt sick.

I was so numb, I don't even remember leaving the office. I recall vaguely hearing Gail Carroll's request that I vacate my dressing room immediately and thanking me again for my services to the show. Then we were out.

It really didn't seem possible that I'd walked in to meet a producer and ended up losing my job, and that the one person I'd thought was unquestionably on my side had gone over to the enemy without the smallest signal to me. Or had he signaled, and I hadn't recognized it for what it was?

"That went just great," Craig enthused as we got beyond the secretary's inquisitive ears. "Now we can take the next big step."

I hadn't been able to think of a good exit line for my producer, but I had a knockout line for my agent: "You're fired," I said.

Chapter Two
October 2000

The next hour was a nightmare.

I returned to my dressing room, feeling dazed and sick, to find the show's two uniformed security officers waiting at the door. They let me know, uncomfortably but officiously, that they were there to help me pack my personal belongings, preparatory to moving out.

I felt sicker. Twelve years, and the studio thought I was going to make off with the contents of my dressing room?

A pile of empty cartons, already assembled, awaited me in the center of the room. This firing was choreographed better than some of the scenes I'd played recently.

I packed quickly, automatically, my hands trembling, the security guards watching to make sure I took only what was mine, checking everything I stuck in the cartons.

I parked my blue Beetle in a No-Parking zone right in front of the studio doors and carried out all the boxes myself, disdaining the guards' offer to help. Twelve years' work. Even stuffed in a Beetle, it didn't look like much. I wanted to cry, but as usual, tears didn't come easily to me, which is why they hadn't come easily to Sheila. In fact, I couldn't remember the last time I'd cried, over anything. As much as I needed the relief of tears today, I knew I wasn't going to get it.

I finished loading the trunk and banged it shut. I swung myself into the driver's seat and saw Craig coming toward my car. He'd waited for me. It took more than being given the boot by a client to make him give up.

"Cady, come on. We've got a contract. You're not going to fire me. Look, I know I should have called you. But I figured I could tell you on the way—"

"—Tell me I was being fired on the way to Gail Carroll's office? That's your idea of tact?" I could feel my voice rising to a shout; from being numb with shock before, I was rapidly becoming furious. "Collude with her to get me thrown out in the street?"

"I wouldn't do that to you, Cady, I swear. *I've got a plan for you.*" He leaned in the window. "Give me a lift, will you? I've got a meeting at 6:00."

"Take a cab." I turned the key in the ignition.

Craig crossed in front of the Beetle with quick strides, yanked open my passenger door and planted himself in the seat next to me, pulling the door closed. "Let's try again. We have a meeting at 6:00—with your new producer, John Staub."

I sat very still behind the wheel.

"I know you've heard of him," Craig went on, unperturbed. "I probably should have mentioned that up front, about how John Staub contacted me *personally* to hire you for the biggest project in his company right now, so big that he's supervising it himself. He also said he needed you at once and that he was willing to pay triple—did you hear me, Cady?—*triple* your previous salary. Oh, and did I mention that you're playing the lead, with all the perks, of course … am I getting through to you?"

John Staub. The Hollywood special-effects genius who had revolutionized the F/X industry with his vision and brilliance. If you had an 'A' picture that needed top-notch special effects, you went to Staub Enterprises, hat in hand, hoping they could somehow fit you in.

It wasn't likely. Their waiting lists were filled two years in advance. Their prices were astronomical—ten minutes of their effects in a picture could cost a third of the entire production budget. Their work won Oscars every single year. Every major Hollywood production boasted of special effects by Staub Enterprises, and to have your production supervised by John Staub personally could cost up to fifty percent extra. He was the top of the line.

And Staub had asked for me, in his own production? Staub wasn't a producer, so what was he producing, and why had he asked for me, a minor soap-opera actress? The words fell crazily on my ears, like an over-chiming clock.

It had to be some kind of macabre West Coast joke, but I didn't get it. But what else could it be?

"Since when is John Staub a producer, instead of an F/X guy?" "Since now, babe. He's branching out. You want to bet against him?"

Craig's cell phone rang. He whipped it out. "Craig Bronkle." His eyes widened. "Oh—yes, Mr. Staub. Yes—just a minute—"

Craig snapped his fingers at me. Out of habit, I dug a notepad and pen from my purse and held them out. He scribbled for a moment. "Yes, we know the area—she'll be there shortly—wonderful—thanks."

He hung up, handing the pad and pen back. "Slight change of plans. You're going to Larchmont." He'd written down the address.

"Larchmont?" I repeated. "I thought Staub's company was based in White Plains."

"You're meeting one of the associate producers in Larchmont. You're to go out there right now, and watch the speed limit, Cady." Trust an ex-husband to remind you of your imperfections.

Larchmont would be easy. I lived in Tarrytown, in mid-Westchester County, which was northwest of Larchmont, where I'd grown up. It would be on my way home.

Craig swung himself out of the car and shut the door.

"You're not coming with me?" I asked.

"Staub wants to meet with me privately, here in town," Craig explained loftily, doing his best not to look smug and failing miserably. "You're to meet a guy named George. He'll probably give you a script. Call me afterward, and I'll finish the deal. You're *in*, Cady. Staub just told me you're the only actress they're considering for this. This is your big break."

I looked at the pad. Craig had scribbled "Coup D'Etat Ltd." and a street address in the commercial section of the village. I'd have no trouble finding it, even in the dark. I could stop by my mother's house on the way home; she lived only ten minutes away.

For the first time that day, my cell phone rang.

"Forget it," Craig said sharply as I made a motion to answer. "Let it go to voicemail. You've got to get to that meeting. And stay sharp, Cady. You need this job."

I thought of several pungent responses but said nothing. However, I did take childish satisfaction in gunning the Beetle in a tight circle that missed Craig's shins by less than an inch.

* * *

The drive to Larchmont started on the traffic-choked West Side Highway, which never cleared until I passed under the George Washington Bridge, onto the snaking roads of the Henry Hudson Parkway. As city skyline became suburban parkway, and more and more trees, shedding crisp brown leaves, swayed in the October wind along the road, I thought about the last few hours. From steady employment to sudden unemployment, to being the only contender for a leading part in a top-notch production … and Craig's unexpected re-appearance on top of everything … it was just too much for a Friday. I'd had whole years where this much hadn't happened to me.

I tried not to think about my mother along the way, but worrying about her was reflexive. Being unemployed meant more than worry about my finances. It meant worry about hers. I had helped out for years with her household expenses.

My mother was not a thrifty woman. She spent fortunes on trifles. If this job didn't work out, I could see my unemployment checks melting like ice cream in the sun before my mother's formidable shopping habits.

I'd tried to explain to her a few months ago why she shouldn't buy six pairs of Italian pumps, at $250 per.

My mother had pursed her mouth. "Cady, just because you dress like a ragamuffin doesn't mean I have to." She didn't like my frugal shopping habits, which had developed in self-defense because of the percentage of my paycheck that I was handing her every month. I had learned to shop for bargains, and when I wanted something extravagant that I couldn't find for less, I let it go by. Unfortunately, my mother didn't, and shopping was only a temporary fix for her pain.

I had always wished she could wash out some of the pain by loving me, her only child. But it had never quite worked out that way. She stood beside me dutifully in photographs and smiled at me with her mouth muscles. She didn't watch my TV show, as she hadn't attended my college theatrical productions. She saw no need. She was still busy with her own grief.

I'd tried hard as a child to win her love, by watching and helping her and being with her through her difficult November moods. I'd hoped for hugs but instead had gotten locked bedroom doors and shouted admonitions to leave her alone. I'd worked to earn high grades so she might be tempted to drop a kiss on my hair. She had hardly bothered to read my report cards.

I married Craig eight years ago because he offered such a dazzling display of affection and attention, something I was thoroughly unused to but had craved for years. I had basked in his demonstrativeness, which disappeared approximately a year after our wedding. When it was gone, we didn't have much left between us. I knew now I had married Craig seeking the warmth I'd never felt from my mother.

All I'd ever really wanted was for her to tell me she loved me.

She never had.

Coup D'Etat Ltd. was a small bookstore set between two other equally small stores at the end of a strip mall I'd passed absent-mindedly for years. The glass display window held a rack of thick books with lurid titles and garish covers, like *I Spied for the CIA and Assassination Folklore*, both spotted with red (for blood, I guessed). The store billed itself as 'the center of conspiracy theories in America'.

This was where a special-effects-genius-slash-budding-film-producer hung out?

Inside, the lights had been switched on. I did a quick breathing exercise to nerve myself, turned the knob on the blood-red door and walked in.

I got exactly four steps inside.

"Cady Cuyler?" asked a male voice.

From behind a packed bookcase set at a slanted angle on the floor stepped a man in his '60s, though he looked vibrant and energetic, even at dusk. Easily over six feet, his posture was sloppy, and the very slight swelling of his stomach was accented by the hunching of his shoulders. His clothes were good but rumpled and oddly matched: Gray slacks with brown shirt and ivory sweater under a leather aviator jacket, the leather so old it was cracking. *This was a man,* I thought, *who was comfortable with himself, but definitely a little off.*

He beamed at me and came over to shake my hand. "I'm George. Happy to meet you. I've been studying your work for a long time."

"Thank you," I said tentatively, but already feeling more comfortable. This man was so friendly and relaxed that I already knew the meeting would be all right.

"Come in, come in. We can talk in the back." He locked the door behind me. I walked with him past endless rows of bookshelves, all neatly tagged with handwritten labels: "JFK Assassination", "Lincoln Assassination", "RFK Assassination", and other labels I didn't understand: "Mongoose", "MK/ULTRA", "Paperclip", and more.

To me, a bookstore focused entirely on political murders and conspiracies seemed a ridiculous waste of time and retail space. But to each his own, I thought. I was here because they had a job to offer me. I'd keep my opinions to myself. If he was willing to pay triple my previous salary, I guessed someone was buying those books in the window.

George moved remarkably fast for a man with a head of solid salt-and-pepper hair; I was almost skipping to keep up. He motioned me to one of the comfortable-looking chairs by a round oak table along the back wall. It was the second time today I'd been offered a seat in a strange office; in the last one, I'd lost my job.

No matter what, this meeting had to be better, I decided optimistically. I sat down and waited.

"Smoke?" he asked. I shook my head. "Mind if I do?" I did mind, but it was his shop. I shook my head again.

He lit a Salem from a pack lying open on the table, and puffed like an addict, drawing in long, deep breaths and holding the smoke in. Then he smiled. "Don't worry. John doesn't smoke, and if I die, he'll still carry on with the project... I understand you majored in American history in college."

I started, both at the swift change of subject and the topic. No one had ever asked me about my college career during casting. It was an odd way to start an interview.

"Yes, I did," I answered after some hesitation.

"Then you switched to drama?"

"Well, I got my degree in history. I took a drama class for a humanities requirement and liked it."

"And apparently, were good at it. Then what happened?"

"I took more classes and did little theater, and eventually the job came up at—" I swallowed, "at—*The Wind and the Stars, and*—"

George nodded, puffing away. "I understand that job is about to end."

"Wrong tense," I said shakily. "It ended today."

"Well, fine. John was prepared to buy out your contract there. He'll be pleased."

Buy out my contract? What kind of money did these people have, and why were they so willing to spend it on me? As actresses go, I wasn't unique in the marketplace. Sheila could have been played by literally hundreds of actresses. So why had they decided I was so special?

"This character you play—played—" George corrected himself, "—I've been watching over the last few months. She's... amazing."

"Sheila's a lot of fun." I didn't want to think at the moment of how much I would miss playing her.

George nodded. "Smart, interesting, independent... do viewers ever confuse you with her?" He asked the question as though making casual small talk.

I laughed. "All the time. They think I'm courageous and resourceful and quick-thinking and practical... I hate to tell them I'm just an actress playing a part."

He smiled at me and tapped out the ash in the cigarette. "Don't tell them. They probably wouldn't believe it anyway."

I thought of a few encounters I'd had with fans, who clustered around me for autographs and peppered me with questions about Sheila's exotic life and her romantic duels with the men she worked with. They'd asked me about my life too, about where I'd traveled, what kinds of perils I had faced. I hated to tell them that I had faced no perils and traveled to no exotic countries. In fact, far from regarding Sheila's character with derision, as other soap actors I knew did, I often felt closer to an active envy. Hers was the life I would lead if I could choose... but of course, I couldn't.

"Are you one of those people who believes life was better in the past?" George asked next, still keeping me nicely off balance.

"Yeah," I said wryly. "Like yesterday."

His eyebrows lifted, as though by themselves, though his green eyes gazed steadily at me. "Then I assume it wasn't your idea to leave the show."

"I wasn't even consulted."

He nodded gently and settled back in his chair. I could feel the shift in the atmosphere. The interview clearly was beginning.

"Well," he began. "I should start by telling you that you're our only choice for this project. We considered quite a few others, but it seems you're really the only person who can do it." He fiddled with his fingernails, deliberately looking down and away from me, as he added, "Or would be motivated to do it."

A vast relief began to flood my chest. Whether I wanted the job or not, it was comforting to know that I wouldn't have to sell myself. Apparently, they were already sold on me.

"Tell me more about yourself," he invited. "Mr. Bronkle said you lived in Westchester."

"Yes."

"And—?" he prompted. "Have you lived here a long time?"

"Pretty much all my life. Why is this relevant, George?" "You sound like you don't like talking about your private life."

"Not to a complete stranger."

"Fair enough. How about I tell you about yourself, instead?"

I looked at him. He seemed calm and straightforward, intelligent, and… normal. So why did I feel a creeping uneasiness?

He glanced down at some stapled sheets of paper in front of him. "Born Catherine Marie Cuyler in Larchmont, July, 1964. Your mother Sandra still lives in the same house you grew up in, on Rockland Avenue. Your father, Donald Cuyler, disappeared in Dallas on November 22, 1963—your parents were living there at the time—and has never been heard from again. Presumed dead."

My head came up. I fixed my eyes on him. Whatever he knew, he'd gotten from no friend or studio dossier. So where had he gotten it?

George continued. "You were raised by your mother and won full scholarships to several prestigious universities, though you chose instead to attend a local college and live at home. After college, you auditioned for Sheila on *The Wind and the Stars*—a two-week role became a twelve-year gig—married your agent, Craig Bronkle, from whom you're recently divorced, no children." He glanced at his notes. "You've been unwilling to leave your mother alone for long periods of time to promote your career— and I get the feeling Mr. Bronkle would prefer to be married to a superstar. Hence the divorce." He looked at me for confirmation, but I was feeling tight all over and breathing shallowly. George paused for a moment, then went on. "That's also why your career hasn't ever reached the level of your talent, which is considerable. And I'm just guessing now, but I believe that your mother's habit of spending large amounts of money on private detectives and whatever catches her eye in the department stores is the reason that you don't spend much yourself—you've been supporting her for years. You don't take vacations, you don't buy expensive clothes, you don't live anywhere close to your means. You deprive yourself so she can keep spending."

I could feel the flush rising from my neck to my cheeks. "All right, George, enough." I was surprised at how heated my voice was. "I don't know who the hell you are, or what you're doing, spying on me, but whatever it is you want, I'm not up for it."

I started to rise, but he stopped me, raising a hand as if to ward off my rage. I was angry and unnerved, but his expression was rueful and his eyes were kind. I had intended to bark some more reproaches about the right to privacy, even for actresses, but his eyes, fixed on me, his lips curved in a half-smile, stopped me cold. "I know this isn't a typical interview. But I had good reason for finding out about you." He waited till I stopped moving, till I was just staring at him, before he went on. "We wanted to know why you were so close to your mother, and what we learned is that your mother has been drifting in and out of serious depression for many years, and one of her symptoms is spending money like a drunken sailor." He didn't wait for a response. "And that depression is directly related to your father's disappearance on November 22, 1963." He stopped and waited for my reaction. I said nothing.

After a moment, he went on. "I think it's really quite simple: Not knowing what happened to your father has left your mother in a sort of—well—suspended animation. No human being can bear that for 37 years. It's like the families of soldiers in Vietnam who went missing and haven't been accounted for: Either you go on with your life, or you go a little crazy." Before I could protest, he went on again. "Your mother chose not to go on. It must be very hard for both of you."

I was breathing hard, as though I'd just run a mile flat out. My eyes, I knew, were wide with rage, and some fear: how could anyone learn what he had learned about me? I never discussed this with anyone. No one else knew what he knew, and he didn't even know me. Or did he?

George's eyes bore in on mine, as he leaned across the table. For the first time, I saw in his face not just casual interest, but real passion.

"Ms. Cuyler, how would you feel about… a treasure hunt?"

A treasure hunt? I had no idea what to say to that. The rule in job-seeking for actresses was always to express enthusiasm. One could always demur later.

"Sounds like fun," I offered, and realized to my own surprise that I actually meant it.

George nodded. "Ever know anyone who collected things? Stamps, coins, baseball cards?"

"I've seen some stuff on TV about it. They always seemed a little—" I wanted to say *crazy* but caught myself and settled for "—well—obsessed."

"Yes, they can be. And there's no one more obsessed than a collector who dreams of one special prize. The Holy Grail of stamps. The Mount Rushmore of baseball cards." George paused to shake ash into the tray in front of him.

I sensed where this was going. "What do you collect, George?"

He'd obviously been expecting the question. "Historic artifacts and documents. Come on, I'll show you."

He took me into a small room that might have been meant as a second conference room. When he snapped on the lights, though, I saw that the floor space was empty, except for a round table and chairs in one corner. The walls, however, were crammed with squares and rectangles, sometimes separated by less than an inch. Framed and held under glass were documents and photographs, some handwritten, others crudely typed, all bearing dark signatures. I was fascinated.

I started at one end of the room and worked my way around.

There was an entire wall of Presidential documents—letters, notes, policy memos—signed by Theodore Roosevelt, James Garfield, FDR, Abraham Lincoln, and even, set off by itself, a directive on faded parchment signed in flowing ink by George Washington. On the opposite wall were memorabilia from famous artists, composers and sports figures—photographs, Playbills, signed baseballs and footballs, sports pennants signed by entire teams.

The center wall—the most prominently displayed and lighted—contained nothing but artifacts from the Kennedy Administration.

Memos and letters, signed by President John F. Kennedy, Attorney General Robert Kennedy, Secretary of Defense Robert MacNamara, National Security Advisor McGeorge Bundy, Press Secretary Pierre Salinger. A short portion of a speech, scribbled on a yellow legal pad and then heavily lined out, bearing the initials T.S., probably for Ted Sorensen, Kennedy's Special Counsel and chief speechwriter. Tons of photographs of JFK and his Cabinet.

It was, literally, stunning.

George said nothing while I examined the collection, just smoked and waited.

When I finally turned to him, I felt as though I'd just met him afresh. It must have been apparent in my face.

"You see now, don't you?" He sat at the table and gestured to me to sit. "And you see why adding to it is important to me."

"George, what is this Holy Grail you're after?"

He gazed at me for a moment. "What do you know about John F. Kennedy?"

Another unexpected question. I fumbled for a moment. "Well—he was the 35th president; from a rich family; he was married to a gorgeous woman he cheated on all the time. His father got him out of all the scrapes he got into. A lot of show; not much substance."

George's half-smile disappeared. "You really think that?"

I shrugged. "The Kennedys are public-relations geniuses. They put most actors in the shade. I do know that Joe Kennedy, the President's father, once said, 'We'll sell Jack like soap flakes'. And they did, didn't they? Even today, people still think he was the greatest."

George cocked his head. "But you don't."

"He was a mediocre president, at best. And a thousand days in office doesn't give anyone a chance to make much impact. If he hadn't been assassinated, do you honestly think anyone would still care?"

George lit another cigarette. I got the distinct impression he was using the small movements—shaking the cigarette out of the box, putting it to his lips, puffing from his lighter—to appear calm.

It seemed to work. He faced me with that half-smile again. "And who killed him?"

"Lee Harvey Oswald," I said, a little forcefully, "despite what your shelves of books might say."

"Why are you so sure?"

"Oh, George, come on! Conspiracies are so—" I looked for the right phrase and couldn't find it. "They happen in novels and movies, not in real life, and not in this country. Why can't you just accept that some little guy, a real loser with a grudge, resented Kennedy, with his money and his good looks and his great-looking family? And decided to put him out of the picture?"

"Because," George said in an easy tone, "it doesn't make sense. Oswald, by all accounts, admired the President very much, and found his family interesting. He said so, when he was in police custody. Why kill a man you admire?"

I gave up. I should have realized, walking into a shop called Coup D'Etat Ltd., that I wouldn't be winning any arguments involving lone assassins. "Fine, George. But I don't believe in conspiracies, and you're not going to change my mind. Just tell me about the project, okay?"

George got up and went to a set of drawers built into the wall behind us, the only wall not paneled with memorabilia. He chose a drawer and opened it, extracted something, and slid it across the table to me. I turned it face up.

It was a famous photograph, one I'd seen many times. In the center of the photograph was a tall, burly man, with thinning hair slicked back, a large face, big flappy ears, right hand raised piously, facing a small brisk woman with dark hair and glasses. On the man's right, crowded next to him and seeming crushed by his vitality, was another small dark woman, her face blank with conflicting emotions.

But the man, for all his bulk and heartiness, was not the magnetic force in the photograph. The woman on his left was. Younger than anyone else, with dark glossy hair, in a bulky light suit, her profile regal even in her anguish, blood spattering her clothes, she stood watching sightlessly. Her beauty and grief drew all eyes. Her pain was almost visible on the photo itself.

"This is the swearing in of Lyndon Johnson as president on Air Force One in Dallas, on November 22, 1963. His wife is on his right. Jacqueline Kennedy stands on his left. Sarah Hughes is the judge administering the oath. John F. Kennedy had been assassinated only a couple of hours before."

"I know the photograph, George."

"Good for you. Look here." He pointed carefully at the almost invisible edges of the book under Johnson's massive hand. "Johnson, of course, needed to be sworn on a Bible. Here it is, being held by Mrs. Hughes."

"You want the Bible Johnson took the oath on?"

"I do. That Bible belonged to President Kennedy."

I looked up in surprise. "It was Kennedy's Bible? I didn't know that."

"It was the only Bible on Air Force One. Kennedy supposedly traveled everywhere with it. When they were scrambling to find a Bible—Johnson insisted on taking the oath before he left Dallas—they remembered Kennedy's Bible and used that."

"Well, can't you buy the Bible from the Kennedy family? Even though I can't imagine they'd give it up."

"Well, now, that's a problem. The Bible disappeared right after this picture was taken."

I hated to admit it, but that intrigued me. It was getting harder to remember that I'd just lost my job a few hours before. "How could it disappear?"

"Well, the story goes that Sarah Hughes actually had it in her hands when she left Air Force One in Dallas. You have to understand—that day, the whole country was in a state of shock, and people did crazy things without realizing it, half the time. Coming down the ramp, Mrs. Hughes met a man dressed in a suit and tie and sunglasses, a man she believed to be a Secret Service agent. He asked her for the Bible. I don't think she even realized she still had it in her hand. She gave it to him immediately; she thought he would return it to the Kennedy family."

He paused. I was riveted. "At least, that's what she said. But the Bible disappeared that day and was never seen again." George paused again and gave me a devilish grin. "JFK's own Bible, used to swear in Lyndon Johnson on November 22, 1963... what do you think an item like that would be worth?"

I shook my head. I couldn't imagine.

"Nobody can," he said softly. "Do you understand now? As a piece of history, part of one of the twentieth-century's most pivotal events... that Bible would be beyond price. And I intend to have it."

"But... how? If you don't know where it is? Unless... do you think Sarah Hughes actually kept it herself? And that story about an anonymous Secret Service guy was just a way to cover her tracks in case anyone asked for it back?" I was beginning to get excited about the possibilities.

He laughed out loud. "You sound like Sherlock Holmes."

I shrugged and tried not to blush. "I read a lot of mysteries... you pick things up."

He smiled. "You don't learn thinking like that. It's instinctive. I was right; you can handle our little project."

"You want me to find the Bible?"

"Not exactly. I know where it was on November 22, 1963. Sarah Hughes had it at Love Field."

"Well, a fat lot of good that's going to do!" I exclaimed. "Unless you're somehow going to travel back in time and pick it up—"

"I'm not," George said reasonably. "You are."

That stopped me dead. I searched his face, but there wasn't the slightest hint of humor in it. I would have been surprised if there had been. George was a man obsessed, and people like that can't usually laugh at themselves.

"Oh, come on!" I said heatedly. "As if that was even possible!" Unaccountably, my heart had begun to beat faster.

"Oh, it's possible. In fact, it works quite well. All we want you to do is return to November 22, 1963 and intercept Sarah Hughes at the bottom of the ramp after she administers the oath. Say or do anything you have to, but get that Bible and bring it back to me. John will send you back to 1963, and then he'll bring you back here. Simple and safe. The question is... will you consider it?"

"George, come on. You want me to believe that you've somehow come up with a way to travel back in time? That's science fiction, not reality."

"Will you consider it?" George repeated patiently.

My mind was so full of questions it was hard to pick one. "Why do you need me? Why can't you do it?"

"Simple. I was alive on November 22, 1963. We've learned that no one who has a living counterpart in any time can travel back to that time. Two of the same person can't exist in any given time period—which means we have to use someone born after that date. You were born in July 1964. Therefore, you can go back. Now, will you?"

I literally did not know what to say. It was absurd, and yet—I hated to admit that part of me, the actress and closet sleuth, thought it could also be exciting. If time travel really could work. If I wasn't going to get stuck in 1963, or even worse, between times... wait, what was I thinking?

I struggled for a sensible question to ask that wouldn't reveal my inner turmoil. "How is John Staub involved in all this? I mean, he's a movie guy; he does special effects. How do you know him, anyway?"

George smiled. "I've known him since before he went into the movie business. He's my son."

I stared. On this Friday night, it suddenly seemed anything was possible. I made a mental note to look for a headless horseman when I went home to Tarrytown. The fact that our town council was trying to rename the place "Sleepy Hollow" suddenly made a lot of sense to me.

George went on. "John figured out the time-travel part. Before the movies, he had quite a career in computers and the sciences."

That reminded me. "Why did he want to meet with Craig alone?"

"What? Oh." George suddenly looked abashed, even slightly guilty. "Actually, I just wanted to explain the project to you without him being here. We don't need some skeptic putting the kibosh on it. So John called him and pretended he'd have to meet him in first one place, then another. If I know John—" he glanced at his watch, "—he's sent that poor guy all over the city. He's probably called him six times, and each time told him to go to a different place."

I think it surprised him when I suddenly roared with laughter.

He looked up, his expression guarded, but his eyes beginning to sparkle. "I take it you don't—er—disapprove?"

"Are you kidding? I just wish I'd thought of it." The idea of sending Craig all over Manhattan, just to prevent him from hearing what George had to say, was priceless. It was also fitting revenge for his collusion with Gail Carroll.

"Then you'll do it?" George said, a sunny smile coming to his face.

As intriguing as it sounded, I wasn't anywhere near as excited about his treasure hunt as he apparently was. "Look, George," I began, choosing my words carefully. He was nice, if a bit odd, and I didn't want to insult him. "It's a good story, but I'm not convinced time travel is even possible. If I were to do this—and I'm not saying I would—I'd want to know a lot more."

George spread his hands out to the sides, palms up, in an open gesture. "Ask me anything."

"How does it work?"

He answered promptly, looking me in the eye. "*That* I don't actually know. John can explain it. It's his invention."

"Is it safe?"

Now George nodded vigorously. "Yes. I do know that. Think about it: if we couldn't be sure of transporting you safely to 1963 and back, I couldn't be sure of getting the Bible. And that's what this is all about, after all. So we'll be damn sure you get there and back safely."

"How long would I be—gone?"

He shook his head. "We're not sure. It could be just fifteen minutes—or time might expand, and while it would be fifteen minutes in Dallas, you could be gone from here for several days."

He smiled. Maybe he thought all my questions meant I would finally say yes. I hated to break the goodwill between us, even though I knew I had to. If truth be told, I even hated the idea of giving up the job. "I'm sorry," I said now. "I can't."   It was his turn to blink. "What?"

"I can't be gone that long. My mother—" I stopped. It was too complicated to explain. "I can't be away for days at a time. Not in November." I stood up.

"But—you want to do it, don't you?"

I looked at him. "Look, George," I said somberly, "you're hitting all my hot buttons, with history and a treasure hunt, but I'm really not convinced it's even possible, and I have obligations here. I can't just turn my back on them. I'm sorry." I stood up to go.

That silenced him. It was clear he could think of nothing more to offer me. The money didn't move me; a hundred times the amount wouldn't change my mind. My mother had no one, and November was the worst month of the year for her, the anniversary of my father's disappearance. I couldn't leave her alone during November; I never had. I'd always arranged my vacation from the show for November, and I'd always stayed close by in case she needed me.

Leave her alone on the very day my father disappeared? It wasn't even a question. Yes, I was intrigued; I was interested; I was even curious about George's offhand references to my father, but it wasn't enough. I couldn't risk it. She was too close to the edge in November.

As I started toward the door, I said, "I wish you well with the project."

He didn't answer. When I glanced at him from the doorway, his eyes were staring sightlessly at the rows of documents on the wall. He looked like a man who'd just lost everything in this world he had to lose.

Chapter Three
October 2000

I was so bone-weary, and so dazed by George's remarkable proposal, on top of the rest of my day, that I had driven back to Tarrytown before remembering that I'd planned to stop at my mother's house.

I swore inwardly, but decided, since I was almost home anyway, to skip my usual Friday-night visit. I regretted it, though a small voice inside whispered that my mother wasn't likely to care whether I stopped by or not. All I did was play audience for her multiple grievances.

The truth is, too much had transpired in my life today. I needed to recharge my batteries.

Home, at least, looked as it always did. Eight years before, flush with a steady income and good prospects, I'd spotted an ad—"For Sale by Owner"—and driven out to see a rundown but potentially charming carriage house on a piece of Tarrytown property dating back to the eighteenth century. Finding a Westchester carriage house at an affordable price wasn't easy. I'd immediately bought it and committed myself to spending the next few years fixing it up. Now it had a new roof, a more open floor plan, shining hardwood floors, kitchen walls bared down to the original brick, and a master bedroom with lacy white curtains, simple oak furniture and a lovely private view of the majestic elms and maples in the backyard. In the spring and summer, after a long day of taping, I could eat dinner on the flagstone patio as the sun set into the Hudson, going over the next day's script until it was too dark to see. Craig once admitted that leaving my house was a lot harder than leaving me.

I believed him.

I lugged the boxes from my car into my cluttered office and dumped them on the floor. Looking around, I really saw, for the first time in months, the piles of paper perched precariously on the large walnut table I used as a desk, along with a jumble of pens and pencils in a plastic Mets cup. On the walls, scotch-taped at jaunty angles, were more full-color travel posters I'd cadged from African safaris and Caribbean cruises. I really *had* to clean the place out. While Natalie, my very reliable maid, kept the rest of the house sparkling, I always forbade her to touch the office; I kept thinking I'd get to it one weekend. But my weekends were usually spent at the gym, catching up on email and fan mail, paying bills, seeing friends and watching over my mother, which didn't leave much time for housekeeping.

I glanced over at the bookshelves against the library wall. Eight feet high and twelve feet wide, and still the books spilled over and hunched against walls, waiting for me to find time to stack them away neatly. Maybe I was always too tired and too sleepily content when I came home, but I suddenly saw the clutter of my house as synonymous with the clutter in my life.

Craig, my ex-husband and bitter, resentful agent. My mother, grieving eternally for a love lost while ignoring me and withholding the love I craved from her. My job, a dead end that had turned around and dead-ended me. Stuff collected during my childhood, during my marriage, during my busy studio years… stuff I had intended to do so much with, and instead… it gathered dust while my life stumped on, in a flat line. No excitement. No goals. No heights to scale.

Grimly I surveyed the rest of the house and decided on some immediate goals: I would sleep twelve solid hours, and then my first priority would be cleaning out. No maids, no cleaning services. Just me and my two hands and a lot of big garbage bags. If it were dirty or broken, I'd sweep it out; if it didn't fit my life anymore, I'd bag it for Goodwill. Either way, I promised myself, I'd been cluttering up my life for way too long with things that didn't belong there. Starting tomorrow, I was going to make a crusade of clearing out all the debris—physical and emotional.

But before I could sleep… something nagged at me, something I hadn't done. I thought back over the whole crowded day and remembered the cell phone call Craig had prevented me from taking. At least I could check my messages before turning in, though I suddenly had no energy even to cross the room. I sank onto the heavy rug which covered the shining hardwood floors and took out my cell phone.

There was one message.

"Ms. Cuyler," said the oily voice of my mother's latest detective, "this is Josiah Morgan. I'm back from Central America…" I sighed; I could just imagine the size of the bill that was coming. I hoped, between my mother's other bills and this one, that I could afford my mortgage this month. He paused and sucked his teeth, a habit which drove me quietly crazy. "I have some new information I think you'll be quite interested to hear, so call me…" He left his number. I expected the message to end, but his slick voice continued, "Our investigation is now complete, and we can close this case for you."

Close the case… ? My father had been missing for almost 37 years, and my mother had spent a fortune on private detectives to try to locate him. He had kissed my mother and gone off at the usual time to his job on Friday morning, November 22, 1963. It was the day Kennedy was shot in Dallas, and from 12:30 onward, the city was in the grip of chaos. My father had not turned up after work. My mother assumed he was spending time with friends, mourning the President.

But 9:00 passed, and then midnight. Nothing. No call. No trace.

My mother, frantic, finally phoned the police, but they weren't interested in the disappearance of a businessman with no bad habits or outstanding debts. The President was dead, a Dallas police officer, J.D. Tippit, had been shot, and a suspect in both murders, Lee Harvey Oswald, had been arrested. They told her soothingly they would look into it.

By the time they got around to it, weeks later, the trail was cold. There were no witnesses to Don Cuyler's disappearance, and no clues.

My mother wept and prayed and grieved. In answer to the prayer came two pieces of luck: a brown sack full of cash arrived anonymously in the mail, which was enough to pay her bills for some years, and some good friends, knowing she was pregnant, helped her move from Dallas back to Westchester, New York, where I was born the following July. My mother carried her baby with resignation. I doubt she felt any joy at my birth, though I'm sure she would have been thrilled, had my father been with her. She was a person whose life force appeared to have gone with my father. All she had left was the vague, tissue-thin hope that he might someday re-appear.

When I began earning steady money in television, my mother begged me to help her learn what had happened to him, and thus began the steady monthly outflow to private investigators, one after another, who took mountains of cash and came back with nothing.

My mother was undeterred. She found new investigators, spent more cash. Each new investigation was an infusion of hope to her. The constant buzzing activity was like a sickness, the desperate need for a shred of information. It kept her feverishly busy, which I thought was positive. However, with each new negative report, she spiraled down further into despair.

Eventually I told her I would stop paying for the investigations unless she allowed me to receive the reports myself. That way, I could cushion the shock for her. With her own cash depleted and no other options, she reluctantly agreed. Now, at least once a month, I was subjected to these `reports', which were little more than excuses for failure. I'd become used to it.

Results? New information? That I wasn't used to.

I dialed Morgan's number. It was almost ten. I was so weary it might have been 4 a.m. I leaned my head against the overstuffed chair in the corner.

He answered on the third ring. "Ah, Ms. Cuyler. I'm so glad to hear from you. We're very pleased with the results of our investigation. In fact, we've found your father."

"What?" My head jerked off the soft chair cushion. "You've found him?"

He heard the wild hope in my voice. "Not alive, I'm sorry to say, no. He apparently died in Central America in 1971."

I breathed deeply. The end of the road for my mother and her dreams. She'd spent the last year re-decorating her house on Rockland Avenue so it resembled her home in Dallas the day my father left it for the last time. Tracking down the companies that manufactured the old fabrics and furniture cost a small fortune, but it had been worth it to see her busy and involved.

Now all that would come to an end, too. I devoutly hoped she would turn her energies into a new channel, once she realized the old one had been irretrievably closed off. There was an end, at last.

Morgan was droning on about sending an itemized bill along with his final report.

"Just a minute!" I interrupted. "What did you find out?"

Morgan whined. "I was asleep—"

"My mother's waited 37 years for this," I snapped. "At least tell me the highlights, so I can break it to her."

"No need," Morgan yawned. "I talked to her right after I left the message for you."

"You—*you what?*"

Chief among my instructions to new investigators was the caveat that they must never talk with my mother about any aspect of the case without talking to me first. She was still too fragile, too bruised, and these guys were not the most diplomatic bunch. Even good news from their lips could lead to a trauma.

Morgan apparently didn't hear the alarm in my voice. "She called me, right after I called you. I figured you wouldn't mind if she called me. I told her how we tracked your dad first to Miami, then to Central America, where he was apparently in hiding with friends, and then—well—she insisted, so I told her we'd had confirmation from a buddy who took a photograph…"

"You *idiot!*" I said furiously, now wide awake and raging. "What did I tell you before you took this job? You never tell my mother *anything* about the investigation! Why did you talk to her?"

Morgan's voice now sounded wide awake, too, and humble. "I've talked to her every day for two months, Ms. Cuyler. She calls me, with information about the case, asking if she can help, offering us stuff—"

"You bastard!" I felt an anger swell up in me that was almost uncontrollable; I didn't know whether it was his total disregard for instructions or a culmination of everything else I'd been through today.

I snapped the cell phone off and almost threw it across the room, so furious I could hardly contain myself. All the precautions, all the protections—all blown to hell because some gorilla can't keep his mouth shut!

Oh, God. *What was my mother thinking?*

I snapped open the phone and pressed the speed dial. A caustic busy signal flashed back at me.

I looked at my watch: 10:15. My mother never called anyone at 10:15. She was almost always in bed, asleep. I tried again, dialing the number manually, slowly and carefully. Busy again.

I stood thinking for a minute, as my gut twisted in fear. Then I ran to the door and grabbed my handbag and car keys. My blood was running cold in my veins. All thought of sleep was behind me.

I slammed the Beetle into gear and roared off toward Larchmont. The Auto Club said you could make it in 25 minutes.

Tonight I broke my own record. Fourteen and a half minutes, door to door.

But I was still too late.

Chapter Four
October-November 2000

The coroner told me, with great sincerity and sympathy, that there was nothing I could have done. Barbiturates mixed with alcohol, in a frame as small and slender as my mother's, had done the job effectively. They can go fast, he said comfortingly, so fast, when they want to. And clearly, your mother wanted to.

I had found her, curled up tightly in her bed, the covers pulled up to her chin, fingers limp on the quilt, and for a long moment I'd breathed a sigh of relief, thinking, S*ee, Cady, you panicked. Over-reacted. There was nothing to be afraid of.* Then I looked at her again, sharply. Something was wrong.

All the CPR training I'd had to play Sheila came back. I shook my mother, placed my fingers on her carotid artery, felt for a pulse. Nothing.

I summoned the real paramedics as fast as my trembling fingers could dial 911 and started resuscitation measures myself. Nothing.

The paramedics arrived in less than five minutes and told me after using more sophisticated techniques and better equipment that my mother was dead, an obvious suicide. I found the bottle of sleeping pills on the bathroom sink. She had filled a prescription for a hundred pills that morning, and the bottle was empty. A bottle of Jack Daniel's stood half- empty on the kitchen sink.

She'd left no note, no farewell. I'd never said goodbye to her. It was the thought I woke with, slept with, and dreamed of. The anguish was unbearable.

I looked out over the pitifully small gathering of mourners at her funeral— Craig had come, surprisingly, and several of my co-workers on *Wind*—and the few people my mother had had contact with regularly; her hairdresser, her banker, her insurance agent, a few of the salespeople she'd given thousands of dollars' worth of business to over the years. No one was really a friend; my mother hadn't had friends, just the people she did business with, and others she danced out onto her puppet stage to complain about.

I was numb. In the week after the funeral, I found myself staying in her house, sleeping in her bed, trying to feel her body warmth in the impressions of the sheets. Impossible, of course. She hadn't left much of an impression while she was alive. Everything human, everything warm, had vanished after November of 1963.

My mother's life had been such a waste.

I never realized how much until the gray, windy morning in early November, when I started clearing out her house.

According to her lawyer, everything of hers was now mine. No real surprise; my mother had no siblings or parents, no one who would treasure a memento of hers. I was the only person she'd had ongoing contact with, so it was to me that she bequeathed it all.

I wanted to divest myself of it as quickly as possible, starting with the house I'd never been happy in. I had spent the most agonizing years of my life there. It was a lovely house, the realtor said repeatedly, walking through it, and I agreed. A lovely house... for someone else.

So I worked upstairs, methodically clearing out boxes of useless papers and setting aside a few items to take to my own home.

My mother was a record-keeper. She had tax documents, bank statements, party invitations dating back to 1950. Those I discarded with hardly a glance. More interesting were her early years in Connecticut, much of it neatly preserved in boxes from exclusive department stores, most of them pink. Even the paper was pink: pink was my mother's favorite color.

I found diaries filled with entries in pink ink—pink ink! My mother!—in a coy, girlish hand, detailing boyfriends desired, boyfriends evaded, parties, small sins (smoking, several glasses of sherry at someone else's debutante ball, necking that got out of hand). There were small souvenirs: Pieces of a corsage from a college dance, photographs of her with friends I recognized and friends I didn't, matchbooks from New York nightclubs like the Stork Club, and even, pathetically, a carefully preserved copy of her wedding invitation.

A separate box, covered in pink brocade, held a collection of letters from my father, all scratched hastily, it seemed, on thin sheets of cheap ivory paper. It looked like he had written on whatever was handy at the time. I'd be willing to bet the missives my mother sent in return were carefully lettered on pink paper, probably in a deeper shade of pink ink.

I opened the envelopes curiously. My mother had spoken of my father only in superlatives: the one carefully framed Polaroid of him (who frames Polaroids?), a blurry, squint-at-the-camera kind of photo, the last taken before his disappearance, had remained on her bureau for the rest of her life.

I often wondered cynically whether she kept it there to discourage other men from trying to take his place or to keep herself vigilant, lest her own quite human feelings sweep away his memory on the tide of her needs. I never asked, and now I would never know.

Each envelope bore my mother's name, starting with "Miss Sandra Gorham" and progressing to "Mrs. Sandra Cuyler", with various addresses ranging from Connecticut to Washington, D.C. to Virginia to Dallas, Texas. All were lettered in my father's sharp print—no cursive—all capitals, all the letters the same size. Easy to read. Hard, I imagined, for my mother to forget.

The first letter, postmarked from Washington, was dated September 10, 1957. It read: "Dear Miss Gorham, I am sure I was not the only man taken with your radiance last weekend, but I have determined that I will be the man who wins you..." God, had people really written stuff like this?

I wondered again what kind of man my father had been. I had heard stories of his heroism and courage all my life, in the Naval Intelligence unit he commanded, in active service around the world, but when I asked my mother specific questions— *What colors did he like, Mommy? What was his favorite song?*—she often could not give me an answer, and I would hear her later in her room, weeping. I think when she realized that year by year, memory was taking him from her even more thoroughly than reality had, she turned to endless, pointless shopping to help her forget it.

From the letter: "I was so impressed, not only with your parents' elegant entertainment, but also with the welcome I received from them, and from you. Are you always so kind to strange men?"

This is getting good, I thought, and then my cell phone rang.

I thought about ignoring it. I wanted to finish reading the letters, but the phone rang again, persistently. Out of habit, more than anything else, I picked it up.

It was Mel, my personal trainer. I hadn't seen him since the funeral. We had been best friends for years, since I'd been married to Craig, and in the time since our separation, Mel had never so much as flirted with me. Since he was clearly heterosexual, I figured I just wasn't his type.

Now, though, without preamble, he said, "I'm picking you up in half an hour. We're going to have some fun."

I gaped into the phone. "What? Mel, I can't. I'm cleaning out my mother's house."

"Half an hour," he said again, as though I hadn't spoken, and the call clicked off. When I tried to call him back, he didn't pick up.

Mel seldom took no for an answer, and never with me. I might as well clean up, because when he arrived—and it would be in less than half an hour—he would expect me to be ready and would likely drag me out half-dressed if I wasn't. Besides, a small voice said clearly into my guilty conscience, *you haven't had any fun for weeks. Might as well have a night out.*

I showered hurriedly, unfolding a brand-new bath towel with a monogram worked into it—"DSC"—which my mother had clearly ordered just before... no, I wouldn't think of that. Tonight, I would forget. Fifteen minutes later I was downstairs in jeans, a pale oxford shirt and a black V-necked sweater.

Mel was there in 25 minutes. While I hastily brushed my hair in the hall mirror, he inspected the living room: the few photographs of my father, my mother's wedding pictures, the piano she never played, the fireplace tools she'd never used because she never lit a fire, even on the coldest nights. It was nothing but a stage set for a life that had never really been lived.

I came into the room.

Mel was always quick with a joke, but now his face was sad. "What a waste," he said, nodding around the room.

"Yes," I said quietly. "It was. She wasn't a very happy person."

"How could she be? She spent her whole life living in the past." He looked around. "She never redecorated, did she? This stuff looks like it's from the '60s."

"She redecorated all the time. This was the latest motif—Dallas housewife, circa 1963. It cost a fortune to replace every piece of furniture she'd had when she lived in Dallas, just before my father—" I choked off my words. My throat felt tight.

Mel gazed at me unsmilingly. "What about you, Cady?"

"What do you mean?" I asked, stung. "You think I live in the past, too?"

He faced me somberly, his dark eyes troubled. "Are you going to? Or are you going on with your life?"

"How should I do that, Mel? Go back to my job? Go back to Craig?" I began to feel a rising anger.

"How about going forward for a change? All those travel posters on your walls are just as futile as your mother's decorating. When are you going to go somewhere, do something for yourself?"

"Is this about that project with John Staub?"

I regretted now ever mentioning it to him, but after the funeral I'd been distraught, and talking about anything other than my mother seemed to help. I didn't remember much, but I suspected I'd told Mel a lot more about the project than I ordinarily would have.

"You're damn right," Mel replied with conviction. "It'd give you a chance to be what you've always been capable of being, Cady. Why won't you do it?"

"It's not exactly an acting job. Besides, they probably got someone else long ago."

"I happen to know that's not true."

I stared at Mel. "You happen to know?"

He studied the arrangement of furniture deliberately. "I've been talking to Craig since the funeral. He's worried about you."

"Let's go out," I said bleakly.

*   *   *

Mel hassled me straight through dinner at a quaint-looking '50s-style franchise restaurant with waitresses whizzing around precariously on roller skates and sporting blouses full of snide buttons. Mel liked `fun' places, which meant quirky, with a relaxed dress code and food that tasted great and was terrible for you. Naturally, there was a large sign advertising "Karaoke Tonight!" on the wall.

I ordered a double cheeseburger with everything and ate it with relish, not caring for once about the damage to my body, while Mel lectured me about living my life to the fullest.

"You've settled for things," he insisted as I washed down crinkle-cut French fries with cherry Coke. "You've settled your whole life! A safe job, a safe husband—"

I had said nothing during the meal, but now I felt a flame of anger rising in me again. "A safe husband? You mean the kind that walks out?"

"Christ, Cady, did you really want him to stay? You married a friend—ugh, and what a friend—so you wouldn't have to deal with any deep feelings. What you need is someone to drag you into adventure. The funny thing is, I think that's what you really want anyway, even if you try to deny it. You're just scared."

I glared at Mel.

"Hey, it's Sheila!"

I turned toward the sound of the female voice. A young girl and a group of her friends were approaching with smiles, reaching into pockets and purses for paper and pen. "Wow, it's really you!"

I smiled automatically. They seemed about 16 and claimed to be 'huge fans' of the show and of Sheila, particularly. They asked eagerly what would happen when Sheila got out of the library—apparently the last show I'd taped had just aired Friday.

"Oh, I couldn't give it away," I parried, leaning close to the first girl so her friend could snap a photo of us.

"You're the greatest!" one of the boys chimed in. "I just hope when I get to college, I meet someone like you!" As usual, he'd confused me with Sheila. I was used to it. We looked alike, after all.

They thanked me nicely for the autographs and the photos and apologized for disturbing me. I said, as usual, that it was my pleasure, thanks for watching, thanks for coming over.

Mel gave me a look when they finally walked away.

"You're just scared," he said. "And there's no reason. You're smart and funny and brave—"

I was getting annoyed. Bad enough to be reminded that the job I'd loved I no longer had. Now I had Mel pushing me to take more chances, when I still felt bruised and vulnerable. "The trouble with you," I said icily, "is that you're like those kids. You think I'm Sheila, too. How can you? You know me."

"Yeah, I know you," he said, the corners of his mouth pulled down. The waitress slapped down the check, and he reached for it. "And I'm not your fans. I don't think you're Sheila. The truth is, Sheila's you. She always was. You never needed a safe harbor, Cady. You can fly on your own. You're the only one who doesn't seem to know it."

I refrained from pointing out the mixed metaphor as Mel fumbled for his wallet. It seemed to me he was taking an unnecessarily long time about it, too. I wondered if he was going to try to stick me with the check.

Behind us, the lights dimmed and flashed, and a thump of music sounded.

"Karaoke!" he said, pretending to be surprised, as though he'd just discovered it. "Hey, tonight's Karaoke Night! Let's stick around!'

"Let's not," I retorted. I wanted to crawl back onto the dusty loveseat in my mother's attic and continue perusing my parents' love letters.

"You'd rather sit in that old house with that ugly old furniture and rot away," Mel accused me, "than belt out the best of the '70s, '80s and '90s here with me?"

"Exactly." I stood up. "Thanks for dinner." "May I join you?" asked a male voice above me.

I turned to say coolly that no one could join me because I was leaving—and stopped cold in my tracks.

The best-looking man I'd ever seen stood smiling at me.

He was in his late thirties, tall and slim, his hair wavy and dark, his skin almost porcelain—did men actually have skin that soft?—with warm green eyes and a wide mouth that turned up naturally, as though his usual expression was a smile. He wore a rough windbreaker over an aqua sweater and an oxford shirt, and starched khakis. No actor I'd ever seen could compare to this guy.

Every word I'd intended to speak died in my throat.

Mel scrambled from the booth. "Cady Cuyler, John Staub," he muttered. And to me, in a whisper, "You're welcome."

I was simply stunned. This was John Staub? This was the nerd who fiddled with computer special effects and commanded his own empire?

John looked after Mel, who had disappeared toward the men's room. Then he turned another smile on me.

"Okay if I sit down?"

I still couldn't speak. I had thought, at the end of my marriage to Craig, that something must have permanently affected my sex drive, because I felt nothing. I'd been asked out on dates but refused; I preferred to sit home and read a book. I wondered if I would spend the rest of my life in a chaste state. I suspected I'd never feel passion again for anyone.

Apparently, I need not have worried. One glance at this Adonis and the feelings came roaring back. I was glad I was sitting down, since my legs felt rubbery under me.

John waited, but since I had made no sign, he sat anyway. "You look poleaxed," he observed, settling down in the booth. "Just like Sheila did the time she found out Cole was stealing surgical supplies and selling them to that doctor who'd lost his medical license."

That brought me down to earth with a bump. I'd forgotten that John Staub and his father George had their own agenda. If Mel was right, they might still feel there was some point in pursuing me. But I had no desire to do anything. I had plunged into my mother's past and for the time being, I wanted to stay there. I didn't have the energy or the interest for anything else.

"I'm sorry," I said. "I told George I wasn't going to do it."

"We heard about your mother. I'm really sorry." He looked sorry, too, but I wondered a trifle cynically whether it was just easier to accept noble-looking behavior when it came in such terrific packaging.

I shook myself mentally. *What was I thinking, being attracted to a stranger when I was mourning my mother?*

I took a deep breath. "So why are you here?"

He tapped his slender fingers on the table. "Well—there's no tactful way to say this. To be honest, my father is hoping—praying—that you'll change your mind and join us. Time is running out, and—we need you."

"And he thought you should meet me right after my mother died, figuring that now I'd have no excuse to say no. Is that it?"

He looked at me and shook his head, and I wished I could somehow ignore the fact that he was the most attractive male I'd met in years.

"Don't blame my dad for this," he said. "It was my idea. If we don't do it now, we'll have to wait at least a year before we can try again, and—I thought—well—you should realize your mother's life could be different, if you went back to 1963. And maybe if you realized that—"

"What do you mean?" I spoke slowly, because my heart was thudding in an entirely different way now. To our left, I heard the opening notes of"Time in a Bottle", and before I heard him, I knew that Mel had taken the microphone and would be singing directly to me. It was his idea of encouragement.

"We've decided we're willing to—" he hesitated now, "—expand the experiment. Give you a chance to find out—"

"What?"

"What you need to know about your father. To maybe—maybe, if it's possible—change certain—little things."

"Are you saying," I said quietly, "that if I do this time-travel thing, it's possible to change things so that my mother's life—so she might not die?"

John gazed around the room, now filling up with the raucous Saturday-night sounds of karaoke. He looked down at the aged wooden table. Then he looked up. "I can't say that," he said slowly, "but I don't believe history is written in stone. I think if you add or take away certain elements—well—you'd have to be looking at a whole different outcome. Not the big events," he said hastily. "I don't mean you could stop a war or anything, but if your father hadn't disappeared, your mother would have been a lot happier, wouldn't she? I mean, that's why she—why things happened the way they did." He seemed to be having trouble presenting the idea, fumbling for the right words. It made me like him. "If you could prevent your father's disappearance, then your own life could be—" He gave me a quick glance, and I felt as though he knew every heartache I'd felt in the last 20 years. It was exhilarating, it was extraordinary... it was frightening.

"You really think I can?" I asked. The blood was now pounding in my ears. It was as though someone was matter-of-factly suggesting I become an astronaut. I felt lifted to the clouds but still wary that I might also be dropped suddenly onto cold, hard concrete.

He looked at me steadily, and his eyes were not kind now. They were appraising, intelligent, and rational. "That depends," he said.

"...if I have the courage?"

He flushed but kept his eyes steadily on my face.

I thought of my mother's wasted life, the years of waiting so patiently, so hopefully, for word from an army of private detectives who never had a word of hope for her. I thought of the years I'd waited for some indication of her love, while she pursued a man who had been lost to her years before, never lifting her head to look at the opportunities she had now.

I thought of the desert my own life had been.

I thought of Mel telling me I could fly on my own.

I thought of the lack of opportunities that awaited me elsewhere.

I thought of this man who had dropped into my life, the first one in years who had aroused any feelings in me that could be called passionate.

I looked at him, and I could feel a warm, inviting smile stretching across my face. I had a direction. I had a *chance*—which is all we can ever ask. "You got me," I said. "Where do I sign?"

John's face lit with relief, and Mel, seeing that smile, began to sing "Fly Me to the Moon".

Chapter Five
November 2000

The contract I finally signed described the project as `a short documentary'. Craig didn't inquire too closely into its nature: I assured him it was interesting, a period piece set in 1963, and that I'd be doing some improvisation. What satisfied his agent's soul was his pleasure at wringing an additional 20 percent out of John, making my fee per minute higher than Marlon Brando's for *Superman*. When Craig was finally happy, he left me alone, and I went to work.

With the contracts signed, John invited me to see his operation in a former business park in White Plains.

A sweeping drive in a cluster of trees led past the "Staub Enterprises" sign to a maze of buildings. The guard at the gate politely asked my name (obviously he did not watch daytime drama), checked it against a list, and nodded me through. "Building 4, on the right. Suite 500."

Suite 500 was an enormous, state-of-the-art editing bay. John was there, surrounded by youngsters in faded jeans and T-shirts sporting logos and psychedelic colors, sipping Diet Cokes and munching what looked like granola, all of them intent on the film footage flying by on the huge screen in front of them. By contrast, John looked remarkably well-groomed, in pressed khakis and a starched, rolled-up shirt. I wondered if he always dressed this well at work.

"Look, John," said a young guy with glasses and a beard."The edits don't match."

"I see," John said grimly."It came to us this way?"

"Straight from the director's loving arms," volunteered a young girl, her face a mask of disgust."And he also sent an audio cassette telling us not to screw it up."

John stood in front of the board, and his fingers played over the keys for a few moments. Click, click—and suddenly the pieces matched perfectly.

Silence.

"Back to it, guys" John said pleasantly. "And don't tell Mr. Hollywood I screwed with his epic, okay?"

There were murmurs and headshakes and a fair amount of awe in those young faces, along with an editorial comment from the back: "Effing genius."

They drifted back to the editing console, chattering amongst themselves, as though there had been no interruption.

John joined me at the door. "Ready?" he said without preliminary.

"Sure," I said.

For the next hour, John showed me buildings full of digitized computer equipment working on expensive Hollywood 'A' pictures I'd been hearing or reading about in the trade papers for months. I counted eight films being constructed in the various F/X bays and screening rooms.

Finally, John led me down a long, narrow corridor in the last building, quieter and starker than the others. The walls were a harsh white, the lights overhead an institutional fluorescent, unlike the warm yellow lights, framed prints and other homey touches I'd noted everywhere else. At the very end was a steel door.

John nodded to me. "Open it."

I tried. I twisted it, pulled on the knob, shook it, even pounded on it. There was no lock and no card swipe terminal on the doorjamb, no one controlling it from the other side. The blasted thing just wouldn't move.

I finally looked up. "I give up."

John reached out to the knob. It turned easily under his fingers. I stared at him. "Biometrics," he said, flicking his fingers at me. "The knob read my fingerprints, recognized them, and opened for me. It read yours and decided it didn't know you… so you were denied access."

"Pretty sneaky," I said, at the same time secretly impressed.

He shrugged. "Look at the bright side. You can never forget your keys again."

We walked into a quiet open atrium with corridors leading off in all directions. "These are my private suites," John explained. "No one else comes back here, ever."

"Of course not. How would they get in?"

At the end of the farthest corridor was another steel door. *More secrets*, I thought.

In a moment we were inside a spotlessly clean computer room, with large mainframe-type machines set at either end of a rectangular space, along with a cluster of smaller desktops atop flat Formica tables.

Near the back, standing alone, was what looked like an airport scanner, a frame one could walk through. It was set with a variety of light bulbs and dials. I looked to John for an explanation.

He perched on a stool next to one of the smaller computers and nodded to me to join him. "Here's the heart and soul of the project, though I'll grant you it doesn't look like much. This is where we make the rubber meet the road."

"Send me back to 1963?"

"Right. How much do you know about the Internet?"

I was startled by the question. "Well, I can pick up my email and get around, but I don't know how it works, if that's what you mean."

"That's okay. Most people who use the Internet don't know how it works. The important thing is that it does. Think about it. How many times have you heard the term `cyberspace'?"

"All the time," I said promptly.

"Right," said John like a benevolent college lecturer, "and `cyberspace' is that mysterious place where all websites exist. That's what they mean, right?"

"I think so. Yes."

"It occurred to me one day that `cyberspace' could only be one dimension of the Internet. If you could have `cyberspace', by definition, you also had to be able to have `cyber-time'. Make sense?"

"Yes," I said slowly. "It does. I just never thought about it before. But time and space *do exist together, don't they?"*

"I certainly think so. I also think that 'time' in cyber-time might be a little elongated." John pulled the keyboard on the counter toward him and typed rapidly. "Look. If what Einstein said was true, that time is like a river, it occurred to me that the one place where that river was flowing both forward and backward was out in `cyber-time'— online—instead of in any dimension we can physically touch. And since we can access cyberspace—well, I just applied a little of what I knew and took the next logical step—to access cyber-time, as well."

He finished typing and swiveled the extra-large color monitor toward me. He had typed in www.backto1963.com and clicked Enter. The Internet connection was very fast ("Satellite," John said quietly), because instantly the monitor brightened and focused in front of me. In just a moment, I was looking at what looked like a camera's-eye view of a distinctive-looking city park.

"Dealey Plaza, Dallas, Texas," John said.

"The place where Kennedy was killed?"

"Right. We have a 24-hour webcam in the Plaza itself. It's tiny and virtually unnoticeable. That view of Dealey Plaza you see through the camera is virtually untouched since the day of Kennedy's death. That's important: it gives us a window into another time. I've linked that camera view to a website that—" He broke off. "How much do you know about quantum mechanics?"

I grinned. "Absolutely nothing."

His face fell. "Then I can't really explain—"

"You can't tell me how you're doing it?"

"Well, only in the crudest terms. The website I've linked the camera to basically narrows time, until 1963 is just as close as an hour ago. And as long as you weren't actually alive in 1963—you weren't, were you?"

"No. I was born in July of '64."

"Good. Because you can't time travel to a time you once actually existed in. The real you of that time would push away the you we're creating to send there, which is artificial, even though you'll feel you're actually there, and function just like everyone else. Your own original presence there would be too strong, you see… is this making sense?"

"Yes. George explained that part. I'm with you."

"Good. Then what we'll do is create a biometric file on you, and I'll upload it to the website. We'll combine your biometric information with computer languages to create a working file inside the hard drive. Then we can insert you anywhere we want."

"As long as I didn't already exist there."

"Right. You were alive in 1977, so we can't send you to 1977. But anything before 1964 is okay."

Wanting to be perfectly clear on the process, I asked, "If I left the year 2000 on November 22nd, then I'll arrive back in 1963 on November 22nd?"

John seemed pleased that I was thinking things through. "That's right."

I looked around the bare room. "Who else is working on this project?"

John grinned. "Just me."

I turned to him, surprised. "Just you?"

"My dad is rabid about the secrecy of it. He made me swear I'd never bring anyone else into it. And you know what? Now I'm glad. I'm a little paranoid about someone else getting the technology, and he's still paranoid about what went on back then." He motioned to a series of file cabinets with extra-thick steel sides neatly stored beneath the Formica computer tables. "So I designed those. Every specification and every file stays locked in those cabinets. They'll only open for me or my dad. Of course, our best defense is simply never telling anyone what we're doing. It's amazing how that helps you stay below the radar."

"I'm impressed," I said.

"I hope that means you're also confident, because it works, Cady, it really does. I've been experimenting with it for more than a year. Come on. Let's get you registered into the system."

He led me into another biometrically-locked room. In the center of the floor was a large counter fitted with yet another computer, monitor, and keyboard, as well as a console consisting of buttons and levers. Underneath the counter were two painted yellow footprints.

At John's direction, I kicked off my shoes, stood on the footprints and waited until I felt a strange flash under my feet. John then placed my hands into palm-shaped glass cutouts on the counter. He lowered an optical imager over my face, which looked and felt like the instruments opticians use to test your vision.

Behind me, the keyboard clicked as John entered commands. A blue-white light flashed over my left eye, then over my right eye. I felt a pinch in my index finger and glanced downward to see an ultraviolet glow coming from the glass beneath my hands. It was gone in a moment, and John moved the imager away. A drop of blood oozed out of my fingertip. John wiped off the blood and offered me a Band-Aid. I noticed, though, that he didn't stop. If anything, he seemed more and more excited as the console flashed with each new piece of data entered.

Next, he asked me to lean in to the countertop microphone and speak into it. "Testing, one two. Testing, one two."

"Say something else. I need at least fifty words." I thought for a moment, then rolled into the Gettysburg Address, and though he had asked for only fifty words, I gave him the entire speech, with inflections.

John fiddled with the keyboard again, and my own voice boomed back at me. "…

so that government of the people, by the people, and for the people, shall not perish from the earth."

There was silence for a moment. Then John looked up. "You're done."

I was a little disappointed that he hadn't seemed impressed with my elocution, but also surprised and curious that the process was so quick. "That's it? What did you do?"

"I took biometric samples of you. Voice recognition, fingerprints, footprints, and iris scans. That pinch you felt in your finger was for blood typing and DNA sampling."

He continued to key in commands for several minutes. I slipped my socks and shoes back on and came over to watch curiously.

The main computer monitor began to flash: Building Integrated File: CadyCuyler2000. The hard drive beside me hummed to life. "You're being recorded in terms of time rather than frames per second," John explained to me. "The computer then mixes the biometric information we just took with the real-time video to create a three-dimensional file of you. You'll exist in the computer."

"But how do I actually—?" I couldn't figure out how to say what I meant, but John knew.

"Your file becomes active once you're actually in it." He pulled me back to the first room, where he'd shown me the big computers and the odd-looking metal detector in the center of the room. I noticed with some surprise that his hands were big and warm, and his arms had surprising strength.

"And when you walk through that metal detector, I can key you into 1963," John was saying. I pulled my thoughts away from his hands with difficulty and tried to concentrate on what he said.

"The metal detector?"

"Well, it looks like an airport metal detector. Actually, it's a biometric scanner that integrates you with your computer file. Your actual living body presence links up with the encrypted biometric information—like putting a key in a lock—and that activates the file."

"How?"

"Well, to put it simply—"

"By all means," I said dryly, "keep it simple."

He grinned. "Oh, stop it. You may not have the scientific background, but you're getting everything I'm telling you. That's obvious. However," his grin broadened, "I will put it simply: sensitive electronic equipment has a technology that prevents it from overload or burnout. It's commonly called a spike, and it's engineered right into the operating system." His eyes nodded toward the monitor. "This is a time spike. It's engineered into your active computer file. When the spike is activated, it pauses your existence in the present time, like hitting the 'pause' button on your VCR. You cease to exist temporarily in real time, and you begin to exist in cyber-time. You're alive, all right, but in cyberspace, in cyber-time. The spike becomes the bridge between now, and then.

"We keep a link between here and where we're going to send you." He left-clicked the mouse, and a drop-down menu appeared. "We click 'Send', and you're there. Just like that." He snapped his fingers. Actually, he tried to snap his fingers, but all that came out was a sound like a wet noodle.

I gave him a look.

He looked embarrassed. "Don't worry. I click better than I snap."

He did, too—his fingers were flying over the keyboard, and eventually, a set of lights around the rim of the metal detector began to glow. "Then we have to get you back here afterward." He opened a drawer and fumbled around inside for a minute, eventually holding up what looked like a cell phone.

"This will help us monitor you in 1963. It should take you absolutely no longer than 20 minutes to get the Bible and get to a quiet area where we can begin the extraction process. So at precisely 3 p.m. on November 22, 1963, I'll close the file on you from here. As soon as it's closed, you return—as long as you have this with you. If you lose it, we can't extract you." He grinned. "So don't lose it!"

"Then what?" I asked.

"That's it. Nothing has changed in you, except that you once more exist in the year 2000, as you always did. You'll be back, and exactly the same as you were."

"And with luck, I'll have the Bible," I reminded him.

He smiled. "You'll have the Bible. Sheila never fails." He closed down the program and showed me out of the office, but the familiar sinking feeling had begun in my chest again.

He thought I was Sheila, too. They'd contracted for Sheila; she's the one they really want. What will they do when they find out they got Cady instead?

*　*　*

The historic research was more fun, and right up my alley.

As an actress, I'd spent lots of time on research. To play Sheila convincingly, I'd learned CPR and Red Cross lifesaving techniques, driven ambulances, and drawn blood (not human) into a syringe. I could also monitor blood pressure readings and splint broken limbs. Did I use it all? Of course not; but like most actors, I enjoyed learning it.

So I expected to enjoy my research on the 1960's, too.

I walked into Coup D'Etat at exactly 2 p.m. one Wednesday, George checking his watch approvingly. He locked the door, hung a "Closed" sign on the inside and took me to the back of the store, where he'd set up a big-screen TV and VCR. There was also a large pile of books on the table. "For you," he said, pointing at the pile.

I looked at the stack of books. They were all, as I feared, on the Kennedy assassination, and every one, just by the title, appeared to endorse the notion of conspiracy. Five thousand pages, at least. George was looking at me as though wondering whether I was going to balk and become difficult and `actressy'. Given the grim look on his face, I didn't think it was prudent to ask if I could skip the footnotes. "Okay," I said.

"Good," he said, looking somewhat less forbidding. "Let's get on with it."

Before I slid completely into the one uncluttered chair, George started his lecture: "Here are some of the images of the early '60s." He flicked on the VCR.

Some I recognized at once; some I'd never seen before. President Kennedy, of course. Bobby Kennedy. Young kids dancing the Twist on American Bandstand.

Mushroom clouds hovering over unspecified cities. Dr. Martin Luther King. Civil-rights protests with demonstrators, both white and black, being beaten bloody, set on by dogs, and sprayed with fire hoses. The Berlin Wall. Fidel Castro. Nikita Khrushchev. A variety of singers and pop groups I didn't identify quickly enough before they faded off the screen. Wonder Bread. Tang, the orange drink of the astronauts. Women's skinny pants and flat-heeled shoes. Pageboy hairdos. Pink lipstick. Men wearing pastel shirts in a stretchy synthetic material—was that Banlon? Big American cars with fins, whitewall tires and automatic shift on the steering wheel. Room-sized mainframe computers. Black and white TV's with dial tuners and trident-like rooftop antennae. The murder of Medgar Evers in Mississippi. The Mercury space missions, with Alan Shepard and John Glenn. Cigarette commercials on TV. Sean Connery as James Bond. The *Ed Sullivan Show.* Frank Sinatra, Dean Martin, Sammy Davis, Jr., and the rest of the Rat Pack, singing and dancing onstage in Vegas. Cocktails before dinner. Nuts and other snacks packed into cans that opened using a key. Yo-Yos. Separate water fountains labeled "White" and "Colored". Governor George Wallace barring black students from entering the University of Alabama. Teenagers bending supplely backward to slither under a limbo stick.

The footage ran about twenty minutes. I sat staring into space when it was over.

"Well?" George said.

"It doesn't look so different," I said slowly. "It was so long ago; everything should have been much different."

"It is." George turned off the TV. "Everything's very different. But you're right: it doesn't *look* all that different. Cady, this isn't some sci-fi book where I have to show you all the old clothes and the carriages and how these people got light and heat, for heaven's sake. It's just a younger version of what we have today. What's changed, really, is us."

He flipped open a coffee-table-sized book and began to show me photographs on every page. "Look. In 1963, there were still Jim Crow laws in some parts of the South—laws telling blacks they had to use a different restroom or sit in the back of the bus, and most blacks in the South weren't even registered to vote. And don't use 'black', by the way. It was 'colored' or 'Negro'. Blacks didn't start referring to themselves as black for another five or six years; calling someone black at that time was a vile insult.

"Women were housewives and that's all—and if they did work, they got paid almost nothing. Men made the big decisions in the families, even if women ran the households. Men brought home the paychecks, and they were in charge of the money. And forget equality in the labor and delivery room: women had the babies, men waited outside till it was over.

"There hadn't been a sexual revolution yet. The Pill hadn't been invented, and girls were supposed to remain 'good girls' until they got married, though of course quite a few of them didn't—and there was no generation gap yet because the Vietnam War hadn't happened, which was one of the big issues that tore the generations apart."

He showed me more photographs of 1960's cars and houses (some of which closely resembled my mother's), kitchens, fashions, classrooms, and technology. I was surprised to learn that the NASA computers which sent men to the moon in 1969 were less powerful than the one I had at home today, and that the Women's Liberation movement had begun with the 1963 publication of *The Feminine Mystique* by Betty Friedan.

George was showing me silently how easy it would be for me to fit into 1963, that it was a time more familiar to me than I realized. He encouraged me to name my favorite TV shows as a child, and I found that a lot of them—*My Favorite Martian, The Flintstones, The Dick Van Dyke Show, The Beverly Hillbillies*—had all been on the air and very popular in 1963, and many of my favorite Golden Oldies songs were also popular then. I found I could easily name many different brands of cigarettes (Winston, Pall Mall, Marlboro, Salem, L&M, Kool), because they were still being advertised in musical jingles on television in 1963, which, when he hummed them for me, I actually remembered. (*"Happiness is ... the taste of Kent. More taste! Fine Tobacco!"*)

He stopped. I was singing the commercial, until he chuckled. I stopped,confused, and he laughed. "You see? I don't have to teach you about the '60s. You *remember* them."

"I didn't realize," I said slowly. "But what does all this have to do with my father?"

George nodded. "Well. That is the question, isn't it?"

I was on him like a flash. "What did you learn? Do you know who took him?"

"Not so fast!" George spoke severely, though his eyes were laughing. "I didn't find much. But it's enough to put together some interesting pieces."

He reached behind the stacks of conspiracy books and retrieved a large manila envelope, which he slid over to me. I hesitated, then opened it.

I felt as though I'd been struck in the face. Here were photos, clear, non-Polaroid photos of my father, in black and white but sharp and full of detail. *He was so handsome*, I thought, a little surprised. The fuzzy old Polaroids my mother had framed so painstakingly didn't really do him justice. His hair was thick, cropped close to his head and brushed faultlessly, his strong-planed face bare of stubble, his tan—obvious even in black and white—glowing like a movie star's. His high-bridged nose was as perfect as his beautifully shaped eyebrows and the thick crescent of lashes rimming deep-set eyes—eyes that appeared to be the same gray as my own.

Wow, I thought, but didn't say it. He looked vibrant, confident, and in control, a man at the top of his game. Yet he had been lost.

It was such a tragedy.

"Where did you get these?"

George shook his head. "We have our sources." Abruptly, he changed the subject. "Quite a resemblance," he said quietly, nodding at me.

I looked at the photographs again. While some of my features might resemble his, somehow I felt like the negative of the photograph, with him as the positive. That energy and the sense of firm purpose—I swear I could see it in his face—was missing in my life.

"We don't look that much alike."

"That's debatable. Apparently, though, you also share a talent: your father was a devoted amateur actor. He was in acting troupes everywhere that he lived from adolescence onward."

"My father?" My mother had never told me this.

"Mm. And he was good: great at accents, great at imitating people, great with makeup—he certainly had the looks. Even did Shakespeare with one group."

"She never told me," I said slowly. Why not?

I knew I idealized my father, because she had. How often had she told me what a kind and loving man he was, how thrilled at the thought of becoming a father, how solicitous of her... how often had she sighed, when she thought I was out of earshot, "I had everything then"? What she'd been left with—an unborn child and an unknowable future—was a real comedown from what she'd had. I'd always accepted it, because she did try to help me be a part of this family that had never lived together, telling me of the walks they'd taken, the laughing arguments they'd had over my name, their picking out furniture for the nursery she'd never furnished in Dallas, because they were planning to place the order the day after he disappeared...

I shook myself out of my reverie and asked, "What else?"

George gave me a sharp look. "You knew your father was in the Office of Naval Intelligence during World War II?"

"Yes, I think so." I'd heard my mother talking vaguely about this, but because she knew no details, my childish mind had easily jumped to other topics, where she could supply precious pieces of information, and those were the stories I'd demanded over and over: how they met at a coming-out party for one of her friends, how he pursued her through letters (some of which I'd read) until they finally married in 1959, how they'd moved from Connecticut to Miami to Dallas, finally, in 1963. His war service, unknown to my mother and presumably not much discussed between them, interested neither her nor me.

But George surprised me. "Did you know he knew President Kennedy?"

"Really?" I looked up.

He nodded. "They apparently met in ONI early in the war. JFK had a desk job in Washington, where your father was stationed, till he could get past the medical exams and go into active service." He chuckled. "Unlike other men, Kennedy lied about his medical condition to get *into* combat." There was admiration in his voice.

"He did?"

"He did. He was completely unfit for service. Ulcers, colitis, Addison's disease, you name it. 4F by anybody's standards. Didn't matter—he wanted to see action, and he persuaded powerful friends of his father to lie on his behalf to the Navy, so they wouldn't give him a physical. They inducted him and put him on the PT boats. And of course you know what happened there."

I looked at him blankly. "No."

George stared at me. "Cady! Come on—PT-109!"

I stared right back, thoroughly clueless and slightly ticked off about it. "What is PT-109?"

"And you a history major!" George shook his head in mock sorrow. He looked like he was going to razz me some more, but seeing the look on my face, he relented.

"Oh, all right. During World War II, the war in the Pacific was fought against the Japanese using small fast boats, called Patrol Torpedo boats: PT boats. They were quicker and more maneuverable than the big Japanese destroyers, but they didn't carry as much firepower, or nearly as big a crew.

"The Navy recruited young men with sailing experience on small boats back home to captain them. One of them was Kennedy.

"Kennedy wasn't the smoothest pilot—they called him Crash Kennedy because he kept slamming the boat into the dock whenever he came in to refuel—but apparently he had it where it counted."

George paused.

"Go on, George."

George grinned devilishly but continued. "Well, the PT boats did mostly night patrols, without radar, and out there in the South Pacific, you're talking bugs and heat and a night so black you literally couldn't see your hand in front of your face. One night in August of 1943, Kennedy's boat got in the way of a Japanese destroyer. They couldn't see it, you see. There was no radar on those boats."

"What happened?"

George shrugged. "PT-109 was sliced in half."

I gasped. No doubt about it, I was getting caught up in the story.

George went on. "Two of Kennedy's men were killed outright. The rest, including Kennedy, were flung off the boat into shark-infested water, nearly three miles from any shore. Kennedy got the survivors to cling to a plank from the wreckage and swim toward shore together, so they could help each other. One guy, though, was badly burned and couldn't swim. He told Kennedy he was going to die anyway, to leave him and get the others to safety."

"And Kennedy did." I was certain of it.

"No. He told the guy he wouldn't leave him, that they were all going to make it. Kennedy loaded him on his own back—and he had a bad back even then—and held the strap of the guy's life preserver in his teeth. And he towed him to shore—hours and hours swimming in the darkness, with the Japanese all around them, sharks in the water, and coral reefs cutting his legs to bits."

I sat back. I could see it all in my mind. The thought of those men swimming to safety in that terrifying darkness gave me the shivers. Finally, I said, "He was a hero, then."

"That wasn't the heroic part."

"There's more?"

"Kennedy got them to an uninhabited island where they could rest. There was very little to eat, though, and almost no fresh water. He knew he had to let the Navy know about them. But they weren't likely to send PT boat patrols out to such a remote area. So that night, when he figured the patrols were out again, he swam out alone, almost naked, with a pistol, a knife and a lantern, to find help. He swam all night in the darkness, looking for help, but the PT boats were patrolling somewhere else. They figured there were no survivors from 109. So, they didn't even go back to look for them.

"At dawn, Kennedy made it back to the island. He was at the end of his strength, and he knew he was in no condition to swim out there again, but somebody had to. He told one of the other men it would be his turn to swim that night. Then he passed out."

"And then?"

"They moved to another island, with more food and water. Kennedy again towed the injured man on his back. Kennedy and the other swimmer went out into the water together the third night. Finally an Australian coast watcher found out about them from some natives on the island. Kennedy carved a message in a coconut saying he had eleven men alive and needed a small boat." George paused and smiled. "That coconut sat on his desk in the White House."

I sat quietly for a moment. This was a story I'd never heard. And hearing it swept away many of my doubts about the man who'd occupied the White House in the early '60s.

Finally, I said, "He was a hero, wasn't he?"

George shrugged, trying to look nonchalant. "Maybe. His was the only PT boat ever cut in half by the Japanese. Was he a hero or an idiot, for letting that happen? Some people said he should have been court-martialed. Others—PT captains—said it was just plain bad luck. It could have happened to any of them.

"Kennedy himself was asked years later, by a young boy, how he became a war hero. And he answered, `It was purely involuntary. They sank my boat.'"

I couldn't help laughing. Still, this had nothing to do with life in 1963. "George, why did you tell me this?"

He looked at me, like a little boy stealing candy under his mother's nose, his eyes bright. "Maybe I just wanted you to care."

"About Kennedy?" I thought for a moment. "George, are you saying if he and my dad were friends, maybe my dad's disappearance in Dallas on the day of Kennedy's death was not a coincidence?"

George shrugged. "I don't believe in coincidence." He stood up. "Go home and read your books."

I did.

Chapter Six
November 2000

Two weeks later I was ready.

At John's request, I explained to Craig that I'd be rehearsing at a cabin in the Poconos and would be back for shooting in Westchester in a week. I'd further said lamely not to be concerned if my cell phone didn't work and he couldn't reach me: the signal wasn't that great in the mountains. Email me, I'd told him brightly, and I'll email you back that I'm okay. I gave John my email address and password, so he could monitor my ongoing life in the year 2000 while I explored 1963.

At this point, I was feeling very confident. John's preparation and attention to detail was all-consuming; unfortunately, it was so all-consuming that I saw almost nothing of him while I made my own preparations. He worked in his studio, while I labored with George or on my own. John never said or did anything to indicate he liked me, while I felt constrained and unable to flirt with him. It was becoming clear to me that Sheila was the kind of woman John could fall for in a big way; perhaps he'd even chosen me for the experiment because he and George confused me with Sheila. I felt a little depressed sometimes, thinking I'd set up a rival for his affections, and it was a facet of myself!

Most of the time, though, I was exhilarated. This was more fun than I'd ever had on *Wind*, and I was allowed more latitude as an actress than ever before, to the point that George sent me to choose my own wardrobe.

Rob, the costumer, ushered me into his private salon on the Upper West Side of Manhattan. It was the size of the studio floor I'd worked on in Wind, with heavy lights and big mirrors everywhere. He showed me racks of women's clothes—slacks, sleeveless dresses, light sweaters.

"It's November, you know," I said.

Rob shrugged. "It's Dallas, darling. It'll be warm enough." He waited patiently while I examined the row of clothes, finally settling on a quiet, classic-looking dress near the end of the rack.

It was sand-colored linen, the palest beige, with a matching jacket, and a hemline that would demurely brush my knees. There was a large black patent-leather belt that cinched around my waist and matched the large jet buttons on the jacket. It looked as fresh as though it had been taken from tissue paper yesterday. It fit me perfectly.

"Excellent," Rob purred. Next he produced a black handbag that opened and closed with a gold clasp and was half again the size of my current bag.

"Looks matronly, but it's all the rage," Rob said, dropping the patent-leather strap over my arm.

Rob turned me over to Claire, who cut my hair an inch, then wound it onto heavy wire curlers, which I remembered my mother using. She slipped me under a large old-fashioned hair dryer, and then after an hour of blasting hot air, coaxed my '90s bob into a '60s pageboy, just like my mother's. She sprayed on heavy hairspray and provided me with a comb and flat brush.

Claire also gave me a short course on cosmetics use in the early '60s. Women were expected to *look* made up when they used cosmetics. We experimented until she approved the right combination of colors—a beige foundation, ivory powder, reddish rouge ("It's *rouge*, Cady, not blush!"), and heavy eyeshadow in a shade of mauve I wasn't crazy about. I got a small makeup case for my handbag and a lipstick in shell pink, to match the pearl-pink nail polish Claire applied for me.

The target date we had chosen to insert me into was Sunday, November 17, 1963, which meant I had to be ready to make the trip by Friday, November 17, 2000. That would give me six days back in 1963, enough time to learn how to possibly prevent my father from walking out of his home early one Friday morning—and never coming back.

John did no more than look up briefly when I came into the studio carrying the dress on a hanger, with my handbag and makeup kit. He was focusing on the computer console and scrambling between the console and the scanner device, whose lights were blinking alarmingly.

George was there too, his fingers drumming on the console in a tattoo of impatience while John worked. His fingers kept inching toward his jacket pocket, while his eyes wandered to the sign taped on the wall—"*Positively No Smoking!*"— then looked away.

I used a small room off the studio to change and hang up my own clothes. Once I was satisfied with my makeup, I scrambled out of my jeans and sweater and into the '60s-style undergarments Rob had supplied. I wore a girdle with attached garters, a lace-trimmed brassiere, and nylons that attached to the garters, which it took me three tries, in my excited state, to fasten properly, though I'd practiced at home. Women didn't use roll-on deodorants in 1963, so I sprayed deodorant into my armpits, then gently lifted the dress over my head and fastened the belt, carefully centering the buckle at my waist. Over that I put on the jacket and used the flat brush to carefully lift the curls away from my head.

When I finally emerged from my dressing room, John was flicking keys on the keyboard, testing systems individually, and scribbling down numbers and notations on a pad next to him.

George, looking glad to be doing something, helped me check off items for my handbag using a checklist. "Wallet," he said.

I flipped open a new woman's long red wallet, with space for bills and ID in the back and a change purse sewn in front. "Check. Where's my money?"

"Typical woman," George cracked. "Always wants to know how much she's got and where she can spend it." He produced a worn-looking cigar box and opened it in front of me. It was filled with bills and coins, none of which carried a date later than 1963. He counted out three hundred dollars in bills and another five dollars in coins.

"George," I said, impressed, "the coins look almost new."

He gave me a smug look. "We bought them from coin dealers and washed them in acid to get rid of the aging—and make them look freshly minted. A 1963 dime that looked like it had been around for 37 years might raise some eyebrows."

George then produced an official 1963 New York State driver's license with my assumed name, Catherine Roberts, inscribed on it, along with my mother's Rockland Avenue address (though her house was not actually built until 1964) and some vital statistics that approximately matched the woman I was playing: 28 years old, born July 17, 1935, brown hair, hazel eyes. New York State didn't require a photo on driver's licenses in 1963.

"I have some other things for you, too. John," he called, "we'll be back in a minute. Cady's dying to see JFK's autopsy photographs."

John snorted, and I turned to stare at George, even as he was hurrying me out.

"What's this about?" I demanded. "When have I ever—"

"Hush," George interrupted. "I won't bother John when he's working through his final calculations, and I do have some things you need. Besides, showing you autopsy photographs would be a complete waste of time."

"Because I don't believe in conspiracies."

"Because the autopsy photos were faked," George said, opening a door down the hall.

The room inside was almost completely bare, except for a large desk. I looked around, trying to figure out what George had in here that might be useful to me.

Meanwhile, George was calmly emptying his pockets. He brought out two objects and set them on the desk. The first looked like my own cell phone.

"John explained this, didn't he?"

I shook my head. "He just said to carry it so you can monitor me."

"It's easy," he said patiently. "Press 0 to tell us you're okay. Do that at least once a day—we'll be monitoring all the time. Press the star key to activate the re-entry process to bring you back to the year 2000. Press the pound key if you'r e ever in trouble, and we can activate the re-entry process from here. You can use the phone—it's a real cell phone, only with better technology—but for heaven's sake don't lose it. We can't get you back if you haven't got it with you."

"Will it run down, like a real cell phone?"

"No, but the signal won't be as good—it'll be cutting through space and time now, remember. You don't need to recharge it. Just keep it close by."

The second object was a key ring with a black plastic spray tube attached to it.

"Pepper spray," he said succinctly. "Ever used it?"

"Not really," I said doubtfully. Working on *Wind*, I'd once been given the spray for a scene, but an assistant director had taken it from me when they'd rewritten it.

"Aim right for the face and give a good squeeze," George said. "If you hit the eyes, great—if not, anywhere on the face will still incapacitate for up to thirty minutes."

"George," I said quietly, "are you expecting me to get in trouble?"

He hesitated. "Dallas in 1963 wasn't safe, Cady. And you'll be asking some tough questions, maybe of the wrong people. So better safe than sorry, huh?"

He looked at me, his eyes flickering. Clearly, he was a little nervous about finally revealing to me the full scope of this job. He could have said nothing. He could have let me go without precautions, knowing that if he gave them to me, he'd have to spell out the dangers. Yet he had put in my hands something that might help if I did get in trouble. For some reason, it gave me confidence.

"Don't worry, George," I said, tucking the cell phone and pepper spray away. "I have too much at stake to back out now."

"Good girl." He patted me on the shoulder. I refrained from suggesting that I was a woman, not a girl. It was an innocent slip, and I'd better get used to it: In 1963, every female except the oldest hags were called 'girls'.

Around 5:30, John announced that all systems were 'go', and we took a break for a light dinner: Deli sandwiches, packed with turkey breast and Swiss cheese, slathered with mustard, mayonnaise, tomato and lettuce. It was delicious, but I couldn't eat more than a few bites. I noticed John and George didn't manage much, either. What a waste.

John insisted I drink a concoction of his that looked like a floating island and tasted a bit like fruit. "Anti-matter cocktail," he said, smiling. "To keep your electrolytes high and your balance stable. In other words, I'm hoping a big glass of this will help you feel better after you get to 1963."

"What, no Dramamine?" I was already getting tense. It was nearly show time.

George carefully closed, bolted and sealed the outer door of the studio. Once they were in and I had stepped through the frame into 1963, events might change drastically, and if so, the two men insulated in the studio would be the only ones who still had knowledge of the world as it had been. They had to be isolated and protected while everything outside changed. *If* it changed.

Their excitement, which they'd kept under wraps for so long, was mounting now. Their eyes were glittering; John's hands kept clenching into fists. The line around his mouth was white. George kept swallowing and taking high, shallow breaths. I smiled sympathetically. He'd get over it—once I brought him the Bible.

John started the computer program, clicked open www.backto1963.com, and signaled me to put my hand lightly on the screen, to activate the identity process.

In three minutes the computer clicked its "Done" signal. "All systems up," John announced.

He took the cell phone from me to synchronize it with his own computer program. "Remember," he said again, "your window of opportunity to get the Bible on November 22nd is 20 minutes long at most. Sarah Hughes will leave Air Force One between 2:40 and 2:45 p.m. local time, and your extraction process begins at precisely 3:00. You've got to get the Bible from her within 5 to 7 minutes and get away. At 3:00 the window closes, and you're back here, with or without it. One shot. Right?"

I nodded. I knew if I got the first one wrong, there wouldn't—couldn't— be a second take.

As I'd rehearsed with George, I walked over to the scanner and stood waiting, handbag looped over my upturned arm. Now the rehearsals were over, and the lights and cameras were on. There were no coaches, no instructions, nothing but me and what I had prepared for. I was as ready as I could be.

"Good luck, Cady," George called softly. His fists were clenched, his knuckles white.

John simply smiled at me. "Ready?" he asked.

I nodded, a lump in my throat. I'd had opening-night jitters before, but these felt uncontrollable. I pressed my lips together tightly.

"Now, Cady!" John called. I stepped resolutely through the scanner.

I heard a roar, saw a flash of white light, and then... nothing more.

PART TWO
BIT PLAYER

Chapter Seven
SUNDAY, NOVEMBER 17, 1963

… Outdoor sounds.

Cars driving past. Car horns blaring. A cool breeze on my face, and something hard underneath me.

Slowly, I opened my eyes.

I was alone, lying outside on a patch of soft grass, and it was growing dark.

My head felt like it was about to split right open.

My eyes were sore.

My body felt bruised and banged up, as though I'd fallen down a flight of stairs and hit a number of hard objects along the way.

Altogether, I had had better days.

For a moment, I couldn't think what I was doing here… wherever *here* was.

It came to me slowly, as I lay there, that I had stepped through John's DNA detector, that I'd sensed a flash of light behind me and heard the tapping of keys on his keyboard. And now… I was alone and outdoors. I could feel a fresh evening breeze on my face and hear the rustle of trees above me.

Where was I? And more important, *when* was I?

I took a deep breath, braced my hands against the grass, and pushed myself into a sitting position. My head hurt worse when I forced myself to open my eyes.

I sat on a slope of lawn facing a curved street leading down under a railroad overpass. To my left I saw a blaze of light and a cluster of taller buildings. In the distance to the right, I could see dingy, weary-looking freight cars sitting still on a railroad track. Directly behind me, in the darkening sky, I saw the outline of a classic-looking curved pergola.

Behind that, on the corner, was an old-looking faded brick building. Wherever I was, it was a city.

I sat still for a moment, gathering my strength and assessing my condition. I did feel pretty beat up, as John had theorized I would. But it wasn't really debilitating; I suspected I'd feel a lot better as soon as I had a good meal and a decent night's sleep.

I lifted my eyes, painfully. The light hurt.

My legs, when I tested them, were sore but would hold me, so after a moment I got to my feet. I walked cautiously down the slope of lawn toward the street. I stopped on the sidewalk; cars continued to flow past.

Big cars. Unusually big cars. Some with… I peered at them…

tailfins?

I turned to look behind me at the lawn I'd lain on.

… And knew, suddenly, where I was.

I was in Dallas. There could be no doubt about it… because the curved lawn I'd been lying on was known in my world as the Grassy Knoll, and the entire pretty little park was better known as Dealey Plaza.

The place where Kennedy had been shot.

…Which meant that the seven-story, faded-brick building on the right could only be the Texas School Book Depository, the clock on the Hertz Rent-A-Car sign on the roof telling me it was 6:40 p.m. The curved street in front of me was Elm Street.

John's program had transported me to precisely where he said it would. The question was… had he also transported me to another time? To the *right* time?

The fresh air was helping ease the pounding in my head, and I remembered I had to send a message. I reached for my purse, felt for the cell phone, and pushed the '0' button to communicate that I was safe. I was rewarded with a quick beep.

Now, to learn what year I was in. George's instructions on this point rose in my mind: "Observe, then confirm." I stood for a moment, watching cars passing under the streetlights lining Elm Street. There were some long boat-like cars, almost all American—Chevrolets, Pontiacs, a Ford Fairlane, an old-looking gray Plymouth.

Many of the tires were whitewalls.

It looked promising.

I headed up Elm Street, a brilliant flash of red neon in the sky catching my eye. Several blocks ahead, a 30-foot high Pegasus spun atop a 50-foot-tall metal tower in the shape of an oil derrick looming up from the roof of one of the tallest buildings. I recognized the winged horse as the Mobil Oil Company logo, spinning high above the company's headquarters. To my right rose the red sandstone and blue granite splendor of the old Dallas Courthouse, its high turrets and castle-like parapets standing silent guard over Dealey Plaza.

I headed for the newsstand on the next corner, pausing to peer at the parked cars lining the streets. Almost all appeared to be automatics, with the gearshift on the steering wheel, the kind you notched down to go into reverse or drive. The door handles had a button underneath. You pushed the button to open the door, instead of just lifting the handle. Each car's windshield bore inspection stickers in the lower left corner, and every expiration date said '64'.

My heart began to pound faster as I approached the newsstand. The old man running it looked up irritably from packing away his papers as I approached.

"I'm closed," he said.

"Please…" I said quickly. "I just need—"

"I'm outta Sunday papers," he retorted, and I heard a distinctive Texas drawl.

My heart sank; all I wanted was to know the date. On the other hand, he'd just told me it was Sunday—why else would he mention a Sunday paper? "No. I need a *TV Guide!*" I said and snatched up a shiny copy from atop a stack.

"Oh, all right." He waited while I fumbled with my purse and came up with a shiny silver 1962 quarter. It was all silver, too: no copper band threaded through it. The addition of copper in coins, I remembered, had been okayed by President Johnson in the mid-'60's.

"Where can I get a taxi?" I asked.

He jerked his chin to his right. "Union Station. Coupla blocks." "Thanks." I handed him the quarter.

I set off in the direction he'd indicated, through the thickening darkness. Oddly, in the middle of the downtown area, there was what looked like a log cabin. A sign next to it said that it was the oldest building in Dallas.

But just now I wanted to know what Dallas I was currently in. I began to look through the *TV Guide*, standing under a streetlamp as the sky darkened. The cover featured two men: an actor I recognized as James Franciscus, in a jacket and shirt, blond hair slicked back, and a bigger, brawnier man next to him, identified in the caption as actor Dean Jagger. Both men, the caption noted, appeared in *Mr. Novak*, a TV series I thought vaguely had been on in the early '60's. Franciscus certainly looked young, but there was no year on the cover date. I kept looking. The first page I turned to happened to be Sunday, and I presumed it was today: I saw a photo of a dark-haired, smiling girl—clearly a beauty-pageant contestant—in a tiny crown. Above, in bold capitals, was "SUNDAY", and underneath, "Evening". And next to that, the date that took my breath away: "November 17, 1963."

I had made it. My heart began to pound harder.

"Hey! Lookin' for a cab?"

A bubble-shaped yellow cab swerved to a stop in front of me. I could feel my mouth hanging open in shock, and I snapped it closed with a pop. A Checker cab! I couldn't remember the last time I'd seen one. "Yes," I said, recovering quickly, and hopped into the roomy back seat, fighting the urge to sit in the folded-down jump seat, something I'd loved as a child. According to the sheet posted in front of the passenger's seat, cab rates started at 30 cents.

The cabbie—actually wearing a little yellow hat—turned, dangling a cigarette from the corner of his mouth. "Where to?" he asked.

"Er—2153 Rosebud Lane."

"Sure thing," he said, and jerking the gearshift on the steering wheel downward, he rolled away from the curb.

2153 Rosebud Lane had been my parents' last home together in Dallas.

I was going home, though not to a home I knew or remembered.

I wondered if my mother would welcome me when I got there.

* * *

The cabbie noticed my wide-eyed stare out the window. "First time in Big D?" he asked gruffly. I nodded, and in a moment, he became my self-appointed tour guide.

"Wilson Building," he announced as we passed a three-cornered intersection, with H.L. Green's department store on the bottom story of a building modeled after the Paris Opera House. I'd never seen the original: Paris was a place I'd always wanted to visit but never had. On the other hand, right now I was further from home than I'd ever been in my life. I decided to enjoy the adventure of it.

My guide pointed out the buildings that headquartered the big oil companies, including the Magnolia Building. I learned about the underground complex of the Gulf, Colorado & Santa Fe Railroad, the almost-new Union Tower, and got a full recap of every play in the upstart Dallas Cowboys' thrilling victory over Philadelphia earlier today.

The cab drew up ten minutes later before a small two-story house set far back in the middle of a block of others that appeared exactly the same. There were just a few streetlights, and I had to peer hard into my wallet to come up with the cab fare: $1 for the ride plus a quarter tip. George had told me to spend cautiously and tip reasonably, and not draw unwanted attention to myself. I thought a quarter tip was reasonable, considering his lengthy and detailed tour. I'd have liked to give him more but thought regretfully that it would make him remember me; that was something I had to avoid.

He thanked me politely and roared off. I was on my own. I straightened up and started up the walk.

There were pale smears of yellow light in the downstairs windows, pale blue light from what was probably a television set turned on, and muffled sounds which I took to be canned laughter. I took a deep breath and rang the bell.

The muffled sound of the TV laughter didn't change in volume, but there were soft hurried footsteps behind the door, and the door opened halfway. A slender young woman in a clean and starched blue and white housecoat with a Peter Pan collar, soft brown curls subdued into a pageboy hairstyle, and dark blue eyes, looked at me inquiringly, a dishcloth in her hand.

This was the young Sandra Cuyler.

This was my mother.

I was rocked by her startling resemblance to the old photos that I'd pored over in our family album. Here she was, as she had been, cared for and happy. For a moment I couldn't speak.

Finally, I said, "Mrs. Cuyler?"

"Yes?" The voice was soft, too, softer than I had ever heard it.

"My name is Cady—er—Catherine Roberts. I've come from New York, and some friends of my family said they knew you, that you rented out rooms?" I waited for her hesitant nod and went on. "I was wondering—I know it's Sunday night—so sorry to impose—but I was wondering if you might have something available for me?"

Her eyes narrowed. There was something immediately cold and untouchable in her, something I didn't understand. I gave her my best smile and hoped my dress wasn't too wrinkled from lying on the grass and that I looked moderately presentable, because I needed to get past that door if I had any hope of saving my parents.

I waited without fidgeting for what seemed a long time but was probably only half a minute. She examined me silently from head to foot, and I was dimly aware, while I waited, of the moment when the canned laughter was replaced by the bouncy, full-bodied orchestral rendering of a cigarette commercial.

Then she said shortly, "Sorry. We're full."

The door started to close in my face.

I might have pushed my foot at the door to stop it from closing, if another voice, a deep, rich, male voice, hadn't interrupted. "Who is it, Sandy?"

She turned to answer, and I could see into a gaily-papered hallway—the very same cheerful wallpaper she would later carefully restore to her house on Rockland Avenue. It made me want to cry.

Behind her stood a man I recognized. He was more handsome than his photos, standing relaxed but straight, his hair (brown with chestnut highlights, I saw) now slightly rumpled, as though from lying on a couch watching TV. He wore a short-sleeved yellow Banlon shirt and beautifully pressed gray trousers.

This was the man my mother had idolized.

This was Don Cuyler. My father.

I stared: he was so much more glamorous than his photos. It was like watching a mannequin come to life.

He peered at me. "Yes?"

My mother hadn't missed my gaping at her husband. "She wants to rent a room," she said coolly. "We don't know her. I told her we're full."

He came closer to inspect me. I gave him the same hopeful smile I'd given her—and saw at once from the tightening of her face and the flowering smile on his that it was not the right move. Though of course my father was just being kind; he would never look at another woman…

I plunged into explanations, talking quickly. "The Milfords told me to look you up. They said you always have rooms for friends."

Don Cuyler cocked his head at me and gave me a smile. His straight, even teeth could have been featured in a Pepsodent ad. "You're a friend of the Milfords?"

"They've—uh—known me and my family for years."

It was no lie: the Milfords had been my parents' friends in Dallas. Later, after my father's disappearance, they helped my mother move to Westchester County.

"Go stay with them, then," Sandra said curtly to me.

He regarded her with bemusement. "Sandy, really. It's Sunday night and she seems quite—respectable. And the Milfords are in Hawaii." I had known that—George had found it out and told me—and I counted on it in making my explanation. Don Cuyler looked at me thoughtfully, as though weighing his options. Sandra made as though to close the door again.

He put out a hand to stop her.

She stopped at once.

"Now let's think about this," he said slowly to Sandra. "How long do you need a room for?" he asked me.

"Well—till Friday? I'm sure I'll find something else by then."

"You have a job here?" Sandra asked suspiciously.

"I was supposed to, but my luggage was stolen at the bus station, and I found out the job I'm supposed to start tomorrow was given to someone else—" I screwed up my face, putting on my most wretched look, hoping that just this once, I could cry on cue if I had to, as I'd never managed to do in twelve years as Sheila.

Don peered at me. "What do you do?"

"Well… telephone operator, receptionist. I can type and file, too."

Don looked at Sandra. "We need someone to fill in at ISI. Looks like she just dropped in our laps." He held the door open for me. "Can't let you sleep out there. I think we can fix something for you till Friday."

"Oh, thank you!" I said, relief flooding me and spilling over into the smile I bestowed on him and my mother, who regarded me sourly as I stepped inside.

"But your friends are coming—" Sandra protested to him.

"It'll be all right. The room near the kitchen, Sandy," he said. "Don't worry."

"Yes, dear," she said dully.

He smiled at me. "Welcome, then, Miss—?"

"Roberts," I said quickly. "Catherine Roberts. Cady for short. C-A-D-Y."

He smiled again.

Before I could thank him again, he'd vanished in the direction of the TV, which now sounded as though the commercial was over. I could hear a high-pitched voice I remembered as Ed Sullivan's speaking over the applause of the audience. "And now, we've got a real treat—"

Sandra didn't speak as she led me straight down the hall to a door on the right.

Without ceremony she pushed it open and snapped on an overhead light.

The room was small but rigidly clean, with patterned blue wallpaper, soft blue flowered curtains looped back at the window and a neatly-made single bed. The open closet showed off plenty of space for my non-existent wardrobe, and extra blankets piled on the shelf. The window, raised an inch to let in the misty night air, overlooked the now-dark backyard.

I was very pleased and started to say so, but before I could, she said stiffly, "I hope you'll be comfortable."

I didn't know what I'd done to her, but from the moment she set eyes on me, it seems, Sandra Cuyler had disliked me: more than disliked me—almost loathed me. I had no idea why. She had no way of knowing I wasn't telling the truth about the Milfords. How could I have offended her?

I turned to her, determined to thaw the ice in her eyes. "It's lovely," I said sincerely. "I can't thank you enough. Oh!" I suddenly remembered. "I didn't even ask you—how much is the rent?"

She hesitated. "This one is—" she paused, obviously sizing me up, "—three dollars a night. If you want breakfast, it'll be an extra two dollars a day."

"That's fine," I said enthusiastically. "I'll take breakfast too."

There was a flicker in her face, as though my response somehow bothered her. Why?

"Fine," she said stiffly. A little of the ice seemed to melt in her features as she added,"You can watch TV in the living room, if you like."

I started to open my handbag. "I'll pay you for the week—"

Before I could finish, a peculiar look came over her face. "Excuse me," she said abruptly.

She rushed out and headed through a door opposite the kitchen. She threw the door shut, but in a moment, I heard the unmistakable sounds of retching.

I would have gone to her, but I sensed this was a household where appearances counted for a good deal. Instead, I sat on the bed and looked around at the quiet, well-appointed little room.

I had made it, so far. I'd managed to insinuate myself into the Cuyler household, which was imperative to the rest of my mission. I'd met my parents. One seemed quite pleased to know me, the other was sullen and unwelcoming.

Well, I would sort out those attitudes in time. Meanwhile, I was here, and Sandra had invited me to watch TV with them. The hall was empty, though the retching sounds were still coming from the bathroom. Quietly I walked into the living room.

Don Cuyler looked up from a glass containing what looked like a whiskey sour and said, "Come in! Ed Sullivan's on."

"A really big shew?" I asked, remembering the phrase from somewhere deep in my childhood, and he laughed.

"Right. We never miss Ed Sullivan. Nancy Sinatra and Tommy Sands are on tonight."

I remembered dimly that Nancy Sinatra had been briefly married to singer Tommy Sands; a duet of theirs might be worth watching.

The room was a comfortable size; still, it seemed stuffed with furniture. Don was lounging on a big upholstered black and white tweed sofa. Against the opposite wall, below a wooden shelf filled with knick-knacks, sat a big console-model TV set with wood paneling. It was black and white, and the screen was larger than I would have expected. In another corner was what looked like a very expensive hi-fi set closed in with wicker doors. In a second corner was a wheeled glass cart stocked with almost-full bottles of scotch, gin, bourbon and vodka, along with several small bottles of mixers and jars of olives and maraschino cherries. Large standard lamps, crystal ashtrays and lacquered coasters covered the end tables scattered about the room. Lying across the beautiful glass coffee table in front of the TV were copies of *The Big D Shopping News*, *Dallas Times-Herald* and what looked like a neighborhood gazette, *The Oak Cliff Tribune*. It occurred to me that my parents seemed quite prosperous.

Don's eyes were on me. He didn't speak for a moment, as I made myself comfortable opposite him. Then, "Room okay?" he said.

"Just fine," I said happily. "You and Mrs. Cuyler saved my life."

He smiled briefly and glanced at the TV set; Nancy and Tommy were singing, and the audience was eating it up. Then casually, "I meant it about the job. My company just lost a telephone operator. We'll be looking for someone."

He glanced back at the TV. He seemed intent on the show, but somehow I sensed he was downplaying his real interest. I remembered suddenly that he'd done amateur acting for years, and I wondered why that seemingly unrelated piece of information had occurred to me just then.

"It's our busy season, too," Don went on. "We were going to bring in a temp from a local agency this week, but I'm sure you'll do just as well." He glanced at my legs before looking back at the TV.

This was more perfect than I had dreamed. To see the people he was surrounded by at work—any of whom might just have been responsible for his disappearance, or known about it... I tried to be casual in my answer. "What kind of company is it?"

He gazed at me now, not hiding the fact that he was studying me deliberately, and I met his gaze, trying to look brisk and professional. "It's called Import Spirits International, Incorporated," he said. "We import and export wines and other alcoholic beverages all over the world."

He gazed at me, obviously waiting for a response. "Must be a very good business," I offered.

"Yes, it's very interesting." His eyes met mine. There was something cool and appraising in them that I found disconcerting. "And you look like the kind of girl my people will just eat up. If you like, you can come to the office with me tomorrow. I'll tell them to put you on right away."

"You can do that?" I asked innocently.

He merely smiled.

The sounds of Sandra's retching had begun to fade. I hadn't realized until I heard the water begin to run that every sound from the bathroom came through loud and clear in here. I wondered why Don hadn't gone to help her.

He gave no indication of having heard her. He simply looked at me and waited. I forced a delighted smile to my face and said, "Wow! A great room and a new job. I guess this has been my lucky day."

* * *

I managed to stay up through *The Ed Sullivan Show* and T*he Judy Garland Show to the beginning* of *Candid Camera*, with its cheery opening theme song (*"When you least expect it, you're elected, you're the star today... Smile! You're on Candid Camera!"*). Finally, though, I began to fade. I was exhausted, it was past 9:00, and a headache was pounding behind my eyes, so I excused myself to Don and headed for the bathroom, where the air was filled with a heavy spray scent. Sandra was carefully covering up the signs of her retching. I wondered why.

I found a bottle of Anacin in the medicine chest, along with a curious assortment of other bottles, including Miltown, which I remembered was a mild tranquilizer, like Valium today. It was prescribed for "Mrs. Sandra Cuyler" and had been filled only a few weeks before, and it was a refill.

Wondering why my mother needed tranquilizers, I splashed water on my face and tried to scrub my teeth using my finger as a toothbrush. I really had to stop at a drugstore and pick up a few things. I would also have to buy more clothes. My beige dress was good, but I couldn't possibly wear it all week.

But this wasn't the year 2000. In 1963, stores closed early every night except Thursdays, according to George, and I could expect to work at any office job until 5:00.

Ah, well. That was a problem for tomorrow. The Anacin was helping my headache, but I still felt weary all over. I needed sleep desperately.

I'd traveled back to Dallas, in November 1963. I'd met my parents and secured a room in their house and a job with my father's company. Though I might not be a clotheshorse while I was here, I couldn't help thinking, a trifle smugly, that for a woman from the year 2000, I was doing okay...

Chapter Eight
MONDAY, NOVEMBER 18, 1963

ISI, Inc. did business in a shabby, low-slung building on the outskirts of Love Field, the Dallas airport, about a twenty-minute drive from my parents' home. It was circled by a huge parking lot and jostled against an adjoining warehouse, and seemed to be squeezing itself tightly between them, as though trying to become invisible.

It was 10 a.m. I had caught the bus from Oak Cliff after asking Don for extra time to shop for a few items, to make a presentable appearance. Given my story of lost luggage and the wrinkled state of my dress, he had agreed, and instructed Sandra to point me in the right direction. I had expected her to give me directions to the smart shops along Harry Hines Boulevard. Instead, frowning, she had grudgingly pointed out a row of cheap shops nearby that opened at 9:00, shops she clearly didn't patronize herself. If I wanted makeup, there was a new cosmetics retailer that had opened in Exchange Park a couple of months before, called Mary Kay. They also sold custom-styled wigs, if I was interested, she said doubtfully. I thanked her as she ran for the bathroom again.

"Flu," Don said succinctly over the sounds of her retching.

I don't think so, I thought, but said aloud, "I hope she'll feel better soon."

Thanks to a helpful young clerk in an all-in-one, Woolworth's-type store, I emerged with enough to see me through for the week: toothpaste and a toothbrush, a hairbrush, three extra pairs of nylon stockings, and two inexpensive dresses, a simple blue sheath with short sleeves and a bright red dress with a matching belt and a full skirt.

I shuddered when I thought of wearing the same high-heeled, constricting shoes for the next week, but there was nothing I could do: I wouldn't find more comfortable shoes in 1963 unless I wore sneakers or sandals, which no girl in business would dare do.

However, when I walked into the lobby at ISI in my new blue sheath (more conservative, to make a good first impression), the air was distinctly cool.

"Miss—?"

"Roberts," I supplied, smiling at the sour-faced woman who intercepted me. She had a bun twisted high on her head and harlequin-shaped bluish-gray glasses with tiny cameos on each corner. Her lipstick was a deep red, and the corners of her deeply lined mouth were turned down.

"I'm Miss Bradley, the office manager," she said, her tone chilly. "Mr. Cuyler said you'd fill in for our telephone operator, who's not—er—not here, at the moment. You can operate a switchboard?"

"Yes," I said confidently, thanking George for his seemingly endless lessons on arcane subjects and understanding, finally, why he'd insisted on them. "I have experience."

"Where have you worked before?" she said doubtfully.

I gave her my cover story. "In New York, at some small advertising firms. A year at one agency, six months at a grocery firm—"

"Which one?" she said suspiciously.

"Gristede's. In Manhattan."

"I've heard of them," she said coldly, "though we don't have them here in Dallas. And you came here why?"

"For another job," I said quickly. "But they told me they'd given it to someone else."

My answers seemed to satisfy her, though she seemed reluctant to acknowledge it. "Fifty dollars for this week, and then, if our regular operator isn't back—" She seemed to follow her own thought silently, and tightened her lips, "we'll talk about keeping you on." She handed me a stack of forms to fill out. "Bring them back to me before lunch. This way, please."

I followed her past a seedy-looking reception area with a high counter to a splintered wooden desk set with a high clumsy-looking metal switchboard, where a girl sat, talking softly into a headset and plugging long brown snakes of telephone cord into small holes in the board in front of her. She was in her twenties, small-boned and too thin, with large nervous eyes, wearing a navy dotted-swiss dress.

"Here," Miss Bradley said abruptly. "Toni will show you what to do."

As she marched off, I turned back to the girl in navy. She finished her call and turned to look up at me, her face serious, even anxious. When I smiled at her, the corners of her pink-lipsticked mouth turned up for just a moment; then the little smile vanished and she was staring at me tensely.

"Hi," I said tentatively. "You're—Toni?"

She nodded, her eyes scanning me. "I'm Cady," I began. "I'm filling in for a few days. Mr. Cuyler recommended me."

Toni immediately stiffened, her face going dark, her eyes flicking up and down my figure. I didn't like the implication.

"I'm here to *work!*" I said, a trifle sharply. "Miss Bradley said you'd show me what to do."

"Sit down," she said, pointing at a precarious-looking wooden chair. I seated myself gingerly, but before she could say any more, the switchboard began to light up.

"Good morning, ISI Incorporated," Toni said in a suddenly cool, professional voice. She listened, pulled a snaking brown rubber line from its hole and plugged it into the board in front of her. "Mr. Cuyler, Loewe's Trucking. Go ahead, please." Another bulb lit on the board. "Good morning, ISI Incorporated," she said to another caller, and in a moment, there was another line snaking to another hole.

I sat watching, remembering George's instructions on operating a switchboard. The reality was faster and a lot more daunting than my rehearsals, but I thought I could handle it. Finally, Toni finished with the callers and handed me a tattered card listing the names and extension numbers of the salesmen and executives. All but Miss Bradley were men.

My job, Toni explained, was to patch through all calls when the lines were open. If someone was out or their line was busy, I was to take a message on a white slip (pads of them littered the desk), then put it in the appropriate mailbox in the chipped wooden cabinet behind us, where each executive's secretary would periodically pick them up.

"Except Mr. Cuyler," Toni told me. "No secretary. He prefers to do everything himself."

I looked at the list. There were only a dozen names on it. My father, Don Cuyler, was listed as Executive Vice-President, the highest title I saw. I'd had no idea he was that important and commented on it to Toni.

Her eyes went wary immediately. She didn't answer at once, instead fumbling inside a desk drawer for a pack of Parliament cigarettes. She offered it to me—I waved it away—then lit up herself, breathing in the smoke deeply.

"Yes, he's the boss," she said finally. "I thought you knew," she added bluntly.

I explained that I was staying at the Cuyler boarding house and told my story about just coming to town, and Don's generous job offer. The tension in Toni's face eased, and the appraising look left her eyes.

"So you really haven't—met him—before?"

"Never," I said honestly. "He told me about the job and—well, I was lucky."

Toni nodded gently, as though confirming something to herself. But her face, when she turned back to me, was friendlier. I ventured another question.

"If he's the Executive Vice-President, who's the President?"

Toni shrugged. "Mr. Feigert. He's not around much. Lives in a fancy house in the suburbs and checks in about once a month. Mr. Cuyler is the boss."

She looked as though she wanted to say something else, but just then the switchboard lit up again.

Mischievously, Toni motioned to it. "Wanna try?"

"Yes," I said resolutely. I put on the other headset, snapped down the switch as I'd seen her do, and said, "ISI Incorporated. How may I help you?"

Toni's eyes widened in appreciation as a young male voice said, "Don Cuyler, please" into my earphones.

I checked the extension for Don Cuyler. "He's on another line right now. May I take a message?"

There was a pause. "No, I'll call him back. When do you think he'll be available?" I could detect a very faint trace of a Southern accent. Not Texan, but southern.

I had no idea. "You might try back in a half hour. Can I tell him who called?"

There was silence. "You could tell him Alec called."

"Alec," I repeated. "Fine. Thank you."

I pulled the plug from the switchboard and turned to Toni, who was nodding. "Al for Mr. Cuyler, right?"

"He's called before?"

Toni nodded again. "Sometimes three times a day. Nice guy, though. Mr. Cuyler always takes his calls. He—" She stopped abruptly, and I could almost see the thought in her mind: *She's temporary. She doesn't need to know this.*

To take the onus off the sudden silence, I said cheerfully, "I'll remember, then, when he calls again." I scribbled a message slip for Don Cuyler and pushed it into his box.

She crushed out the cigarette into an ashtray on the desk and lit another one. Though it was just past 10:30, the ashtray was already full. Her hands were trembling, and she had trouble holding the cigarette tip to the lighter.

I had no idea why.

She took a deep drag but finally, her fingers shaking uncontrollably, she dropped the cigarette into the ashtray.

"Are you all right?" I asked before I thought.

To my surprise, Toni dropped her head into her cupped hands and began to cry.

At the same time, the switchboard began to light up with calls.

She was in no condition to do anything about them. I plugged in the calls and did my best, while Toni wept.

At least half the calls were for Don Cuyler. I took messages from three different trucking companies, asking for return calls 'immediately', and pushed the message slips into his box. As soon as his light went off, I had patched through a call to him from yet another trucking company. When the switchboard finally quieted down, I rummaged in my bag for Kleenex for Toni.

"Can I help?" I asked quietly.

Toni shook her head almost violently. "No, no!" But she accepted the Kleenex, blew her nose and mopped at her eyes.

"Are you sick?" I knew she wasn't. "Or just scared?"

She was still trembling, but the tears had stopped. I looked steadily at her, and she said, in a quiet, hopeless voice, "It's Debbie. She used to work here." She gestured at the switchboard.

"The girl I'm filling in for?" Toni nodded and gulped. "What happened to her?" I asked as gently as possible.

"We don't know!" Toni whispered into the handkerchief. "She just—didn't show up for work one day last week. Miss Bradley called her and went by her apartment—she even called the hospitals—but—no one's seen her since last Tuesday."

I had a sinking feeling. This was the person I was replacing? Someone who'd simply vanished? Like Judge Crater or Amelia Earhart?

Toni, who hadn't noticed my frozen expression, babbled on, "And Mr. Cuyler says not to talk about it. He says it isn't *good for business!*" She sobbed again as the switchboard lit up.

At a break in the action, I sent Toni into the ladies' room to wash her face and repair her makeup. Her handbag, like mine, was about twice as big as what I usually carried. I had also noticed on the bus that unlike most women today, the young women of 1963 kept makeup kits in their bags and checked their faces regularly. Being told to fix her face was something Toni considered quite normal.

I sat alone behind the switchboard, wondering about the vanished Debbie. Where was she? Why did no one here at work know where she was? Did someone else? If so, why weren't they coming forward? What about her family—didn't she have one, and did they know where she'd gone?

I shook my head as the switchboard jangled. *You're a soap-opera actress*, I told myself. *And you've been playing with dramatic storylines for so long, now you think it can happen in real life.*

Could this have anything to do with Don Cuyler? He's going to disappear as well. Could the two disappearances be related? How could they not be related? Two disappearances from the same place of business in less than two weeks?

In less than 24 hours in 1963, I'd landed myself in a very strange situation.*You'd better start asking the right questions, I told myself, or nothing will change on Friday.*

But what are the right questions? George had assured me I would know. Well, he had more faith than I did, at the moment.

"Well, hello," said a male voice above me, and I mentally shook myself out of my reverie and looked up with an automatic smile. The speaker was young, mid-'20s, I judged, in a starched white shirt and striped tie held by a gold tie pin, and carrying a light gray jacket rakishly over his shoulder.

"Fresh blood," he said, looking me up and down, and gave me a smile that was just short of sly. "I must be slipping if it's lunchtime and I haven't noticed you yet."

I glanced at the clock above my head. Sure enough, it was just past noon. The morning had flown by, between my concentrating on my job and my speculations about Debbie.

Well, every contact helped. I smiled encouragingly and said, "I'm Cady."

"Nice to meet you, Kate," he said jovially, but before I could correct him he went on, "I'm Stan Marchand. Top sales guy for ISI. Gonna be with us long?"

"I hope so," I said. I explained that I was staying at the Cuylers' and how Don Cuyler had suggested I work here temporarily.

"Then you'll be here for the party tonight!" he exclaimed, his eyes roving up and down my body. At the same time, his hand seemed to snake out independently and snare the pen lying on top of the counter. Without taking his eyes off me, he slipped it into his jacket pocket. I decided prudently not to notice.

"What party?" I asked.

He actually stared at me. "*The* party, babe! The big party for the whole company—I mean, everybody—out at the boss man's pad!"

I looked at him again, bewildered. "Sounds—big," I said.

He nodded vigorously. "You know it. The biggest. Primo food, serious booze—and all where the other half lives, if you get what I mean." He winked at me. *Crude*, I thought, *but probably thinks he's a real suave operator.*

I knew what to do with guys like this. God knows, I met enough of them as an actress. I leaned on an elbow, widened my eyes and said, "Stan, that sounds marvelous. I'll bet you're going, huh?"

"Wouldn't miss it," and he winked back at me.

"I bet you've already got a hot date, huh?"

But the wink and leer I expected from him didn't materialize. Instead, Stan just looked uncomfortable.

Toni came back from the bathroom. Powder was caked heavily under her eyelids, but the traces of tears were gone. She gave Stan a quick nod and sat down next to me.

Stan rummaged in his jacket pocket, not looking at her. "Toni—" he began.

"Nobody knows nothin'," Toni said stiffly. "Especially me."

Stan's lips tightened. "And what am I supposed to do … ?"

"Find someone else," Toni said. For a moment she looked up at him wistfully, but he didn't notice; he was busy running a plastic comb through his hair.

Toni continued to look at him hopefully, but when he began to straighten his tie, she sighed and put the headset over her ears again. He still hadn't looked at her once.

Finally finished, he straightened up and threw the jacket over his shoulder again. "See you, Kay," he said. "Kinda nice having new scenery around here." He gave me the once-over again and said, his eyes twinkling, "Very *nice* scenery." With a flick of his fingers that he'd probably copied from James Bond, he strolled unhurriedly out the door.

Jerk, I thought. Toni gave me one quick look, and in it I read condemnation: the age-old look of the unpopular toward the chosen. She didn't say a word to me but continued to plug in the calls and scribble down messages. I wanted to speak to her, but she kept her eyes carefully averted.

There was nothing for me to do at the moment, so I studied the office. The reception area where I sat faced the double glass entrance doors, and all visitors obviously came through here. It was a small area scattered with a few wooden straight chairs, some so old the wood had splintered. They looked anything but inviting.

I looked at the walls. Apart from magazine covers of picture-perfect models in brief costumes enjoying various cocktails, which had been crookedly scotch-taped to the walls, the whole area looked drab. The pale green paint on the walls was now faded and peeling right off, and the ashtrays hadn't been emptied in weeks. An odor of stale cigarette and cigar smoke hung over the whole area.

It looked not just unprofessional, but downright seedy. *If I ran this place, I'd hate for visitors to see this*, I thought. It would give people a terrible impression of the company.

I waited till Toni was finished with a call and had stuck a message slip in one of the little boxes before I said casually, "Do we get lots of visitors coming in here?"

Toni looked past me at the clutter of old chairs and the full ashtrays and the ugly stained linoleum floor. Clearly, she knew what I was thinking. "Not many," she said reluctantly, and I was careful to put on my most neutral expression. "Mr. Cuyler says we shouldn't encourage people to come here and plop themselves down in our reception area; he says that's how work doesn't get done."

If I didn't know better, I thought, I'd think that Don Cuyler was trying to keep people from coming here.

But that made no sense. My father was a terrific businessman hadn't my mother always said so? I was just missing something, something very obvious that would explain it all…

The trouble was, I couldn't figure out what it was.

*   *   *

By 12:30, the office had mostly emptied. About a dozen nicely-dressed young men—the sales force, Toni explained—poured out of the door leading to the warren of rooms in the back, saying hello to me and flirting mildly. When they'd gone, the place was starkly quiet. Even the air felt heavy.

"As I was eying the clock and wondering when I might get a bite to eat, the switchboard buzzed again." By now I was feeling much more confident. "Good morning, ISI Incorporated, may I help you?" I intoned for the hundredth time that day.

"Is Don Cuyler there?" The same young male voice from this morning, the same faint Southern accent.

"Is this Alec?" I asked.

There was a pause. "Well, yes."

I checked Don's lines. "I'm sorry, he's still on his phone. I've left your message for him. Would you like me to leave another one?"

"… Is this Debbie?" he asked.

"No, I'm filling in for Debbie. She's—uh—she's not here right now." I found myself instinctively tiptoeing around the truth—whatever that happened to be.

There was a pause. "Well, I'm getting ready to leave my current location for a short while—but this is a matter of some urgency. Perhaps I could hold on until he's free?"

I checked with Toni. "Can we let Mr. Cuyler know someone is waiting for him?"

She shook her head violently. "No! Never! You never interrupt Mr. Cuyler for any reason!"

I went back on the line. "I'm sorry, that's not possible. Can you give me a specific message and I'll get it to Mr. Cuyler as soon as possible?"

He paused. "Will you please tell Mr. Cuyler that Alec called at his direction, and that frankly, I'm rather perturbed at being put off. It's not easy for me to get to a telephone all the time, as he well knows."

"Alec—" I was spelling it out as I wrote down the message. "Very unusual. Sounds English."

"Well—no—actually. It's—uh—it's Russian. Alek with a 'k'."

"Russian?" My eyebrows went up. This was the Cold War, after all. "But you sound American."

"Yes."

"Let's see if I have this right—" I read him back the message.

"That's perfect," he said. "You must be much better educated than most of the young ladies who answer the telephones in Dallas. You got every word of it right."

"Oh, well—" I didn't know what to say to that. "I've—uh—I've traveled a little. Maybe that's the difference."

"Really? So have I."

"An American with a name like Alek—I should say so," I retorted, but I was smiling, and I'm certain he could hear it in my voice, because when he replied, I could swear he sounded like he was smiling, too.

"From your accent, I'd say most of your traveling was up North," he announced.

"From your accent, I'd say most of your traveling was down South," I retorted.

"You'd be wrong. I've been around the world."

"Really?" I said, my voice scaling up, along with my interest. "Where?" I hoped he'd been to some of the places I'd always wanted to go: I could ask him about them.

"You haven't answered," he said. "Have you traveled up North?"

"Yes, and lived there," I said. "New York, mostly."

"Oh, New York. It really is a wonderful town. I've spent time there."

"Really? And what did you like about it?"

"The Empire State Building," he replied promptly. "And the Bronx Zoo. Both great."

"You sound like a typical tourist," I said, and when Toni stared at me. I realized I'd been on the call much longer than I needed to be. I was enjoying this back-and-forthing with Alek—and as long as the phones were quiet, I supposed it was all right to keep chatting for a while.

"I was no tourist," he insisted. "At one time I could have named you every single shop in the Empire State Building—I knew 'em all, and where they were located. And I knew the subway system backwards—most tourists never figure that out."

"Then you must have spent a lot of time there," I said.

"Not really," he said. "I've spent more time overseas."

"Overseas?" My voice scaled up. "You are unusual, then. Where overseas?"

"Oh—Japan. Finland. Holland." He hesitated. "And the—well, other places."

"That's amazing," I said, and I meant it. For someone who sounded so young to have been in all those places was nothing short of astounding, particularly in a Cold War environment. I wondered if he had been in the military, which would explain at least part of his list.

I started to ask, but then realized the question was impertinent, at best. For all the energy in his voice—I could tell he was enjoying this conversation, too—I had the distinct feeling that Alek might not be too free with information about himself. People didn't readily spill their life stories to strangers in 1963, the way they often did in the year 2000.

Instead, I said sincerely, "I've always wanted to travel a lot. You're one up on me. I envy you."

"Oh?" he said, and I could tell he was pleased.

"Oh, yes," I went on. "You must have had some real adventures. I haven't really been anywhere. I'd love to see other places."

"That's nothing," he said. "Just going to other places isn't a big deal. It's living in those places that really broadens you."

"You've lived overseas?" I asked, and I couldn't help the admiration in my voice; I really was impressed. "You sound so young—were you with your family?"

"No," he said. "I went on my own."

"Alone? Really?" This guy had more going for him than I'd thought. "Where?"

There was a pause, and the guardedness came back into his voice. "Is Mr. Cuyler off the phone yet?" he asked abruptly.

I was getting too personal; he had pulled back. Why had I asked? I checked the board. "Not yet. Should I give him your message?"

"I think that's best," he said, and there was a formality in his voice now. I had gotten too close.

Then he surprised me. "What's your name?" he asked. "After all, you know mine."

"Cady," I said quickly, realizing belatedly I had to get back to work. Toni was handling all the calls herself, and while there weren't many, I felt slightly guilty.

"Cady," he said musingly. "With a C?"

He stopped me cold. No one ever got my name right the first time. "How did you know?" I asked.

"I told you. I've traveled a lot. Talk to you later, Cady with a C." And he hung up.

"Lunchtime," said Toni unsmilingly some time later, when we'd untangled the phone lines and it was once more quiet.

To my surprise, Toni told me that we took lunch at the same time, with another girl, Hilda, to relieve us. I saw Hilda slide around the switchboard and into Toni's seat as soon as Toni stood up, in one practiced motion. Hilda's stiff black hair, obviously buffered by great amounts of hairspray, didn't move as the headset went on, and in her hand was a worn copy of *Photoplay*, which she flipped open at once.

"There's a little luncheonette on the next block," Toni told me. "We usually go there."

Outside of ISI, Toni seemed less jumpy, more sure of herself. I wondered aloud why the company didn't have a lunchroom for the employees.

"Mr. Cuyler," Toni said promptly. "Says lunchrooms cause disruptions in work. He prefers that employees go outside for lunch."

I was perplexed. The impression I'd formed of Don Cuyler the night before— jovial, concerned and thoughtful—was at odds with what I was learning today. Perhaps he was one of those men who separated their personal lives from work so thoroughly that they developed completely different personalities for each.

We cut through the parking lot, past more than a dozen shiny new cars parked neatly in rows. Several Thunderbirds, a Cadillac and a Chrysler Imperial glistened in the midday sun.

"Company cars," Toni said promptly when I asked her. "Mr. Cuyler insists the salesmen make a good impression when they visit clients. And the executives sign them in and out when they're making a pickup or delivery at the airport." A descending jet roared directly overhead, and Toni added, "Love Field is only five minutes away."

I confessed that I hadn't known that.

Toni looked at me strangely. "But I thought you just came to Dallas. Didn't you fly here? I mean, from New York?"

"Ah... no. No, I came... on a bus."

Luckily we were at the luncheonette now, its entrance marked by a blazing red and white Coca-Cola sign overhead. Toni shrugged and made for the counter, where a round fan blew the warm air around ineffectually. Toni slid onto a high stool, and I perched next to her and looked at the large handwritten menus posted on the wall, but something teased at the back of my mind. Something she'd said bothered me.

"What'll it be, Toni?" The young counterman grinned as he approached us, wiping his hands on a formerly white towel. "And when's Debbie coming back?"

I could feel Toni stiffen next to me. "I'm in a hurry," she said abruptly. "I'll have a tuna sandwich and a Coke."

The counterman looked at me. "You,

Miss?"

"Same."

I tried to think what Toni had said that raised a question in my mind. Nothing jogged my memory. I glanced around. Big colored posters on the wall advertised Kool cigarettes, Marlboro cigarettes, Lone Star beer, and of course, Coca-Cola. I noticed with amusement that the Cokes the counterman set in front of us were frosty glass bottles he'd simply uncapped and left by our places with straws.

I needed to know more about Debbie, and being out of the office was a good opportunity. Toni looked more relaxed, daintily sipping her Coke through the straw, so I said casually, "Debbie seems pretty popular, especially with the guys."

Toni blinked, and I thought there might be another cascade of tears, but she merely said grudgingly, "They all liked her."

The counterman slid our plates in front of us. The tuna sandwich tasted surprisingly good, and the Coke tasted wonderful. I'd been drinking sodas from cans for so long, I'd forgotten how good it could taste out of a glass bottle. The sandwich came with a small bag of potato chips.

I was so surprised that I liked the food that I'd almost forgotten my query to Toni when she said in a rush, "Debbie was—I mean, is—everything any guy would want. When the guys sassed her, she always knew something funny to say back. And she was so pretty. All the guys at ISI liked her, too." She sighed; it was a sigh of envy.

I didn't think Toni should be envying a girl who might just have been easy.

"She sounds," I said deliberately, "like a party girl."

Toni's eyes flicked up as she finished her sandwich.

"Well, that's what you thought I was, didn't you, when you met me? Is that what Debbie was?" I remembered something. "You thought that when I told you Mr. Cuyler recommended me for the job. Why?"

"I didn't!" Toni gulped down her soda and stood up, fumbling at her purse. "I've got to get back."

"I'll get it," I said. "For both of us."

Toni looked at me, surprised, and then smiled for the first time. "I—well, thanks." Then she added, with a glance at the clock overhead, "We'd better hurry. Hilda'll scream if we're late."

On the way back to the office, passing the ISI parking lot, I suddenly realized what had been bothering me. "Toni," I said, "did you say those cars were for pickups and deliveries at Love Field? And that the executives signed them out?"

She nodded.

"Well, does that mean the people doing the pickups and deliveries are the executives?"

Somewhat doubtfully, she nodded again.

"Why do the executives do it? I mean, you could send a messenger, couldn't you, to pick up and deliver? And why are the cars so fancy? Just to go to the airport and back?"

"Mr. Cuyler has a messenger," Toni explained, a little exasperated with my probing. "The other executives pick up and deliver clients to the airport, take them to their hotels, and then take them out on the town. That's *business*," she emphasized. We had reached the doors of the ISI office, but she made no move to walk inside. Instead, she turned to me, her hand on the glass door. "Don't ask so many questions, Cady, okay? You're just a temp. And besides, I—I like you."

And with that startling statement, she pulled open the door and walked inside.

* * *

The switchboard, which had been quiet while Hilda tended it, lit up like the Fourth of July as soon as Toni and I sat down. I could handle the lines without mishap now. Next to me, Toni relayed calls and took messages so smoothly and quietly I could hardly hear her as I did the same.

The fifth caller, a man with a hoarse midwestern voice, asked for Don Cuyler, who was on his line. "May I take a message?" I asked.

"Tell him Jack called. From the Carousel. He'll have that shipment of gin by 10:00 tomorrow. I'm having it sent directly." He hung up. I wrote out the message and pushed it into Don Cuyler's box, which I noticed was full. Obviously, he'd been too busy to collect his messages yet, including Alek's.

A few minutes later, Alek himself called again. "Hello, Cady. Mr. Cuyler available now?"

"Sorry. I'm afraid not."

A pause. "I'll wait. Maybe you and I can talk for awhile, instead."

I glanced around. Toni had taken a bathroom break and, I thought, might be taking advantage of the time away to sneak a cigarette. Hilda had drifted along to Miss Bradley's office, still perusing her movie magazine. I was alone, and I would enjoy another conversation with Alek.

But Toni's warning stuck with me, too: "Don't ask so many questions, Cady… you're just a temp."

So I stayed silent and waited for him to open the conversation.

He paused, too. "What are you doing in Dallas? That's pretty far from New

York."

"I could ask you the same question," I retorted, smiling. "If you liked New York so much, why didn't you stay there?"

"It wasn't my decision," he said promptly. "I was a kid when we left."

"Ah—no wonder you liked the Empire State Building and the Bronx Zoo. Kids love things like that."

"You haven't answered my question," he insisted. "What are you doing in Dallas?"

I considered. "I'll tell you if you tell me." It was just banter, of course—I would never think of telling anyone where I was really from—but I realized that Alek's was the friendliest voice I'd heard since I arrived in 1963. I sensed that he liked me, and I knew I was beginning to like him, too. It would be nice to have a friend in what was turning out to be surprisingly hostile territory.

There was a longer pause. "Well, I'll probably be leaving Dallas pretty soon, although I've done some pretty interesting work here."

"What kind of work?"

Instant and reproachful silence. *Stop asking questions, Cady, I berated myself. Girls who ask too many questions can disappear...*

I felt stricken. Until that moment I'd never allowed myself to infer that Debbie's disappearance had anything to do with anything she might have found out at ISI. I sensed that there was a real-life mystery here and Debbie had known something about it, and it was up to me to solve it. Maybe Alek was even a part of it, without knowing it.

When the silence continued, I said, "Sorry. I'm always asking too many questions. You don't have to answer that."

But he did answer, very quickly. "I did some photography work I really liked."

"You're a photographer? How interesting."

Another pause. "No: darkroom, developing, things like that." Before I could speak, he added, "How do you like working at ISI?"

"It's—different. I never worked for an import-export company before." Or as a telephone operator.

"It's lucky they got you, since Debbie's disappeared."

I froze. What did he know? Had I told him something I shouldn't have? Somewhat stiffly, I said, "What do you mean?"

"Oh, I keep tabs on what goes on over there. It does seem—strange—that you just happened in from New York and got this job. Don't you think?"

I laughed. "It was just lucky. They needed someone to fill in and I was here. I'm not a spy." And this was the Cold War, when there were spies everywhere...

Another pause. "That's not so farfetched. Anybody could be a spy, these days."

"I think you've seen too many James Bond movies."

Now he sounded puzzled. "Too many? There's only one. *Dr. No.*"

Oh, my God! Of course.

"Did I say James Bond movies? I meant—"

"—You meant the books," he finished, to my relief. "I've read a lot of those myself. They're very good. Ian Fleming, the author, knows how the Russians think, and he was a spy himself. That's why his stories are so believable."

A thought flashed into my mind from our earlier conversation. "Oh!" I exclaimed, pleased at having made the connection. "You said you'd lived overseas. It was in Russia—I mean, the Soviet Union. You've lived in the Soviet Union, haven't you?"

"Curiosity kills the cat, Miss Cady. Is he free yet?" Was his voice suddenly abrupt and repressive? I didn't know.

I noticed with dismay that the board was beginning to light up, and Don's light was still unblinkingly on. "Sorry—no. And I have to go, too—"

"So do I." And like a flash, he was gone.

I concentrated on putting through the calls with dispatch, and midway through a major telephone traffic snarl, Toni appeared, slipped into the second seat and helped me work it out. At last all the lights were lit, and we had a moment to scribble down messages.

"Whew!" I said when we were done.

"You said it," Toni said. She seemed to be feeling better. She hadn't lit a cigarette since she came back from her break, and her eyes were clear and smiling.

Suddenly I felt hungry, in that compulsive, gotta-have-it-*now* way that only seems to happen during a lull on busy afternoons. I wished I'd thought to buy a candy bar at the luncheonette. I'd noticed a glass case there full of candy, packages of Cracker Jack, Good & Plenty, Hershey bars, and candies I remembered from childhood, like Sugar Daddys and Mary Janes. It seemed so strange to see them in the case, in shiny new wrappers, when I hadn't seen them in so long.

Right now I would kill for one of them. "Toni, I'm starving," I said. "Is there some place here that I could get a candy bar?"

Toni shook her head. "Cady, we're not supposed to eat out here. But—" Her eyes brightened conspiratorially. "Debbie and I always keep some snacks in our desk—"

She started to reach into it, but just then, a young man came whirling through the door. He was medium height, beefy and dark-complected; it took me a minute to realize he was probably Hispanic. His silky hair was the giveaway; glossy, dark and wavy. He grinned at me and said, in heavily accented English, "I come for car. Jou know?"

I started to say I didn't know, but Toni was quicker. She reached under the counter for a logbook I hadn't noticed before. It was flat and heavy, with a red marbled cover and black binding. When she spoke, her voice was brisk and professional.

"Cady, you fill out the log," she instructed me. "That way, you'll know how for the next time. I'll help you with all the information we need." She turned to the young man. "Driver's license?"

He gave her a look.

She shrugged. "Those are the rules."

"But jou know me, Toni!" the young man protested, plainly dismayed. "How often I am here?"

Toni shrugged again. "Sorry, Jose… no license, no keys."

Scowling, the young man produced a card, which she gave me to copy into the logbook. I wrote down his name, which was listed as Jose Martinez, the license number and the state, Florida, and noted down his address. He signed alongside the entry, at Toni's insistence.

Then Toni, using a key from a small key ring in her desk, unlocked a metal cabinet filled with labeled keys dangling from tiny hooks. "Sedan or station wagon?" she called to Jose.

"Sedan, *por favor,*" Jose requested. Toni handed him a set of keys, asking me to note down the tag number and time in the log.

"Here you go. Number 17, in the lot. Blue Thunderbird. Stan had it last, so it probably needs gas."

"Back soon," grinned the young man. He took the keys and vanished.

Toni put the logbook away. "We sign out the company cars and check the count on them first thing every morning. There should be twenty at all times, including those in the lot and those logged out. Count them twice a day; if the count is ever wrong, tell me right away. Okay?"

"Sure," I said automatically, but my mind was on Jose. "Toni, that guy—"

She was inspecting her manicure. There were some chips in the pale pink polish. "Jose? What about him?"

"Is he—Mexican?"

"No, he's Cuban. Didn't you know? A lot of Cuban exiles live in Dallas. Cute, huh?"

"He can't be an ISI executive!"

"No," Toni admitted. "Jose works exclusively for Mr. Cuyler. He signs out a car almost every day."

I started to say, "But—", when the front door opened.

The man who walked in wore a trench coat and hat, though it was still warm outside. His hair was grizzled at the temples, but his posture was straight and his step energetic. He headed for the switchboard and leaning over the counter, addressed me. "I have an appointment with Mr. Donald Cuyler. My name is Ran Taylor. Taylor & Sons Trucking."

He was our first visitor of the day, and for just a moment I gaped, not sure what to do. Toni smoothly took over. "Thank you, sir. Will you wait just a moment, please?" She plugged in the call and said softly, "Mr. Cuyler, Mr. Ran Taylor to see you… thank you." She looked up. "He'll be with you in a moment."

The man bowed slightly and seated himself in one of the sagging chairs, reaching for one of the tattered magazines on the low table in the center.

Before he had started to read, however, the front door burst open, and Stan came in.

He was breathing hard, his hair rumpled as though he'd run his hand through it in frustration, sweat dampening his cheeks. "Where the hell is Don Cuyler?" he demanded.

We stared at him, and Toni made quick, silent motions toward Ran Taylor, who had looked up with interest.

Stan obviously didn't notice.

"Never mind, I'll go see him myself!"

Before he could hurtle past us, the door behind us opened, and Don Cuyler came out. His shirtsleeves were rolled up, tie slightly askew, but his movie-star tan glowed as much as ever, his eyes morning-fresh.

Stan stepped straight into his path. "What's goin' on?" he bellowed, his mouth only a few inches from Don's ear. "I thought we settled this last week! You're not gonna to do this to me, not again!"

Don gazed at Stan. He seemed not the least intimidated, though Stan was at least half a head taller and perhaps thirty pounds heavier. Don's expression never changed, but the look in his eyes was dangerous. I shrank back instinctively, hoping he wouldn't look my way. Stan himself, after trying and failing to stare him down, took a half step back.

Don turned once more to Ran Taylor, who was now standing, looking questioningly at him, and as though there had been no interruption, strolled over to meet him, his hand outstretched, his eyes suddenly cordial again. "Mr. Taylor," he said, "a pleasure. I'm Don Cuyler. Let me show you our operation."

"If this gentleman," Mr. Taylor began, looking at Stan, "needs a moment of your time now—"

"Not necessary," Don assured him smoothly, not glancing again at Stan.

He led Taylor out the door.

Toni busied herself at the desk, rewriting messages she had just written down, carefully looking away from Stan. Her lips were trembling. Stan's chest heaved as he struggled to control himself. He strode angrily from one end of the desk to the other, on the way picking up a handful of rubber bands from a bowl on the counter and pocketing them absently.

With visible effort, Stan finally calmed down, recovered his usual bland self-possession, and ran a plastic comb through his hair. By the time he pocketed it again, he was smiling.

"So, Toni," he said easily, "what time is that shindig tonight?"

"Er—7:00, I think," Toni said, her eyes still wary. From her demeanor, it was clear that she had never seen Stan in such a mood, and it shocked and frightened her.

"And me without a date," he said, but the corners of his mouth were tight. "'Course, I had a date, a honey of a date, last week, but what happened to her?"

Toni glanced at me but said nothing.

With an abrupt change of mood, Stan swung around and gave me a you-know-you-want-me-honey smile, like the one he'd given me this morning. "Well, Kate," he said jovially, "I suppose no one's asked you to come, have they?" I shook my head. I hadn't given it a thought.

He threw back his head, and now his sunny smile was unforced. "Well, honey, today's your lucky day. You get the hottest date in Texas."

As I gaped at him, he said, grinning, "Me." And he added, in case I had any doubts, "Believe you me, honey, a date with Stan the Man is a once in a lifetime treat, though if you're good—" he chuckled in a way that felt like bugs crawling along my spine, "why, who knows? Maybe we'll have a return engagement." He smiled down at me and leaned over to pat me on the head. "You staying at the Cuyler place? I'll pick you up at 6:30. Wear something *fun*," he emphasized, looking me over lecherously. "What we want to do is make an *entrance*."

He sauntered off to his office, letting the door swing shut behind him.

I stared after him. "Did I say I would go with him?" I wondered to Toni. And Toni, for the first time that day, burst into a gust of real, unforced laughter.

"That's how he got to be top salesman," she burbled. "He doesn't take no for an answer. I don't think he even hears it."

Who was this guy? I'd discounted him as a braggart, someone I was sure was pretending to be more than he was. But this other side of him—the unguarded, almost violent side—made me wonder.

My first instinct was not to go near him.

But my father had disappeared on November 22, 1963. And here he was, just four days before, facing down a young man with a hair-trigger temper and a serious chip on his shoulder.

Could there be a connection?

If I wanted to know, I'd have to spend more time with Stan Marchand. I could also observe my parents, who would no doubt be at the party as well. I'd like to see more of the relationship my mother had described wistfully as so adoring.

I thought of the ice in Don's eyes, and of the trepidation he inspired in Toni. I thought of Stan's unconcealed rage and Debbie's disappearance and my own misgivings.

Clearly, it was going to be a long night. The good news was, I had forgotten all about being hungry.

* * *

At ten to five, the day was slowing down; the switchboard had been quiet for twenty minutes, and some of the other men had come out of their offices. There were about eight others, all in white shirts that were beginning to crumple, and ties that were beginning to droop. But they were joking, and this seemed to be an afternoon ritual.

I noticed Toni blushing a little and flirting, gingerly, with one of the youngest men. He finally whispered something to her that I would bet had something to do with the party that night, because she blushed harder but nodded yes, looking away from him.

Good, I thought. I hope she has a great time. It's about time she got out from Debbie's shadow.

I hadn't really thought of Debbie all afternoon, but now I wondered if any of these guys had dated her. It seemed to me a good-time girl could have a very good time in a place like this—young, mostly single men, and who knew? Possibly Miss Debbie didn't mind if some of her escorts were married.

When Don Cuyler came in the front door, the noise level was beyond professional tones. He shook his head at the men but smiled, as though reluctant to indulge them but knowing he was going to anyway.

He slid behind me to pick up the messages in his cubbyhole, glancing through them and frowning. He turned to me.

"These messages from Al—why didn't you call me?"

I glanced at Toni, who turned away, clearly agitated. "I'm sorry, sir," I said. "I thought I wasn't supposed to disturb you on the phone."

He grimaced, but his voice remained pleasant as he said, "Well, for Al I tend to make exceptions. He's not easy to reach."

"Yes, sir. He said the same thing himself."

"And you didn't even think to slip me a note?" Don's eyebrows went up, almost comically. Behind me, I could see Toni's face going pale.

"I'm sorry, sir," I said, furious that I hadn't obeyed my natural instinct.

"Well, I need to know when Al calls. You just slip me a note the next time, like a good girl."

"Yes, sir." I tried a smile, but I could feel my face flushing with humiliation.

"Now, now." Don smiled at me; his smile was pleasant, but his eyes were flat and cold. "It's your first day. I'm sure you're doing fine." He patted my hair for a moment. The pat turned into a stroke down my head. I felt uneasy and breathless; I could feel myself going stiff.

He may have sensed it too, because he took his hand away but kept his smile. "I have a feeling, Miss Roberts, that you're going to fit in beautifully."

He turned his smile on Toni, whose face seemed suddenly frozen. He said to her playfully, "How has Miss Roberts been handling the job, Toni?"

"Oh, she's—doing great, Mr. Cuyler."

"Dealing with the clients okay?"

She swallowed. "She's—she's trying very hard, sir. She follows directions well."

To me, Don said casually, "Toni's gotten to know our clients quite well, haven't you, Toni? You should watch how she handles them. They all seem to like her."

"I like them too, Mr. Cuyler," Toni blurted out. "Especially Al."

Don drew back, in mock surprise. "How can you tell, just from the phone,Toni?"

"Oh, not from the phone, sir. I've met him."

Don lifted his head, this time in real, unfeigned surprise. "You met him?"

Toni's voice took on a defensive edge. "Not—not on company time, Mr.

Cuyler. He just—he asked if we could meet for coffee." The nervous look returned to her face.

"And you thought he was nice?"

"He was nice," Toni said, a trifle defiantly. "Thoughtful. A gentleman."

Don raised his eyebrows at her. "I do hope, Toni, that you didn't let out any company secrets."

Toni didn't realize he was kidding her. Now she was actually panicking. "Oh, no, sir! I would never—"

"Good girl." He raised his voice to the other men without looking at them. "Back to the grind, gentleman. It's not 5:30 yet."

The others, who had been joking amongst themselves, paying no attention to our conversation, drifted away at once. Apparently, no matter how pleasantly he phrased it, Don's word was law.

When they had gone, Don pulled a crumpled slip of paper from his pocket. "Bill of lading, Toni," he said briefly. "Between ISI and Taylor & Sons Trucking. We're using them for a special delivery at the end of the week. These are the terms. Type it up for me, will you?"

"Certainly, sir." She took it.

"And you'll take a delivery for me, won't you? To the Mills Building? I'll have it ready very soon."

"Yes, sir."

He smiled absently at her and went through the door.

Toni's face went rigid.

"Toni," I said quietly, "what's the matter?"

She looked down and traced a finger along the edge of a blotter. "When Mr. Cuyler said you—" she gulped, "fit in beautifully—" She stopped.

"Yes?"

"Well—that's what he said about Debbie. The day before she disappeared."

The switchboard began to light up insistently, but for a minute I couldn't move.

ddDon Cuyler had spoken in admiration of Debbie, and she had vanished. He'd joked with Toni about her job, and she was terrified. He inspired fear and rage in everyone who worked under him.

And someone obviously was engineering his disappearance even now.

But who? And why?

* * *

At 5:30, Toni said, "You can leave now."

We'd been surprisingly busy in the last few minutes of the day, so busy that she had put aside the bill of lading for Don.

I motioned at the handwritten notes Don had given her. "Aren't you going to type it?"

Toni shook her head. "He won't want it tonight. I'll do it first thing tomorrow, before he's in." She stretched her arms upward. "Got to get ready for my big date!"

I went to punch out, smiling at the thought of Toni's good time tonight. When I came back, Don was at the desk, handing Toni a sealed manila envelope. "Here you go. Don't wait for the bus; it's just a couple of blocks. I want that delivered immediately. You won't miss any of the party."

"Yes, sir," Toni said. She went off through the door with a nod at both of us.

Don turned to me. "Well, Miss Roberts, you do know there's a company party tonight? You're invited, of course. I'll give you a lift home, so you can freshen up."

"Thank you," I said. "Stan—Mr. Marchand—asked me to go with him. He's picking me up at your house."

"Oh?" Don seemed perturbed. "Well, he's wasted no time, as usual." He was smiling as he said it, but I thought I heard an edge in his voice. "Come on, let's head out."

See? I thought. *Don knows what a jerk Stan is, and he doesn't want me associating with him. He's looking out for me.*

Night had fallen by the time Don wheeled his black Cadillac out of the ISI lot.

I noticed he wore no seatbelt and kept his foot down hard on the accelerator. The moment we cleared the lot, the car was clipping along at sixty.

Don said nothing personal, but he pointed out the various neighborhoods we drove through, like a tour guide. I saw the houses getting progressively smaller, shabbier and closer together. Finally, he said, "Here's Oak Cliff, where we live," and swung into the shabbiest neighborhood yet. The houses were identical: two-story affairs on tiny plots, as I'd noticed last night. The streets were cramped, and many houses had "Rooms for Rent" signs in front.

The question I'd asked myself last night jumped back into my mind. If my father was a top executive with a successful company, why did they choose to live in such a rundown neighborhood, when they could clearly afford better? This had to be one of the cheaper neighborhoods in Dallas, and yet my father drove a Cadillac and my mother's furnishings were of excellent quality. They couldn't be starving. So why live here? And why, come to think of it, did they rent out rooms at all? Did they really need the extra income?

Don pulled into the driveway at five to six. I turned to him and said impulsively, "Mr. Cuyler, thank you for helping me get this job. I really—I'm very grateful."

"Well, now, it's my pleasure," he said, reaching over to pat my hand. "Who knows—maybe sometime you'll be able to do me a favor, too."

He collected his briefcase and jacket and, not waiting for me, strode into the house.

I hoped what had just happened didn't mean what I thought it meant.

It couldn't.

The man my mother had described didn't behave like that.

But the man I was getting to know behaved a whole lot differently.

* * *

I heard the hum of male voices as I came in. Don was talking quietly to three dark-complected men in the hallway. I started: they all looked like the young beefy guy who'd signed out an ISI car. They all had cheap suitcases piled around the hall. These were the new boarders? Young, strong-looking Cubans?

I went back toward my room and almost ran into Sandra, carrying a plastic laundry basket. "Sorry! I didn't see you," I said, smiling. "Hello, Mrs. Cuyler."

She looked pale, but her hair was wound into a bun and her makeup looked fresh. She wore a housecoat, and I guessed that she'd soon be dressing to go with Don to the party.

The basket, filled to the top with clean-smelling, just-folded laundry from the line outside, looked heavy: she was breathing hard. I tossed my handbag into my room and turned to her, taking the basket from her hands. "Which way?" I asked.

"You don't have to do that," she said quickly.

"I know," I smiled. "I'd like to help. Where to?"

She looked a little flustered but nodded me ahead of her, up the narrow steps to the second floor. We went toward the door at the end of the hall.

Sandra opened the door and motioned me inside.

I walked into a lovely room with deep, soft rose carpeting and a double bed covered with what looked like a handmade quilt. The wallpaper was in soft pastels, gray, rose and ice blue, and the whole room was clean and thoroughly tidy.

"How beautiful," I said in wonder, looking around. "Did you do all this yourself?"

She nodded, a little shyly, and pointed to a corner. "If you'll set it there, that will be fine," she said, and then, making an effort, as though trying not to talk as lady-of-the-house to a paid servant, "I mean, please. And thank you for bringing it up for me."

I set the basket down for her and decided to take the bull by the horns. Don intimidated me, with his nice-as-pie attitude mixed with undertones of a sexual come-on. But Sandra I knew much better. I wanted to reach out to her.

"Mrs. Cuyler," I said confidentially, "you're expecting a baby, aren't you?"

Her face went paler, but she managed a nod. "I haven't told my husband yet. I was waiting for the right time."

"How about after the party tonight?" I suggested. "I'm sure he'll be delighted."

"Maybe." Abruptly she sat down on the bed, her eyes on the floor, a frown creasing her forehead.

"Which do you want?" I asked. "A boy or a girl?"

"Oh!" She looked up, a reluctant smile lifting her lips. "I know Don probably wants a boy, but—I'd—I'd really like a little girl."

I smiled at her. "I predict you'll get your wish."

"You think so?" She wanted to hope so much but didn't dare: it was in her eyes, the fear of having it snatched from her.

"I'm dead certain," I assured her.

"Ohh! I hope so!" She smiled at me now, her first genuine smile since I arrived. "Thank you," she said. "For—well, everything. It helps so much."

Then she hesitated. "About the rent—"

"Oh, yes!" I remembered I hadn't paid her. "I'll get my bag—"

"No." She put out a hand to stop me. "I mean—" This was difficult for her to say. "I think I'm—overcharging you. For meals. You shouldn't pay two dollars a day for breakfast. A dollar is fine, and you're welcome to have dinner with us, too."

"Oh?" I was distinctly pleased. That's why she'd looked odd last night—she hadn't liked me and had wanted, deliberately, to cheat me, though she didn't seem very experienced at it. I was glad we'd cleared the air.

She looked at me shyly, and I suddenly felt, without knowing it, that my mother hadn't had a friend of her own in a long time.

"Well, thank you," I said. "I'll see you at the party tonight."

She looked surprised. "You're going?"

I nodded. "With Stan Marchand, ISI's top salesman," I said, throwing my head back and hunching my shoulders in imitation of Stan. "Do you know him?"

Sandra started to laugh weakly. "Oh! That's just like him!" Remembering, though, that he was my date, and obviously trying to encourage me, she said doubtfully, "I hope you'll have a good time."

"With Stan the Man? It's guaranteed," I said, and we burst into companionable laughter.

* * *

It had taken Toni longer than she'd expected to deliver the manila envelope for Mr. Cuyler: Her wristwatch told her it was already 6:00. She'd had to find the janitor and then wait for him to open the door for her. But Mr. Cuyler had always specified delivery right to the company, so she had trudged up to the fourth floor and slipped the envelope under the office door.

She'd labored long and faithfully for the company, Toni thought, often doing part of Debbie's work and staying late, never asking for extra pay. She hoped that one day her efforts would be recognized, but so far, Mr. Cuyler seemed to prefer Debbie. Debbie had skipped out early, done her work sloppily, sometimes disappeared altogether after lunch, yet he preferred her. *Every* man seemed to prefer Debbie. Toni sighed. It didn't seem fair.

As she came out to the sidewalk, the silence was a little unnerving. The sky was black. Night had fallen, and there were few lights. The shadows were long and ominous.

Toni felt a chill of uneasiness. She wore only a thin sweater over her dress, but she pulled it closer to her and started toward the corner, her eyes trained on a single streetlight at the end of the block.

As soon as I reach that streetlight, I'm safe, she told herself. There's no reason to feel scared. I'm just jittery—anything sets me off, after Debbie—

She wished she had a cigarette, but that would have to wait until she got to the party and found Steve, her date; she had forgotten to buy them at lunchtime. That strange girl Cady asking all those odd questions had flustered her.

Almost running, Toni reached the welcoming circle of yellow under the streetlight and took a deep breath. S*ee, there was nothing to be scared of, after all.* She turned and stepped off the curb.

Suddenly, the roar of an automobile filled her senses. A sedan that looked blue under the thin yellow light was now headed straight toward her.

Hastily, Toni jumped back on the sidewalk, but something seemed to be wrong. The car, instead of staying on the road in front of her, peeled off, heading right for the streetlight where she stood…

Toni saw the back of the car as the light splashed over it—it appeared to be piled high with an untidy array of… guns?

Then the car swung around again, and she realized the car was aiming at her… the driver holding the wheel steady, his shadowy face grim…

She took a step, then two, in a moment of crazy panic and disbelief: *He can't mean to hit me! Why?*

Terrified now, she broke into a run, back toward the dark building she'd just come from, the engine roaring behind her, but blessed safety just a few feet ahead…

Something solid slammed into her left hip. The jolt threw her straight into the air and then she was falling… falling… toward the heavy unyielding pavement…

She landed on her arms, instinctively cushioning her head from the impact. The thud felt as though it had broken several bones. She almost wept with the pain and shock of it, in her knees, her hip, her shoulder… but she couldn't seem to scream for help… as though it would do any good… no one there… no one to hear her, except maybe the janitor… oh, God, could he hear her? If she screamed to him… ?

She opened her mouth to call out, but once again there was a roar around her ears, And this time the shock that she felt was the thud of metal against the left side of her head and her left cheekbone. Toni sank back on the pavement, not knowing that the Thunderbird had roared off, its distinctive silver lettering plain on the blue grill in front, her mind already going dark, her head falling once more, with a noisy final snap, onto the concrete.

* * *

The party took place at a house in an affluent suburb nearly thirty minutes away, so I had plenty of time to learn more about Stan as we drove.

He had shown up precisely on time and given a wolf whistle on seeing me in my new red dress with the matching belt and swirling skirt. I wasn't sure I liked how well the dress fit me: this guy thought he was a real swinger, and I didn't relish the thought of a wrestling contest at the end of the evening.

Stan drove an immaculate candy-apple-red Pontiac Star Chief, its creamy trim matching the sparkling whitewall tires, with lots of chrome on the fenders and mirrors. The roomy bench seats could seat six comfortably and eight in a pinch. Stan was obviously proud of it. When I said hesitantly, "Cool car," he told me proudly that it was a 1957 model but that he himself kept it in mint condition and that it had the best ride of any car on the road, with a V-8 engine that boasted 270 horsepower. Since my 2000 Beetle had only 115 horsepower, I was impressed, and said so. He warned me sternly not to smoke in his car; he didn't like having butts in his ashtray. I started to say I didn't smoke, but he wasn't listening.

Conversation with Stan wasn't difficult; it consisted mostly of his bragging about his work performance and his score with girls. According to him, he was both ISI's sales savior and the biggest stud in Texas. I had no idea why he thought that would impress me, but soon I began to realize that Stan talked to hear himself talk, not for feedback from anyone else. He talked a lot about his fascination with the Rat Pack: "That Sinatra guy, now you take him, he knows how to live! The best times, the best booze, the best girls… I bet he can get laid three times a day if he wants, and more in Vegas!"

Was this how guys courted girls in 1963?

Stan went on, "Dean Martin, I don't know, he sings good, but he's too—I'm not against good-looking guys, y'know, but a guy can only be so pretty before he starts looking like a fag. No, Sinatra—he's the real thing. Dino can't hold a candle to him."

"And Sammy Davis, Jr.?" I asked.

Stan snorted. "Skinny little black bastard… hanging out with big white guys so he can score with white chicks… somebody oughtta take care of him good… " In the end, Stan told me I was lucky, as he'd been watching Sinatra so long he'd absorbed all his cool and I could be assured of a real good time.

At last, Stan drew the Star Chief toward a brightly-lit modern-looking house at the end of a cul-de-sac lined with tall trees and high manicured hedges. There were many other cars, stolid-looking station wagons mingling with sleek convertibles, their tops prudently raised on this cool mid-November night, parked at various angles on the street. A harassed-looking man, perspiring in a sport jacket, directed traffic with big movements of his arms.

Stan followed the man's wave and carefully pulled his car to a piece of unoccupied curb. "Ring-a-ding-ding, baby!" he yelped. "Let's show the local yokels how to have a good time!"

"I can't wait," I said.

He smiled and patted me on the thigh, through the folds of the new red dress. "And if you're very good, big Stan'll give you something real nice later on."

Like hell you will, I thought, jerking the handle of the car door.

"Hey, baby, show some class. I gotta get out and open the door for you."

I debated whether to tell him what he could do with his class, but in the end, I let him open my door and followed him docilely toward the mecca of lights and music.

The front door was open, and a cacophony of music and talk and feminine laughter spilled out as we walked toward it.

"Just a minute, Miss." A hand dropped on my shoulder.

The hand belonged to a tall, muscular guy with a ruffle of dark hair across his forehead. His eyes were the kind popularly described as 'smoldering', and his lips were overly full. He had a clipboard in one hand. "Name? This party is by invitation only."

"She's with me," Stan said aggressively, pushing close to me. "Stan Marchand from ISI. Mr. Feigert's expectin' me."

The other guy, unimpressed, looked down his list. "Yeah … okay." He made a mark on the clipboard with the attached pencil.

"Jerk," Stan muttered to me as we went past him. "These private security guys are all mouth."

We squeezed into the doorway. Ahead of me was a virtual wall of strangers, all chatting and huddled in knots, holding glasses and cigarettes; behind me was Stan, blocking the only exit that I could see.

I plowed straight into the hallway, where dense clouds of smoke were already drifting toward the ceiling. The women wore tight-fitting sheath dresses, many off the shoulder, revealing various shades of suntan; the men were in sports jackets, some quite loud, a few in ten-gallon hats, and many eschewing wedding rings for big pinky rings and heavy crested class rings.

I felt a heavy hand on my shoulder. It was Stan. "Nice layout, huh?" he shouted at me when I turned my head in his direction. "Feigert always goes first class."

Stan was pushing me toward some destination he had in mind, which I found was the curving built-in bar in a corner of a big den at the back of the house, now crammed with people. Black-uniformed Negro waitresses moved softly and unobtrusively among the guests, emptying ashtrays and bringing in clean new ones, picking up beer bottles and abandoned glasses with melting ice, while others carried trays of hors d'oeuvres which they offered to guests with lowered eyes.

Stan reached a long arm around me and seized a small roll-wrapped frankfurter, which he popped whole into his mouth and chewed so I could see his molars. I tried to remember what it was about my ex-husband Craig that I'd once found so offensive: Next to swingin' Stan, he suddenly seemed like Sir Galahad.

"Mr. Cuyler! Hey, Mr. Cuyler, over here!" Stan yelled, his voice shattering.

I saw my mother and father just coming in the door. They had seen Stan too, and now they came over, Don responding drily to Stan's eager glad-handing.

"Can I get you a drink? Both of you? Gee, seems like we just saw each other an hour ago!" Stan chortled, as Sandra looked away from him and Don gave a tight grin.

"Gin and tonic for me, and Sandy—"

"Oh—" Sandra gave me a quick look. "I think I'll just have a ginger ale."

Don shrugged. "Guess she won't be much fun tonight. Gin and tonic and ginger ale, Stan."

"A-OK, Daddy-o. I'll be right back."

I watched as Stan headed toward the single bartender, who was slopping down drinks as fast as he could for eager patrons on three sides of the bar. Stan joined them, waving at him, and succeeding in engaging his attention, if only because of his gangling height.

Don was looking at the others, and Sandra murmured to him, "It's packed. Are all of these people from the office?"

"That and our other branches," he answered, his eyes settling on two couples in the corner. The man was joking with another man, both middle-aged at least, clinking beer bottles and roaring at each other's sallies, while their girls (or wives?) were considerably younger and slimmer and dressed to kill. The first one was trying to laugh, too, but the men were deaf to her attempts to fit in; the second, bored, with bright auburn hair teased into compliance and a jangling charm bracelet on her tanned and rounded arm, looked around for stimulation.

I saw her eyes light on Don, though Sandra didn't seem to notice.

Don saw it too.

"I'd better say hello to Feigert," he said abruptly, and weaved off through the crowd. Not surprisingly, I didn't see him go anywhere near the bar; instead, he seemed to make his way in a circuitous fashion toward the bored girl with the auburn hair.

When he reached her and smiled down into her eyes, I felt sick. How must Sandra feel?

I glanced at her. She had deliberately turned her back to Don, and was saying too brightly to me, "I love your dress! That red looks just wonderful on you!"

"You too," I said feebly. She did know, then. And she handled it by ignoring it.

I caught a glimpse of Don settling down next to the bored girl, who had brightened and was talking to him animatedly, swinging her hair away from her face. He was smiling down at her, touching her cheek lightly, leaning close to light her cigarette. Practiced, graceful gestures, all of them. It told me he had done this before. Done it often.

I felt for a minute as though I couldn't breathe.

Then I realized I really couldn't.

The room was getting steadily more packed, and the hum of conversation was rising. Glasses were clinking on the bar, and the room was getting hotter and hotter. I needed fresh air desperately.

I helped Sandra find a couch and sit down. When Stan brought her the ginger ale, I excused myself hastily. I wanted to be alone with my thoughts.

Instead, I found the crowded kitchen, where a variety of women in brightly-colored, clingy dresses, were smoking and sipping cocktails. None of them appeared to be the hostess, which I found odd, since the only people handling the food, unsupervised, were the hired help. They deftly shifted trays of hors d'oeuvres from the oven and slid them onto serving trays, with napkins and fresh ashtrays, while the women talked to each other as though they weren't there.

I felt a chill as I watched: the kitchen was not overly large, but in it were two groups of people co-existing, yet not interacting with each other at all, ignoring each other's very existence. *Black is black and white is white,* I thought, *and never the twain shall meet.*

The guests, seeing me, hitched over a little so I could sit down. I was white and wearing a party dress, and as long as I didn't speak, they could assume I was one of them...

Instead, I took out my compact and pretended to be checking my makeup as I eavesdropped on their gossip:

"Antoine says everyone will be wearing it next year

I'll be the first on my block to have this shade of blonde... "

"Half the price of Neiman-Marcus but with twice the style... and none of those annoying bills at the end of the month to explain to my husband... "

"That little tramp, serves her right... disappeared! As though I believe that! I hope she stays gone for good... All she ever did was stir up trouble... "

I jerked my head up, trying unsuccessfully to locate the source of that remark. Was that a jibe at Debbie? Who else could it be?

No doubt about it, life in 1963 was anything but simple. I felt as though I'd swung a baseball bat at a hornet's nest, with poison suddenly spewing from all directions. So far, the poison wasn't directed at me. But there was enough of it to make me wary, just the same.

So far, I hadn't spotted Toni. I thought if I continued through the house I would eventually find her, since it appeared that guests were now spilling into all the rooms, public and private. There must be two hundred people here, I calculated, and most of them did not work at ISI. This was no office party for the hired help. I wondered what it was really for.

The three bathrooms were unfortunately crowded with guests, looking for quiet places to neck and start the motors running for romantic interludes to come. Toni was not among them.

I had reached a bend in the corridor by the five bedrooms and was wondering where to go, when I saw the auburn-haired girl. She was stumbling along the hall, unsteady on her feet, giggling. She opened a door that I assumed led to a bedroom and slipped quietly inside. In a minute, a Do Not Disturb tag with a blue and orange Howard Johnson's logo on it was stuck onto the doorknob.

At least Don had finally detached himself from her. I hoped he had gone back to be with Sandra and not embarrass her anymore.

But he wasn't with Sandra; he was sidling down the same side of the hall, stopping at the Do Not Disturb tag and tapping lightly. The door opened, and he slipped inside.

No light clicked on, and I could hear the faint sound of the door locking. In a moment, I heard moans and grunts issuing from within. There wasn't much doubt what they were doing.

I retreated down the hall, feeling sick with despair.

They were still at the party, within earshot of anyone walking by... it was so flagrant. He might as well have worn a sign, for God's sake!

This was the man my mother had spoken of with such reverence, such adoration— this pig who turned his eye on every girl in sight—including me! For one vicious moment I was glad he would disappear on Friday, never to return.

My mother had needed, somehow, to retain the picture of him as upright and heroic, and the picture of their marriage as unblemished. Yet that false picture, repeated often enough to herself, became the basis of a miserable, unsatisfying half-life where she spent too much money and waited for my father to return.

I remembered how she used to whisper to herself, "I had everything then," when she thought I couldn't hear.

Was this what passed for happiness in her life before all those years of desolation? The thought was unbearable.

* * *

I didn't find Toni anywhere. I wondered if she had left before I arrived, or whether she had slipped away with her date and was behind one of the locked doors. I tried not to think of Don and the auburn-haired girl. I found the porch door and slipped out to stand in the garden, where the air was wonderfully cool and fresh, and I could be alone.

An hour went by as I savored the quiet.

Finally, though, I decided regretfully to go find Stan. He had brought me, after all, and I couldn't dodge him for the rest of the evening, though I would have liked to.

When I returned to the den, the women had split into small groups to gossip and a few couples were dancing, but the majority of the noise was being made by the men clustered around the bar, the melting ice in half-empty glasses and their reddened faces mutely testifying to their condition.

"... Roger Staubach, the kid from Navy," a burly man in a wide Stetson hat and bolo tie bellowed to no one in particular, his forefinger crooked over a pungent cigar nearly an inch thick, using it to make his point. "That's who the Cowboys need."

"... pickin' her up tomorrow, a '64 Cadillac convertible... "

"...vacation properties, that's where you wanna invest... "

They were egging each other on, one shouting something and the others backing him up. I saw Stan sitting loose-limbed on a barstool, gently twisting from side to side, obviously drunk. To my fascination I realized Don was sitting unperturbed in the center of the group. His trysting partner was sitting demurely in the corner, twisting her bright auburn hair over her finger and talking innocently and earnestly with the middle-aged, paunchy man, who was patting her approvingly. I noticed they wore matching wedding rings. But while she managed to flutter her lashes slyly at Don every other minute, he never glanced in her direction.

"Big week here!" a man by the bar shouted happily. "Big guns coming to the Big D—the *President's* coming to Dallas!"

The way he said it, it was clear to me that JFK shouldn't ask these people to stage a fund-raiser for him. The voice was jeering and nasty, and everyone else began to shout approvingly at his words.

"Just what we need—"

"Spoiled Yankee rich boy—"

"Tryin' to tell us how to run our lives and our business—"

"Never worked a day in his life—what does he know about real people and real problems?"

Suddenly Don whipped around and shouted at the knot of drunken men, "Shut up!"

In just a moment, there was absolute, hushed silence.

Even I held my breath.

He had an almost empty glass next to him, but he rose straight as an arrow with infinite grace and glared around the room. Every remaining sound choked off; women's giggles stopped; drunken men tried to straighten too, in imitation of him, but ended up clutching their barstools. The waiters and waitresses stopped walking about and held their trays quietly.

Don surveyed the room; every eye was on him. "I'll have you know," he said loudly, "that I served in the Navy with Jack Kennedy. I've known Jack Kennedy for over twenty years."

No one spoke. I began to feel a flutter in my throat; as corrupt as he might be in other ways, my mother had always said he admired the President. And for all his faults, standing up to a room full of drunken rednecks took courage.

"Twenty years I've known him," Don repeated, "which makes me better qualified than anybody to know what a son of a bitch he is!"

A stutter of sound; then the room erupted in laughter and cheers. I saw women clapping, their faces shining with glee.

I felt sicker than ever.

Don surveyed the room again, his eyes brilliant, his color high. "I know better than you do," he went on, "what a whining, lily-livered coward he is—I know that he's never done anything without his old man's money—he's a spoiled rich brat who has no idea what real Americans are like or what they want and need—which is why we're going to *boot his ass out of the White House* come next November!"

I caught a glimpse of Sandra, standing ten feet behind me, staring at her husband. Her face was chalky; her lips pressed together tightly; there appeared to be a shimmer of tears in her eyes. She clutched her purse with fingers so tense that her knuckles were white. She was quite alone in the crowd. No one even glanced at her.

The rest of the crowd loved Don's impromptu speech. The men cried, "More! More!" and Don, grinning rakishly, spread his arms and turned his head to make eye contact with the entire room. "It takes more than a pile of money and a great-looking wife and a good tan to make a President. He's no leader—you know he should've been court-martialed for letting the Japs sink his boat—instead, his old man's money bought him a damned medal! Commander in Chief—he's a Commander in Chief like I'm Captain Kangaroo! A real Commander in Chief knows when we have to fight— and all Kennedy's done since he's got into office is hide! Anybody remember the Bay of Pigs? He let those brave men get slaughtered on the beach! Do you think he cared? And last year, when Russia had missiles pointed at our heartland—Kennedy cut a deal with the Russians, instead of standing up like a man and fighting back! When is the rest of the country going to figure out what we here in Texas have always known— Jack Kennedy is a traitor—he's out of control—and he's damaging the prestige of this country so badly we'll never be able to build it up again!"

This last comment prompted the largest cheer yet. The bartender, the women in their jangling bracelets and the men with their pinky rings and cigars—all were shrieking approval. The black waiters and waitresses cautiously retreated from the room. The noise level rose unbearably.

A couple of men were clapping Don on the back, speaking softly to him. The urgency on their faces was diametrically different than the slack smiles I'd seen in the den. These men had clear eyes and taut mouths and something important to talk about. Don nodded, his face serious, and followed them across the hall and through a door I hadn't noticed before. They slipped inside, quietly locking the door behind them.

I wondered if this was the real reason for the party—to allow them to slip away and chat in the context of a social situation.

The irony was that one of the men Don was conversing with was the paunchy man who had held the hand of the auburn-haired girl earlier. I wondered if he knew how his wife had been entertaining Don an hour earlier.

Given the urgency of their conversation, I wondered if he'd care.

I couldn't stand anymore. I had seen enough, heard enough, had more than enough of this company.

I decided to ask Stan to take me home.

* * *

Stan was in the act of casually pocketing a cocktail coaster when I reached him at the bar and made my request.

"Leave?" Stan's voice rose in astonishment. "You kidding? Before I get to talk to the big man? Before I make my *connection?*"

I had found him at last, maneuvering his way through a crowd of drunken women toward the closed door, behind which I knew Don and his compatriots were talking urgently. Stan wanted to be in that meeting, and I knew he wasn't going to get there. Still, when I asked him to take me home, he broke into a storm of protest.

"You crazy? What do you think these parties are for? Talkin' to people, makin' connections, so people remember you for the future—you think I'm leavin' now, you're crazy—"

"But I told you, I'm feeling sick. Please—"

"Nah. I'm stayin'. First that two-bit tramp stands me up, and now you wanna drag me out, for—what? Cramps? The hell with you."

He turned on his heel.

If I wanted to go home, it would be under my own steam. Thank God for the little pack of bills in my handbag.

I called a taxi, with the help of one of the young maids in the kitchen.

An hour later I was back at the Cuyler house.

Sandra had instructed me to go inside through the back porch, which she had left unlocked. I let myself in with shaking fingers, and I could feel my legs just about folding up under me. My feet were aching horribly, and I'd have to wear the same shoes tomorrow. If I expected to function, I'd better find a way to soak my feet before bed.

So after dropping my bag and my belt in my room, I headed to the kitchen, thinking that Sandra might not mind if I borrowed a shallow pan overnight.

I clicked on the kitchen light—and gasped as a man let himself in through the same back door I'd just entered. It was one of the Cubans I'd seen that afternoon.

I was very startled to see him cradling a rifle.

I couldn't think what to say. I pointed at the kitchen sink and tried to say, "Water," but nothing came out. Then I wondered if he could speak English anyway.

Finally I managed, "My feet hurt," and I pointed at the sink again. "I'm going to soak them—make them better for tomorrow."

He was holding the rifle casually, its barrel pointed toward the floor. But what was a man doing in a perfectly ordinary American home on a weeknight, standing in the dark with a rifle?

I didn't want to know. I just wanted to get my pan of water and get away from him.

I rooted around in the cupboards while he watched me silently. Finally, I found a small aluminum pan I hoped Sandra wouldn't need immediately. *I'll fill it up in the bathroom, I thought. Just let me get out of here in one piece.*

"Well," I said, as lightheartedly as possible, "good night."

"Buenos noches," he said, nodding. I fled.

I washed up and brushed my teeth in record time, then carefully carried the filled pan to my room, and gratefully soaked my feet. *I could sit like this all night,* I thought. The relief was unimaginable.

I snapped off my overhead light and lay back on the bed, keeping my feet in the water. I stared at the ceiling and reviewed the day in my mind.

My parents ran a boardinghouse in a shabby section of Dallas and were obviously living way below their means. Why? Why did they run a boardinghouse? Couldn't they easily afford a house, without having to take in paying guests?

And what guests! Their new boarders were silent Cubans who apparently thought it was normal behavior to carry rifles around. I had no idea where my parents had found them or why they'd agreed to rent them rooms.

On top of that, my father's place of business featured a switchboard operator who'd gone missing and her compatriot who panicked when I asked questions about it. I frowned, thinking of Toni. I hadn't seen her anywhere in that crush tonight. I wondered if she'd gotten there at all. She had been so looking forward to it...

What was worst, in my mind, was that the life my mother had described for me, the life she'd made so blazingly clear in her words and attitudes for as long as I could remember, was clearly a fantasy. My father, far from being the kind, loving, virtuous man she'd adored in memory, was reactionary, overbearing and promiscuous. Just as clearly, he was making my mother's life miserable.

The water over my feet had warmed up a bit, and I decided I'd treat myself to another cool panful before sleep.

In the bathroom, I emptied out the used water and ran clean, cold water into the pan. Then I turned off the light and stopped, trying to balance the rocking water.

Suddenly, there were footsteps and a door slamming. Then loud voices.

The raised voices were clearly Sandra and Don's. "That's all you know!" he was saying furiously as they came closer and closer to the bathroom. "It wasn't like that at all!"

Sandra's voice was lower, but no less furious. "I'm supposed to turn my back when you waltz out of a party—a party for your business—following the hostess, of all people?"

"I was not following anybody!" Don shouted at her. "And since when is it any of your business?"

"My business?" Sandra sputtered. "You're my husband!"

"Well, if you aren't happy with the way I'm being your husband, we can easily arrange to change that," Don said nastily.

There was a gasp, and a pause. I think Sandra was shocked at the very suggestion. This was a time, after all, when few people with any social pretensions got a divorce.

Then she spoke again, very quietly. "I didn't say I wanted to change it."

"Then you'd better learn your place," Don said to her coldly. "You're my wife. You don't interfere with my business, and you don't interfere with any other part of my life. I provide for you, I give you my name and all the social position any wife can hope for. Being Mrs. Don Cuyler is an enviable position for any woman, Miss High-and-Mighty. And pretty soon I'll be riding even higher. In fact, I'll be more of a hero than that horse's ass, Jack Kennedy!"

"Don, don't!" There was real distress in Sandra's voice. "I thought—I thought you were just—you know, showing off. To fit in with those awful people. Those terrible things you said about the President—you don't really mean them. You couldn't."

"Couldn't I?" he sneered. "Listen, you and your kind are living in a dream world. Kennedy is not only no saint, he should never have been in the White House to begin with. He stole an election and paid off the right people, and next year he'll do it again, if he isn't stopped! My God! Have you forgotten? We still have a thousand dollars' worth of canned goods stored out back because you were so panicked during the missile crisis. Who do you think was responsible for that?

"Oh, no, Sandy, you'd better get over your hero worship. Kennedy won't be around long, and you'd better get used to it. This country needs a real man in the White House, a man like Lyndon Johnson, not some daddy's boy who doesn't know anything except appease the enemy and make a deal. And as for the rest of it—if being Mrs. Don Cuyler isn't enough for you, let me know. There're plenty of others who would relish the title."

"Don, wait! I have—something to tell you. Something I think—I mean, something we both want." There was a pause. "I'm going to have a baby."

Another pause, heavy with displeasure. Then Don's voice, still cold. "Are you sure?"

"Oh, yes! I've been to the doctor, and—"

"Get rid of it, Sandy. The last thing I need right now is a baby."

I heard heavy footsteps stomping up the stairs. There was silence, and then the sound of Sandra's soft sobs. They continued for a long time.

Finally, Sandra's footsteps tapped slowly up the stairs.

It was a long time before I opened the bathroom door.

It was even longer before I slept.

.

Chapter Nine
TUESDAY, NOVEMBER 19, 1963

I arrived at ISI early the next morning. Don had offered me a lift, but I mumbled some excuse about promising to meet Toni and ran for the bus: After what I'd seen yesterday, I wanted nothing to do with this guy.

Miss Bradley was already at her desk, the corners of her mouth turned sourly down, but the rest of the office was empty. Everyone else must still be nursing their hangovers.

There were no messages on the desk to be sorted into the executives' boxes; there were no letters or packages to deliver. I found myself feeling restless: I wanted to lose myself in my job and forget what I had learned last night. I needed to find something to do.

My eyes lighted on the bill of lading Don had given Toni to type. She had left it to do this morning and had pulled out an old bill of lading for reference. I decided to type it for her. I would leave it on her desk when I was done, as though she herself had typed it last night. No one would be the wiser.

Around the corner from our desk was another desk fitted with a Royal manual typewriter, carbon paper and a stack of company letterhead. I checked again for prying eyes, found none, and sat down to type, using the old bill of lading as a template.

The handwritten notes Don had scribbled were dated yesterday, November 18th, and specified a bill of lading between Taylor & Sons Trucking and ISI, Incorporated, for the transport of freight from Dallas to Miami, for pickup on Thursday, November 21st, and delivery on Sunday, November 24th. Contents were listed as "Vodka, bottled".

Though I was accustomed to the light touch of a computer keyboard and the manual required more force on the keys, I managed to type it without mistakes and placed it on Toni's desk, wondering all the time about the terms.

The shipment's final destination was the University of Miami campus, which I thought was a little odd: To me, shipping vodka to a college campus was like taking ice to Alaska. Don was paying the trucking firm two thousand dollars to make the trip from Dallas to Miami, which I thought way out of line with normal business costs. Under "Remarks" in the notes was a clear specification that the truck was never to be off the road except to pump gas or pick up food for the drivers, and that the drivers were expected to drive around the clock to reach the campus by Sunday morning, which was illegal in the year 2000 and might also be in 1963.

I saw Don Cuyler talking quietly on the telephone in the small office off the lobby. He said, "Right" decisively, hung up and wandered out to the reception area.

"All right, Hilda," Don said to her dryly. "Suppose you open the board this morning. I'd like to talk to Miss Roberts."

As Hilda scrambled to obey, Don stopped beside Toni's desk. The finished bill of lading lay there, face up. He picked it up and scanned it as I furtively slipped on the high heels I'd kicked off under the desk and stood up. I noticed he folded the paper and slipped it into his inside jacket pocket before motioning me to the small office off the lobby.

I braced myself for a repetition of the subtle proposition of the night before. But there was nothing like it. Instead, he closed the door unceremoniously and looked down at me.

"Something has... happened." He paused, seeming to look for words. When he spoke again, his words were a terrible shock: "It's about Toni. She was hit by a car last night. Hit and run accident. She's dead."

Dead? Toni? I stared at him, dumbfounded.

Dimly, I heard the outer door swing open and the padding of soft footsteps, then the low murmur of a male voice. The door opened behind me, but I couldn't look up; I was literally gasping. I couldn't think of a thing to say. When I finally did turn around, I was in for another shock.

A tall, slim man in a loose-fitting gray suit, his back to me, was holding up a leather-backed identification folder for Don's inspection. "Dallas FBI," he said in an officious tone. Then he swung around to glance at me—and I gasped again.

It was *George.*

George—the architect of this whole time-travel experiment, owner of the Coup D'Etat bookstore in the year 2000—37 years younger and far stiffer and more pompous than the man I had known in New York. Unlike the man I knew, who moved lazily, fluidly, as though he were boneless, this man stood as though there was starch in his spine. But without a doubt, it was George. The hair was light brown, parted neatly and slicked back, the suit and thin dark tie standard issue for the Bureau, I supposed. The penetrating eyes were the same, as was the firm set of the nose and the slight upturn of his lips.

No wonder he had such an interest in Kennedy's assassination! He'd been here in Dallas at the time!

George and Don shook hands, measuring each other. "You're the—er—Executive Vice President of ISI?" George asked.

"I am," Don confirmed. "We've been expecting you." He nodded to me. "That's all for now. We'll call you when we need you."

I found myself outside the little conference room, still stunned, unmoving, while my mind raced.

I shook away my thoughts and headed for the switchboard. Time and tide waited for no man, and neither, apparently, did Hilda, who resented every minute she spent away from her movie magazines. She was slipping off her headset as I put mine on, and as I slid into the seat Toni usually occupied, the board began to light up. I plugged in lines and announced calls in a daze.

How could Toni have been hit by a car? The last I'd seen her, she was on her way to deliver an envelope. Who hit her? How had it happened? And—worst thought of all—was it an accident? Or had there been a reason, in someone's eyes, for her to die?

Just as disturbing was the presence of George Staub—my friend George, from the year 2000. George had to have known that I would run into him, in his younger incarnation. Or did he? Had I somehow, by my presence here, altered events in such a way that these new developments were springing up? Had my mother known of Debbie's disappearance and now Toni's death—both of which occurred in the last few days before her husband's untimely disappearance? Or had they not happened in the untouched past? Had they happened somehow because of *me*?

One thing was certain: if Toni's death did have some connection to the company, then there was a hell of a secret about the place. It would mean that Debbie's disappearance was not an accident, and it would further mean that the two incidents were somehow related. I couldn't prove that, of course, but felt it instinctively.

But what did two switchboard operators know that was so important that their lives were endangered by being here?

I pondered this.

A half hour went by.

"Miss Roberts. Come here, please." Don opened the door and beckoned to me.

Hilda slid reluctantly into my chair.

My hands beginning to tremble, I made my way to the little office.

George was waiting for me. He acknowledged me with a cool nod as I walked in on shaky legs. He looked over a sheet of paper for a moment before he said to me, "Your name is—er—Catherine Roberts."

"Yes."

"And you started working here yesterday."

"Yes." I'm sure I sounded puzzled.

George consulted a stack of papers in front of him for a moment. "And—let's see— you keep the log of ISI's company cars at your desk."

"At the switchboard, yes," I said uncertainly. "Toni kept it."

"Can I see it?" George asked Don. Don nodded and went out; he came back with the red marbled book and gave it to George.

George flipped to the back. I sat unmoving. I still couldn't believe Toni was dead; that fact was simply astounding.

"Did you write this?" he asked me suddenly, pushing the book toward me.

I glanced at the entry.

"Yes," I said, feeling more confident, "Toni was showing me how to fill out the logbook."

He looked down at the entry again. "Blue Thunderbird. Signed out yesterday, but not signed back in." He glanced at Don. "How many pool cars you have here?"

"Twenty. They should all be in."

I'd forgotten to check this morning myself, though I could remember Toni saying, *If the count is ever less than twenty, let me know right away.*

"Why don't you check them now?" he suggested to Don.

"Sure thing," Don answered.

He left, while George continued to examine the log. "It's interesting, Miss Roberts, that this blue Thunderbird signed out yesterday is the only entry in your handwriting."

"Why?" I asked, genuinely surprised. "I only started here yesterday."

"And before that, you worked—where?" George prompted.

I gave him the highlights of my phony resume, praying he wouldn't check up on me but knowing he almost certainly would. I swore vividly to myself, at the bad luck that had my handwriting in the logbook at all.

But why is it important? I asked myself.

The answer wasn't long in coming.

Don returned a few minutes later. "Number 17 hasn't been checked back in." He opened a cabinet holding a set of hooks, from which glittered rows of keys. "That's a 1962 Thunderbird."

George nodded, as though he expected it. "License number?"

"Number RJ601." Don showed him the note in the logbook, another note I had written quite innocently, with Toni explaining.

"Right," George said briskly. "And the car that crashed downtown last night was license number RJ601." He began to make notes rapidly in his pad.

Don looked at me. I knew what he was going to say. "We just learned this morning," he said tautly, "that our other telephone operator was—er—hit by a car last night, a few blocks from here. Hit and run accident. I wonder if—"

George nodded. "I'll look into it. Could be a connection."

He jotted down the information in the logbook and flipped his pad closed.

I began to feel very sick.

"I'm sure," he said in a level voice that didn't deceive me for a minute, "that there's a perfectly reasonable explanation."

"I just gave it to you," I said slowly, feeling as though I was caught in a spiraling nightmare. "Toni told me to write this, for practice."

George tried to cut me off with a raised hand, but I persisted. "The courier," I said quickly, "can't you talk to him?"

"Courier?"

"Jose," I said quickly, relieved that I could remember. "Toni called him Jose. Not too tall, broad shoulders, dark silky hair, heavy Cuban accent—"

Don shook his head. "We don't have a courier named Jose. We never did."

"Toni called him Jose!" I insisted. "She seemed to know him very well. She said he was your personal courier."

Don and George exchanged tolerant smiles. In George's I could also read something that looked like regret. He stood up. "I'll get to work on this. Oh, er, Miss Roberts?"

I looked up at him dumbly. What could I possibly say that would help me?

"Your driver's license, please," he said politely.

A little dazed, I got out my wallet and handed him my beautifully-forged New

York driver's license. *Thank goodness*, I thought numbly, *George of the year 2000 thought to take care of these things… or the George of 1963 might arrest me right here and now.*

He wrote down the license information and returned it to me without comment. Then he shook hands with Don and departed, holding that infernal notepad in his hand.

"You can go back to the switchboard," Don told me. "We'll call you when we need you."

Hilda stayed sulkily on switchboard duty as my second, though she spent every spare minute avidly reading a tattered copy of Motion Picture, a magazine I'd never heard of, its pages ruffled from many readings, open to a story about Troy Donahue, his blond hair gleaming in the Malibu sun, his teeth gleaming almost as brightly.

Bad as I felt about Toni's death, it was a pinprick compared with the panic rising in my throat now. To be completely alone in the world, away from everyone and everything I knew and who knew me, and to be possibly implicated in a possible homicide, was terrifying.

Don made a formal announcement of Toni's death a few minutes later. Gossip spread like a tidal wave through the office and then, through the chattering salesmen, to outsiders. Several callers even asked me about Toni, but I kept my tone professional and refused to talk. Near noon, when the calls had momentarily slackened, a solitary light buzzed on the board.

"Good morning, ISI Incorporated," I said for the fiftieth time that day.

"Good morning. This is the world traveler."

Alek. I'd forgotten all about him.

"Cady? Are you there? Are you all right?"

All morning, I'd kept off the subject with other callers. With Alek, it just burst out of me. "Toni's dead," I said flatly. "She was killed in a hit and run accident last night."

There was a sharp intake of breath. Then, "That's terrible," he said, but slowly, absently, as though he were thinking of something else.

"And," I went on, suddenly feeling a compulsion to talk, "I think the FBI thinks I have something to do with it."

There was no sound at the other end, but I had the feeling I'd startled him. "The FBI?" he repeated. "They've been in to talk to you?"

I don't know why, but I suddenly blurted out all the important points of the story, including how frightened I was of the possible consequences. "And my handwriting was in the logbook," I concluded, "because Toni was showing me the procedure and she had me do it, so I could learn. It was totally innocent. But I think this guy thinks there's something sinister about it."

I expected Alek to throw me some glib words of comfort and then ask for Don—why should he care about the fears of a temporary telephone operator?—but he didn't.

"Look," he said at length, "there are a couple of strange things going on here. First, why is the FBI investigating?"

"What do you mean?"

"A hit and run car accident isn't a federal crime. If someone's investigating Toni's death, it should be the Dallas police. Have they been around today?"

"No. I haven't seen them." But a small tide of relief was beginning to surge inside me. Alek was right, of course, and if I hadn't been so shocked by the whole turn of events, I would have realized it. Hit-and-run car accidents were not FBI jurisdiction; so what *was* George Staub doing here?

"Meet me tonight for coffee," Alek was saying. "I think we should talk about this. You need somebody to talk to. You sound pretty shaken."

He was right, I was; but I couldn't help blurting out my first reaction: "Meet you for coffee? The last girl from ISI who did that got hit by a car!"

He sounded offended. "Well, I wasn't driving it." He stopped and drew a deep breath. "I'm sorry about Toni, really. She was a nice girl. Maybe I can help."

I remembered Alek's implying that he knew a lot about what went on at ISI.

I wondered if I could learn more by talking to him. I wondered where he spent his days, and what he did that allowed him to keep such close tabs on ISI. I wondered, also, if Don knew that Alek was watching.

Then I realized that, however tempting it was to think about it, I couldn't confide in anyone, not in my situation. Though I genuinely liked Alek—he was intelligent and friendly—this was no time to start blabbing to near-strangers. I needed to figure out some answers on my own. And I couldn't discuss ISI business with him, if only because it might somehow get back to the people responsible for Don's impending disappearance.

"I—well, no, thanks," I said reluctantly. "I—don't think I'd better." Then lamely, I added, "I wouldn't want you to get in trouble."

There was a pause. "You need a friend, Cady," he said quietly. He paused again. "But I can understand if you don't trust me yet. Don't forget, though, you've got rights. Don't let 'em push you around."

There was a rustle behind me. Hilda raised her head from her magazine.

It was Don Cuyler.

I hadn't slipped him a note about Alek.

And I was already in trouble.

"Hold on!" I hissed into the receiver. Then, waving frantically at Don, I called to him as softly as I could manage, "Sir, Alek—I mean, Al—is on the phone for you."

He raised his eyebrows but nodded and went back through the door. A moment later, I plugged in the call.

Hilda barely lifted her head from Rock Hudson. "You're not gonna win any friends if you keep calls from the boss."

"I wasn't—" I began.

She tossed her head, stood up and flipped the magazine closed. "It's no skin off my nose. Besides, I'm on lunch. It's your turn to stay in."

"Don't I get to eat?" I asked, my stomach starting to rumble.

Hilda flipped her black hair back so it tumbled over her shoulders. "You can take a break around two, but since Toni's—" she hesitated, "—not here, somebody has to stay at the switchboard right now. I guess you're elected."

She was out the door before I could protest further.

Twenty minutes later I was so hungry I could have eaten the pencils in my pencil cup.

Sandra had offered me eggs and bacon at 7:00, but since she was clearly queasy, I had thanked her and mumbled something about not being hungry. I couldn't bear the thought of her standing at the stove with those smells rising to her nostrils when she should be in the bathroom. Besides, sitting at breakfast with Don Cuyler was anything but comfortable. Instead I'd bolted a few bites of a bun, which was so sticky and sweet I could hardly swallow it.

I was paying for it now. I was starting to feel lightheaded.

The office was unnaturally quiet. The air was still. The switchboard had been silent for ten minutes. Even Miss Bradley had stumped out of the building, the first time I'd seen her leave during a workday.

Toni had said she and Debbie kept snacks there. I knew it was against the house rules to eat at the switchboard, but I no longer cared. I was ravenous.

Quickly, I rummaged through the desk.

Toni kept few personal items—a used handkerchief, a worn-down lipstick in a scarred case, a packet of matches.

I peered into the second desk, Debbie's desk, then felt with my hands.

Chewing gum wrappers. A crumpled pack of L&M cigarettes with two forgotten bent ones in the bottom. A gold lighter.

Then my hand reached the very back of the desk and closed on something.

Holding my breath, I carefully drew it out.

It wasn't one object; it was two.

The top object was wrapped in a plastic case, which had been zipped partway closed. I unzipped it with difficulty and drew out a bright red vinyl head scarf. There were bright loops spaced along the length of the scarf. I realized that the bright loops were small round metal picture frames sewn into the vinyl itself.

Each frame contained a tiny photograph.

Each photograph featured a beaming girl with long dark hair—Debbie? It had to be. She had a ravishing smile and deep dimples and the kind of mischievous little-girl look that told me she loved being photographed and probably also loved being the center of attention. I could see how she could upstage Toni without even trying.

One photo showed her with Toni, obviously at a party. Toni looked ill at ease in a dowdy brown and black dress with an unsophisticated Peter Pan collar, while Debbie sparkled in a white dress with a low-cut neckline and tight bodice.

Two other photos showed her with an arm draped companionably around the neck of a man in a well-cut business suit, holding a cocktail glass, a man I clearly recognized... Don Cuyler.

One photo showed Debbie with her lips close to Don's, her eyes closed, head tilted back, as though about to be kissed. Don was leaning toward her, a sardonic smile on his face. The second photo showed her cheek to cheek with him. Both photos had obviously been taken at the same time: In each one, Debbie wore a tight shimmering red dress and jetty earrings; Don had on a gray suit and figured tie, the tie pulled askew, his hair slightly rumpled. Both held cigarettes high in their fingers.

There were a few other photos of Debbie alone, all with that beaming touch-me smile for the camera and the provocative lowered eyes and lifted lips. She was, as Toni said, a very pretty girl—and obviously a good-time girl.

It occurred to me that Debbie's accepting a date with Stan allowed her to be in easy proximity of Don at a crowded social occasion. Perhaps Debbie had decided, before her disappearance, to use Stan as a beard. She could go to the party with him, which obviously would gratify Stan, and then disappear discreetly for some fun and games with Don. He'd shown no compunction about accepting sexual favors on the spur of the moment, even in a place where his colleagues and their wives would note it. And if the dialogue I overheard at the party was any indication, the women, at least, knew that Debbie had cast lustful eyes in the past on some of their husbands.

I was so mesmerized by the photos on the scarf, I had almost forgotten the second object. The crackle of paper under my fingers reminded me, and I found myself fingering a standard-size window envelope.

There was something inside. I slid my fingers under the flap.

And pulled out… a paycheck. ISI's name and address were printed on the top. The check was made out to Deborah Fuller and was dated November 15, 1963. The amount was one hundred and eight dollars and change. The stub noted that this was pay for the two weeks ending November 8th.

My hunger was suddenly forgotten.

Curiosity had taken over.

Debbie worked as a switchboard operator, and if the amount of her paycheck was any indication, she earned about sixty dollars a week, less deductions. Judging by the photographs on the scarf, she liked pretty clothes and jewelry, and they can't have been cheap. Yet here was a paycheck—her most recent paycheck—stuffed in the back of a drawer and forgotten.

How many girls, I brooded, *innocently left their paychecks in the backs of desk drawers at work?*

The answer was: None that I'd ever heard of.

Working girls needed every penny of their paychecks, and many still had trouble making ends meet—no girl would unthinkingly leave it at work.

There was only one logical conclusion: Debbie hadn't known she wouldn't be coming back—which meant her disappearance had not been her decision.

I was even more convinced now that Toni's death was related to Debbie's disappearance. After all, the two girls worked together at ISI, and Toni was undeniably frightened of *something* here. And if Toni's death was related… then it couldn't have been an accident.

I'd had those thoughts earlier, but there'd been no way to connect them. Now here was positive proof. It was clear to me that both girls were no longer here *because of something they knew about ISI.*

I felt very cold inside.

I thrust Debbie's check and scarf back into the drawer, and tried also to thrust away Alek's comment that had popped, unwanted, into my mind: a hit-and-run accident should be investigated by the local police. *Why, instead, is an FBI agent nosing around?*

* * *

Special Agent George Staub stubbed out a cigarette in his FBI-issue metal ashtray and lit a new one in almost the same motion, inhaling deeply. A small cloud of smoke rose from his nostrils and hung gently in the air over his head. It was an absent, automatic motion: he was concentrating fiercely on the folder in his hands.

It contained the police report of last night's crash of a 1962 blue Thunderbird and details of the man who had been killed driving it. More important, to George, were the details of the interesting cargo the car contained: boxes of military rifles, some of them twenty years old, but all apparently recently oiled and in good repair, along with cases of ammunition. The car had been wrecked when it wrapped around a telephone pole downtown, but the bashed-in fenders still contained traces of blood and hair that George made sure went straight to the FBI lab in Washington for analysis. Unless he really was barking up the wrong tree, he'd bet next month's salary that the report would come back with a match to that poor girl, Toni LaRoux, who had been a hit-and-run victim the same night.

But… something just didn't add up.

The girl was killed only about three blocks from the ISI building, yet this guy was finally stopped by that intrepid telephone pole several miles away. Carrying contraband like that, George certainly could understand why he was driving so recklessly, but what was he doing in that area after dark, when she was probably the only person on the street? The area where the car got wrecked, sure: there were tons of people and plenty of parking lots and buildings where he could meet a contact. Not so with the area where Toni LaRoux died. And the description of the accident he'd shaken loose from Don Cuyler indicated that she died where she was found.

So *why?* How did it happen?

George smoked another cigarette down almost entirely, thumbing thoughtfully through the ISI logbook, before his reflections began to jell. He didn't like his thoughts.

George Staub had joined the Dallas FBI office only two months ag, re-assigned from his home district in New Orleans, to follow a curious trail involving stolen weapons.

These weapons were traveling along an established pipeline in the Deep South, and George was the right man to hunt them down. Not yet thirty, he projected a calm and confident demeanor that commanded respect, and he was a thorough and relentless digger for facts. New Orleans bred, his Southern accent could be gentle and winning when questioning witnesses; it could also drip like acid when he was confronted with incompetence, incomplete reports or inaccurate information. In short, George Staub was a Southerner by birth, an investigator by inclination, an FBI agent because it gave him satisfaction: working for the FBI was being a good guy and fighting evil.

He'd picked up the illegal arms trail in New Orleans two months before, from the files of another FBI investigator who'd been inexplicably reassigned to another state. He'd traced the weapons to an office off Lafayette Square, but that was the last stop before, apparently, they were sent off further east. The weapons came from somewhere else, and in migrating to Dallas he was following his nose and a couple of good tips from informants. Who got the weapons and who procured them and most important, *what they were for,* were still questions for which he didn't have definitive answers. But without a doubt, he had some pretty good leads, and he was following them conscientiously.

This girl, though—this Catherine Roberts—she was another corkscrew in the whole nasty puzzle. He'd run information on her driver's license as soon as he returned and was waiting for results, but she didn't smell right to him. There was something—off—about her. From Don Cuyler, he'd elicited the information that Miss Roberts was rooming at his and his wife's boardinghouse here in Dallas temporarily, and Cuyler looked like a pretty fair judge of character. He wouldn't let her stay at his home unless he thought she was all right.

It did seem odd that she arrived out of the blue to take this new job right after the first girl at the switchboard disappeared, and that on her first day, the second operator was killed.

George didn't notice that he'd smoked the second cigarette down until he felt a burning in his fingers. Hastily he stubbed out the tip and was contemplating lighting another when a veteran Dallas agent named Terence Miller stopped by his desk. George liked Miller, who had been helpful without being an overbearing jerk when he first joined the Dallas office. Miller, in turn, liked George: among other attributes, Miller found, George wasn't an asshole. On such mutual admiration are friendships firmly built.

"Curiouser and curiouser," said Miller.

George merely raised his eyebrows.

"This—Catherine Roberts," he said, glancing at his notes. "Come in my office a minute. You'll want to see this."

Once they'd closed the door of his closet-sized office—the FBI didn't waste operating money on frills—Miller offered George a sheet of paper. "Just over the teletype."

George scanned the sheet, his eyes moving swiftly at first, then slowing down. He glanced up at Miller, who nodded and lit another cigarette for him, which George accepted absently while he read very slowly to the bottom of the sheet.

Miller waited until George raised his head.

"That's peculiar," he said finally.

Miller lit a cigarette of his own and puffed carefully. "This girl doesn't seem to exist anywhere that we can trace her." He paused. "George—how did you read her? You think she might be—well—some kind of plant?" In other words, a foreigner posing as an American, for some sinister reason?

George thought about the girl he'd met at ISI. Quiet, polite, probably jittery, though he also read her as unusually intelligent and poised—but every movement, every word authentic. "No. Whatever she is, she's American." He tossed the teletype back on his friend's desk. "You're right, though. Something smells awfully fishy."

"What's your gut feeling?"

George shook his head slowly. "I don't think I have one yet. That girl, Toni LaRoux, gets killed in a hit and run accident—by a guy who's killed himself a half hour later, crashing into a telephone pole, in a car full of stolen weapons. I'm waiting to hear from the guy out at the army base, but I'm pretty sure those rifles started off as standard Army issue, and somehow got 'liberated' from the base just not long ago."

"And then?"

"And then this guy—a courier, let's say—he's taking them to make a delivery but still manages to kill a girl along the way, who's nowhere near the site where we found him. Did he get lost and hit her accidentally? Or did he go out of his way to hit her deliberately—and if so, why? And on whose orders?"

Miller shook his head. "This is sounding worse and worse, but George, before you go off half-cocked—"

"Who, me?" George said innocently.

"—just remember that accidents do happen. Every once in awhile."

"I wish I could believe that. But too many accidents add up to coincidence, and you know what too much coincidence tends to add up to."

"George, not everything in this world is a conspiracy."

George snatched another cigarette from the pack on Miller's desk. "No," he agreed gloomily. "Just the cases I tend to work on."

The truth that he didn't tell Miller was that his gut instinct was to believe this Catherine Roberts. She was fresh and polite and seemed startled at being tied to Toni's death. He couldn't be wrong about how his suspicion had thrown her off balance. And she had accurately described the guy who'd died at the scene, though his ID listed him under another name and said he was Mexican, not Cuban. But in a Cold War, there were lots of talented operators. She could just be one of them, even if his gut said differently.

It was looking more and more as though he'd have to have another conversation with this Catherine Roberts, but he'd wait till the Crime Lab boys told him what they knew.

* * *

I spent the rest of the day carefully not thinking about anything except my job, until 3:30.

Don had gone out to the warehouse. Stan and the other half dozen ISI salesmen were out on their calls, jollying customers to buy more liquor for Thanksgiving next week.

Hilda had reluctantly put down her movie magazine (Silver Screen) to deliver the afternoon mail, and I was alone. The switchboard was quiet, but my thoughts were racing: Debbie's disappearance, Toni's death, George's appearance, his suspicion of my complicity, Don's upcoming disappearance, my parents' marriage. Every thought I had was unpleasant; some were downright frightening.

Stop thinking, I told myself. I reached for Hilda's magazine and tried to lose myself in gushing stories about "Dean Martin, Swinger AND Family Man" and "Why Eddie Still Cries Over Liz". I couldn't concentrate on the words or the photos. I needed something more distracting.

…Which was why I was more relieved than otherwise to see a nervous-looking man come through the front door. I supposed he was a deliveryman: he was carrying a metal clipboard and wore a plain blue shirt with navy slacks. But he didn't quite look the part: the wrinkled shirt was only partly tucked in; his hair was uncombed; the hems of his pants were fraying. No delivery company I'd ever heard of allowed their drivers on the street looking so disgraceful.

He came to the counter and nodded to me, holding out the clipboard. "Afternoon, ma'am," he said in a soft Texas twang. "Brought ya that shipment y'all are expecting from the Carousel. Five hundred units of scotch. You want it in the usual spot?"

I signed the clipboard and answered automatically. "Oh, yes, that's fine."

I had no idea where 'the usual spot' was. And a memory clanged in the back of my mind. When 'Jack called from the Carousel' yesterday, he'd said he was sending over gin, not scotch. And the bill of lading I'd typed for Don had specified vodka.

Strange.

I held the front door open as the deliveryman wheeled in a cart stacked with long wooden boxes. I was stunned when he pushed the cart straight past me and opened the door to the back, where I had not once set foot since arriving yesterday morning.

This was my chance to see past that door, so I marched behind him, trying to look self-assured and confident.

To my surprise, behind the door a cluster of offices sat under a soaring warehouse-type ceiling at least twenty feet high. The office walls, held together in a large rectangle, only rose about seven feet, the space above being open. It looked like a hastily-constructed TV set, the kind I had worked on so often in *Wind*. The high ceiling and dead air above each office meant that many, many sounds floated past me as I followed the deliveryman down the hall. I wondered fleetingly just how long ISI had occupied these offices. I would have bet it wasn't very long at all, a matter of months at most. These were not offices constructed for permanence.

He pushed the cart unhesitatingly to a door at the end of the long hall.

The other doors had laminated name tags in slots next to them, but the slot on this door was empty, and it was situated far away from the others.

He pushed the door open with his foot—I was surprised it was unlocked—and wheeled the cart in, unerringly finding and flicking on a light switch with the ease of long practice.

I followed, as quietly as possible. I doubted he knew I was behind him.

We were in a room almost bare of furniture: several rows of wooden crates, identical to those on his cart, were neatly stacked against the walls. A large blackboard, maybe six feet by four feet, was mounted on one wall, and had a rough diagram sketched on it in chalk. I glanced at it fleetingly: the center of it appeared to be a curving horizontal line with a rectangle sitting on it, about midway down. Above it was an arrow pointing to the rectangle's left side. The arrow was drawn from top left to lower right. There was another arrow on the right of the rectangle, zooming from upper right to lower left. A third arrow went from the right side of the rectangle on a perfectly straight line to the right of the diagram. All the arrows pointed at the rectangle.

I wondered idly what it might be—there was no label, but the arrows seemed painstakingly drawn. Someone had gone to some trouble constructing the diagram.

Meanwhile, the deliveryman, not looking at the blackboard, unloaded the cart. Now that he was alone, or so he thought, he became careless: Instead of lifting all the cases off the cart, he nudged the bottom ones off with his foot.

They'll fall, I thought, and they'll break open, and we'll have liquor flowing all over the cheap linoleum...

"Please," I said quickly. "Can't you—"

He turned, startled. Until that moment he obviously hadn't known I was behind him.

His foot, in the act of moving to push the last case off the cart, caught the cart instead, flipping the boxes in an untidy sprawl, topside down, all over the office floor.

The sound of the crash was thunderous.

The man swore, but instead of bending to pick up the boxes, he simply yanked his cart upright and almost ran out of the office.

I was left alone with the mess.

I got down on my knees at once, hoping to right the cases before the liquor seeped out. I sniffed, but smelled nothing. Maybe gin was odorless, like vodka. I tried to remember if I'd seen a freight manifest. No, he'd only had me sign the clipboard. I had no idea what bottles were supposed to be inside. I didn't even know if he'd delivered the right items.

I hadn't heard glass shatter, either.

I'd better stack the boxes upright, I thought. Then I can slip out and no one will ever know I was here. I had the distinct feeling that no temp should be poking around back here—which was precisely why I intended to.

I reached out to pick up the closest box.

I'd expected it to be heavy, but it wasn't. The box was about four and a half feet long by a foot wide, and I lifted it easily. Inside, I thought I could hear the clank of metal.

I bent over to be sure. Yes, that sound was metallic pieces clanking together.

Something about this whole thing seemed very odd to me.

I pushed my finger under the top wooden slat. A nail was loose in the box, and I pulled on it, bruising my fingers, so I could peer inside. Eventually I loosened it enough to lift off one corner and hold it under the bar of fluorescent light above me.

Though the side of the outer box was conspicuously stenciled "Scotch Whiskey" and "Inspected by U.S. Customs", the inside had certainly never been seen by a customs inspector.

What I saw through the loosened board made my heart begin to slam against my ribs. It was a dark mass of metallic objects stacked carelessly together.

Rifles.

Chapter Ten
WEDNESDAY, NOVEMBER 20, 1963

I slept badly that night and woke abruptly to a light rain drumming on my window. I looked at my watch: 4:15.

I was wide awake, until the demons chasing themselves in my mind were sorted out.

Whatever was happening was much bigger than I'd thought back in the year 2000.

It was something that involved most-likely-illegal arms like the rifles I'd uncovered, something that also involved ISI as a conduit. Someone was using ISI to pass these arms, but to whom? And why?

Two telephone operators had already learned something they shouldn't at ISI. One had vanished, and if the paycheck I'd found was any indication, not of her own volition. The second was dead, and it was becoming horribly clear to me that her death had been no accident. George Staub—the 1963 FBI version of him—had confirmed that the car that hit her was an ISI pool car. It couldn't be a coincidence. The George of the year 2000 had made it clear to me there was no such thing as coincidence.

I wasn't connecting all the dots yet, but some threads seemed obvious.

The first thread was that those rifles were part of the shipment being sent on Friday, the one whose bill of lading I had typed, which had clearly and conspicuously said "Vodka, bottled". Were there more boxes of rifles I didn't know about, slated to go on that truck?

The destination was the University of Miami. I racked my brain. What was going on in Miami in 1963?

The answer rose in my mind, schooled by the hundreds of pages George had insisted I read:Cuba.

Anti-Castro Cubans were training by the thousands for a second invasion of Cuba. The Bay of Pigs, in 1961, had been a spectacular failure, the first blemish on Kennedy's administration. The Cubans hated Kennedy for what they saw as his betrayal of them by refusing to provide air support for the forces trapped on the beach at the Bay of Pigs.

So they had started again, planning a second invasion, an invasion, I reminded myself, that had never happened. Though Kennedy's death had created a new Commander-in-Chief, Lyndon Johnson was just as cautious as JFK had been about committing the U.S. to war with Cuba. We had, after all, promised just a year before that we would not invade Cuba. Besides, Johnson's primary concern was developing an all-out war in Vietnam.

I suddenly connected my reading to the situation at hand. The University of Miami was the site of JM/WAVE, a huge CIA station in Florida, which was almost certainly providing arms and training to Cuban exiles eager to try to re-take their homeland from Fidel Castro.

So the rifles were almost certainly intended for shipment to the JM/WAVE station. They'd be traveling overland in a commercial truck, direct from Dallas to Miami.

The second thread was the enmity between Stan and Don. When they saw each other in the office, they ignored each other; when they spoke, they spoke curtly. There was rage simmering under Stan's genial surface, and resentment toward Don. And Stan was a guy, I sensed, in whom violence was bubbling just below the surface.

It was clear that Don was in danger. As little as I liked him personally, as much damage as I felt he was doing to my mother, he was nonetheless going to be the third person to vanish, on Friday morning. Debbie and Toni were telephone operators, menial workers who just happened to have caught wind of something they weren't a part of.

Don was Executive Vice-President of ISI.

"Whatever was happening couldn't be hidden from him—after all, he'd given Toni the instructions to type the bill of lading. He knew something about this operation; therefore, he was dangerous to the powers that be. Someone, to shut him up, was going to make him disappear in 48 hours.

"I lay still as that thought penetrated.

"I had to warn him.

"I had to learn more about the operation."

How could I do that alone?

I thought of the people I'd met in 1963—my mother, Don, Toni, Hilda, Stan, the Cubans… all with their own agendas, their own suspicions. I knew that just by being an outsider with a non-southern accent, I excited their skepticism. There wasn't one whom I felt I could trust completely.

… Well, there might be one…

You need a friend, Cady…

There was one person who'd remained honest and steadfast from the first day. He knew more about ISI than he was saying, so telling him what I'd learned wouldn't shock him. Toni had described him as a gentleman. She'd liked and trusted him. Most important, he didn't work at ISI.

I understood at that moment that I could talk to Alek. He'd told me he'd been 'keeping close tabs' on ISI.

An odd thought crossed my mind. Could he be 'keeping tabs' for some reason related to the rifles I saw?

I thought about it as light crept into the room and the hands of the clock moved toward six. Whoever he was, he was young and kind, and I was certain that he was one of the good guys.

I hoped he'd call early in the day, so I could arrange a time to meet him tonight.

* * *

I had wondered how I could reach Alek if he didn't telephone, but my worries were groundless: he phoned around 10 a.m.

Unfortunately, almost as soon as he identified himself, the outer door swung open to admit the ominous figure of George Staub. He strolled purposefully toward the reception desk, just close enough to hear every word I said. My stomach began to churn with tension.

Oh, no, I thought. *I can't have him overhearing my conversation.* But I had to connect with Alek, and I couldn't be sure he'd call back. And I couldn't say anything that would sound even faintly suspicious to an FBI agent. He was suspicious enough of me already.

"Cady? Are you there?"

"Mm – yes, indeed. And there is a message for you about yesterday's conversation." I prayed he would figure out what I was trying to tell him. I scrambled for some paper to pretend to read from. George looked at me curiously. "The answer'to your question yesterday is yes."

Alek was silent. Finally, he said, "Is someone listening?"

"That's right," I trilled brightly.

"Are you saying you've changed your mind? You'll meet me after all?"

"Yes, indeed," I confirmed, relief coursing through me that he understood. I turned to smile and nod at George, who nodded back, and raised a finger to indicate I'd be right with him. He sat down in one of the less-dusty chairs and gazed around thoughtfully.

"Okay." Alek had taken charge. He spoke quietly, as though someone might overhear him. "Meet me at 5:30 at that luncheonette near the ISI building. You know it?"

"Yes, sir, I certainly will," I said, pretending to jot down a message.

"Good. We can talk there. Is that what you want?"

"Oh, yes, absolutely," I said, still scribbling madly.

"I'll be wearing a gray zippered jacket and a blue shirt. See you then."

He hung up, and I crumpled up the slip of paper and turned to George. "Hello. Do you want to see Mr. Cuyler again?"

"Actually, I'd like to talk to you."

The churning in my stomach became worse. I wondered wildly whether I was going to throw up. "I—I can't leave the switchboard," I began.

George glanced behind me. "You," he said abruptly. "Take over the board until we come back."

Hilda, looking sulky, was just sidling out, another copy of *Photoplay* in her hand. She seemed to have an endless supply.

George didn't wait for her to slip into my chair. "Let's go," he said brusquely to me.

I found myself on the sidewalk in front of the building a moment later, feeling the slight chill of the November day bite through the light fabric of my dress.

Abruptly, George said, "Why don't you tell me who you really are?"

I snapped out of my reverie. "What?"

"Well, Miss Roberts, we've been checking on you. Your driver's license, for instance, is quite interesting. I don't think I've ever seen so many lies on the same document." He paused, waiting, no doubt, for my outraged denial. I said nothing.

After a moment, he continued. "The New York Department of Motor Vehicles didn't issue it. No one at your New York address recognizes your name. No one named Catherine Roberts was born on the date you listed anywhere in this country. Your Social Security number is phony, and none of the companies listed on your ISI personnel forms has ever heard of you. So who are you?"

"My name is Catherine Roberts."

"You're lying," George said pleasantly.

This is it, I thought. *This is the critical moment.* I remembered the old saying that the best defense is an offense. I remembered Alek's remarks to me yesterday and took the offense with gusto.

"Agent Staub, I find it curious that the FBI is investigating a hit-and-run accident. That's a police matter… especially if it wasn't an accident. So why are *you* involved? What's *your* interest?" I looked up at him with the same icy glare I'd used the day Sheila found out Peter, her great love, had been seeing his ex again. "What gives you the right to investigate me?"

George didn't retreat, but I could sense him hesitating. Still, he held his ground. "I'm not investigating Miss LaRoux's death. I'm working on something that could be related, which has to do with that 1962 Thunderbird you signed out Monday." He started to speak again, no doubt to reiterate his questions.

I cut him off. "No matter what the entry in the logbook says, you should know by now that I wasn't driving the car that killed Toni."

"I know that," George said calmly. "The driver was killed a few miles away, and he was in the car." He added grimly, "If you looked at a newspaper once in a while, you might have seen something about it."

My eyes narrowed. "I don't suppose the driver was a guy named Jose?"

"No," George answered.

My heart sank.

"But," George went on, unperturbed, "perhaps his Texas driver's license is a forgery. The license said he was Juan Rodriguez, and he had other ID indicating he was from Mexico City."

I saw a glimmer of light in the situation. "But," I began, "Mexican or Cuban— that's awfully close… "

"I agree." George looked at me purposefully. "And I'm willing to suspend my—er—suspicions about you, in return for a little, well, help on some things that are puzzling me."

I didn't like the way this conversation was going at all. "What kind of help?"

He shrugged, trying to look casual while watching me with bright eyes, like a cat a mouse hole. "Well—how about some idea about why exactly you showed up at ISI two days ago, just as one telephone operator disappeared and right before a second one is killed? Who are you working for, really? And what are you trying to find out?"

I was struck literally dumb for a moment. Who was I working for? It was on the tip of my tongue to reply, "For you, of course, dummy", but I didn't think humor was going to get me very far at this point, especially since a sense of humor wasn't exactly young George Staub's strong point.

Perhaps I could have tried reasoning with him, if I'd felt calmer and more confident. But I wasn't in the mood to be baited by a suspicious FBI man, even if he was someone I already knew pretty well in another time.

"Look," I said icily, "if you're planning to arrest me, you'd better just do it. But you'd also better know that if you do, your career at the Bureau is over. Hoover doesn't take kindly to agents who make mistakes that hit the front pages. You'll end up emptying wastebaskets at the North Dakota office, if you're lucky."

I expected a backlash of rage. I thought it was even possible that he might produce handcuffs then and there and snap them on me. I braced myself.

George merely looked at me, with what I could swear was a dawning respect in his face. "Fine," he said calmly. "I'll delay arresting you, then. Meanwhile, I need someone inside ISI. The Bureau has some concerns about it, and we need some eyes and ears that can help us figure it out."

I waited, saying nothing. Did he mean the Bureau was looking at ISI as part of a gunrunning operation? What else could he mean?

George looked at me sharply, almost as though to see if I was listening. "Now, you may be just who you say you are, though," he added wryly, "I rather doubt it. But you're right. I don't suspect you in Toni's death, and I'm not investigating that, anyway. I'm investigating matters related to the crash of that Thunderbird. I came to ISI because the Thunderbird is part of ISI's carpool. What I do know, Miss Roberts, is that without a doubt you're not really a part of ISI, and that can be valuable to me."

He reached into his jacket pocket, took out a business card embossed with the FBI seal and handed it to me. "Will you call me if you see or hear anything that sounds odd to you? Anything at all. You can reach me anytime. Someone will always answer that number."

I should have been relieved. I should also, I suppose, have told him everything. But explaining my suspicions meant explaining how I knew what I did about the U.S. involvement in Cuba, which was so secret I was so sure even George didn't know about it and might not give it credence. It certainly would blow any lingering possibility that he might regard me as a normal girl just doing a temp job.

Besides, I was meeting Alek tonight, and I placed more trust in him. He had never treated me with suspicion, but I knew with certainty that he was affiliated with something powerful, too—perhaps as powerful as the FBI. He was calm and rational, and I knew I could tell him the story and get his help without feeling as though if I gave the wrong answers, I would be hauled off to jail.

George Staub, G-man, was simply too suspicious and perhaps too cynical to suit me.

I took the card. "All right, I will," I said, not meaning a word of it.

George gave me a more generous smile. "Good girl," he said. "I don't even care who you're working for. And you don't have to tell me. We'll keep this between us. I'll be in touch."

I might have said something even then, but the 'good girl' part rankled. Since I'd returned to 1963, I'd seen enough to understand that no matter what information I had or how much more I knew than any man, my information would be treated with disdain, disbelief and more than a little contempt because I was a woman.

Alek wouldn't treat me like that.

I'd save my observations for him. The hell with George Staub.

George nodded to me and walked toward a green sedan at the curb. He probably thought he'd handled our conversation with real tact.

I thought he'd be lucky if I ever spoke to him again.

* * *

My mind kept circling back to the blackboard with the chalked diagram that I'd seen yesterday in the empty office. It had looked like a clumsy spider, I remembered, with three arrows pointing from different directions to the rectangular shape in the middle of a wavy horizontal line.

I kept thinking I should recognize it.

I was sure it wasn't doodling. But what was it?

Did it have anything to do with the shipment slated to go out Friday morning?

Maybe the rectangular shape was intended to represent the truck traveling to Miami? But then, the arrows would point *away* from it, not toward it.

I decided I had to have another, longer look at the diagram.

But how would I get past the door to the inner offices?

I got my chance at 3:00, when the late mail came in.

Hilda had let me know loftily, from the first day, that it was *her* job to sort the mail and wheel the little mail cart around the back of the office, delivering to the salesmen and executives. She alone had the right to flick through those important envelopes, and only she was trusted enough to hand the piles of mail to their owners. Until now I hadn't cared to challenge her.

Getting behind that door with the mail cart would serve my purpose admirably. When the mailman, in his starched blue uniform, brought in the sheaf of mail and deposited it with a smile on the counter, I had ripped off the headphones and was already sorting the letters before Hilda could move.

"Hey, that's my job!" she protested, as I swiftly sorted the mail into the slots for each person. I paid no attention. As a final touch, I snatched the message slips from the box; I would personally deliver them while I delivered the mail.

"You can't do that!" she insisted, as I got the cart ready to roll behind the door.

I looked over at her. "I saw the new *Silver Screen* at the newsstand. If you keep quiet and watch the board for a few minutes, I won't say anything if you want to slip out and get it before they run out. Did you hear that Elvis is breaking up with Priscilla?"

And I left her, mouth open, staring at me, as I pushed the cart through the door, trying to act efficient, relaxed and confident. I wondered if Elvis was even married to Priscilla at this point, or whether anyone in America even knew who Priscilla was; I couldn't remember, but I figured either way, I'd left Hilda flummoxed enough to do as I said and not follow me.

I got through the door easily, walking briskly behind the cart. At least twenty people worked back here, their voices, slightly distorted from the acoustical freakishness, rising past me as I rolled the cart. I double-checked the name on each door before I knocked discreetly and went in, bearing my handfuls of letters, message slips and circulars.

I found two of the young salesmen playing dominoes and eating cheese sandwiches. One of the older guys, Isaac, who ran the shipping department, was laboriously pasting strips of S&H green stamps into books; Miss Bradley was hunched over what looked like timesheets, initialing furiously in the margins.

I walked almost on tiptoe past Don's door. For once, he had no mail, and the door to his office was closed. I thanked God silently and continued quietly to the last door at the end of the hall.

I stopped there and waited. No one was around. Everything was quiet. I turned the knob and walked inside, flicking on the light switch with a sigh of relief, then almost let out a scream.

Don Cuyler was standing in the center of the room.

We stared at each other for a moment. I think he was as stunned as I was.

"What are you doing here?" he said eventually. His voice was calm, his eyes fixed on me.

"I was—" My throat was closing up fast; I had trouble getting the words out, "I'm—delivering the afternoon mail."

He recovered his composure quickly.

"You must have made a mistake," he said pleasantly, with a half-smile. "As you can see, no one works in this office."

"Yes—yes, I must have," I said, my heart going like a trip hammer. Impulsively, hardly knowing what I was saying, I blurted out, "Mr. Cuyler?"

"Yes?" I could see a muscle working in his cheek.

He saw me glance at the stacked crates in the corner. I could swear one was open just slightly, and peeking out were—

"Miss Roberts," he said, "you can go back to the front now." The smile remained on his face, but I felt a chill. This was not a suggestion. It was an order, and one with so much force and hostility behind it that it was all I could do not to run out of the room. I didn't dare glance at the blackboard. I didn't think I would dare come in here again. I could see why people ran to do Don Cuyler's bidding.

"I can't go," I blurted out. "Not—not before I warn you."

"About what?" His expression hadn't changed, but his eyes were wary.

"Mr. Cuyler," I said desperately, "I'm sure someone's going to try to—hurt you—if you aren't careful. I just have this strange feeling, I can't help it. I worry about you, especially with Mr. Marchand being so—" I hunted for a word other than 'violent' and finally settled for "—so hostile to you! I worry that he might do—I don't know what!"

I prayed that I sounded rattled enough to make some crazy kind of sense. If not, I was tipping my hand and leaving myself open to all kinds of problems. Distraught, I looked down at the floor.

And felt his hand caress the top of mine.

This wasn't the reaction I'd expected from him.

As I stood there, frozen, his fingers moved up my fingers to my arm, to my neck, and then my cheek. "Thank you, Cady. I appreciate your—er—vigilance."

"Don't you—don't you—want to know more about it?"

"If you knew, I'm sure you'd tell me." His hand was caressing my cheek now, his eyes still on my face, but the tension in them had relaxed, and there was a warm light that had been missing before. He wore a look that told me he was very satisfied with the way things were going.

Abruptly I stepped backward. He moved closer to me, but I stood my ground and gave him the 'touch-me-not' look I'd perfected on Craig during the last days of our marriage, which had easily kept him at arm's length.

It worked now, too.

Don muttered something about getting back to his office. "Oh, Miss Roberts?" He held out a folded sheet of paper. "Please give this to Miss Bradley on your way."

I took the sheet numbly. "Yes, sir."

As he walked past me, he said casually, "I appreciate your taking the trouble to let me know about this—er—situation. It makes me feel I have a special friend here." He smiled, not chastened in the least.

I escaped.

* * *

By 5:00, almost everyone had cleared out. Hilda was gone as soon as the time clock ticked past 5:30; she clocked out and was out the door, the new *Silver Screen* in her hand. Don had left earlier, at 4:30, saying he had an appointment.

The warehouse manager had come in to drop off some papers. He was chatting with Miss Bradley as I went to clock out.

On a hunch, I waited a few moments, until she collected her handbag and gloves, slipped on a jacket and went out with the warehouse manager, talking earnestly. Then I walked boldly into her office. Running into Don Cuyler had terrified me; the worst Miss Bradley would do if she found me here was fire me. It didn't seem, anymore, like such a terrible end.

Miss Bradley's door had no lock on it. Her desk was bare, except for a green blotter, a pen in a penholder, and a calendar.

I looked quickly for any papers she might have recently received, especially the one I'd hand-delivered to her earlier.

I spotted it finally in a wire basket behind her desk, on a small credenza which looked like it doubled as a filing cabinet.

The white paper was still folded in half. I snatched it up and opened it.

The slip Don had given me for Miss Bradley was filled out in his own firm, staccato handwriting, in blue ink. He'd requested vacation time from Monday, November 25th through Sunday, December 8th. He'd signed the slip himself, as his own supervisor, and added the words "Executive V.P."

I stared, thoroughly surprised.

Don had requested *vacation time* for two weeks, starting right after the assassination. He was expecting to be away from the office.

But he had never mentioned it to Sandra, who had not known where he was. She had assumed—and passed that assumption on to me—that he had disappeared involuntarily, that someone else was responsible.

I realized now that might not be true.

If so, it made matters much worse than I'd thought. I thanked heaven that I had someone I could talk it over with.

Alek hadn't called that afternoon, and my stomach was starting to twist into knots, as I got ready, finally, to meet him. It seemed like I'd have a lot more to pour out than I'd originally intended.

I could only hope he was as sympathetic and kind as I'd intuited, and as Toni had said. I needed a friend badly, and between Agent Staub and Don Cuyler and the Cubans with their rifles in the Cuyler kitchen, I was feeling shaky enough.

Don's behavior upset me the most. The thought that my own father had tried to seduce me made me slightly sick. Of course, he had no idea he was my father—but I knew it, and I also knew that his wife was newly pregnant (with me!) It was enough to make me wish I'd never laid eyes on him and kept my mother's memories intact.

Of course, I mused as I walked across the street five minutes later, *they weren't her memories: they were desperate wishes, transformed into memories to block out the real memories of a man she could hardly bear to live with*. I wondered if Don Cuyler didn't disappear on Friday, whether my mother would ever be able to summon up the backbone to leave him. She seemed so dependent, so tender, so trusting—and he used all of those qualities to kick her in the face, again and again.

I reached the luncheonette door and checked my watch. It was just past 5:40, and though night was rapidly falling, I could see a number of people still sitting inside. The sign on the door said that the luncheonette closed at six. A gray zippered jacket and a blue shirt, Alek had said.

I took a deep breath and pulled open the door.

At the end of the counter, a young man sat by himself, sipping a Coke. He was in profile, reading a newspaper, occasionally glancing at the clock on the wall. His hair was brown, thinning in front, and he was quite slender—and wearing a gray zippered jacket with a hint of a blue shirt underneath.

He looks familiar, I thought, staring at his profile. *Why?* I knew he'd never come into the office, and I didn't know anyone else here in 1963…

Suddenly, I recalled the diagram I'd tried to sneak another look at only this afternoon. It had looked like a silly spider, with three arrows pointed on straight lines to a rectangular box on a curving line…

Why had I remembered that now? Why, when I was staring at Alek, had it occurred to me?

He glanced up again at the clock and gazed around until he saw me staring at him. His eyes were startlingly blue as I saw him full face for the first time.

My heart turned to ice.

I *had* seen him before, in black and white pictures, scowling, his face bruised. I had seen him in a cluster of a hundred reporters shouting questions; I had seen him handcuffed and defiant.

I had seen the famous footage of him being shot to death in the basement of Dallas police headquarters.

He slid off the stool and started toward me with long quick strides, smiling, while I realized with sickening clarity that Alek, the man I'd instinctively trusted and believed I could confide in, was no savior.

Alek was Lee Harvey Oswald.

* * *

I couldn't think what to say, or what to do.

He was smiling at me, coming closer and closer, his eyes never leaving mine.

Panic seized me.

I didn't want him near me.

My hand caught at the doorknob behind me, and before I could think, in one movement, I'd yanked it open and run straight into the road.

I heard him shout after me, but I was blindly intent on putting as much distance between us as I could. I pushed past a woman with a baby carriage and two giggling teenagers in faded pedal pushers, bumped an old man who cried out, "Hey!" and flew across the sidewalk, trying to reach the crosswalk where I could catch the bus that was pulling in at the corner…

By now I was so frightened I could feel my teeth chattering, even as I urged my shaking legs, in those tight uncomfortable high heels, to run harder. I focused on the bus, which was lumbering slowly to a stop, its red blinker on, letting the cars behind it know it was dropping off a passenger.

The streetlights were on, and it was harder to see, but suddenly a light flashed off a sleek piece of chrome, which was heading toward me… straight toward me…

In a flash I knew that it was a car, and that the car was headed for me deliberately, callously. I couldn't back up far enough on the sidewalk or run fast enough to outrun it. My mind wouldn't work, wouldn't help me to evade it, and I knew I was going to die just like Toni, which was so stupid, and I couldn't do a thing about it…

Then a strong arm snagged me around the waist and yanked me back, so far back that the car, swooping down on me, knocked instead against the curb, and a fist banged against the side of the car, too, and the arm knocked me down, though it seemed as though I was being cushioned all the way, even as I was falling…

"Don't move," whispered a familiar voice. "Don't get up. Wait for the crowds. They'll protect you."

The car was bumping off, and I knew it was going to come back and hit me, that my pseudo-fall hadn't fooled anyone…

But that was all I knew for quite awhile…

* * *

It was fully dark, and water was dripping down the side of my face when I woke up. "Hush, you poor little girl," cooed someone above me. "You're going to be just fine."

I looked around, as much as I could. I was partially sitting up in someone's lap, someone who turned out to be a large, motherly-looking woman in some sort of white uniform. Someone else—the old man I'd bumped into during my panic-stricken run—was clumsily pressing a wrinkled square of handkerchief, soaked in water, to my forehead. A few bystanders were clucking and gossiping quietly; I caught bits of murmured conversations:

"That car just came right up at her!"

"Lucky she wasn't killed."

I pressed the handkerchief to my head, more to contain the water than succor a bruise, and handed it back to its elderly owner. "I'm much better," I said gratefully to the motherly woman. "Thank you so much for stopping."

The old man carefully wrapped the wet handkerchief in another (slightly) cleaner and much drier one and stuck it in his pants pocket. "Lucky that nice young man saw what was happening," he remarked.

Nice young man?

Oh, God. Did he mean Oswald?

The motherly woman nodded. "He pulled you back from the curb and put his own body between you and the car. I'd say he probably saved your life."

I peered at her, stunned. *Oswald saved me?*

"And then he ran off," said one of the bystanders wonderingly, shaking her carefully-coiffed head. "Didn't even wait for you to come around."

By now I was so completely flummoxed that if I was hurt, I couldn't feel it. I tentatively wiggled my fingers and toes, moved my arms and legs experimentally, and decided nothing was broken; nothing was sprained. Nothing else much mattered, including the tear in the back of my dress and the bang on my elbow. Too much had happened—way too much had happened—since Sunday night, and the only thing I was certain of was that it would be prudent to spend tonight away from my parents' house.

With many thanks and appreciation, I got somewhat shakily to my feet and asked my newfound friends to hail me a cab. I asked the driver to take me straight to a reasonably-priced hotel.

Whatever might be waiting for me at the Cuyler residence, I didn't want to run into it tonight.

Chapter Eleven
THURSDAY, NOVEMBER 21, 1963

I had nightmares.

I was standing on the grassy knoll in Dealey Plaza, watching the President ride by, a clanging in my ears. Two men with guns pursued the President on foot, running behind his limousine, which was traveling oh-so-slowly in the motorcade. One was Oswald, his eyes crazed, firing, each shot coming closer and closer to the President, who seemed to hear nothing behind him. Oswald was shouting incoherently; with each step he was coming closer, while no one in the motorcade saw or heard him.

The other man wore black clothes and was veiled in the mist. I couldn't see his face, but I knew who he was. Though silent, he ran just as fast as Oswald, and was even more terrifying, because he was running toward the car from the front, his rifle cocked, and I knew his would be the shot that would not miss...

Then the man in the mist changed into a giant spider that was suddenly pursuing me to bite my legs off...

I woke up drenched in sweat, the bedclothes torn apart, the top sheet held in a death grip in my fist.

I was more frightened than I'd ever been in my life.

The clanging noise I'd heard in my dream was sounding outside my window. I was in a small house at the other end of Dallas, where the cabdriver had brought me last night, assuring me this little `motel' would be clean and quiet.

I checked over my body, which felt sore and bruised. There were scratches and minor pains on my back, my elbows and my chest. I didn't especially hurt anywhere, but I felt bleak.

Cuba is the key.

I heard George's voice in my mind, the George of the year 2000, as clearly as if he stood next to me, lecturing. The voice was an admonition to view all the information in one context.

The nighttime dreams had somehow coalesced all the threads of knowledge that had lain in my mind for days. Without wanting to, I suddenly knew things. And with that knowledge came responsibility.

I knew who was behind the wheel of the car that almost hit me yesterday.

It had been dark on the street, but the car had hurtled under a bright streetlight for a long moment, and the glitter of those eyes and the hulk of those shoulders had been unmistakable.

I had known, even as I tried to evade the car, that it was Stan trying to kill me.

I further knew that with Lee Harvey Oswald phoning *Don Cuyler* at ISI every day this week, ISI was somehow tied to JFK's visit to Dallas and to his assassination, which would happen a little more than 30 hours from now.

For the first time, all that reading on the Kennedy Administration and the assassination made sense. George had told me I'd be thankful for it.

I wasn't feeling too thankful, but I thought I finally understood.

Cuba was the key.

Oswald was talking *every day* to Don Cuyler.

It had never been mentioned anywhere in my reading that Oswald had any connection with ISI. Further, his connection was specifically with Don Cuyler. Here the knowledge I'd tried hard to push away was unmistakable. I quailed, but I had to face it.

Both Debbie and Toni had known Oswald, under the name 'Alek'. Toni had mentioned her meeting with him in Don's presence on Monday—and a few hours later, she was dead. I had talked to Don, in veiled terms, about a threat to *his* safety, had gone off to meet 'Alek' myself—and less than an hour later Stan was speeding toward me on a crowded street full of pedestrians, probably on a mission to keep me from identifying Oswald, soon to be notorious, as a frequent caller to the company.

… Which meant that, however bitter their personal rivalry, Don and Stan were working on the same side. Stan, despite his bragging, didn't have the brains to organize a fraternity party, let alone a murder. But Don could easily have sent Stan to do the dirty work. It's the only way it could have happened.

Even more disturbing was the revelation that Don *intended* to leave Dallas tomorrow. The vacation slip was positive proof. Obviously, Sandra didn't know it. That disappearance, though, had been meticulously planned. It was his own idea, not a crime perpetrated against him.

But why? *Why?* I thought of everything I'd seen and heard—and overheard— in the past few days. I thought about Cuba. And suddenly the answer was in front of me, and I knew I was right.

The gunrunning. George was investigating a gunrunning case in Dallas, a case where guns were stolen from military bases and shipped out on a pre-arranged pipeline. Many, many guns. Sent through the pipeline on a regular basis.

Who would need a regular supply of military weapons, outside of the military?

Someone planning a military-style attack.

Where?

The guns stolen from military bases in the South were to be used in another invasion of Cuba.

The anti-Castro Cubans who had seen their dreams shattered in 1961 at the Bay of Pigs and perhaps destroyed forever in 1962 by Kennedy's agreement with Khrushchev not to invade Cuba again were going ahead with their own illicit invasion, an invasion planned and fueled by the CIA.

ISI was being run by Don Cuyler. My father. Who *had* to know that those guns were coming in illegally by the hundreds.

Who—*face facts, Cady*—had to know all about Operation Mongoose, the notorious secret CIA program to kill Castro and overthrow his government. Had to be involved in it, if ISI was part of the pipeline.

Who, far from adoring JFK, as I had thought, hated him and everything he stood for. It was clear that Don Cuyler was mixed up in something that was targeting Kennedy.

I thought of the diagram of the spider and how I'd thought of it as I looked at Oswald in the luncheonette. At the time I'd thought it was irrelevant. Now I realized why I'd thought of it as he was walking toward me.

I went to my handbag on the little bureau in the corner of the room and rummaged in it for a pad of paper and a pen. Swiftly I drew the diagram as I remembered it in my quick glimpses of it.

In a couple of minutes I was satisfied with it. Next to the bureau was a folded newspaper I'd picked up late last night. It was the early-morning edition of *The Dallas Morning News* and featured a diagram on the front page, a map of the President's motorcade route on Friday, November 22nd.

I laid the thin, almost translucent paper I'd drawn over the diagram.

A perfect match.

A rectangle with three arrows pointing at it on a curving horizontal line... Kennedy's car, targeted by three gunmen in different positions, as it drove west on Elm Street...

Once his limousine turned from Houston onto Elm, he'd be shot—from three sides, that infamous 'triangulation of crossfire', according to George—within half a minute.

The arrow to the left of the rectangle referred to a gunman on the grassy knoll to JFK's right front, where George's books still insisted a rifleman had been stationed. The top arrow to the right was the School Book Depository. The famous 'sniper's nest' had been set up in the sixth floor east window, but certain witnesses, who somehow were never called to testify before the Warren Commission, saw men in the sixth-floor west windows, where a sniper firing toward the freeway underpass could get off a much better shot. And that third arrow on the bottom... well, there'd always been speculation that there was a third sniper, firing from another high building, perhaps the Dal-Tex Building, across the street from the School Book Depository, in Dealey Plaza.

It didn't matter anymore what I could prove. I knew the mastermind of the operation.

It had to be someone who knew Dallas and could pick the best kill zone, someone intelligent, cool and able to meet sudden emergencies calmly and capably. It had to be someone for whom that second invasion of Cuba was crucially important.

It had to be someone with an intelligence background. Only an intelligence operative could misdirect attention so skillfully from the real culprits. That someone would already have set up his own escape route and planned to blame a Cuban-directed operative (Oswald) firing on their President.

The planner *had* to be… Don Cuyler.

I thought of the secrets I'd discovered here, of my dismay when I realized that everything I knew, except his photographs, was a lie, supplied to me by my mother.

My pride in him was gone forever.

I thought of the stealthy passage of military rifles into the hands of cold-eyed men training to face Fidel Castro, one of the world's most notorious dictators.

They wanted a war with Cuba. They were going to kill the President to incite it.

But there never had been a war with Cuba, from the '60s onward. I had nothing to worry about. No invasion would come about, despite all their fanatical plans.

On the other hand, who knew what I might have said or done, however innocently, to push that invasion to fruition?

I needed to stop that shipment of rifles. It was probably the last shipment of arms before the invasion started.

How? And to whom could I turn as an ally?

That thought made me smile for the first time that morning. I dressed quickly and used the downstairs phone to dial the telephone number on the business card Agent Staub had given me yesterday. I had thought I'd never use it, but things had changed.

When he came to the phone, I asked him to meet me for breakfast.

* * *

When I walked into the coffee shop at 7:15, it was already crowded with working men gulping coffee and eating hearty plates of eggs, bacon and hash.

I headed to one of the small two-person tables in back that remained unoccupied. It was quieter and more inconspicuous, and right now, I didn't feel safe at all.

The waitress was bringing my coffee when George strolled in and came over to join me.

"Thank God," I whispered as he slipped into the seat opposite me.

"What's all this? You're suddenly cooperating with the Bureau?" He was smiling, as I panicked inside.

"With you, George. You personally. You're right, I've got information, and I don't know who else to call. I don't think anyone else would believe me."

George raised his eyebrows and waved to the waitress for coffee. When she'd poured him a cup and left, he leaned back. "Okay," he said. "I'm listening."

I kept my voice low. "The President is coming to town tomorrow.

When he gets here, he'll drive through town in a motorcade." I tried to keep my voice from trembling. "And when that motorcade turns from Houston Street onto Elm, he's going to be shot."

George didn't even blink. He merely lit a cigarette. "Go on."

"He'll be shot driving down Elm Street, just before the car reaches the freeway underpass. You've got to stop it, George. You've *got* to."

George said nothing for a moment. He stirred sugar into his coffee, then took his time adding cream.

As I waited for him to speak, I noticed a well-built Dallas police officer in full uniform saunter into the shop and choose a seat close to the door. He looked oddly familiar.

Then I realized he was the security guard who had stopped me at the party Monday night and demanded to know if I had an invitation, the guy who had irritated Stan.

Suddenly, there was a commotion at the counter. Everyone turned to look at the young man shouting at the waitress.

"You didn't give me what I ordered! I said scrambled, not over easy!" he said loudly, pushing his plate away. "These are terrible! I can't eat eggs over easy!"

The hairs prickled on the back of my neck.

The young man complaining vociferously about his badly-cooked breakfast was Lee Harvey Oswald.

"High-strung fellow," George said quietly.

Someone up front said something, probably asking him to quiet down. "I'm not making a scene. I just want the eggs cooked the way I asked for them. I don't think that's so much to ask. I'm a paying customer!"

The police officer was frankly staring at Oswald, making no effort to hide his interest.

I glanced at George. I'd have expected him to be watching Oswald. Instead, his eyes were on the police officer, who continued to look curiously at Oswald even as he opened his breakfast menu.

"Why are you telling me this?" George asked me, bringing me back to our conversation. "The Secret Service is in charge of Presidential security. Why don't you talk to them?"

"You're an FBI agent. You're federal law enforcement. They'll listen to you."

"You need to talk to them," George repeated patiently. "They investigate these things all the time."

"George, you know if they can't verify who I am, they'll throw out everything I'm trying to tell them. I can't explain who I am, and they won't take my word for anything. Please."

"I'm not putting myself in the middle of this." George glared at me. "Especially since you're lying again, Miss Roberts."

He unfolded the newspaper I'd brought to show him. "You said the President would be shot on Elm Street?"

"That's right. Look—"

He spread the paper over the table and folded it to show the bottom half of the page, the map of the President's motorcade route.

George stabbed a finger at the diagram. "He can't be shot on Elm Street, Miss Roberts. He's not even going to be on Elm Street."

"That's impossible," I began, frantically studying the paper myself. I hadn't looked at the motorcade route on the map, just at the horrifying similarity between the spider sketch and the layout of Dealey Plaza. But the broken line representing the motorcade route was unmistakable: the President's limousine was scheduled to drive straight west on Main Street to the freeway entrance. No turn at Houston. No hairpin turn onto Elm. No detour through Dealey Plaza. No drive into the killing zone.

"The map is wrong," I said positively.

"It was given to the newspaper by the Secret Service," George said quietly.

"Then they're going to change it at the last minute. Kennedy's car will drive down Main Street and right onto Houston, then left onto Elm." I leaned across the table. "You've got to tell them, George. Even if you don't believe it yourself, *you've got to tell them.*"

For a moment, George didn't speak or move. Then suddenly, he grabbed my wrist and pinned it to the table, smiling pleasantly for the benefit of the people in the restaurant, but his eyes glittered at me in a way that unnerved me considerably.

"You listen to me. I don't know who you are, but if this is your idea of how to discredit me, getting me to tell the Secret Service something this crazy and having them tell my boss and have me fired or transferred or whatever you're trying to do—it won't work.

"You can talk all you want. But until I know who you really are and why you're here, lady, I'm not doing a damned thing. I like the Bureau and I intend to stay here. And mouthing off about some wild assassination plot and setting up a wild-goose chase that'll come back to bite me is not the way to do it. I go with my gut on these things, and my gut is telling me *you are not to be trusted.*"

I knew my face was flushed, and my wrist hurt from the grip of his fingers. He released me, and I knew there would be a bruise on the bone; my fingers hurt from the pressure of his hand, and the skin was quickly turning a livid red.

It was hopeless to ask for more help. George wasn't interested in what I knew; the morning paper and his own prejudices had pretty much sealed his mind against me.

I stood up. George made no move to stop me; his eyes had gone back to Oswald, now sitting sullenly on the stool at the counter. They must have brought him a breakfast he finally approved of: he was eating in quick motions, his eyes on the overhead clock, whose hands were crawling steadily toward eight.

Near the door, I passed the officer I'd seen only three nights before. His ruffle of dark hair was combed neatly this morning; his skin was swarthy in the morning light. He was just starting his coffee. On his gold uniform tag glittered his name: "TIPPIT".

J.D. Tippit? The police officer who would be shot in Oak Cliff (near my parents' house) tomorrow, supposedly by a desperate Oswald, after his escape from the Texas School Book Depository?

Wait a minute. Oswald was here, making a fuss over breakfast, in a loud voice almost deliberately designed to carry to everyone in the restaurant. Tippit was here, quietly sipping a cup of coffee and watching Oswald's antics attentively. If Oak Cliff was his regular beat, this was a strange choice for breakfast; it was miles from that neighborhood. George was here, too, supposedly also 'on assignment'.

It couldn't possibly be a coincidence. But what did it mean? Did George already have suspicions about Oswald that he wasn't telling me about? Did Officer Tippit?

I also noticed that the only people being seated in the coffee shop were white. Though there were several Negroes standing quietly in line, and though most were well dressed and apparently had been standing there for some time, including one nice-looking couple with an obviously hungry little boy, the white people just walking through the door were being seated ahead of them. None of the Negroes made a fuss; they simply kept their heads down, stared at the floor and waited. This was the order of things in Texas in 1963. They had long ago accepted it.

I was not the only one who had noticed this.

Oswald was paying his bill at the desk near the door. While waiting for his change, his eyes met those of the Negroes waiting. In them I read anger for the way things were.

It surprised me. I hadn't thought a man like Oswald would care much about anything except himself.

As the hostess handed him his change, he said loudly, "You ought to seat people in the order they come in. First come, first served."

The hostess saw where he was looking. "We're not breaking any law," she whined. "We're not doing anything wrong."

"You're doing plenty wrong," Oswald said tightly. "And I'll never eat here again till you start doing things right." He turned to leave and caught sight of me. For a moment we just stared at each other.

I didn't know what to think about this guy, but my instinct was stronger than my intellect at that moment. All I knew was that I had to get away from him, fast.

Outside, a city bus was just pulling in at the curb.

I didn't care where it was going. I ran for it and caught it with seconds to spare.

* * *

An hour later, sitting at his desk, George lit up another cigarette and thought about Catherine Roberts as he'd last seen her, running out of the restaurant to catch a bus.

She was odd, but she certainly seemed sincere... all but clutching at him, imploring him to use his influence as an FBI agent—that was a joke!—to wring some action from the Secret Service, as though they'd listen to him with any more respect than they would anyone else.

And there was that strange look on her face when she saw Oswald, the guy he'd been sent to check out. That was really peculiar—she seemed spooked. Why? Even if she had met him, he was pretty harmless, as informants go.

Oswald's contact at the Dallas FBI office had suggested George have breakfast at the coffee shop. The agent had said vaguely that Oswald was making contact with someone there and that George should spot the contact, if possible. Unless he was very wrong, the person most interested in Oswald's deliberate outburst was the police officer in the corner, that guy Tippit.

...Which said to George that talking to the Dallas police about this girl's passionate declaration of an assassination attempt was a waste of his time. That uniform was the real thing. If this Tippit guy was somehow mixed up in this strange brew, even at the lowest levels, he wasn't going to see a lot of interest or cooperation from Dallas's finest.

But the Secret Service? Well, it was their job. And he was an officer of the law himself. It was worth a phone call, even if he couldn't tell them much.

Out of curiosity, he had stopped in Dealey Plaza on his way to the office. The spot the Roberts girl had pointed out on the map in the newspaper was a good spot, he saw, for snipers to aim at. There were good hiding places for shooters in the Plaza, with lots of tree cover and easy access to the railroad. That's not to say there really *would* be snipers there tomorrow, but...

George sighed, hesitated a moment, then dialed a number.

"United States Secret Service."

He asked to speak to an agent and was connected right away. He found himself stumbling through the explanation Miss Roberts had given him so lucidly just a short time before. "It's worth checking out," he concluded.

There was a pause, as though the person at the other end was still jotting notes. Then the guy said, agonizingly slowly, "You say the name was Catherine Roberts?"

"Yes," George said, stifling his impatience.

"You wanna give me that again?"

Now George had to stifle a curse that rose to his lips. The Secret Service wasn't known for employing idiots, but it was always possible for one to slip through the cracks, and apparently, he was talking to him. Slowly and clearly he repeated the gist of the message: the possibility of an assassination attempt on the President's life tomorrow in Dallas, the very specific change she had given him in the motorcade route, from straight west on Main to the turn onto Houston and then Elm Street, and the concern for extra security.

He had to wait a long time before the voice at the other end said slowly, "Thank you, Agent Stone. Someone will get back to you."

The line went dead. George swore out loud. The moron couldn't even get *his* name right?

Now what? Should he talk to Hoover? The Special Agent in Charge of the Dallas office? Terence? Who would believe him? His information came from a girl whose very existence he couldn't even verify; what value could her wild tale have to any of them? He didn't even really believe her... but as a federal law enforcement officer, he knew that correct procedure involved passing on information, whether or not it was always accurate.

If she'd only been right about the motorcade route—or if he knew who she was, whom she was working for—but he didn't, and what he did know was the Bureau's usual reaction to the passing on of complete fiction. It wasn't a medal and a corner office.

Had he done all he should do? Yes. He'd done *more* than he should have. He'd taken an unverified story from a completely unreliable source and given it to the right department. It was their job now to investigate. So why did he feel uneasy, as though he'd left something undone?

He swore again and went back to work.

* * *

I used the key under the mat to open the Cuyler back door. Everything seeme
quiet. Don's Cadillac was gone, as was Sandra's wood-paneled station wagon, and
they were both gone, as were the Cubans—who, I now realized, were probably hired
guns who would be in Dealey Plaza tomorrow. The thought of encountering them in
the house was unnerving.

There was no sound anywhere. I slipped into my room and stared in confusion.
The bed was made. The room was swept, but all my stuff—toilet articles, underwear,
dresses—had been dumped in a big carton, which stood open on the floor.

Someone was sure that I wasn't coming back.

Was it Sandra?

Had Don told her *I'd* met with an 'accident', too?

Swiftly, I scrabbled through the box, fishing out fresh nylons, some toiletries and
the two-piece beige dress I'd worn on my first day. I wasn't sure why, but I didn't want
to leave it behind.

I had the quickest shower of my life, hid the wet towel in a bin of dirty laundry,
and dressed quickly. I stuffed my toothbrush and makeup into my handbag, thanking
heaven for the first time that it was so huge and capacious.

By now it was 10:30. I didn't want to go near ISI, but I had something to do there,
and once it was done, I could leave forever.

I realized that the truck Don was so carefully preparing for an overland journey
tomorrow was to be loaded with illegal guns and driven directly to Miami, unlike other
shipments which had gone along the established pipeline to New Orleans. There wasn't
time for this shipment to go to New Orleans and then on to Miami; they planned to
start an invasion as soon as Kennedy was dead and public opinion could be sufficiently
inflamed.

I also realized why Toni had been killed and why, most likely, Stan had attempted
to run me down.

Toni had met Alek.

She could tie him—Lee Harvey Oswald—to Don Cuyler at ISI.

It was her fatal mistake that she'd mentioned it to Don, who coolly had her
dispatched only a couple of hours later.

And I? I was to be killed, perhaps, because Toni might have confided in me—or
because they thought I might have learned something I shouldn't have, maybe just to
be on the safe side. Why not?

Stan had derived a savage sort of pleasure in aiming for me; I saw it in his face as
he held the car straight at me. My whining to him at the party was excuse enough for
him to resort to violence. I was luckier than I'd imagined in evading him last night.

I was, let's face it, lucky that Lee Oswald had been there and thinking quickly.

I didn't want to face my conflicting feelings on that subject, but I had to, sooner or
later: for a guy I was certain had killed the President, he certainly had acted differently
than I'd expected.

When I'd thought his name was Alek, I'd liked him: he was polite and interesting to talk to.

The truth was, I owed him.

If history repeated itself tomorrow, I knew he would be behind bars and facing the wrath of the entire world before the end of the day. The least I could do was spare him that.

Despite his loud protestations at the coffee shop, I felt instinctively that this guy had no real capacity for violence. At the coffee shop, he wasn't throwing punches or picking fights, he was just being a pain in the neck. There were too many people, including my ex-husband, who were experts at that, too. It didn't make them criminals.

He couldn't kill Kennedy any more than I could, and as an actress, the one thing I knew was that no one—*no one*—could commit any act, large or small, good or evil, that was not in their nature to commit. We did what we were capable of doing, no more and no less.

No matter what the evidence said, I was reluctantly willing to believe now that George—my George, from the year 2000—had been right all along: Lee Oswald was innocent.

It occurred to me that if I could stop him from being at the Texas School Book Depository tomorrow, perhaps I could do more than shield him from suspicion: maybe if there was no patsy in place, there would be no assassination attempt. Maybe the plotters would decide to postpone action until they could maneuver Oswald, or someone else, into a position of vulnerability.

It was worth a try, anyhow.

I owed him at least that much.

The day was already shaping up to be a busy one: I had to divert the truck driving to Miami, get out of ISI without being accosted by Stan or Don, and somehow not only talk to Lee but convince him that my former behavior was an aberration and that I had only his best interests at heart.

Too bad I hadn't had breakfast after all: today I definitely could have used my Wheaties.

* * *

George called in to his office two hours later after checking out a fruitless lead at Love Field and was connected promptly to his friend Terence Miller. "What's the word from the Secret Service?"

"I'll read it to you." There was a pause and a rustle of paper. "Here. 'It is the opinion of the Secret Service that Miss Catherine Roberts does not pose a significant threat of any kind to the President's security during his scheduled visit tomorrow.'"

"That's it?" George said in disbelief.

"That's it."

"But that wasn't the report I turned in!"

"George," warned Miller, "you'd better let this one go. Gordon's not happy about anyone from this office turning in a report to the Secret Service, period. He about hit the roof, and what pisses off the Special Agent in Charge of the Dallas office is eventually going to piss off the Director."

George was silent. He wasn't interested in incurring J. Edgar Hoover's wrath. Agents who pissed off Hoover often ended up in remote outposts in places like North Dakota. Funny that Catherine Roberts should have mentioned that. Only someone who had worked for the Bureau would know that…

He had a bad feeling, but it seemed pointless to try the Secret Service again. The message would likely end up just as garbled, and he could end up worse than garbled, worse than fired. He could end up investigating badger sightings in Fargo. He felt worse when he thought that he'd solicited Catherine Roberts' help, and when she'd finally offered it, he'd done worse than nothing with it.

Hell, you couldn't solve all the world's problems all the time, could you? he rationalized. He reached for his cigarettes and noted that he was down to his last one. He'd better stop somewhere for more; black coffee and cigarettes and a lot of scotch at night were all that kept him going through this investigation.

"George?" Miller said sharply. "Did you hear me?"

"Yeah. Message received, loud and clear." He hung up. He hoped Catherine Roberts wasn't counting on his success with the Secret Service. But she didn't strike him as that kind of girl at all. He had a feeling she'd find a way to get her warning through somehow, with him or without him.

* * *

I timed my return to ISI for 12:30, though it was the last place I wanted to be today.

I had hoped that Hilda would leave the building to take lunch, even with no one there to replace her. Sure enough, at 12:35 I saw her walk out of the building and head for the luncheonette where just yesterday, I'd met Lee Oswald and he had saved my life.

With my hand on the door, I peeked in. There at the desk sat Miss Bradley, straight back, sensible shoes and all.

I dropped the door handle and backed hastily away.

Restless and angry at myself, I walked in the parking lot among the rows of shiny cars, watching the ISI entrance aimlessly. *Why couldn't I come up with a plan? Isn't this why George sent me back here in the first place, to improvise on the spot?*

As I turned down one row of cars, I saw a Cadillac screech up to the entrance and slam to a halt. Curious, I stopped walking and looked over. A man was getting out of the driver's seat, carrying a bulky-looking bag. He was in his '50s, stocky, with thinning hair combed straight back from a ferret-like face topped by a pair of beady, brooding eyes.

I hurried back to the entrance to intercept him.

"Can I help you?"

He eyed me suspiciously.

I gave him back the sweetest smile in my repertoire. His face had clicked in my mind. This was Jack from the Carousel. "Would you like me to take that?" I asked politely.

"No." He held the parcel away as I reached for it. "Is Mr. Cuyler in?"

"No, I'm sorry, you just missed him," I lied cheerfully. I hoped he had; it would mean I'd missed him, too. "But I'll put it right on his desk. He'll get it as soon as he gets back."

"When'll that be?"

"Tomorrow morning," I said, my mind clicking furiously. "He had an emergency and said he'd be out for the rest of the day. He'll be back tomorrow, and I'll make sure he gets this, first thing."

The man's mouth creased with annoyance. Obviously he'd have preferred for Don to receive the package earlier, but I also could read in his beady eyes that tomorrow morning was early enough. He eyed me. "What's your name?"

"Hilda," I said brightly.

He looked at me carefully, as though memorizing my features. Then the tight mouth eased, and an oily smile took its place.

"All right, Hilda." He finally surrendered the parcel. "I'll call to be sure he got it."

"After nine," I said helpfully, fervently hoping to be far away by then, and watched him drive away in the Cadillac, a boneless-looking dog lolling next to him on the front seat.

I juggled the package speculatively in my arms. Not heavy, but bulky; lots of small, light objects inside. Nothing metallic. No guns. I wondered how important this was to Don Cuyler. It was being delivered the afternoon before the big shipment started for Miami and the day before the assassination; the timing to me was suspicious. I thought it was probably very important.

Swiftly I crossed over to the other side of the street. When I was safely out of sight of the ISI building, I hailed a cab and gave the address of the FBI building.

George would almost certainly find the contents of this package to be proof that what I was saying was true.

*　*　*

George wasn't in.

The girls at the switchboard were quite sure that they didn't know when he'd be in, where he was, or where I could reach him. Could they take a message, or perhaps the parcel I was carrying, to give to him?

They could not.

I felt a compulsion to be somewhere far away, very safe, and immediately. At the same time, my curiosity was killing me: what had been delivered to Don Cuyler with such urgency?

I wanted to know, but I had something else to do before I could open it.

I had to reach Taylor Trucking.

I checked out a phone book in a large office building and found the address and telephone number.

I ran the story in my mind, shut myself into the phone booth, dropped in a dime and dialed the number. When a young girl's high soprano voice answered, I asked for Mr. Taylor, keeping my voice at its lowest register.

Mr. Taylor's familiar voice came on a moment later. "Yes?"

"This is Miss Bradley at ISI, calling for Don Cuyler," I said, as calmly as I could.

"I'm the office manager at ISI, Mr. Taylor. Mr. Cuyler had an emergency and won't be in for the rest of the day, but he asked me to call you. There's been a change of plans for our freight shipment tomorrow."

"Oh?" Taylor's voice was apprehensive. I'm sure he was thinking of the $2,000 fee he would be forfeiting. It was exactly the note I wanted to hear in his voice. "My boys were over there this morning, loading up. We weren't told of any change."

"Yes, I realize that," I said briskly. "The destination has changed. Mr. Cuyler has instructed me to tell you to send the—er—shipment to New Orleans, instead."

"New Orleans?" Now he was puzzled.

"New Orleans," I confirmed. "Your fee, of course, will remain the same. However, Mr. Cuyler is frankly concerned about this shipment. We've had some—er—internal problems here, which might affect our security. That's why he's redirecting it. He also asks, until he can deal with these problems effectively, that the drivers *not* call here for any reason while they're on the road. Naturally, if there's an accident, we'll need to know about it, but assuming that all goes according to plan—well, he'll simply expect the shipment in New Orleans by early Sunday morning."

"This is most irregular," Taylor said, regaining some semblance of command. "I'll have to clear it with Mr. Cuyler before I can—"

"Mr. Taylor, have you been listening?" I said shrilly. "Mr. Cuyler is not available to discuss this at the moment, but if you do not send the shipment as I'm telling you, we might well lose it. Do I need to remind you that if we do, since you've been informed of our concern and since the shipment is already in your care, that your company is liable for the entire cost?"

He was fumbling now. Whether or not Taylor actually knew what he was transporting, he was looking for an out. "I'll have to have something more," he said. "How do I know this is on the level?"

I visualized the contract I had typed the other day, and an image of it rose sharp and clear in my mind. "I have the specifications you and Mr. Cuyler discussed," I said coolly. "Isn't that enough to prove I have the authority?" I rattled off the serial numbers of the cases and the license and serial number of the truck Taylor was providing.

I could hear him flipping the pages of the contract. "That's—that's right," he said. He sounded relieved.

"Then you'll follow instructions? Mr. Cuyler is most concerned that you do."

"I—yes, we'll follow instructions. What's the new delivery address?"

I thought hard. In naming New Orleans, I had simply grabbed for the first city I could think of where Don Cuyler would not think to look for his shipment. I remembered back to my reading for George, and an address rose in my mind.

"Please send the shipment to 531 Lafayette Street," I said. "That's in Lafayette Square."

"Yes, we know it," Mr. Taylor answered. "Will the freight dock be open?"

"It might not be, depending on what time you get there," I told him, feeling relieved that things seemed to be proceeding well. "However, ask your men to sleep in the truck and be ready to unload by 10:00 Sunday morning. Oh, and Mr. Taylor?"

"Yes?"

"Be extra careful about security. Someone may call and ask you for information about the shipment; he may even claim to be Don Cuyler. That's part of the reason Mr. Cuyler is so concerned. He suggests that if he has to reach you directly during the weekend, he'll phone you and give a password to prove his identity."

"What kind of password?" Taylor was buying it. I knew I had him.

I thought quickly. "If Mr. Cuyler has to phone—or if anyone else legitimately connected with the shipment does—we'll use the phrase 'Cuban cigar' to identify ourselves. If you don't hear it—I don't care who the person says he is or even if he sounds *exactly* like Mr. Cuyler—*don't* give out any information."

"Very well, Miss Bradley. We understand. I'll instruct my people accordingly."

"Thank you, Mr. Taylor." I delivered the coup de grace. "Of course, Mr. Cuyler knows that this change of plans will incur extra expenses for you. He'll add $500 to the agreed contract price for your cooperation and, er, discretion."

I could hear him suck in his breath. I had no doubt whatever that the extra five hundred would go straight into his pocket. At last, he said smoothly, "Please tell Mr. Cuyler we'll follow his directions to the letter. We understand his security problems and hope he, er, solves them with dispatch."

"I'm sure he will," I said with more confidence than I felt. "Thank you, Mr. Taylor."

I hung up the phone and wondered whether Don Cuyler would ever think to check for his missing shipment with the first link along his regular supply route—the offices of Guy Banister, former FBI agent and now private investigator. I also figured that by the time he could, it would be Monday.

By Monday, with any luck, this whole mess would be over with.

I looked longingly at the package. I couldn't open it here. The building was swarming with people who might at any moment decide to take a break to smoke or use the restroom.

When the going gets tough, the tough go shopping, I thought, and hailed another cab. When it stopped, I asked the driver to take me to a department store where I could buy socks and ties for my boyfriend's birthday.

* * *

Less than half an hour later, I was closed into a dressing room cubicle in the Ladies' Department at Neiman-Marcus, with an armful of dresses so expensive that all the money in my handbag wouldn't pay for them. It didn't matter, though: I'd simply snatched up the dresses as a cover to get into the dressing room, where I could examine the mysterious package without being disturbed.

I kicked off my high heels, though they no longer bothered me. I guess it's true that you can get used to anything, because after the first day, they felt, if not soothing, at least comfortable.

The parcel was hidden under the dresses.

It had been heavily taped, and once opened, the package had been further lined with newspaper. I shook out the contents.

Little books. No, not books… passports!

At least a dozen U.S. passports, as well as leather billfolds with photographs and Secret Service credentials…George's books had mentioned that on the grassy knoll at the time of the assassination, men showed Secret Service credentials to citizens running up trying to find the shooters, and shooed them away. These must be the credentials. And if they were being delivered to Don Cuyler on the Thursday before the assassination…

I had my proof.

By now, it was past three. I went to the bank of telephones in the store, dropped in a dime, dialed the FBI office and asked again for George. Again, he was out but now I was told he'd be in before five.

Now all I had to do was get to Lee Oswald and persuade him to stay away from Dealey Plaza the next day. Maybe, with the patsy out of the way, there would be no shooting. Despite the newspaper diagram George had shown me, I was still certain that the motorcade would come down Elm Street, that the shooting would happen as history had recorded it. But if I lifted a crucial element out of the equation—would the shooting still happen?

I was certain the plotters would be sure Oswald was at the School Book Depository before they started shooting. So my brief plan was to make sure he wasn't.

At 4:30 I left the store, having disposed of the newspaper lining and folded the packet of passports and Secret Service ID's into the lining of my handbag. It felt ten pounds heavier, but clipped closed and over my arm, it looked no different than before.

Another cab took me obligingly, in heavy rush-hour traffic, to Dealey Plaza. Looking up at the Texas School Book Depository Building, I checked the big yellow Hertz Rent-A-Car sign on top with its clock. It was 4:50 exactly. The workday at the Depository ended at 4:45, according to George's books.

The doors had already opened and workers were streaming into the parking lot.

At last I spotted Lee, in slacks and a plaid shirt.

I felt as though it had been years since I'd thought of him as Alek.

He was headed toward a beat-up old car in the lot, following another young fellow who was already turning the key in the ignition and plainly about to give him a ride.

I cut across the lot to intercept him, but couldn't bring myself to call out to him. I wouldn't have known what to call him—if I called him Alek, everyone would stare, since they knew him as Lee. If I called him Lee, he'd wonder how I knew his real name.

Instead I put an urgent hand on his arm. He turned, surprised, and then dark color flooded his face as he recognized me. "What do you want?" he asked.

"I have to talk to you. Please. It's very important."

"Now you want to talk!" he complained. "I was there to talk to you last night, but you ran away from me."

"I know. I'm sorry."

He looked toward the boy in the car, who had seen us talking through his rear-view mirror. "You ran away from me this morning, too, and now I'm going somewhere," he said stiffly.

"Home to your family in Irving. I know."

He jerked his head up in surprise. "How do you know that?"

"Have coffee with me. I'll explain everything. Really, this is urgent." He looked at the car again. I could see that he wasn't going to change his plans for me. "Please, Lee, there's a lot at stake here."

He stared at me again. "How did you know my name?"

I said nothing but gave him a pleading look. He hesitated for a moment, then went over to the boy in the car, who by now was gunning the motor impatiently. He talked through the driver's side window for a minute. The boy nodded, and when Lee stepped back, he drove off.

He turned to me. "All right, let's go."

I expected him to stride toward the buildings downtown, to any coffee shop tucked into the block, but instead he led me into the concrete pergola in Dealey Plaza. Past the shallow steps there was an area that was already covered with evening shadows. He leaned against one side of the pergola. I eased into the shadows of the other, so that we faced each other just a few feet apart. There were no pedestrians on the sidewalks, and cars driving past could see us only in extreme shadow. It was a good place to talk privately.

"Well?" he said peevishly.

I would not waste time, I decided, trying to sweet-talk him or placate him. "The President is coming to Dallas tomorrow," I said abruptly. "And when he gets here, he's going to be shot."

He stared at me, but he didn't try to deny it. *He knows something about this*, I thought, *but he's also surprised that I know it.*

I went on. "After he dies, a man is going to be arrested for killing a police officer and then charged not only with the policeman's murder but also with the assassination of the President, and by Friday night, everyone in the world will know his name." I stopped for a moment and then gave it to him straight: "It's you, Lee. You're going to be accused of killing the President."

He didn't even hesitate. "That's ridiculous," he said.

"It's true!"

"No one would believe I'd shoot President Kennedy. I know tons of people who would testify for me at a trial."

"There won't be a trial. You're going to be shot dead on Sunday morning, in police custody, on national television."

That stopped him cold.

"That's ridiculous," he said again, but this time it sounded unconvincing, and his eyes were troubled.

"You've got to stay away from work tomorrow," I said. "If you don't come to work, they'll have to call off the shooting. They won't have anyone to blame it on, and there won't be a trail to follow."

He looked at me. "You don't know these guys," he said. His words sent a chill through me.

"Will you stay away from the School Book
Depository?"

"I have to be here. You don't understand."

"Neither do you. You saved my life last night. I'm trying to save yours today. If you go to work tomorrow, Kennedy will die."

He looked away from me then.

"Please, Lee!"

He looked back at me. "You never told me how you knew my name. Who are you, really?"

I shook my head. "I can't tell you that."

"Then I can't promise to stay away from work. I have things to do tomorrow, important things. You're wrong, you know. The President isn't going to be shot."

"*You're* wrong," I said despairingly.

Astoundingly, he laughed. "That's not possible." All of a sudden, he was Alek, who had talked to me lightheartedly at ISI. "Look, don't worry. I know what I'm doing. I don't know who you're working for, but your information is wrong. I've got it right. You'll see. In a week everyone will know my name. And they'll think I'm a hero."

He was so stubborn about it, so sure, and so wrong! It was more than not knowing what was going to happen: someone had given him a cock and bull story so convincing, or so appealing, that he'd swallowed it hook, line and sinker. Nothing I could say would dissuade him.

"I've got to go," he said then. He started down the steps toward the sidewalk. If he walked up one block, I knew, he could catch a bus out to Irving and spend the evening with his estranged Russian wife and two young daughters, which I'm sure he was looking forward to. He had no idea he'd never see his children again after tonight. He wasn't listening, like everyone else in this city.

"Lee—" I said in despair.

He turned back to me. "Look, you're worried about something that's not going to happen! Who knows? Even if it should happen just as you say, maybe someone will warn the President himself, tonight. That would change things, wouldn't it?"

A moment later, he was gone, in the darkness. The streetlights illuminated his slender figure for just a moment, and then he vanished around a curve.

* * *

George never returned to the office that night.

I had a gloomy dinner alone in a diner, then sat in my small but safe hotel room, calling every 15 minutes for three hours. Nothing. Finally, I was told he'd be in after noon the next day.

After noon tomorrow would be hours too late, if it wasn't too late already.

The Secret Service wasn't listening.

The Attorney General's office in Washington, where I might have gotten a hearing if I'd called sooner, would have long been closed for the night.

The only person I knew at the FBI wasn't available.

Nothing would change.

Tomorrow Kennedy would ride, smiling, into Dealey Plaza...

But tonight... ? Lee was right, someone could warn him tonight. *I* could warn him tonight.

Where had Kennedy spent that last night?

The answer rose in my mind: Fort Worth. He and Jackie had spent the night at the Hotel Texas in Fort Worth, surrounded by beautiful artwork that had been borrowed from local museums for the First Couple to enjoy. I looked at the clock: 9:30 now. They wouldn't be there until midnight or later—and if I remembered correctly, that was the night that the Secret Service detail had left JFK unguarded in his suite except for two local firemen, while they sneaked out for drinks in a nearby bar called The Cellar. A lot of them reported the next day with hangovers.

Local firemen, no matter how beefy, are easier to get through than trained Secret Service agents. Fate seemed to be taking a hand here, pushing me toward action, which I would rather avoid. Sheila would leap into action; Cady, on the other hand, had to think about it.

Maybe all was not lost, after all.

What if I could reach the President himself with my warning?

He was the one person on earth I could tell my real identity to. If he believed me, he'd understand why he had to change the schedule for tomorrow, even on short notice. It could be done. He was the President.

And really, wasn't this what I had always wanted, to live a life at center stage, rather than watching from the sidelines? Wasn't this the kind of adventure I'd always dreamed of?

I hadn't known that adventure could tie your stomach into knots.

Trying to calm myself, I took a pass at ironing my beige outfit. If I was going to meet the President, I'd better be well groomed

Chapter Twelve
FRIDAY, NOVEMBER 22, 1963

1:30 a.m.

When I walked into the lobby of the Hotel Texas, which was still bubbling with life at this late hour because of the arrival of the President's party, the first person I recognized, looking out of place among the richly dressed men with their ten-gallon Stetsons and thick cigars, was Lee Oswald.

Maybe someone will warn the President himself tonight, he'd said.

He'd shown up to do it himself.

He saw me at the same moment I saw him, and got to his feet as I approached.

"What are you doing here?" I demanded.

He looked at me shrewdly. "The same thing you are, I guess."

I bristled. "I have the right to see the President. I can tell him things you can't."

"And I," said Lee with determination, "can tell him things *you* can't."

Each of us was telling the truth. Neither of us was backing down. Neither of us intended to leave without seeing the President.

For a moment, we measured each other. If you can't beat 'em, join 'em, was the old phrase. I saw the moment when Lee's eyes flickered. It was as though we'd agreed to a partnership, even if it was a limited one.

The hotel elevator, surprisingly, was empty. I punched the button for the eighth floor and it began to rise jerkily. Lee glanced around the high boxy space and frowned.

"These hotels used to have elevator operators," he said in disapproval. "When they put in self-service elevators, they took someone's job away from him. I bet the poor devil didn't even get decent training so he could work at something else."

He saw my incredulous look. "You never think about it, do you?" he flared. "Automation is killing this society! Every time a machine starts to do what a person can do, that person and his family have a livelihood cut off. How long do you think we'll need telephone operators? Do you think you'll be able to work at that forever?"

"That wasn't exactly my plan," I began.

The door opened at the eighth floor, cutting off the rest of my protest. All of a sudden I felt a wave of absolute panic. I'd never been this close to living on the edge before. I couldn't do this. I needed time. I needed to re-consider. I needed to hide under the bed!

I looked over at Lee. He was waiting, none too patiently, for me to precede him off the elevator. I took a deep breath—*You have one chance. Get it right*—and stepped off into a quiet hallway with a musty smell and yellow-flowered, faded wallpaper. Yellow lights burned up and down the halls.

Lee followed as I turned right. Rooms numbered 830, 832, 834… I was headed in the right direction. Then Lee touched my arm lightly and nodded to his right. "Down there," he said.

Two men in blue shirts and navy slacks, held up by haphazard suspenders, slumped against the walls of one dark-painted door, with a scarred wooden desk in front. It had to be the President's suite.

"They're dressed kind of funny for Secret Service," Lee said, frowning.

"They're not Secret Service," I answered. "They're Fort Worth firemen."

Foolishly, I just stood there for a moment, gazing at them. The men appeared not to have noticed us. *Action,* I told myself. *This is a situation where you need to take action.*

Lee was ahead of me on that score. He was starting down the hall, when I caught his arm and pulled him back and around a corner. I had an idea and prayed it was audacious enough to work. Quickly, I unpinned the Secret Service badge from the belt of my suit.

"Take this," I said quickly. "Keep it in your pocket and don't flash it till they challenge you. You're from the Dallas Secret Service office, and you're very shocked to find none of your men here." I took a quick look at the badge. "Oh, and your name is MacDonald."

"What are you going to do?"

"Back you up. Go on."

I watched from behind the corner as Lee sauntered down the hall, doing a very credible impression of nonchalance. As his footsteps echoed, the men turned toward him. His eyes appeared to fall on them at the same time. "What's going on here?" he demanded truculently. "Who are you, and where are my guys?"

The best defense is an offense. Apparently, Lee had already found this out.

The two burly men dwarfed Lee, but he appeared completely unafraid, continuing to raise his voice imperiously. "Where are they?" he boomed. "How did you get here?"

"Let's see some ID," suggested one of them, who appeared quieter but also perhaps smarter than the other, who looked all muscle but very little brain.

Lee gave him a look of distaste but brought forth his shiny ID and held it up for inspection. "MacDonald, Secret Service," he said coldly. "Now you answer some questions. For openers, who are you?"

He leaned forward to inspect the chest of the muscle-bound guy, which was anchored with a gold badge too. "Fire Department?" he read in disbelief. "You guys are Fort Worth FD?"

I rummaged in my capacious handbag for a small sewing kit I'd bought at the Five and Dime store on my first day in Dallas. It was my cue to show up.

"Excuse me!" I strode purposefully toward the suite door.

"Just a second, lady," said one of the thick-necked men, blocking the door. "Who the hell are you?"

I looked at him with narrowed eyes. "I'm Annie, Mrs. Kennedy's maid. She just called me urgently." I waved the sewing kit. "I have a dress to repair for her tonight. She has to wear it tomorrow. If I'm not in there in the next minute, you'll have a *lot* of explaining to do."

The quiet one looked from Lee to me. "You know this guy?" he asked, nodding toward Lee.

I gave Lee a quick, casual glance, and turned a look of puzzlement on the quiet guy. "Of course. Mr. MacDonald. He's on this detail all the time. You should know him." I stopped and gave the others a long stare, as though I were getting suspicious. "And shouldn't you be wearing suits? The Secret Service *does* have a dress code, doesn't it?"

"You don't look much like a maid," the quiet one pointed out. He obviously knew the best defense line himself.

I glared at him. "I've been in and out of cars and on planes all day! Did you think I'd be in uniform while I'm traveling? Now please let me through!"

Lee glowered at them, his mouth a pinched, thin line. "Oh, they'll do more than that, Annie—these gentlemen were actually just on their way out. Weren't you, gentlemen?"

They gave us a glare, but Lee held up his Secret Service badge once again, and that seemed to remind them of the several nasty scenarios that could occur if they were there when the door opened. They began to shuffle off, reluctant but apparently relieved.

Praying they'd be gone quickly, I planted myself in front of the door and knocked firmly, as though I was expected.

They weren't moving as fast as I'd hoped. Lee seemed to understand that. He turned to them, his posture ramrod straight, hands in his pockets, eyes cold, and gave them some free advice. "Beat it."

They were gone in 30 seconds.

I knocked again.

"How did you know there'd be firemen here instead of Secret Service?" Lee asked, as the elevator doors closed softly behind them.

"It's a long story," I assured him.

"You're pretty good at this," he said grudgingly.

"So are you." We exchanged glances that were slightly less hostile.

When the door finally opened, I blinked and took an involuntary step back.

Lee, beside me, straightened even more, and his eyes brightened.

The man in the doorway was yawning, and his bright chestnut hair, flecked with threads of gray, was tousled. He wore half glasses down on his nose and held a thick typewritten report in one hand. His navy silk tie was pulled down, his white shirt was rumpled. His eyes, though bloodshot, focused on us politely.

I was face to face with President John F. Kennedy.

He looked at us, puzzled, and glanced around the empty hallway.

I knew if I didn't speak that I'd never have another chance, but I couldn't think of a thing to say. The President looked at us, raised an eyebrow.

Quick, Cady, say something. "Mr. President, my name is Cady Cuyler." Beside me, I felt Lee start at the words. "I've come a long way to speak to you. Please, it's very urgent."

He was still puzzled. "Where's my Secret Service detail?"

I took a deep breath. *In for a penny, in for a pound.* "They're out drinking at a nightclub called The Cellar, here in Fort Worth. They left some Fort Worth firemen to guard you. They'll be pretty hung over in the morning."

Kennedy looked down at me. His eyes were a bit brighter, though it was now close to 2:00 a.m. He looked over at Lee, who gave him a tense smile, and stood almost at military attention. He looked back at me and asked quietly, "And how do you know this?"

It was time. His hand was on the doorknob. Almost imperceptibly, he was inching it shut.

I took a deep breath. "I'll tell you, but you're not going to believe me." I waited; he waited too. But he was listening; I still had a chance.

"I'm from the future. I don't live in Dallas in 1963. I live in New York in the year 2000. I'm here to warn you, sir, and save you if I can. If you don't listen to me now... *you're going to die in less than 12 hours.*"

Oswald had turned to me in alarm. Kennedy's gray eyes never left my face while I spoke. When I stopped, hoping, praying I had reached him, he glanced down for a moment, then down the hall. All was quiet, the annoying yellow lights still burning overhead. Like casinos in Vegas, it was impossible to know from the artificial light in the hotel whether it was noon or midnight.

"You're right," the President said in that distinctive accent. "I don't believe you." He started to close the door in my face.

Before he could, I was talking again, as quickly and persuasively as I could. "Why would I make up a story like that? It makes no sense. Unless it was true!"

His gaze was even and noncommittal, but at least he'd stopped closing the door. "Can you prove it?"

I thought quickly. What could I say that would make it real for him? Quickly, hardly thinking, I said, "I knew your Secret Service detail wouldn't be here. That's how we got to you so easily; I knew you'd be guarded by firemen who didn't have a clue about Presidential security."

"That's true, Mr. President," Lee put in, trying quickly to make an impression. "She also knew you'd be staying on the eighth floor."

"Is this the eighth floor?" Kennedy rubbed his eyes wearily with the back of his hand and glanced at the suite number on the door. Then he straightened again. "That's not enough."

He was going to close that door in a minute; I could feel it. I had to persuade him that I knew more than he did, that I knew something no one could know in advance. But what?

I rubbed my damp hands on the front of my beige dress, which suddenly reminded me… "Wait a minute!" I said quickly, as he started to shut the door in my face. "Your wife wore a white dress today with a black belt and a black beret—"

The President looked at me coldly. "Miss Cuyler, my wife's fashions are photographed by the press every day. That's hardly impressive."

I had him now, and I knew it. I looked him straight in the eye and delivered the coup de grace. "And this morning, she's going to wear a pink suit with navy-blue trim and a pink pillbox hat and short white gloves. Ask her, if you don't believe me. "

The President stared at me for a long moment. Then the door closed.

My heart sank into my stomach.

"No," I moaned. "No, no!"

I felt sick with frustration. There was nothing left to try. I didn't dare look at Lee, because I knew I was so exhausted and frightened that I might just pound on the door and shout until the real Secret Service came to haul me away…

The door opened again.

It was the President, and he was smiling. "You're right," he said, the edges of his mouth curling up. "She will be wearing a pink suit… I suppose under the circumstances you'd better come in."

* * *

The suite opened into a small living room, where the President stretched out in a rocking chair lined with lumpy pillows. He carefully tucked away his reading glasses before turning to us. Lee and I settled on the not-too-comfortable print couch opposite.

"Five minutes," he said, but his tone was gracious, and now I heard the famous Boston-tinged accent. "You're Miss Cuyler, and you are—" He turned politely to Lee.

"Lee Oswald," Lee supplied. They shook hands, and I couldn't help smiling: George of the year 2000 would literally kill for a photograph of these two men shaking hands.

The President was eying Lee appraisingly. I decided to stop him cold.

"Lee's part of Operation Mongoose," I said brightly. "He's doing a wonderful job. In fact, I think this whole plot to kill you is part of Mongoose."

Kennedy looked startled. Operation Mongoose, the plot to kill Castro and overthrow the Cuban government, was, after all, one of the deepest, darkest secrets of the Kennedy Administration. That a mere woman would know of it in 1963 defied common sense. "You know about Mongoose?" he said wonderingly. "But it's top secret… "

"I told you. I'm from the year 2000. It's common knowledge there."

He gave me a sardonic look. I could see him decide to take it in stride. "All right, Miss Cuyler," he said, a hint of humor in his voice. "You have my full attention."

I had Lee's, too. "Cady Cuyler?" he said. "Are you related to Don
Cuyler, then?"

"He's my father," I said matter-of-factly.

"That's impossible," Kennedy and Lee said together. Then they looked at each
other and laughed.

"Don Cuyler?" Kennedy said. "Tall, muscular guy? Very good looking? Married
a girl from... Connecticut, I think." He was rocking the chair gently, and I could see
the fingers of his right hand drumming on the armrest, as though impatient.

"That's the one," I confirmed.

"We were in the Navy together," Kennedy enthused. "I haven't seen him in...
oh, must be twenty years." His face clouded. "He couldn't have a daughter your age."

"I was born in July of 1964," I said. "And none of this is coming to the point, Mr.
President. You have a motorcade this morning in Dallas. It's going to take you through
a park called Dealey Plaza, which leads to the freeway entrance. When you get into
that park, there'll be gunmen hidden at different locations. Professionals... they won't
miss."

His fingers abruptly stopped drumming. "Who are 'they'?"

I shrugged. "History's been arguing about it for almost forty years. All I can tell
you for certain is who was blamed."

"Well, who?" Kennedy said impatiently.

"Lee Oswald," I said. "The lone assassin."

Both men reacted instantly: The President snapped his head around to stare at Lee,
and Lee snapped his head around to stare at me.

"Stop saying that!" Lee said sharply, finding his voice. "It isn't true!"

I looked at him. "I didn't say it was true! I told you you'd be accused of the
President's murder, and of killing a policeman, on the same day. And that you're going
to be arrested and shot and killed while in police custody on Sunday morning. So you
can see why I've been a little hesitant to trust you. All the history books say you're a
crazed killer."

"I would never shoot the President!" Lee flung back, his irritation at me
outweighing his awe of Kennedy.

"I didn't say you would!" I yelled back.

"Enough!" Kennedy ordered. "You two are worse than the United Nations!" He
stood up, and we automatically stood, too. I had never realized it from looking at his
photos, but seeing him now, in person, tired as he was, all alone with us in the middle
of the night, eyes bloodshot and blinking with fatigue, he still carried such... majesty.
The grandeur of the Presidency fit him so perfectly. It was clear to me that no one—*no
one*—had inhabited this office better than John F. Kennedy, whatever his missteps and
mistakes had been. For that reason alone, my resolve stiffened. I would not let history
happen the way it was set to. I couldn't.

"Is there anything else you think I should know before tomorrow morning?"

His eyes were smiling, but they were also filled with disbelief. In them I read an
effort to be polite but also the stirrings of pity. Nothing I said had made an impression.

I had failed.

"Well," the President said, and the note of amusement in his voice was prelude to a farewell, the windup of a none-too-successful meeting. "I feel rather confident that Mr. Oswald means me no harm tomorrow."

"Oh, no, sir," Lee assured him. "I'd never—"

The President cut him off, gently, and turned to me. "But somebody does. That's your message, after all. Who is it?"

"I told you, no one is really certain," I said, my voice shaking now with my own fatigue. "But I think—no, I know—that my father planned it all. I think the company he works for is a CIA front operation. It's called Import Spirits International—ISI, for short—and it's located near Love Field. I'm sure he's in Mongoose too, and this whole thing has to be a Mongoose operation... "

The President had clearly had enough. He began to walk toward the suite door, and we trailed after him.

"... So I think it's people in the CIA who really want to get rid of you," I went on, talking quickly as the distance to the suite door shortened perceptibly. "And organized crime, of course, and J. Edgar Hoover, and Lyndon Johnson, and maybe even Richard Nixon—who's here in Dallas tonight, attending a secret meeting—and the Texas oilmen, and the military-industrial complex—they want a war in Vietnam, and you're planning to pull out at the end of 1965—"

The President's red-rimmed eyes widened, but he did not break his stride. "Thank you, Miss Cuyler, Mr. Oswald," he said courteously. "It's been a most enlightening evening."

I stared at him. "Mr. President, you can't—I mean, knowing what you know now, you won't—you won't go on to Dallas, will you?"

"Miss Cuyler—" He pronounced it 'KY-la', "No American President can be afraid to enter any American city. I promised to come to Dallas."

"But you can't!" I all but grabbed his shirt. "You'll die! There's no one else to help—I've tried—no one is listening! And no one can save you! You can't do it, Mr. President!"

"Miss Cuyler—" He was opening the door. "The Secret Service has already checked out the city thoroughly, and they're satisfied it's safe for me to visit."

"The Secret Service?" I said bitterly. "The same ones who left you high and dry tonight? Their protection is less than sterling, wouldn't you say?"

"I'll take your warning under advisement," the President said firmly. He opened the door wide and sighed at the empty hallway beyond. "And now, good night."

We walked out. The door closed behind him.

Lee was staring at the closed door, his eyes brighter than ever. I was thoroughly discouraged. To come all this way—to try so hard—and still to fail—*he'll take it under advisement?*

Nothing would change. George was right. The big events couldn't be changed, no matter what small details did.

I'd been a naïve fool.

"Let's go," Lee said quietly. "We can't do any more here."

He steered me toward the elevator. From the other end of the hall, a man came on the run. Dark hair, disheveled suit, face puffy with sleep, he sprinted toward the President's door. I paused and turned to stare at him.

He tapped on the door lightly. It opened immediately, and with a whispered word, he slipped inside.

"The President must have called him right after we left," Lee guessed. "Maybe he'll check out your story between now and tomorrow morning."

I hoped so. I hoped a miracle would somehow come from this low-key, thoroughly undramatic meeting. Lee pushed the bell for the elevator, and we waited dispiritedly to walk out into the dark Texas night.

PART THREE
CENTER STAGE

Chapter Thirteen
FRIDAY, NOVEMBER 22, 1963

10:20 a.m.

After an early-morning rain, the late-emerging sun, garishly bright overhead, was drying the trees and grass along the deeply sloping patch of cropped grass on Elm Street. It had yet to become known as the Grassy Knoll.

I felt apprehensive, my mouth dry, my heart thudding in my chest. Lee had instructed me to meet him outside the Book Depository at ten. "And can you get a car?"

I thought of ISI with its pool cars, gleaming Chevys and Fords and Pontiacs, sitting quietly in the unguarded lot next to the office. "I think so," I'd said. That morning, as soon as Miss Bradley had opened the office but before anyone else had arrived, I slipped quietly into the reception area, headed straight for the cupboard of keys and snatched a set from the board. This was one car I wasn't signing out in the logbook.

Now I was standing outside the soon-to-be notorious faded red brick building on the corner of Houston and Elm Streets. There were few pedestrians, since the motorcade was not scheduled to pass through until 12:25, but traffic was bumper to bumper. I kept my back to the curb as much as possible.

I'd been strolling the sidewalks of Dealey Plaza for almost 20 minutes, surreptitiously eying everyone who passed by. I suspected everyone of being a shooter, suspected every truck that passed me of hiding the assassination weapons. I stopped in my pacing toward the School Book Depository, pretending to check my makeup, tilting my compact mirror to check for movement behind the picket fence on the knoll. Nothing.

The air was heavy, and despite the earlier rain, I felt sticky, and my freshly ironed beige two-piece dress was already wrinkling. I could imagine how uncomfortable Jackie Kennedy would be in a few hours in her heavy pink suit and pink pillbox hat.

Behind the wooden fence, shadowed by trees, rose the control tower overlooking the parking lot and railroad tracks. A railroad man named Lee Bowers would be working there now, directing freight train traffic. He would later involuntarily witness what he described as a 'commotion'—a puff of smoke or flash of light—by the picket fence, which could have been gunfire. He would die only a few years later in an odd, single-car accident.

I thought of all these things as I made my way slowly back to the ISI pool car, a brown Chevy sedan, parked on Houston Street, on the east side of the Book Depository, and got into the driver's seat. At 10:24, a side door opened, and Lee's head peeked out. He waited until the sidewalk was empty and then trotted to the car, a brown wool driving cap on his head.

"Go," he ordered almost before he'd finished closing the car door. Immediately he slouched down beneath the window to stay out of sight. I drove three blocks before I asked anything.

"Where are we going?"

"Love Field," he answered. "Get on the freeway going north and follow the signs."

"Why are you wearing that silly cap? It's stifling outside."

"Stop talking back," Lee snapped, easing himself up in the passenger seat.

I steamed inside. Wait till the Women's Liberation movement caught up with this guy.

Traffic was still moving slowly, so I had to keep my eyes on the road, and as usual, he didn't volunteer any conversation.

I glanced at my watch: 10:37.

The closer we came to Love Field, the more traffic dragged.

I parked the brown Chevy in the first lot I came to, hurrying behind Lee, who was striding swiftly toward the International Arrivals terminal. Inside the building, Dallas police officers stood sentry at key points throughout the concourse. I was certain at least one would intercept us, but we reached the gathering crowd unchallenged. It was 10:50.

High-spirited Kennedy supporters lined the area behind the chain-link fence that separated the terminal from the tarmac. They were chattering and cheering. The women talked about what Jackie would be wearing, the men about Kennedy's bid for re-election. It was a rally-like atmosphere.

Lee and I blended into the crowd easily, smiling with the others, edging ever closer to the chain-link fence, where the early comers had swiftly staked their claim in case the First Couple deigned to look their way or even, if they got very lucky, walk over to say hello.

The crush was unbelievable. I don't know how many minutes we swayed in the crowd, trying to move in one direction while being squeezed into immobility. But the excited buzz grew louder when someone with a transistor radio clutched to his ear shouted, "Air Force One just left Fort Worth!"

Not everyone was cheering. I caught sight of a few signs with ugly slogans: "Yankee Go Home" and "You're a Traiter" (sic), then caught my breath as a large Confederate flag rose above the last row of spectators. Nearby, a group of high school kids began shouting anti-Kennedy slurs, giving themselves laugh after laugh. Dallas police scanned the crowd, but they did nothing.

What made me nervous were the silent men milling about the crowd, watching everything around them without emotion. Many of the Kennedy supporters paused their conversations or lowered a sign when these men passed by. On the surrounding rooftops, snipers with high-powered rifles stood ready. Despite the buzz of his supporters, this was hostile country to the President, and it was nearly impossible to tell who was friend and who was foe.

We saw the long, navy-blue Lincoln convertible, the Presidential limousine, with its bright fluttering flags and sleek whitewall tires, sitting in place on the tarmac. My heart fluttered. I knew once the President got into that car, he would never come out alive.

"We have to get closer!" Lee yelled over the roar of the Kennedy supporters. I still had no idea what he had in mind.

"Over there," I said, pulling him by the hand through the crowd, making our way toward the end of the four-foot-high cyclone fence. "The President will shake hands after he gets off Air Force One." I'd seen the film footage hundreds of times, Jackie holding red roses in one white-gloved hand and greeting the crowd with the other, the President beside her.

Lee moved to my other side, so he was closer to the end of the fence.

"What are you going to do?" I demanded. He ignored me.

Ten motorcycle cops took their positions, a line of convertibles and Cadillacs forming behind them, with a bus for the press corps bringing up the rear. An unmarked police car belonging to the Chief of Police headed the column, the space behind it reserved for the President's limousine. The sound of an approaching jet grew, the crowd roaring just as loudly, as Air Force One headed down. It was 11:25 a.m.

Local politicians and dignitaries moved onto the tarmac. A legion of Secret Service agents escorted Vice-President Johnson, who had already arrived on Air Force Two, to the makeshift reception area, where Texas Governor John Connally greeted him with enthusiasm, and Johnson just as enthusiastically pumped his hand, smiling broadly. They had done precisely the same thing in Houston yesterday and Fort Worth this morning: this was nothing but theatrics. Nonetheless, the crowd here in Dallas lapped it up. But the pop of flashbulbs was light. The crowd seemed to hold its collective breath.

Then came the moment they had all waited for. Hundreds of heads leaned forward in anticipation.

Air Force One touched down lightly and taxied to the reception area. Airport personnel rolled portable steps to the passenger doors, set high in the side of the plane, and the door swung open. Aides and Secret Servicemen deplaned swiftly.

There was a pause. Nothing happened.

Then there was a stir at the door, and a flash of pink, and a roar went up from the waiting crowd.

The First Lady, in her lovely pink suit, short white gloves and pink pillbox hat stood at the open door, and smiled automatically toward the fence, where the crowd had exploded into cheers and waves. Behind her, the President, in his elegant dark suit, striped shirt and figured blue tie, smiled and waved. The glare and heat of the Dallas sunlight was overpowering, but they looked cool, poised and genuinely pleased to be there.

Talk about star power.

They moved graciously through the official reception line—where Mrs. Kennedy smilingly accepted an armful of blood-red roses—then made their way, as I knew they would, toward the waiting crowds behind the fence.

It was eerie to be living through this moment now, just as it was happening, the dashing young President and his beautiful wife in her unblemished suit, with the matching pillbox hat set lightly back on her dark hair just a few feet away. The crowd roared and waved, cameras clicking endlessly. A tall, lean Secret Service agent shadowed the President.

Working his way through the crowd, Lee followed the President's movements, pulling me along behind him. "Stay close!" he insisted.

The President's driver eased the convertible toward the fence, to be ready when the President finally decided to leave his admirers. Kennedy was coming to the end of the fence. There wouldn't be another chance. Lee was leaning toward Mrs. Kennedy, who was moving slowly along the fence.

I reached out for the Secret Serviceman next to the President. "Secret Service!" I yelled.

Involuntarily, the man's eyes flicked to me. He could see I had nothing suspicious in my hands. "Don't let him get in the car!" I shouted, trying desperately to be heard above the roar of the crowd. "Don't let him—"

The Secret Serviceman, unable to hear me and uninterested, was moving away, his eyes trained on the President once again. I reached out and grabbed frantically at his sleeve and managed to yank him back.

I had to tell him. He could stop it, but only if he knew.

He hadn't expected anyone to grab him. I had pulled him off-balance, my strength increased by my terror.

He fell back a step from the President, then two, then three, as the President, not noticing, moved toward his wife and the admirers at the other end of the fence. Meanwhile, I was transfixed by what was happening down there; I didn't say anything more to the Secret Service agent because I couldn't stop staring in that direction.

Lee had a fixed smile on his face and was calling out to Mrs. Kennedy, pushing through the crowd to the top of the fence. For a moment, he hung precariously there, then leaped lightly down, to land right in front of the First Lady.

With a little laugh of surprise, she jerked back instinctively.

Lee removed his cap with one hand. I thought it was a gesture of exaggerated courtesy. So did Mrs. Kennedy: she started to smile and reach out a hand to him.

When his hand came down from his head, it was holding a revolver. He pointed it straight at her head.

The President saw it, and his eyes widened in horror.

The Secret Serviceman behind him couldn't see it; his view was blocked by the President, and I had unwittingly distracted him by trying to get his attention.

The President, only a few feet from his wife, was at her side before anyone else could move.

"Put down the gun, Lee," he said calmly. Even in this moment of maximum pressure, he recognized Lee and remembered his name.

"Get in the car," Lee retorted. "Now, Mr. President—or your wife gets it."

Kennedy's Secret Servicemen, several feet behind, saw too late the threat in front of them. They started to break into a run, started to draw their guns—but Lee coolly swung the revolver to Kennedy's temple instead.

They stopped.

"Drop your guns!" Lee shouted to them and to the Dallas policemen on the tarmac. "All of you—drop your guns *now!*"

The President hadn't moved since Lee put the barrel of the revolver against his head. He hadn't raised his hands, and he wasn't breaking a sweat. He simply stood there, facing Lee unflinchingly, his eyes tense but obviously calculating. "Put down the gun, Lee," he said again. "I'll talk to you if you put down the gun."

"Put your guns down," Lee warned the Secret Service again, his eyes still on the President.

"Do it," the President said to them, his eyes, unwavering, still on Lee.

The Secret Servicemen on the ground moved back and reluctantly, their expressions mulish and inflexibly hostile, dropped their guns. Lee began to move past them, shouldering the President and Mrs. Kennedy with him. "Move," he told them. "Get in the car." He glanced up long enough to pick me out of the crowd. "You drive."

He yanked at me with one hand, the other training his gun on the First Couple.

I found myself suddenly over the fence, my legs and knees scraped raw from the metal links. He was a lot stronger than I'd thought.

I was being literally dragged into a nightmare. *How could I have been so stupid?*

All hell was breaking loose around me. A huddle of Secret Service agents whisked the Vice-President to the safety of Air Force Two. The police snipers on the rooftops took aim. The crowd behind me scattered, shrieking.

But the gunshots I expected never came.

Lee had moved sideways, his gun trained on the Kennedys, until he reached the Presidential limousine. "Get in," he said quietly.

"No," the President said, equally quietly.

Lee moved the gun. It was aimed directly at Mrs. Kennedy now. "I'll kill her," he said.

The President said nothing. Did nothing. Stood next to the limousine, unmoving.

Lee moved closer to Mrs. Kennedy, cocked the gun, and rested his finger on the trigger. The sound, though soft, cracked like thunder in the now hushed airport. "Get in," he said again. His eyes never wavered from the President's. The barrel of the gun was only an inch from her pink suit.

The President glanced at his wife. Her eyes were wide with horror. She hadn't uttered a word.

"Get in, Jackie," he said softly. "It'll be all right."

The silence was absolute. Even the press had stopped shooting photos, when the glares of the frustrated Secret Service agents turned on them. Nothing was to be allowed to force Lee over the edge. The snipers eased off their triggers. Firing at Lee would almost certainly trigger his gun and kill the First Couple.

The driver of the limousine slid out of the car as I came to the driver's side. He held his hands away from his body, to show he wasn't touching his weapon. The potential for complete disaster was only a breath away.

At Lee's direction, the Kennedys climbed in the front passenger side of the car, Mrs. Kennedy in the middle next to me, the President on the far right. Lee jumped in behind them, never lowering the revolver.

"I'm so sorry," I said to Mrs. Kennedy as I turned the ignition key on the limousine. "I never meant for this to happen."

Her wide brown eyes flickered over to me for a fraction of an instant; they were full of shock and fear. Then they flickered away again. Unconsciously, she still clutched the sheaf of red roses she had been given. It seemed a lifetime ago. It was about five minutes. The President sat rigid, a muscle moving in his cheek. He faced straight ahead, but his hand pressed his wife's reassuringly.

I thought urgently of what I could do to set things right, knock Lee off balance, restore the Kennedys to what they had been just moments ago. I calculated various quick strategies. There wasn't one I could think of that wouldn't end up with one of us dead.

"You're not to follow us," Lee called to the drivers of the various vehicles. "Drop your car keys in here."

A dozen sets of keys clattered onto the floor of the limousine, the drivers running back and forth like participants in some crazed relay race. Lee never took his gun off the Kennedys. I wondered wildly whether the Secret Service taught its agents how to hot-wire a car. It was the only way they'd be able to follow us. I had no doubt they were going to.

At Lee's command, I drove straight out of Love Field, and turned down a wide ribbon of concrete, incongruously named Mockingbird Lane. The limousine, armor-plated, if I recalled correctly, was heavy and hard to move. I had to press my foot to the floor to accelerate up to thirty, then pump it again to get up to fifty.

In the rearview mirror, I could see Lee's eyes darting in all directions, watching for anyone trying to intercept us. No one was following. We were out of view of the airport. I saw Lee relax behind me, tilting the gun away from the President. He pushed the safety on.

"I'm sorry I had to do that, sir," he said. His tone stunned me: it was respectful and courteous.

The President was trembling with rage. "You frightened my wife half to death! What the hell are you doing?"

Lee smiled wryly in the rear-view mirror at Mrs. Kennedy. "I'm sorry, ma'am. I would never hurt you or the President. Please don't be afraid."

"These *idiots*—" the President said furiously, "showed up at our hotel last night, Jackie, with some dumb story about an assassination plot."

"If you'd bothered to check it out—" I began in self-defense.

"I did check it out!" the President yelled back at me, louder than I could ever have imagined. "It was nothing! There's no evidence! I had agents at that company you told me about early this morning, and there wasn't a damned thing there!"

I was stunned into silence. Whatever evidence had been there had obviously been swept away. I still knew, though, as sure as we were all here, hurtling down the highway, that the President's life was still in terrible danger.

The President hadn't finished, though. "You two," he said in barely controlled rage, "are going to the electric chair. I'll put you there myself."

"What did you plan on doing with us?" Mrs. Kennedy asked Lee, voicing the question I had wondered about too. She seemed to be recovering her composure.

Her eyes weren't as wide, and she was blinking a little.

"We need to get the President out of Texas, ma'am," Lee answered calmly, as though he kidnapped heads of state every day. Leaning forward, he guided me through an upcoming intersection. "There's an airfield about ten miles straight down this road. Redbird Airport. Turn when you see the sign." To Mrs. Kennedy, he added politely, "We'll get you on a private flight out of here and straight back to Washington, where he can be protected. I've already got some people out there warming up a plane."

"This is insanity!" the President exploded again. "I have trained protection officers. That's their job! Take me back to them at once!"

"Those trained protection officers," I said dryly, "are the same ones who left you unprotected last night, so it was possible for us to reach you without any interference."

The President glared at me. "At least they wouldn't kidnap me! The only threat to me in Dallas is you two!"

I had spotted the sign for Redbird Airport. Slowing down carefully, cautiously checking the mirror, I turned in the lane. No one was behind us. I felt extraordinarily relieved.

"Who are you?" Mrs. Kennedy asked Lee.

Lee smiled with a hint of pride. "I work for the government."

"Ours?" Mrs. Kennedy asked skeptically.

"CIA," Lee said proudly. "And I also have a relationship with the FBI."

"Jesus Christ," the President muttered.

I thought I heard a wail of sirens in the distance, though there was nothing in the rear-view mirror.

Kennedy heard them too. "They're coming," he said tightly. "They'll shoot you on sight." There was a hint of malicious satisfaction in his voice.

"We're getting you out of Texas," Lee said stubbornly. "Left here, Cady!"

I turned left. The President unleashed a spiral of fury. "You've already done more than enough!" he snapped. "I might never get re-elected after this. Nobody wants a coward for President."

But he wasn't a coward, I considered silently, thinking it prudent not to enter this discussion. The President hadn't budged, even when he had a gun to his head. It was only when Lee threatened Jackie that he acquiesced. I thought his actions were heroic.

We were now driving along a concrete strip dotted with large warehouse-like structures. "Hangar M-10," Lee told me.

I drove past a dozen light planes, more hangars, and a terminal building, which sat near the end of the row.

Just past the terminal building, a red and white twin-engine Cessna warmed up outside the last hangar, a rusting tin shed marked with a small sign, "Texas Aviation Flight School", just yards from the airport's outer fence. Four more Cessnas were parked in two neat rows nearby. At Lee's direction, I pulled up close to the revving airplane. The pilot, in suit pants, shirt and tie, came around to meet us. He was an attractive six-footer, his hair almost the same shade of chestnut as the President's.

"Zachary!" Lee called, jumping from the limousine before I'd fully stopped.

"What are you doing here?" The pilot checked his watch. "You're supposed to be at work." Zachary looked at the Lincoln, his jaw dropping at the sight of the President. "W—what're *they* doing here?" His tone didn't sound admiring.

Lee spoke with cool urgency. "They're trying to kill the President and set me up for it. Instead of flying me to Cuba, we're going to fly the President back to D.C."

Zachary didn't move, staring at the President, dumbfounded.

"Hurry," Lee insisted. "The Secret Service is right behind us."

"You brought the Secret Service here?" Zachary reacted in a rush of fury, looking down the service road. It was still empty. "You idiot! You're going to ruin everything!"

"They're chasing us," Lee said urgently. "Let's go now."

"Wait here," Zachary ordered, briskly moving toward the hangar. "I'll be back."

Lee turned to the President. "Please, Mr. President, get on the plane. We'll be taking off shortly."

"We're not going anywhere except back to Love Field," the President said firmly, not budging from the limousine. "Take us back there. Now."

For the first time, Lee looked genuinely disconcerted. "Mr. President, we're trying to save your life."

Before any of us could say another word, a female voice cried out behind us. "Oh, my God. It's Mrs. Kennedy!"

A slim, curvy brunette with Mrs. Kennedy's pageboy hairstyle and a beaming smile came toward us in a good-looking suit and expensive high heels, a burning cigarette between two dainty fingers. "And the President, too—welcome to Dallas, Mr. President!"

We were all a little dazed at this girl's appearance, none more than me. I recognized her, of course—this was Debbie, the good-time girl from ISI, who had disappeared mysteriously last week but seemed alive, well and quite at ease today. She carried a new calfskin suitcase in one hand, which she set down on the tarmac before coming over to the limousine. I got out to speak to her.

"I am so happy to meet y'all," she said, holding out a gloved hand. She was even prettier in person than in the photos I'd seen. She smiled adorably at the President, so he could see her deep dimples and lovely teeth.

"Debbie?" I asked.

"Yes," she answered, puzzled. "Are you coming with us?"

"Coming with you?" I repeated.

"To Barbados. Don says it's beautiful this time of year."

The pieces of the puzzle worked themselves together in my mind, the picture sharp and clear to me now. Debbie hadn't been missing at all. I knew now why she hadn't been at work…

Tentatively, I tested my theory. "You two are going off together?" I asked. "How romantic!"

She blushed. "We'll be married on the beach, under the stars. I can't wait."

"Don's already married, you know," I said carefully.

"He'll take care of that," Debbie said casually. "That witch he's married to doesn't deserve a guy as sexy as Don."

"Do you mean Don Cuyler?" asked Kennedy.

Debbie blushed. "Don told me he'd known you, Mr. President, but I thought he was just pulling my leg. That's him, all right."

"Get on the plane, Debbie," Zachary yelled, coming out of the hangar about 40 feet away. Behind him came a second man, in his late forties, gray stripes in dark hair atop a six-foot-three-inch frame.

Lee's face lit up.

"That's my contact," he said confidently. Waving a hand, Lee stepped forward to greet his friend. "Spencer!"

Spencer, angling toward the front of the limousine as he approached, raised a hand to return Lee's greeting. The sunlight reflected off something silvery in his hand. Looking to my right, toward the rear of the limousine, I saw the man Lee had called Zachary lifting his arm as well. Halfway to the limousine, I realized neither man was waving.

They were taking aim.

The first shot split the air with terrifying sound, freezing me in place. Debbie's scream snapped me from my trance. I moved around the limousine toward the President.

"Get down!" I yelled, a second shot booming. A sharp, splintering crack echoed behind it. The smell of gasoline singed my nostrils. Still, Kennedy didn't—or more likely, couldn't—move, the restrictive back brace he wore holding him upright. In Dealey Plaza, the third shot had been the kill shot, and he had been helpless to avoid it. Here, I was still a foot away from the President when the third shot sounded. It was followed instantly by a dull, muffled pop.

The President slumped sideways, toward the First Lady. His hand came upward, toward his head, then stopped. Something wet splashed my face, stinging my eyes. I knew it had to be the President's blood.

My heart thudded in my chest till it hurt my ribs.

It was over, just like that, faster than it had happened in Dealey Plaza.

The President had been assassinated.

Only the place was different. Rather than be exonerated, Lee would now be implicated beyond doubt, hundreds of people having witnessed his kidnapping the President just minutes before his death.

I covered my mouth in horror, Mrs. Kennedy's hands reaching for the President's head slouched in her lap. I knew her white glove would turn forever crimson, soaked with the President's blood. Time stood still while I waited for the First Lady to react to her husband's fatal wound.

In the next instant, history changed forever.

"What the hell—?" said the President.

The words echoed in my ears. My breath escaped with a gasp of relief, my senses rushing back to me. "Stay down!" I said.

Behind the limousine, Debbie had crumpled, mouth agape in a horrified silent scream. It had been her blood that had splashed me. She'd died on her feet, two holes through the middle of her blood-soaked jacket and silk blouse. She fell off the limousine's blood-spattered trunk, the burning cigarette between her fingers falling into the jet fuel puddle next to her. More fuel was pouring like a waterfall from two bullet holes in the Cessna's fuselage.

With a sudden *whoosh!* jet fuel on the ground ignited, orange flame leaping into the air. To our right came a shimmering wall of heat and flame.

Zachary closed in from the rear, aiming straight at the President. Then the thread of jet fuel snaked through the ground with incredible swiftness. Zachary probably thought he had time to take his shot before jumping away. He didn't.

The inferno surrounded him suddenly, the flame catching his pant leg and moving higher. He shrieked and threw himself to the ground, writhing and rolling to stamp out the flames. Black smoke thickened around him, till all we heard was the roar of flame and his screams. His gun went off, twice, three times. More jet fuel poured from the broken fuselage. More flames ignited near the Cessna.

"Get out of the car!" I yelled to the frozen First Couple, nearly yanking Jackie's arm off as I pulled her from the President. Feeding hungrily on the steady stream of gasoline, the fire was already licking up the trunk of the convertible, another strip of flame leaping above the driver's door.

The President shoved the First Lady up and out of the burning limousine, his hand pushing her forward so hard he knocked the pillbox hat from her head. Kennedy turned his body upright, a grueling labor considering the back brace. Pushing away my proffered hand, he slung himself out of the burning Lincoln.

Thick smoke drifted up from his suit jacket, smoldering holes burning the sleeves and shoulders.

"Get it off, now!" I yanked at his sleeve to help him along.

The President shed the burning coat, dropping it beside the limousine. Another shot sounded, a somewhat duller blast. In a crouch directly between Spencer and the limousine, Lee fired back with his revolver. Lee's shots didn't hit anything, but Spencer, caught in the open, dropped back to the cover of the airplane hangar.

"That way!" I pointed to the two rows of parked Cessnas, hurrying the President and Mrs. Kennedy to cover behind them.

Lee kept firing while he backed toward us. Finally, he reached us and dropped down between the gleaming planes, where we had a clear view of the service road. It was still empty.

"Where the hell is the Secret Service?" barked Kennedy.

Another shot sounded, this one a lot sharper, more distinct. Where we were now might be safe from the fire, but it wasn't anywhere near safe from the gunfire.

Lee shook his head. He was as unnerved as I was at the way this rescue was coming apart. As I eyed the flames, now licking up the wheels and struts of the Cessna, I realized we had to get out of the airport and take our chances somewhere else. Another five minutes here, and both of the Kennedys would probably be dead.

I looked around frantically. There had to be a way out. I looked at the open spaces between the big barn-like hangars. My eye caught the rows of cars parked neatly on the other side. One of them, please God, had to have its keys in the ignition.

I stood up and pulled off my high heels. "Cover me!" I called to Lee. "I'm going for one of those cars!"

Remembering Sheila's paramedic training, I stopped, dropped and rolled under the shielding airplane. Pushing to my knees, I sprang up and broke into a dead run. The dull crack of Lee's revolver sounded behind me. I hoped he'd brought extra ammunition.

Another sharp *crack!* sounded, a bullet skipping off the concrete a few inches ahead of my feet. Again I heard the sound of Lee's revolver.

There was a fierce *crack!* from the burning airplane. It sounded like a thunderstorm. I glanced back. A tire had burst from the intense heat.

I reached the side of the hangar, out of the line of fire. More gunshots thudded behind me. I ran out the back.

There were several cars nearby, and yes, I saw keys dangling in the ignitions. I slid into the driver's seat of a big blue Ford Fairlane and turned the ignition key.

The Fairlane started immediately. Backing away from the building with screeching tires, I saw Spencer crossing the tarmac, holding an automatic pistol, already half the distance between the hangar and the cluster of Cessnas shielding the President. Debbie's body still lay on the tarmac, surrounded by flames and the First Lady's pink pillbox hat. The flames near the damaged Cessna were licking ever higher.

I had one weapon. My foot slammed the accelerator. The car was much lighter than the President's limousine and leaped forward. Spencer turned toward me, taking careful aim. The bullet pierced the Fairlane's windshield as I ducked to the side. My foot stayed on the gas, speeding up, closing in, giving Spencer no time for another shot. I could see the horrified realization in his face as I held the Ford straight at him and pushed the accelerator straight down.

His desperate leap came far too late. The car's grill hit Spencer's knee at 40 miles an hour, the impact vaulting him sideways. He landed on his back, his head bouncing off the pavement with a vicious snap.

I braked hard, spinning the wheel to bring the Ford around as I did. "Get in!" I yelled, throwing open the passenger door even as the tires squealed again.

The President and First Lady scrambled into the back seat as Lee threw himself in the front. With a quick glance, I saw that they appeared to be unhurt, though the President's shirt was grimy and his tie loosened, and Lee's long-sleeved shirt was torn in several places.

Before they were actually sitting, I had gunned the motor again, my eye on the rear-view mirror. The Cessna behind me was almost entirely engulfed in flame now. It would be only a matter of minutes—if that—before a possibly fatal explosion. I was determined to be far away before that happened.

I steered the Ford toward a road at the very back of the field, praying I could get us safely out of the area of impact. There looked to be a way out through a cut in a cyclone fence.

The ground shook beneath us, the explosion that followed drowning out all sound.

The Cessna erupted into a fireball, thick black smoke and orange flame shooting 50 feet into the sky, debris raining all around. The *boom!* of the gas tank was literally deafening.

I deliberately gunned the motor again, to try to drown out the noise.

"That girl—" the President was shouting. "The girl behind us—"

"She's dead," I said, feeling sick inside. "Don't look back. She's dead."

"We've got to worry about getting you out," Lee said tightly. He, too, was avoiding looking at the mirrors or over his shoulder.

In the rear-view mirror, I saw Jackie's hand tighten on her husband's. He leaned over to her, whispering softly. They must have been words of comfort, because Jackie's eyes filled with tears, and she nodded.

"All right," the President said to Lee and me. "I'm willing to concede that someone other than you wants me dead." To Lee, he added dryly, "If those were your friends, maybe we could try for sanctuary with your enemies."

"I'm sorry, sir," Lee said, and he sounded contrite, but also suspiciously triumphant. I stole a glance at him. His eyes were bright: the President believed him. I think it made his whole day.

"Let's get going," the President said, the ring of command back in his voice. "I've got to get my wife somewhere safe."

I couldn't have agreed more."I aimed the car at the break in the fence and drove through, my heart fluttering, my hands trembling. That was twice in a half hour that we'd somehow fumbled through a dangerous situation." The last line of that section—

"How many more chances would we have?"

* * *

Extreme heat and jet fuel kept Redbird Airport's fire teams at a distance, spraying foam to contain the blazing aircraft. Racing up the taxiway, four police motorcycles and six police cruisers skidded to a halt just behind the fire engines. The Chief of Police himself led the tallest of six broad men in dark suits and sunglasses toward the white-helmeted fire captain.

"Where's the President?" the tall agent demanded. "That's the President's limousine; where is he?"

The confused fire captain looked for an explanation. "Chief?"

"The President was kidnapped from Love Field half an hour ago," the Chief explained. "Mrs. Kennedy was taken with him. We followed them here."

"Jesus Christ!" the captain exclaimed. "We've got two victims down that we know of, a man and a woman. There might be more people inside the plane, but we can't get to anybody until this fire's under control."

The fire captain's hand stopped the tall agent from moving past him.

The agent's face was like granite. "The man and woman—alive or dead?"

"Dead."

"Is it the President and the First Lady?"

"Jesus—"

"Is it?" the agent said insistently. "Is it them? I need to know!"

"We can't get in there," the fire captain said harshly. "We have jet fuel, a plane that's exploded, gases leaking everywhere—it'll take hours to clear it. We can't tell anything for sure until then."

"We can't wait." The tall man's lips tightened.

"Roy, come here! This one's alive!"

A fellow agent knelt over Spencer, a pool of dark blood oozing beneath his head, his eyes fluttering upward in semi-consciousness. The tall man came on the run. "Can you talk?" he asked, his voice soft and coaxing.

"Yeah—I think—"

"Name?"

"Wade Spencer," the injured man answered weakly. "I run the flight school."

"What happened?" Roy asked.

"President's dead," Spencer whispered, coughing up blood. "I—saw it myself. Oswald killed him."

"Oswald?" Roy repeated the name.

Spencer nodded weakly. "Lee Oswald. Young guy. He—came in a few days ago and chartered a plane for today, but wouldn't tell me where he wanted to go. Said his name was Hidell, but he signed the contract Lee Oswald."

"You have a copy?" Roy asked.

Spencer gestured, his hand limp. "... In the files. He shows up here today with a gun on the President, tells me to fly 'em to Havana. Mrs. Kennedy refused to get on the plane. Oswald shot her. Casual. Like it was nothing."

The agent looked sick. Spencer began coughing, blood pouring from the corner of his mouth. "Then he starts hitting the President, and screaming, 'Get on the plane.' I tried to stop him. I had to shoot."

The Secret Service man picked up the pistol at Spencer's side. "Yours?"

Spencer tried to nod and ended up coughing again. More blood spewed from his mouth. His voice sounded weaker. "There's a—girl with him. She ran me down. I—never saw her coming. You—get me some—help?"

"Any minute, fella. You rest now."

Spencer shut his eyes, his skin an icy blue-white and damp. Roy checked his pulse and shook his head at the Chief of Police.

"How'd they get away?" Roy asked Spencer somberly.

"Took my car. '56—" Spencer spat more blood, "Ford Fairlane, baby blue with fins."

His eyes closed once more. They did not open again.

"You believe him?" asked the Chief.

"No reason not to, Chief. Christ, what else *could* have happened?"

Roy wandered closer to the wreckage, heavy coats of foam thinning the smoke and flames. His agents were scouring the site beside the fire teams.

An agent handed Roy the First Lady's scorched pillbox hat. "They found this next to the plane."

Another agent pressed a ripped and dusty dark suit jacket into his hands. "The President's," the agent said shakily. "His wallet's inside."

Roy felt sick. The President and the First Lady. On his watch. His responsibility.

He had not protected them properly, not stood between them and this terrible hazard, when that was his only job. He felt ill. *God, how could it have happened, and so quickly?*

And the son of a bitch who did it was still running around at large. Roy felt the beginnings of a massive migraine. To forestall his consciousness of it, he barked questions. "What about the bodies?"

"Badly burned," the first agent said somberly. "We'll need dental records to make positive ID's, but body size, height and approximate weight match the President's and Mrs. Kennedy's."

"Jesus, Roy," said the second agent, tears beginning to run heedlessly down his face. "Who the hell else would it be?"

The lanky agent keyed the microphone on his two-way radio.

"Charcoal, this is Digest." Roy's voice was barely audible, his words deliberate. "Lancer and Lace are dead." A few seconds passed before an incredulous voice crackled a single word back over the radio, ignoring official protocols.

"What?"

"This is Digest," Roy repeated, his voice louder as conviction grew in his soul. "Lancer is dead. Lace is dead." He cleared his throat and looked at each of the men standing around him, many of them blinking away tears.

"Confirmed?" asked the voice in disbelief.

Roy looked at his men, at the scorched hat and jacket in his hands, and in his heart he knew. "Confirmed."

* * *

Lyndon Johnson, in the cramped spaces of Air Force One, where his Secret Service detail had rushed him, couldn't believe what he was hearing. It was almost too good to be true.

Kennedy, confirmed dead!

His troubles were over. In one smooth move, he had left behind a Vice-Presidency haunted by broad hints of shady associates, financial irregularities and bribery—all of which were true—and ascended to the highest office in the land, the job he'd coveted for years and believed for a while was beyond his reach.

Nothing was beyond his reach now.

He allowed himself one beaming grin that stretched from ear to ear before hastily hiding his elation behind the somber mask of the concerned man who was oh-so-reluctantly taking up the duties of his fallen Commander-in-Chief.

The press, still confused by the lightning-quick events at Love Field, was phoning in strange, contradictory stories, but the Secret Service report to him wouldn't stay secret for long: he'd make sure of it. In ten minutes, he would put out official word of the tragic deaths of President and Mrs. Kennedy while they were being rescued from a madman who had kidnapped them at gunpoint just after they landed in Dallas. It made it all the more imperative that he do what he was itching to do, had been itching to do, for a long time.

There was a quick, impatient knock, and his communications guy came in, along with his own secretary, Marie. "Sir?" Johnson noted that already, the respect in his men's voices was more than that awarded a Vice-President. It had become the ultimate respect accorded a President.

"What is it?" Johnson asked.

"The phone lines are open, sir. We have secure lines."

"Good. Get me Sarah Hughes," Johnson instructed Marie. "She's a judge here in Dallas. She's in my book."

"Yes, sir." A minute later, she announced the call.

Johnson picked up. "Sarah? Yes, it is, a terrible, terrible thing. And especially here in Texas, where there were so many people who loved him. You should have seen the crowds yesterday... yes, I just did receive confirmation. Yes, I'm afraid so. Well, I've talked to the Attorney General... oh, he's shattered. Of course. A terrible thing for the whole family. He advises me to take the oath right away, so there isn't the slightest misunderstanding. We need to make it clear to the rest of the world that there's someone in charge, that the government is strong and going on. Yes... can you come down here to Love Field and administer the oath? We'll get the wording for you... Thank you, Sarah. I'll see you shortly."

He hung up and nodded to Marie. "Get me the Attorney General."

This took longer. Bobby Kennedy wasn't in his office; he was lunching at home with a guest. Finally, Marie nodded to Johnson, who picked up the phone, his tone noticeably subdued. "Bob? You've heard?" He paused. "You haven't heard?" He hesitated. He hadn't bargained for this. "There's been trouble in Dallas. The President and Mrs. Kennedy were kidnapped at Love Field by some crazy guy, a Communist, I think... well, no. No, I'm actually calling to confirm that... Bob, they're both dead. I'm very, very sorry to tell you that."

Johnson listened to the painful efforts of Robert Kennedy, United States Attorney General, to compose himself and ask questions, while it was all he himself could do not to dance with glee right there on the plane.

"Are you sure?" Bobby's voice, with its own distinctive Boston accent, came through shakily.

"I'm quite sure," Johnson said as gently as he could. "I wouldn't call you if I wasn't sure."

A moment passed. "I'm coming to Dallas," the Attorney General said.

"Don't, Bob. The Secret Service will bring the—uh—well, they'll bring the President and Mrs. Kennedy back. We'll be in the air as soon as we get their—I mean, as soon as they're on board. We'll make sure no one disturbs them—" He stopped, realizing how ridiculous that sounded, then rushed on. "What I really need to know about is the oath."

"The oath?" Bobby repeated. He sounded dazed.

"The oath of office. I think it's best to have the swearing in before we leave Dallas, in the next hour. People have got to know there's someone at the helm. They've got to see that the government goes on. I don't have the wording, though. Can you get it?"

Kennedy's voice sounded worse now, like he was trembling uncontrollably. "I don't have the oath. Do you have to do this now? Can't it wait till you get back to Washington?"

"God knows what's going on out there, Bob," Johnson said piously. "We could be heading off God knows what foreign policy calamities by letting people know someone's in charge. President Kennedy's people here in Dallas seem to feel the same way. They've urged me to do it." He hadn't spoken to one of them about it.

Kennedy fumbled for an answer. Finally, he said he'd have someone find the oath and dictate it over the phone. It wasn't very long.

"Thank you. I appreciate your help," Johnson said, his Texas accent going even broader as more pieces fell into place for him. "You'd better keep this line open. I need to be able to reach you... there's a lot of business to take care of before I get back... oh, and Bob? Lady Bird and I send our sincere condolences to all your family on this terrible, terrible tragedy."

He put the phone down and nodded to Marie, who made sure the line would stay open. He looked like the cat who had swallowed the canary, and it was even tastier than he'd dreamed.

* * *

Lee watched the traffic from the front passenger seat, saying nothing. Beads of sweat dotted his forehead, but those could be more from the exertions of the last half hour than from anxiety. All in all, he seemed very cool. I couldn't figure out how he did it.

"Don't speed, we don't want to attract attention." It was the first sentence he'd spoken since we drove out of Redbird. His voice was even, and he didn't look at me.

His eyes were trained outside the car.

"We've got to get off the streets. Someone's going to spot us." I stole glances at the cars around us, expecting every driver to pull a gun at any moment. I figured the lady with her son, the trucker, and the old man ahead of me were all either cops or conspirators waiting to make their move. "We need a plan."

"I *had* a plan," Lee snapped. He waved a hand in the air, vividly expressing his feelings. "Now we have to get him back to Air Force One."

"Are you crazy? How?" I glared at Lee till the blare of a horn made me jerk the Ford back into my lane just before I sideswiped a truck. "We can't take him anywhere close to Air Force One. We just have to be more careful."

"What makes you think we can protect the President better than the Secret Service can?"

"So far, he's still alive. That's a plus."

"Alive but no longer President," came the muffled Boston voice from beneath the back seat. Kennedy pushed himself up from his awkward crouch along the floor. He slid away the jacket covering his face and Mrs. Kennedy's. "You saved my life—I won't argue that—but all the same—" he glared at us, "I no longer have the power of the Presidency. Do you understand that?"

I honestly hadn't given it a thought. From the look on Lee's face, I could see that neither had he. We'd been focusing on saving Kennedy's life. The President was thinking about salvaging his Administration.

"But," Lee said blankly, "you're still President. As long as you're breathing, you're still President."

Kennedy's voice was savage. "Being President means having the power to do things. It doesn't matter a damn that technically, you're right: I am still President. Right now I can't do a damned thing, and until you get us somewhere safe, no one will know we're alive. There's nothing to stop them from declaring me dead and swearing in Lyndon Johnson. They might well decide it's a good idea to have at least an interim President in the meantime."

"But," I began eagerly, "Lyndon Johnson won't take the oath of office until 2:38, and—"

"I *don't* want to hear any more about the future, Miss Cuyler!"

Chastened, I stole a look at Mrs. Kennedy. Her face was paper white, her brown eyes enormous. Her pretty pink skirt had a long tear in it; her hair was in disarray. Her white gloves bore smudges of dirt, and right now one hand was clutching the President's arm. She appeared to be stunned.

Seeing her somehow gave me bravado to go on. "Look," I said, "your Administration is important, but your life has to come first. We'll get you someplace where people who are loyal to you can protect you."

Kennedy looked from one to the other of us, his chin level with the seat back. "And where might that be in Dallas?"

He had a point. "At least," I said, "you have to let them know you're alive. That's important. Johnson won't take the oath if everyone knows you're still alive."

"That is important," the President conceded. "You'd better drive me to a private phone right away."

"No need," I said cheerfully. I was feeling better, since he now saw the situation the way I did. I fumbled through my handbag with one hand on the wheel, till I found the cell phone and turned it on, handing it over my shoulder to the President.

"What's this?" he asked blankly, staring at it.

"A telephone," I said. "From the future. Just push the buttons to dial the White House, or wherever you want to call, and then push the 'Send' button, and you'll be connected."

I stole a glance in the mirror. He and Jackie were gazing at the phone with astonishment. "Jack," she said softly. "It's so small! And there are no cords!"

He was nodding, too, turning the device in his hand. "And it's light. Can't weigh more than a few ounces."

"For heaven's sake, make the call," I said hurriedly.

I had to give him the instructions again. I'd read in George's books that most of the time, no one had to explain anything to Kennedy twice: he was a man of rare intellect. Right now, though, he was so fascinated with the tiny phone that he wasn't taking in what I'd said. Once he understood, he pressed some buttons rapidly, but after a moment he shook his head. "Nothing," he said. "Just static."

"Let me try," I said, still driving. I dialed the number the President gave me, which was unfamiliar. I didn't think it was the White House.

"The Attorney General's office," he said.

Of course: the man the President trusted most was his brother, Robert Kennedy, the brilliant and ruthless legal mind who was taking on organized crime as his number-one target, the only Attorney General ever to make significant strides toward vanquishing the major crime families in America.

Unfortunately, I got static also: I supposed that despite all his preparations, John wasn't quite aware that dialing a number simply across a geographic area required less juice than dialing a number across both space *and* time.

I couldn't blame him for that, but I also couldn't keep us out here, driving aimlessly, when any minute someone was liable to notice us, and the chase would start all over again. I didn't even know who the good guys and the bad guys *were*.

I racked my brain for a place I could go.

And then I knew: the one place I was certain no conspirator could possibly be, not at this time of day.

"Hang on," I said, pulling an abrupt U-turn on a deserted street. "I know just where to take you."

* * *

I circled the block outside my parents' house, making sure the street was empty. Memory told me everyone would be glued to their television sets awaiting further news of the President's assassination (kidnapping, at this point), but a single nosy neighbor could jeopardize our safety. I parked the car in front of the house and reminded Lee and the Kennedys to crouch down until I returned.

I ran up the steps and threw open the door, startling Sandra, who was red-eyed and teary, away from the television set.

"Cady!" she gasped when she saw me. "But—but you're—Don told me you were—"

"All a mistake," I assured her breezily. "I'm fine."

She wasn't: she stood gaping at me, so truly stunned that for a minute I forgot the urgency of getting my passengers into the house. I had no time to comfort her, yet I knew she would need reassurance before she would help us.

"Mrs. Cuyler," I said, going to her, "please, don't look like that. I'm not a ghost. There was an accident, and I think everyone at ISI thought I was… well, you know. I'm really all right. I spent Wednesday night and yesterday at—" I thought quickly, "at Parkland Hospital, but they released me this morning. I'm not here to hurt you. But I do need your help now, very badly. Will you help me?"

Sandra blinked a few times. She was beginning to trust that there was nothing sinister in my sudden re-appearance. Slowly, she began to nod, and then to smile. We had gotten over the hump.

The television set, blaring behind her, brought her back to other concerns.

"Come in," she said quickly. "I've been watching the news… did you hear what happened?"

I had no time to sympathize. "Mrs. Cuyler, I need to borrow some coats and hats, just for a minute." She looked at me stupidly, not following the change of subject. "Two men's coats, two hats, and a lady's coat and scarf."

"But it's warm out, Cady," she protested. "No one needs—"

"Please!"

Reluctantly she cast a look at the set; she wanted to be back there watching, not missing a word. But I drew her into the foyer, and finally she concentrated long enough to hand me a lady's raincoat, a trench coat and a heavy winter coat of my father's. She poked around again and came up with two lumpy, disreputable-looking hats and a motley scarf.

"Thank you," I said quickly. "I'll be right back."

I rushed outside and threw the garments through the open window on the passenger side, indicating that they should put them on.

Lee and the Kennedys complied quickly, clumsily pulling the clothes on while trying to remain unseen. I scanned the street, which thankfully remained empty: everyone, apparently, was glued to their television sets and radios, listening to the latest developments of the President and Mrs. Kennedy's terrifying kidnapping.

Jackie emerged first, her head wrapped completely in the black scarf, her pink suit concealed beneath my mother's winter raincoat. Lee and the President looked like hobos in my father's coats, but at least with the hats pulled down, they were covered from head to toe. I urged them ahead of me up the short stretch of sidewalk to the house. Everyone moved quickly, and I was confident no one on the block had identified them.

Sandra had gone back to the television set. "I'm back, Mrs. Cuyler," I called, to give her time to compose herself.

She came out, a frown of annoyance on her face. I was definitely intruding now, and she was more annoyed still at the three strangers wrapped in the old clothes she had just supplied to me. I had said nothing about them.

"These are friends of mine," I said quickly, reassuringly. "They need a place to stay for a couple of hours. We'll be glad to pay, but they can't be safe unless you promise you won't tell anyone they were here. Please promise me that, Mrs. Cuyler."

Matters were certainly worse when Lee took off his hat and coat.

"Oh, my God," she said, the breath exhaling from her in a rush. "You're that man who kidnapped the President!"

"It's all right," I said soothingly. "This is Lee Oswald, but he's okay. He's not a killer. I swear it."

Her eyes widening now, she looked at the two taller figures behind him. I could see her trepidation, her concern turning to fear: were these his shady accomplices? Slowly, she took a step backward toward the phone.

Then President Kennedy stripped off the trench coat and hat.

Sandra gasped audibly. "Oh, my God!"

She clutched the newel post at the foot of the banisters, staring at him in disbelief, hand over her mouth.

Quickly, I made introductions. "Mr. President, may I present Mrs. Sandra Cuyler, my landlady. Mrs. Cuyler, President Kennedy."

"You can't be here," she whispered. "They're saying you could be dead. All the newsmen are saying it. I don't understand… "

"It's all a mistake," the President assured her, smiling. "I'm happy to meet you, Mrs. Cuyler. Thank you so much for having us here."

Behind him, Jackie was untying her scarf and throwing off her coat. Sandra's eyes flashed behind the President to her, and her face blossomed with recognition and delight. She was obviously thrilled at seeing the glamorous Jacqueline Kennedy in person. "Mrs. Kennedy too! So you're both all right! Aren't you?" she asked, her voice uncertain.

"Quite all right, thank you," the President agreed. "I wonder, though, if we could use your telephone?" He smiled at her warmly, and like so many other women, Sandra fell for it, hook, line and sinker.

"Oh, yes, of course! In the kitchen. I wonder," she turned to him, "would you and Mrs. Kennedy and—er—" she glanced at Lee doubtfully. In her mind, he was still a crazed psychopath; after all, Walter Cronkite said so.

"Lee Oswald, ma'am," Lee said softly, giving her a smile too. He was hanging on every word and gesture of the First Couple, and seeing close up what compelling charm could accomplish. Lee was no fool: as a southerner, he already knew something about manners and charm. All he had to do was turn it on full throttle.

"Mr.—Oswald." She turned to include them all. "I wonder if you might like some refreshments?"

"We'd love it," said Jackie warmly. She saw me glancing out the window and correctly gauged my anxiety about passing neighbors, because she added, "Perhaps we could sit with you in the kitchen? We could have a nice chat there."

You really had to admire this woman who's been kidnapped at gunpoint and then almost killed in a massive explosion and fire. Her poise was unshakeable, her manner winning and soft, so easy for Sandra to relate to. Even Sheila couldn't have pulled that off.

Sandra smiled back at her, as I had known she would, already at ease. "Please come in, then, all of you."

"Ma'am, I wonder if we could trouble you to lock the front door?" Lee asked, his manner just as winning. "So no one accidentally disturbs us."

"Oh, yes." She hurried to lock the door carefully and then led the way into the kitchen. The President went straight to the white princess phone on the counter, those obsolete phones with dials set not in the receiver but on the phone base itself, and dialed quickly. I could see him hoping fervently that this time, he would get through to his brother.

* * *

The Attorney General's office was fast collapsing into chaos. The Attorney General, it was whispered from desk to desk, was on his way back to his office at top speed and would expect answers on his arrival. Up and down the hall at the Justice Department, staffers choked on their sobs as they worked the phones, scrambling for information from Dallas.

Angie, Robert Kennedy's crisp, efficient longtime secretary, refused to collapse. Her boss would have a hundred chores to do when he arrived, and she intended to help him.

Angie considered herself as stoic and businesslike as her boss. She had not permitted herself a tear since she'd heard the news over a tinny radio as she was returning from a late lunch. It was a warm enough fall day for D.C. workers to linger outside, listening to music or chatting with co-workers. She had caught the awful bulletin as she strolled on the Mall, and her first thought had been to get back to the office.

The big television set in the Attorney General's office had at once been turned on, and more than a dozen staffers had piled inside, arms folded, lips bitten until blood poured, heedlessly, as they watched helplessly, reluctant to leave the set for any reason.

Still, when the private line rang, force of habit pushed her into the outer office. She never answered the private line for any reason, but it rang through on her phone nonetheless. Today was exceptional. Today she would answer. But she would answer out of earshot of anyone else, instinctively keeping the call private.

"Mr. Kennedy's office." Her voice quivered as she spoke, her heart almost coming to a stop when she heard the familiar voice on the other end of the line.

"Angie? It's the President."

For the second time today, she covered her mouth with her hand to keep from crying out. The line was full of static, a sure sign of a long-distance connection. Yet there was no mistaking the Boston twang of a Kennedy.

"Angie?"

Angie struggled to keep her voice level, as shock and relief warred inside her. "Mr. President?"

"Yes. Is he there?"

"N—no, sir. He's still at home." Her hands and lips were trembling with shock.

"I just tried him there. The line was busy for ten minutes. Listen. You understand no one can know I called."

"Yes—yes, sir. I understand."

"Good girl. Tell him I'll call later. I'm not sure where we're going from here, but I think we're still in Dallas, and for now, I'm safe. Give him a message for me, will you?"

"Y—yes?" Angie snatched at a pencil and pad on her desk, though her fingers were still shaking.

Kennedy's voice was warm and full of laughter. "Tell him reports of my death are greatly exaggerated."

Angie wasn't sure whether to laugh or cry. "I—I will, sir. You'll call back soon?"

"As soon as I can, I promise. I'm all right, and so is Mrs. Kennedy. Tell him not to worry. Strange as it may seem, I'm in good hands."

Angie started to answer, but the line went dead. Mechanically, her hands shaking, she wrote down the exact message the President had left. Behind her, the television set in the inner office was blaring.

I can't keep control of myself, she thought, not with all these people around. Someone will see my face and guess something… and they mustn't know… they can't know…

She herded out all the staffers, shut the door of her office, which had stood invitingly open every day for almost three years, and leaned against it. For a second she thought she'd imagined the whole thing.

Then she was sure she had not. And she dropped her head into her hands and wept, in relief and thanksgiving.

* * *

The President set down the phone in the Cuyler kitchen. "Bobby's secretary said he was still at home in Virginia. The line there is busy."

Everyone seemed to hear that except Sandra. She was bustling around, measuring coffee into the coffeepot, setting a kettle on the stove to boil, getting down what I guessed was her best china, because it was stored up on the highest shelves, away from her everyday dishes. She appeared to be focusing more on what she could do for the Kennedys than what they could do for her. She went into the dining room with the plates and cups carefully balanced in her hands, still giving no sign that she'd heard anything the President had said.

"We can stay here until you reach him," I said, feeling smugly confident. I'd outwitted Don Cuyler by bringing his quarry right to his door, and he'd never know it.

Lee protested. "That's crazy! What if Cuyler comes back here? We're all dead."

I could feel the grin bursting out on my face and spoke to him in a near-whisper. "Impossible. He's already made plans to get away. He put in for vacation time at ISI after today. He's not coming back."

My mother came to the table. "Please," she said shyly, "come in and sit in the dining room. I'll bring in coffee and tea to you right away. I'll fix some sandwiches, too." She added to Jackie, "If that's all right with you."

Jackie simply smiled at her.

In a few minutes we were settled around the oval-shaped dining room table, which was so eerily familiar to me from my childhood. It was exactly the same dining-room set she'd had right up to the day of her death in Larchmont.

"Your husband and I met in the Office of Naval Intelligence during the war," the President told Sandra, reaching for his cup. "I haven't seen him in years. Will he be home soon?"

I smothered a smile. This was one night I knew Don wasn't coming home early. *Thank God.*

"Don usually gets home around six on Fridays," Sandra said shyly. I think the wonder of holding a casual conversation with the Kennedys just overwhelmed her. Her face was radiant. "More cream, Mrs. Kennedy?"

"No, thank you," Jackie said cordially. "This is just fine."

"I'll fix the sandwiches." Sandra jumped up and stood looking at us wistfully for a moment. "It's—it's just *wonderful,* having you here."

When she started into the kitchen, I followed her, carrying my handbag.

"Oh, Cady," she whispered to me, when the door closed behind us, "it's really them! How did this happen?"

"I'll tell you sometime," I promised. "I keep forgetting to pay my rent here, so I thought I'd just give it to you. I'm leaving today, Mrs. Cuyler."

"Oh, no!" Sandra turned to regard me with troubled eyes. "I had hoped you'd stay."

"I did say Friday, you know," I reminded her. I took out my wallet and handed her two $10 bills, and then a third.

"Oh, Cady! That's too much!"

"No. Thanks for holding my room for me, and for all those good breakfasts."

"Wouldn't you rather give it to my husband? He'll be home soon."

"I'd rather give it to you," I said, holding it out to her. I knew Don was on his way out of town, and thought he'd probably left her without a dime to her name. She could use every extra dollar she could get her hands on in the next few weeks. I was glad to give it to her. Reluctantly, she took it, slipping it into the pocket of her dress.

"I hope we'll see each other again," she said, and there was a genuine wistfulness in her voice.

"I'm sure we will," I said with a smile, "and sooner than you think."

We might have said more, but suddenly, there was a choked cry from Lee. It sounded like trouble.

It was.

Lee was at the front window, staring into the driveway. Don Cuyler was slamming the door of his black Cadillac and starting toward the walk.

For just a moment, I was frozen in horror. This wasn't supposed to happen! He *couldn't* be here—he just couldn't!

Lee's mind was working faster. He saw me standing helpless and grabbed my hand. "Let's get the Kennedys and get out the back!" he barked at me.

We ran straight into the dining room and yanked the First Couple to their feet, scooping up the discarded hats and coats. They understood in a few words what was happening, and sped with us to the back door, everyone scrambling awkwardly back into the outerwear, even as they ran. Lee covered us with his revolver. I prayed he wouldn't have to use it, especially as I recalled with a sinking heart that he was a terrible shot. He was more likely to hit the President than our enemies. As I headed for the door, I saw a set of car keys on a pretty flowered key ring, hanging from a nail on the wall. Praying they were duplicate keys to Don's car, I snatched them and ran.

I was the last one out. As I closed the back door, I heard the front door open.

The others were already around the side of the house, crouched under the hedgerow, when I caught up with them. From where we were, we could see the Cadillac in the driveway. "Everybody in!" I hissed. "Hurry!"

They scrambled in ahead of me, and as I ran headlong to the driver's side door, I could hear muffled shouts inside the house.

I jumped into the roomy driver's seat, and before the doors were closed, had slammed the key in the ignition and roared out of the driveway.

* * *

It hadn't taken Don a full minute to realize that Lee Oswald and the Roberts girl had been in his house—*his house!*—and that they were no longer there. Sandra had blurted it out, as soon as he had seen the cups on the dining room table. In a voice low and tense with fury, he assailed Sandra. "Where did they go? What did they say?"

"Nothing. They didn't tell me anything!" Her eyes were enormous in her white face. *She was hiding something*, Don decided. She had told him so quickly about Oswald, as though trying to forestall giving him other information by shocking him with that first. He had seldom raised a hand to his wife, but now he needed answers fast. Oswald could not be allowed to get away. He had seldom raised a hand to his wife, but now he needed answers fast.

Don slapped her hard in the face. "Talk, damn you! Tell me what he said!" He backhanded her; she was knocked backward and staggered against the wall.

"I don't know!" She began to cry, trying to shield her face with her hands.

He balled his hand into a fist and threw it at her cheekbone. She ducked, but her own sudden movement threw her off balance, and she crashed to the floor, this time clutching her stomach protectively.

He drew his foot back to kick her in the stomach, to force her to tell whatever she was holding back. He knew she was holding something back; it was obvious from the way she avoided his eyes, and besides, if he kicked her hard enough, he could kick the brat right out of her and end one of his problems right there. Then he heard the sound of a car close by.

Very close by.

He rushed to the window and saw with disbelief that his Cadillac was screeching out of the driveway. "Jesus Christ!"

It was useless. The car barreled down the street so fast he knew he could never catch up. Odd. He had thought Oswald couldn't drive.

Thank God there was something he could do. He went past Sandra, who was lying on the floor weeping. "Shut up!" he bellowed at her, picked up the phone and dialed '0' to ask for the police.

A moment later, he was connected.

"Dallas Police," crackled the voice over the phone.

"My car's been stolen, by that fellow who killed the President," Don shouted, giving a credible imitation of an outraged and upstanding citizen. "He came in my house and beat my wife! He might have killed her! I want action on this!" He allowed himself to be calmed down enough to give the dispatcher his name and address, and a description of the Cadillac and its license-plate number. Hanging up, he glared at Sandra. "I'll deal with you later. Now get the hell upstairs before the police arrive."

* * *

The scene at the Cuyler house had shaken me badly. Lee and I had become everyone's enemy, despite our good intentions. Don Cuyler or his henchman or even ordinary Texans could hunt us down and kill us all without a second thought and then virtuously claim self-defense. No doubt they'd even be hailed as heroes for facing down the crazed Lee Harvey Oswald. Too bad the President and First Lady were accidentally killed in the crossfire, the news reports would say; they'd still get medals and kudos and we'd get—I hated to think of what we'd get.

Once we'd turned the corner of Rosebud Lane, I had slowed down, hoping not to attract attention. Lee sat beside me in the heavy coat and snap-brim hat, his eyes scanning the road, his lips set grimly. Behind us, in the back seat, the Kennedys wore their shapeless old coats and hats. They looked thoroughly unlike their public image: Jackie had tucked her sleek dark hair under the brim of a man's hat and hunched her shoulders down in the dowdy tweed coat, her face turned down into the rough material. The President had slouched the other hat over his head and pulled the collar of the winter coat way up. At least no one glancing in the car windows would guess who they really were.

"Now what?" the President demanded acidly. "What's the next great idea?"

Lee and I glanced at each other. We had run out of ideas, but this wasn't something we cared to mention at the moment.

Lee forestalled Kennedy's next comment by clicking on the car radio. "We'd better know what's going on."

The local announcer's voice came up. "… identified one of the kidnappers as Lee Harvey Oswald of Irving, Texas. Oswald is a known Communist, and a man who defected to the Soviet Union in 1959."

"Quite a career you've had," Kennedy said, and I thought I detected a trace of reluctant respect in his voice.

The radio continued: "He is the secretary of the New Orleans chapter of the Fair Play for Cuba committee, a Communist organization, and this summer he was involved in a street fight in New Orleans while defending that organization, which led to his arrest."

"It was my cover," Lee said defensively, looking at the President in the rear-view mirror.

"Christ," Kennedy muttered.

The announcer's voice cut in again. "Dallas police have issued an All-Points Bulletin for Oswald, who is heavily armed and considered extremely dangerous. He may also be traveling with a female companion. Roadblocks and checkpoints have been set up on all roads leading out of Dallas as the manhunt intensifies. The latest bulletin indicates that Oswald is traveling in a 1956 blue Ford Fairlane."

So they were still looking for the Fairlane, at least until Don called in the alarm, which I had no doubt he'd already done: it's what I would have done in his position. Maybe we still had a few minutes before they started looking for a black Cadillac.

The announcer's voice faded to a murmur as Lee twisted the volume dial lower. Through the sudden silence we heard the peal of church bells, slow and mournful, in the distance.

The streets were jammed with cars, mobbed with people, everyone in a state of what looked like almost uncontrolled grief. There were clusters of people huddled around television sets mounted in storefront windows along the sidewalks. Men were shouting and swearing, women stumbled along the streets with tears streaming down their cheeks,"

Add to this, after the comma above: "children whose parents were numb with shock were running free on sidewalks and even into the streets, shouting and laughing, heedless of the oncoming traffic, causing even more chaos. There wasn't a police car or traffic officer in sight."

This comes before: "What's going on?" Kennedy peered at the scene from under the hat.

"They think you're dead," I said matter-of-factly. "People are grieving."

Kennedy sat up so fast his hat fell back on his head. He pressed his face against the window and watched, fascinated, as two women held onto each other for support. "They're crying for me," he said wonderingly. "*For me!*"

Above all the chaos, the church bells were still pealing. Kennedy pulled the hat back over his face and moved away from the window, but his eyes lit with a thought. "Drive us to the nearest Catholic Church," he said in an undertone. I recognized it as an order from the Commander-in-Chief.

Lee asked, "Why a Catholic Church, sir?"

"Sanctuary," Kennedy replied tersely.

The President's idea made sense, I realized. There wasn't a Catholic church in America where the priests wouldn't shield the Kennedys from danger with their own bodies, if necessary. I understood that Kennedy saw the church as a place where he could rest, plan and call for Secret Service escort. It was, in fact, a very smart idea.

The problem was, I had no idea where the nearest Catholic church was. *Follow the peal*, I thought philosophically, and finally, maneuvering through the stumbling, disorderly crowds, I spotted a spire in the distance and after a few more minutes of crawling through the congested streets, turned into a quiet alley.

The church parking lot, fortunately, backed right up to the building. I pulled up to the back door, and Lee jumped out and held the car door for Mrs. Kennedy. The President scrambled after her, clutching his hat over his face still. When he looked up at the modest printed sign on the building, his face broke into a smile. "Look, Jackie," he said quietly.

The First Lady looked up, mindful of the hat over her face, too. The President pointed at the sign. "The Church of St. Jude," he said. "Patron saint of hopeless causes. We've come to the right place."

I saw the first real smile flit across Jackie's face.

*   *   *

The door was mercifully unlocked and opened onto a steep staircase. We started quietly up the staircase to the main floor, with me in the lead, the Kennedys behind me, and Lee in the rear, keeping an eye out for unexpected company.

The long corridor at the top of the stairs was deserted, though we could clearly hear the tones of a broadcast. Otherwise, there wasn't so much as the click of a pair of heels, but somewhere in this silent hallway there had to be some other sign of life. There were scarred wooden doors on either side of the hallway, and cautiously we started toward the only one cracked open, through which we could hear the voice of America's most respected newsman. I took a chance and peeked in.

In a small, cluttered office piled high with stacks of paper, pamphlets and books, sat a priest, another man and a woman, watching a small television set that had been balanced precariously on the paper piles. The woman was dabbing her eyes with a twisted handkerchief, the man clenching his fists as he listened. The priest was sitting behind the desk in a battered swivel chair, his head bowed over his clasped hands. His lips were moving, his eyes closed.

I heard Walter Cronkite's familiar tones clearly: "From Dallas, the flash, apparently official... President Kennedy died at approximately 2:00 p.m. Eastern Standard Time, some 45 minutes ago. The President died of injuries suffered during a plane crash and fire in the middle of a rescue mission to free him from kidnappers. First Lady Jacqueline Bouvier Kennedy was also killed in the explosion."

"Oh, my God," Mrs. Kennedy whispered.

It was enough.

There was a flurry of movement from the little room. I stepped back just as the door opened.

"What is it?" asked the man facing us. He was muscular and stern: four strangers, two muffled in hats and coats on a warm Dallas day, demanded attention, even as news from the small television set poured forth an unthinkable tragedy. "What do you want?"

The President shook off his hat and shrugged out of his coat. The man turned a peculiar shade of olive, and his hand made a quick, automatic sign of the cross.

"God in heaven!" he gasped.

Mrs. Kennedy stepped forward and shook off her hat, as well. The man's eyes flickered to her, and his complexion turned even more amphibian-like. "My God!" he repeated. "Father—Father!"

The urgency in his tone communicated itself to the others. After some bumping and mild swearing, we heard the footsteps of the priest, who gazed from one famous face to the other, his hand, too, moving automatically in the sign of the cross.

The President, clearly the most composed, nodded and smiled. "Good afternoon," he said pleasantly. "May we use your phone?"

The woman fell to her knees and clutched his hand. "Oh, thank God! Thank God! Oh, Holy Mother, it's a miracle!"

Lee edged backward, a little taken aback at this passionate show of faith. The Kennedys inclined their heads gravely. I tried a smile and felt foolish.

The woman rose slowly, brushing at the fresh tears on her face, but her face was aglow.

"Please," I said quickly, "the President and the First Lady need sanctuary. They have enemies here in Dallas, and—"

The muscular man stepped forward, his eyes turning from liquid to steel. "They're safe here," he declared. "No one will get to them." He looked the President in the eye. "You have my word on that, sir."

"I believe you," the President smiled, extending his hand. "And you are—?"

"Miles Everett. I live here in Dallas and do contracting work. Building. Today I was working here in the church, and—" He gestured at the television. "Well, no one has left their radio or TV set. Not since we—heard."

"Thank you, Miles." The President looked toward the priest. "Father—?"

"Mr. President, I'll order the church emptied at once. People have been here to pray, but—"

"No," the President said quickly. "I don't want people to leave church when they came to pray. But we must keep our presence here a secret. From everyone. Please."

Everett, the priest, and the woman nodded. I thought her head bobbed a little too eagerly.

"And," continued the President, "I *must* use your telephone—"

The priest pushed his black desk telephone forward and invited him with a gesture to sit in his battered swivel chair. The President was already dialing, leaning on the edge of the desk.

Quickly, the priest ushered the rest of us out of the office and reverently closed the door. "Privacy," he said.

He looked at Lee and me for perhaps the first time, and his face wrinkled in puzzlement. "And you are—?"

"Lee Oswald and friend," I supplied with a wry smile.

"Oswald? But aren't you—?" The priest shook his head and looked to Mrs. Kennedy.

She looked at us with something like fondness. "Father, they're our saviors. If we live through this weekend, it'll be all their doing. They're risking their lives to help us."

The priest looked again at us, and this time his face was filled with benevolence. "Then I will pray for you," he said simply.

Lee opened his mouth to speak. His eyes were rebellious, which boded no good for us. We needed these people.

But before I could nudge him or make any sign, Mrs. Kennedy fixed her doe-brown eyes on him. Slowly and meaningfully, she shook her head.

Lee met her eyes. Her gaze never faltered. He turned to the priest, and his voice was polite. "Thank you, Father," he said. "That would be very nice."

* * *

Angie had succeeded, with difficulty, in clearing the Attorney General's office and wiping away her tears. When Robert Kennedy appeared in the doorway, she was sitting at her desk and appeared to be typing a letter collectedly, but the paper she was supposedly copying was upside down, she had forgotten to put in carbon paper, and her fingers, usually so strong and accurate, were hitting a wrong key roughly every third stroke.

"Angie."

Bobby Kennedy looked haggard and suddenly old, though he had just turned 38 a few days before. His thick hair was more unruly than usual, as though he'd been running a despairing hand through it, and his deep-set eyes were blank: Pain and shock were warring with the need to remain calm and get things done. Whatever else he was, Bobby was a man who could be counted on in a crisis. With Jack and Jackie both dead, his whole family and the remnants of the Kennedy Administration would turn to him for their cues in the next few days. He dared not fail them or himself, or his late, beloved brother. But it was hard to think of details when his mind was being sealed by grief.

Angie was galvanized into action by his appearance. She jumped up from the typewriter and stuck her head into the hall to be sure they weren't observed. "Inside," she said quickly. "Close the door!" She who had never touched her boss now pulled him into the office, and he who refused to be led except by his older brother now shuffled obediently inside and allowed her docilely to lead him.

Angie beckoned him to his desk. He went to it like a sleepwalker and set down his briefcase and perched on his roomy leather chair.

"Mr. Kennedy," she said in a whisper, though they were quite alone, "the President called. I just spoke to him. He wanted to talk to you. He said he'd call back."

Bobby Kennedy rubbed a hand over his face. "I know, Angie," he said wearily. There was nothing of the famous Kennedy vigor about him now. "Johnson reached me at home. He told me to expect to hear from him again. I'll patch through a call to him on Air Force One. Just give me a minute."

"No!" Angie said forcefully, trying to rouse him from his stupor. "Not Johnson. President Kennedy. *I just talked to President Kennedy.*"

Bobby stared at her in astonishment, as though his dog had suddenly begun to sing. For a moment, what she said was so out of keeping with what he had just painfully learned that his mind refused to accept it. "No, Angie," he said patiently. "President Kennedy is dead. He was killed in an explosion." He couldn't seem to stop saying it, rocking back and forth in the chair. "President Kennedy is—"

"He's not dead!" Angie insisted. "I just talked to him, not half an hour ago. I don't care what they're saying on the news: *He's alive, and he's going to call you back!*"

It slowly began to permeate his befogged mind that Angie was telling him something momentous. She had spoken to the President many times; she knew his voice. She couldn't be mistaken…

The optimism his whole family had always embraced began to come back dimly, then to roar in his veins. He stopped rocking and sat up. "Angie, say that again."

On the third repetition, Bobby seemed to get it. The look of anguish and the shuffle of the old man vanished. He leaped out of his chair. "Tell me everything, Angie, everything he said to you. God in heaven, I have to help him!"

An hour ago, Johnson had told him his brother had been assassinated. Now Angie was telling him she'd just spoken to the President. As she started to repeat the conversation in detail, the private line rang. Bobby snatched it up before the first ring ended.

"Jack?" he said eagerly.

"Bob, it's Lyndon." He paused. Bobby's happy mood suddenly deflated, like a cruelly punctured balloon. "I guess whenever anybody says 'the President's calling' you'll be thinking of him. That's natural."

"What can I do for you, Mr. President?" Bobby spoke carefully, trying to hide his soaring elation. His brother was alive. His brother would be calling back. Thank God. Thank God. For now, he had to play the game, say nothing to anyone, keep this bombshell of a secret tightly under wraps. He knew he could count on Angie's silence; he also had to stay alert himself, to avoid betraying the smallest hint of it to anyone. Everyone he trusted had been with Jack in Dallas. He wouldn't be able to reach them for hours. For now, he would remain the loyal public servant.

Johnson hesitated again. "I just wanted you to know I've taken the oath. On Air Force One. We'll be taking off from here any minute. Should be back in Washington in two and a half hours at the most. I don't—" He listened to someone behind him. "Bob, I'll call you back."

"Yes, Mr. President," Bobby said. He set down the phone grimly. Calling anyone but Jack 'Mr. President' seemed like an obscenity, and none more so than Lyndon Johnson, the jovial Texas bastard Bobby loathed and had urged Jack not to run with in 1960. Bobby was sure he was wallowing in mud, which included accepting bribes, stealing elections and possibly murder. Yet here he was now, President of the United States!

Not for long, Bobby promised himself grimly. *Not while I have something to say about it.*

The phone rang again, almost at once. Bobby braced himself and picked up the phone. "Mr. President?"

"From now until 1968, Bobby." *Jack.*

Bobby's face lit with hope. "Jack? Is that you?" he asked tentatively, unwilling to trust his ears.

"It's me. Don't worry. We're both fine."

"Jack, in God's name, where are you?" Bobby exploded, his joy and relief making him feel weak. "Jesus Christ, do you know what's happened?"

"I've been a little busy, Bobby."

"Jack, it's bad. Lyndon's taken the oath."

There was a pause. "Well, I hope he enjoys the job," Jack said cheerfully. "He won't have it for long. I'm the elected President—now get someone the hell out here to get me out of this godforsaken place."

"Jack, for God's sake, *where are you?*"

Another pause. "A church in Dallas. St. Jude's Church. I don't know the street address, but we'll stay here until you get someone to us."

Bobby's mind was working furiously again, ticking off possibilities and obstacles at lightning speed. "Look, it's a lot worse now that Lyndon's taken the oath. He's the power now, Jack. Your Secret Service detail brought what they think is your body to Air Force One. Lyndon's thrilled at having the Presidency; he'll never give it up without a fight. If he finds out you're still alive, well, you know what he's capable of. I'm afraid of what might happen to you."

There was a pause. Bobby could hear the hum on the long-distance line. "Don't worry," Jack said easily. "We'll stay right here until you get someone out to us. Get our people, Bobby. You're right; it could be very—er—inconvenient for Macbeth if Duncan were suddenly to come back from the dead. So for the time being, I'm staying dead. It's a lot safer."

"Who's with you now?" Bobby asked. He was already flipping through his Rolodex for the names of people in Texas.

"Besides Jackie, a girl named Cady Cuyler and this Lee Oswald character."

"The one who kidnapped you?" Bobby said, appalled. He'd been listening to the newscasts on the car radio and picked up Oswald's name. "The one who tried to kill you? Jack, are you crazy?"

His brother laughed. "No, but I'm beginning to think he is. He's risking his life for me, Bobby. Anyone who sees him here today will shoot him on sight, and instead of running for cover he's trying to shepherd me through this nutty city and keep me safe. I'm telling you, if we get out alive, that kid gets a medal."

The phone lines in Bobby's office were beginning to light up. Word had passed that he was back at the Justice Department. "Okay. I'll have the federal marshals out to pick you up in an hour. *Don't move, Jack.* Don't go anywhere. We'll get you out fast and quiet. Just sit tight. Once we get you back to Washington, we can get the Presidency back."

"All right, Bobby." There was a smile in his voice. "And don't worry—if the Japs couldn't kill me, neither can a few nuts with rifles, okay?"

"Give me the number where you are now. Jack?" But the line had gone dead.

Though he needed to be able to reach his brother, Bobby was smiling as he replaced the receiver gently. The nightmare was over, faded away just like all bad dreams in the daylight, and he was determined to keep any other bad dreams at bay.

He kept smiling as he turned to Angie. "I want the marshals' office, right now. Get me the head guy—" Bobby stopped to think of his name, and in that moment, the private line rang again.

"We need an unlisted number," Angie said, smiling too, as she went back to her desk.

Bobby grinned as he picked up. "Hello?"

The grin faded as he heard Johnson's Texan accent again. "Bob. Lyndon."

"Yes, Mr. President?" Bobby said evenly. It was important, so important, he told himself again, that Lyndon have no suspicion whatever that his brother was still alive. He had to play the game, even as he calculated how best to bring Jack back from the politically dead.

"Bob, I want you to know that I understand your position. You're head of your family now, and they need you. I respect that. At a time like this, your family obligations have to come first."

What the hell? Since when did Lyndon Johnson *ever* believe in putting anyone's family first?

Johnson went on, his voice oily with phony sympathy. "You have big things to do, and you're the only one who can do them. Two funerals. All those arrangements. Taking care of Caroline and John-John—you've got your hands full. I wanted you to know that in recognition of that, I'm relieving you of your duties as Attorney General, effective immediately. You're on indefinite leave until you wrap up all your family obligations. I'll instruct Hoover. He'll work directly with me until you're ready to come back."

Johnson went on talking for a minute or so, but Bobby tuned him out. He was staring at the walls of his office. *He'd been fired, as soon as that bastard took the oath of office!* More than fired—he was stripped of power, so he could do nothing. His word would mean nothing; his ability to get things done was suddenly a thing of the past. His balls were being cut off smoothly and in the name of sympathy for the poor Kennedy family. In the midst of trying to deal with this sudden cataclysm, one terrifying thought stood out clearly in his mind:

How the hell am I going to help Jack now?

* * *

Johnson felt a thrust of the deepest satisfaction when he hung up the phone after his conversation with the Attorney General. By God, he was going to take charge, and sweep out anyone who had had strong ties with the previous Administration, starting with the arrogant and ruthless Bob Kennedy, his personal nemesis.

The door to his private compartment—the President's private compartment—opened a crack. "Sir, they still need a few pictures of the swearing in. If you'd come back for just a moment…"

Johnson complied at once, his vanity well pleased at the thought of being the center of the photographer's attention, for a change. That was the difference between being President and being Vice-President, the difference, in fact, between being President and being anything else. The way he cooperated with the Army photographer on board, jovially turning, straightening and then tipping his head as requested, showed everyone on the plane his pleasure. What did it matter? The Kennedy people were huddled at the rear, talking in low tones among themselves, still stunned with grief. Only his own people would sense his overflowing happiness, that is, unless the photographer somehow caught something on film that he didn't intend to show.

It took just a few minutes to shoot the additional photos. Judge Sarah Hughes, the old friend Johnson had asked to swear him in, posed patiently, holding the black leather-wrapped Bible with its gold cross in the center that the Kennedy people had produced for the oath. It was the only Bible on Air Force One, Kennedy's Bible, and Johnson thought it was more than good enough for him to use at the swearing in. After all, he was taking Kennedy's office—why not take the oath on his Bible? Johnson posed with one hand on the Bible and the other piously upraised, his face solemn, until the photographer was satisfied.

As soon as the photographer released them, Johnson caught hold of Marie and motioned her toward his compartment. "Get me Mr. Hoover at the FBI, right away," he told her in an undertone of urgency. She nodded and disappeared.

He turned back to Sarah Hughes and gave her a smile and a nice hug. "Thank you, Sarah. I do appreciate your coming."

"We're all behind you, Mr. President," Judge Hughes said demurely. She understood that she was dismissed.

She made her way to the exit door, not realizing she was still carrying the black leather Bible she'd just posed with. As she passed through the door into the late-fall sunshine, a security man watching her from the aisle said, "Are you finished with that?"

Judge Hughes looked down. "Oh! Yes. Here." She handed the Bible and the card on which the oath was typed to the security man, who took them, nodded a thank-you and motioned her toward the ramp.

When Judge Hughes arrived at the bottom of the ramp a minute later, her hands were empty.

Seven minutes later, Air Force One began its ascent to 40,000 feet, high above the incoming storms. By the time the flight had leveled off, Johnson was focused on the next item on his agenda, which involved simultaneously extracting information and massaging the massive ego of Washington's best-known bureaucrat, J. Edgar Hoover. "Thank God for you and the Bureau, Edgar. I need your help now more than ever. It seems the Attorney General's office is already starting an investigation into the kidnapping.

He had pushed the right button. Hoover had been a Washington bureaucrat since before Johnson came to Congress, and he jealously guarded his power base. He loathed the Attorney General—in fact, he loathed both Kennedys—a feeling heartily though silently endorsed by Johnson himself. Hoover was also aware that the Kennedys planned to retire him immediately upon his 70th birthday in January of 1965, which was a mandate for all government employees. A more sympathetic President, however, could extend his tenure at the Bureau indefinitely, and since Hoover's life revolved around the Bureau and the power it brought him, he was delighted to make himself useful to the new President, whose own peccadilloes made him anxious to secure Hoover's goodwill.

Hoover took a pause to compose himself, while vicious thoughts circulated in his devious mind. Bobby Kennedy could not be allowed to investigate his brother's death! "Well, that's most irregular, Mr. President. As you know, the Bureau has jurisdiction in kidnapping cases. This is a Bureau investigation."

Johnson's grin widened. Hoover had said precisely the words he'd wanted to hear. "Exactly, Edgar, which is why I'm concerned that your people get into this thing thoroughly."

"Well, that could be a problem. The Secret Service has been quite diligent in— er— repelling my people from the crime scene. We haven't even been able to positively identify the bodies."

Johnson froze. "Now, Edgar, we know who the bodies are."

"Sir, I'm told they were very badly burned. Positive identification will have to come from dental records. Until then… " Hoover let his voice trail off. He knew he'd just planted a terrifying seed in Johnson's mind. That bluff Texan had just barreled ahead to take the Presidential oath of office, hiding his bursting ambition under the guise of stepping in as necessity dictated, a public servant reluctantly assuming the mantle, not out of covetousness but with respect for his fallen leader. If anyone suspected he had jumped the gun, without even waiting to be sure that the bodies were those of the President and the First Lady… Hoover knew Johnson was suddenly contemplating the ruin of his political career in his eagerness to snatch the crown.

He let Johnson wait while he named his price. Hoover knew that he would have to sweep Johnson's previous irregular financial transactions under the rug and help him secure his power base. When he did, Hoover himself would be secure. He wanted that made clear at once. "Frankly, sir, I see this as a failure on the part of the Secret Service. Their responsibilities do not lie in investigation, and they've been hampering our efforts, which do. I think you might consider restructuring their responsibilities. Of course, I could be helpful in doing that, except that I am facing that silly government retirement policy… "

"I'll have something drawn up specifically exempting you," Johnson said, his tone becoming that of the confident leader. "This is your investigation, Edgar. No one else has the experience to get the job done. And of course, I'll make certain we look closely at the Secret Service and see how they might—ah—improve their operations."

"Thank you, sir." Hoover permitted himself a frosty smile at the other end of the phone. "And the Attorney General... "

It occurred to Johnson now that he really didn't like Hoover and had never liked him, the crusty old bureaucrat. He knew, though, that Hoover's files on his financial activities alone, should they ever surface, would destroy him. That was the bastard's insurance policy, those devastating files he kept on virtually every Washington politician. Johnson knew it was in his best interest to keep Hoover as the closest of close personal friends, and he knew Hoover would approve wholeheartedly of the favor he was about to ask him.

"I wonder also," Johnson said, his voice deliberately tentative, "if you'd do me a special service. Personally."

"It would be my honor, Mr. President."

"The Attorney General is really the patriarch of the Kennedy family now. He's requested some time off to handle the family's affairs, and I couldn't refuse him, though he is such a valuable member of the Administration. I wonder if you might step across to his office and perhaps help him wrap things up there, so he can go home quickly? He might be gone for some time, and I'd like him to get on with his own responsibilities and not have to worry about the government now."

"I'd be pleased to help," said the FBI Director, thinking, *The little bastard's been fired, and his brother's body isn't even cold!*

"He's grieving terribly," Johnson went on, "and I am concerned, as a friend, about his mental state. I would feel better if I knew someone was looking out for him on a— uh—regular basis."

"I admire your concern, Mr. President," Hoover said smoothly. "If I might suggest it, I'd be glad to have a couple of my best men looking out for Mr. Kennedy, to be sure he— er—doesn't run into trouble during this difficult time."

"But of course, Edgar, I wouldn't want to hurt his feelings by having it be obvious."

"No, no, Mr. President, I quite agree. I think my men could keep quite a close watch on him without letting him know. That way, he could feel independent, but he would still be fully protected. Don't worry. You can rely on the Bureau's discretion."

They understood each other. Bobby Kennedy was to be expelled from the Justice Department as quickly as possible, cut off from all government privileges and powers, and followed everywhere he went, to be sure of his loyalty and his silence. Hoover knew that Johnson had also just silently authorized him to use wiretaps and any other illegal methods necessary to keep track of his prey. It was the only way either of them could be sure that Johnson's head would continue to wear the crown. Each of them saw the advantage in that.

"Thank you, Edgar. I knew I could count on you."

* * *

I had stationed myself at the window of the priest's office, to keep an eye on the parking lot for suspicious intruders, but the tension had lessened considerably as we waited for the federal marshals. Jackie's pallid skin had begun to glow again, and Lee had carefully put away his revolver.

My original mission had been pushed to the back of my mind by the necessity of saving the President. Now that that was almost accomplished, I felt an obligation to George and John to recover the Bible. I looked at my watch. It was almost 2:00. I would have to leave in the next few minutes to get to Love Field and intercept Sarah Hughes, who would be coming down the steps of the ramp around 2:40.

The President was talking quietly to Lee, who had straightened up from his relaxed posture on the desk and was listening eagerly. "You should come with us to Washington," he was saying. "It won't be safe for you here for a while. Besides, the Attorney General will want to debrief you personally."

"I'd be glad to, sir," Lee answered. "I've been giving my reports to the Dallas FBI office, but I'm not sure they're reaching the right ears."

"They certainly haven't been reaching mine," Kennedy said. He grinned engagingly at Lee. "I need to know what's happening with these Cuban groups. They're getting out of hand." He asked Lee a question in a tone so low I couldn't hear him.

Lee answered, "The gunrunning pipeline was set up by Jack Ruby years ago. They've been using it for Mongoose since 1961. They've moved lots of arms since then."

"And they're using it for the second invasion of Cuba next week," I said, turning away from the window. I wondered if I could get out of the church unseen in time to get to Air Force One at Love Field. What if the timing of the oath had changed? What if Sarah Hughes left the Bible on board this time?

Kennedy looked at me curiously. "What second invasion of Cuba?"

Of course. He didn't know. He'd never known. Silently, to myself, I *said, And he needs to know.*

Rapidly I told him what I knew about the planned invasion and the role of ISI in sending guns along the pipeline, Lee nodding in confirmation. I also told him about the important shipment of 'vodka' Don had been working on all week, about Taylor Trucking, and even diffidently mentioned that I'd tried to divert the truck, to stop it from reaching its destination, if only temporarily. In that pallid way, I'd hoped to head off the invasion myself.

The rage in Kennedy's face dwarfed any emotion I'd seen there since I first met him last night and heaven help me, it was all directed at me. "Jesus Christ! Why the hell didn't you tell me this last night?"

"I didn't think of it," I said meekly. It was true: I was so focused on what *would* happen with the assassination that I had never thought about explaining what *might* happen with Cuba. "Would it really have made a difference?"

"A difference?" Kennedy glared at me and clenched his fists. "A difference? Last night you're babbling about assassination, today you're telling me about a second invasion of Cuba—you don't think it makes a *difference?*"

I didn't really see how it could. To me, they were interrelated issues. When he had calmed down a little, I told him about my deduction that the plotters intended his assassination to be the pivotal event that would turn public opinion in favor of a war against Castro.

Kennedy's face was gray. "Public opinion be damned! An invasion of Cuba is tantamount to nuclear war! We promised last year that *we wouldn't invade Cuba again.* If we invade, it gives Castro the leverage to ask for help from Moscow. Khrushchev will honor his commitment, and this time, he will use nuclear weapons. Millions of Americans will die!" He jumped up. "I've got to get back there and take over—it's the missile crisis all over again!"

He grabbed for the phone, but just then our attention was arrested by the blare of the television set. The priest had come back and turned up the volume. "Mr. President, you should hear this." Quickly he withdrew again, leaving the four of us alone.

Walter Cronkite, his shirtsleeves rolled up, black-rimmed glasses slightly down on his nose, was speaking into the stick microphone set on the desk in front of him, the desks of other newsmen behind him, in the background. "Again that bulletin—we have just received word that Vice-President Johnson has taken the Presidential oath of office on Air Force One. He is now the 36th President of the United States. Air Force One has departed from Love Field and is on its way back to Washington, carrying not only President Johnson, but also the bodies of President and Mrs. Kennedy. Presumably we will learn something of the plans for their funerals in the next few hours."

Kennedy dropped his head in his hands. The power no longer belonged to him, though as long as he breathed he was, as Lee had pointed out, still the President. Until he could regain the powers of the Presidency, he was, for all intents and purposes, nothing more than a private citizen. All of his power, all of his authority, was gone.

I was thinking that I had failed, too, not realizing that the timetable would change as soon as we changed events at Love Field. My one chance to retrieve the Bible from Sarah Hughes had slipped through my fingers. My entire reason for coming to 1963 was moot now, and I was going to be recalled to the year 2000 in—I looked at my watch again—just about 40 minutes.

I thought about what I had done: Kennedy had not gotten into the death car and had avoided assassination in Dealey Plaza. We were temporarily safe in a church in Dallas, with Bobby Kennedy himself sending people to protect us. But the invasion of Cuba was more likely to happen now, not less, and if they did try to kill Kennedy again, I could no longer use the benefit of hindsight to predict where or when.

I had made things worse, not better, for both Kennedy and Lee. Now I was leaving, and leaving them behind. If Lee stayed in Dallas, he might still be arrested, imprisoned, his reputation smeared by powerful unseen forces, maybe even killed in police custody. Kennedy could be killed the next time he was out in public, as I was certain he would be: He believed that presidents had to be among the people, and he was one of the most accessible in the 20th century. I would be safe, when there was no guarantee yet that they would be.

That invasion with Cuba might yet come off. The thought was terrifying. Nuclear war was a very real possibility in 1963; if it did come about, I would die before I was born. So would everything and everyone I had cared for here.

It wasn't right.

I slipped my hand into my bag and fingered the cell phone buried deep under my makeup kit and handkerchief. It had been my safety valve, all along, and my secret. I had always felt a sense of security knowing it was there, and that no matter what my dilemma, I could use it to lift myself out of danger. Now, though, it was beginning to seem more like an excuse.

What more could I do? I asked myself. I had done all I could.

I was so busy ruminating that I hadn't realized the President had leaped to the phone and dialed frantically until I saw Lee starting toward him, saying, "Mr. President?"

Kennedy slammed the receiver down with a crash I thought would be audible to the policemen on the street. "Dammit! Bobby's private line has been disconnected. What the hell is going on?"

He had realized something the rest of us hadn't, something he didn't yet want to believe. He picked up the receiver again slowly, and dialed again, more slowly— obviously trying to remember the number. He waited, then asked in a gruff voice totally unlike his own to speak to Mr. Kennedy.

There was a burst of sound from the receiver. Someone was speaking. Kennedy's face had gone gray again. Dazed, he put down the receiver.

"It's Hoover," he said. "He didn't recognize me, I'm sure of it. He said Bobby wasn't there. He said Bobby… was no longer Attorney General."

I could see the look of grim realization on his face: We were on our own.

Johnson was taking over with a vengeance, and sweeping out anyone who had been loyal to Kennedy. This hadn't happened the first time. Events were changing so quickly I couldn't keep up with them.

The President—I couldn't help it, I still thought of him as the President—was used to thinking quickly and making decisions. "I need to stop that truck," he said. He turned to me. "How big did you say that shipment was?"

I thought quickly, and the details on the bill of lading rose clearly in my mind. "One hundred cases," I said. "Twenty rifles each, I think."

"Two thousand rifles," Lee said. "Enough to supply a small army."

The President was talking to me again. "And you diverted the truck to New Orleans. When will they be there and how long will they stay?"

"They're supposed to get there late Saturday night or early Sunday. I think I got them to wait until at least around seven or eight in the morning."

"So I'd have to get down there in about 30 hours," the President muttered.

Jackie, who had sat down and was sipping coffee quietly, bolted upright. "What? What do you mean, Jack?"

He turned to her, and the gray shock in his face had been replaced, in that split second, by determination and purpose. "Jackie, Lyndon's throwing my whole Administration out. Bobby's gone. I don't know if those federal marshals will even get here; there's no telling when Hoover took over the office, or if Bobby got the order out before he was cut off. We've got to assume the worst. He can't do anything to help us; he has no more power than I do right now."

Jackie shook her head. "What do you mean, you're going to stop the truck?"

The President nodded to Lee. "We're going down there to keep that damned invasion from starting."

We? I looked at him. Did he mean himself and Lee and me? That was crazy; Lee and I were wanted by the police, and Kennedy—we had no way of knowing who was friend and who was foe to him. He was in worse danger than ever: if Lyndon

Johnson even suspected Kennedy was still alive, he would be hunted through the state by people loyal to Johnson, and almost certainly quietly killed. Lee and I couldn't protect him from all those dangers!

"I'm with you, sir," Lee said at once. I stared at him, too. He couldn't mean it. We were going to leave the church, where we were safe, and venture out to meet God knows what perils, just to stop a truck?

Kennedy was already standing, his sense of purpose renewed. "You girls will stay here," he told Jackie and me. "The priests will take care of you."

"What?" I said. Jackie was already nodding obediently, but I was stunned. After I drove the getaway car and risked my life, he was relegating me to the sidelines?

"This is too dangerous for you," said the President, clearly impatient at having to explain something so obvious.

"You're not going without me," I insisted. *Wait, what was I saying?* Five minutes ago, I'd been perfectly satisfied to wait here until the marshals arrived! It was the idea that the President thought he and Lee, simply because they were men, were the only ones fit for battle. The spirit of Sheila was fighting to break through.

The President grimaced. "Miss Cuyler, I can't be worried about your safety."

"Well, I've been worried about yours for most of the day," I answered. "I don't need your protection, Mr. President, but since I'm the only one here with hindsight, you probably need mine."

He glared at me. The idea of being protected by a mere woman did not sit well with a Kennedy.

I turned away from that furious gaze and looked out the window at the alleyway behind the church. A lone police car turned down the alley, edged toward the church parking spaces, and stopped. A lone police officer stepped out.

He looked up at the church building, his face visible to me. I saw the full lips and the ruffle of dark hair. Tippit again. What was he doing here? This was the third time in five days that I'd seen him in connection with the assassination. It couldn't be a coincidence, could it?

"Dallas's finest are outside," I reported. The President came swiftly to the window and looked down. Tippit looked toward the Cadillac. I felt a shiver of uneasiness.

Lee came over too, his eyes concerned. "Some of the Dallas cops are on the payroll," he said. "I'm not sure which ones are clean and which aren't."

"Then we need to get out of here fast," the President said. He turned to Jackie swiftly.

"You'll be the decoy. It'll give us a chance to slip out."

Jackie got unsteadily to her feet, her eyes fixed on her husband. "I'll do whatever you say, Jack."

"Good. Here's what we're going to do." He outlined his idea rapidly.

Lee and Jackie listened intently, while I stood several feet apart from them, wondering if I'd lost my mind in proposing to join them on this lunatic mission. *I should go home*, part of my mind argued. *This wasn't my problem.* I'd tried to help and bungled it, true, but that didn't mean I had to deliberately throw myself into more danger. Kennedy was intended to die today; what I'd done had at least given him a few more hours of life, and wasn't that important?

You didn't do that, the other side of my mind said silently but unflinchingly. Lee did it. Lee put himself into terrible danger for the President. He put himself in danger to save you the other night, too. You're abandoning him along with the President.

What I was contemplating was no less than physically throwing away the cell phone. It was the only way to divorce myself from the automatic extraction sequence and continue my odyssey in 1963. But if I were really thinking of letting the cell phone go—and that would be crazy!—how would I ever return to the year 2000?

Maybe you're not meant to, the voice inside me said again. Destiny counts for something; maybe this is yours.

I thought of John and of my attraction to him, of George, waiting eagerly for the Bible, and of my empty life there. I looked at the three people in front of me. Two had been dead for decades and one for six years, but here they were young and alive, and their lives had value and meaning. I could still help, if I were willing to get involved.

In my entire life, I had never been as involved as I could be now. It was my choice alone. All the adventure and danger I'd ever craved were right here waiting for me.

The President had finished his instructions to Lee and Jackie. They were both standing, waiting for me. "So you're going with us?" the President asked, somewhat doubtfully. He was glowing with life, and with purpose. His energy and charisma were palpable even across the room.

I looked at him, and at Lee. I knew they didn't stand a prayer of surviving without me. With me, we might have enough of an edge to escape disaster.

And if I were honest with myself, I knew I would never again have the chance to live an adventure as big as this one. I had dreamed of adventure all my life. Was I only to be an armchair adventurer? Or did I have it when it counted?

I would never find out unless I took the chance.

It was my choice.

I looked at the President again, took out the cell phone, and threw it in the trash can, under a pile of the priest's papers.

"Yes, Mr. President," I said, blindly committing myself to whatever came next, which I'd never done in my life before. "Let's get going."

* * *

Don Cuyler, looking tired and irritable, was knocking back a double whiskey alone in the Cuyler living room when George rang his doorbell. George said hello and waited until Don waved him to a seat before perching on the couch and taking out his notebook and fountain pen.

"Mr. Cuyler, the FBI has been assigned jurisdiction over this case. Of course, it's related to the President's kidnapping, and kidnapping is a federal offense, so we'll be handling it instead of the Dallas police."

"The police have already been here. They asked tons of questions."

"I'm sorry to ask you to go over it again," George said pleasantly, but his meaning was clear: Don would repeat the details for George's benefit whether he wanted to or not. Don scowled at him, then stared into his glass.

George paused for a moment, to bring down the levels of hostility, then began his questioning. "I understand the suspect, Lee Oswald, stole your car this afternoon?"

"That's right. A black Cadillac." Don rattled off the license number, which George noted.

"What was he doing here?"

"I've asked my wife that. Seems he came here with a girl we had staying with us for a few days."

George had a sinking feeling in his chest. "You don't mean Catherine Roberts?"

Don nodded without looking at him and drank deeply. He had been seriously rattled, George noted. Don's hands were trembling faintly, and his mouth was tight. Despite his suspicions about ISI and his burgeoning certainty that Don Cuyler knew much more than he was letting on, George almost felt sorry for the guy.

Lee Oswald and Catherine Roberts. When she'd seen Oswald in the coffee shop yesterday, the sight of him seemed to alarm her. And now here they both are, in the home of a guy whose company is almost certainly the Dallas link in the gunrunning part of Operation Mongoose. The ties and interconnections in all this were beginning to make George a little nauseous.

He willed himself to focus on the interrogation. "Tell me about what happened."

Don nodded, but he needed another stiff jolt before he could begin to speak. When he did, his voice was low and uncertain. "I came home around—what was it?—around 1:15. I'd heard on the radio that the President had been kidnapped at Love Field and nobody knew anything, but people were crying and panicking, and I figured I wouldn't get anything more done at the office, so I drove back here. As I was coming in the front door, I heard the back door slam. The house was a mess—chairs thrown over, newspaper all over—and my wife was lying on the floor." He stopped and swallowed painfully. "We just found out Monday she's going to have a baby."

George's insides curdled. "Are you saying Oswald—?"

"I think he—he kicked her in the stomach. The vicious little bastard. She was crying and holding her stomach. There's a mark on her face, too. That Roberts girl slapped her when they asked for her car keys and she said her car was in the shop."

George steadied his hand so he could continue to take notes, trying to stay calm. Kicking a pregnant woman in the stomach—there wasn't a punishment bad enough for a man who did that. Yet he would have sworn Oswald was as mild and passive as they came. His gut instinct was usually right. Occasionally, he was beginning to realize, it could be wrong, too.

"Did you go after them?"

Don shook his head. "My wife was moaning on the floor. I ran to take care of her. I heard the car back out, but I had no chance of catching up with them. And even if I did, Oswald had a gun, right? What chance would I have against a guy who'd just kidnapped and killed the President?"

George nodded. "You did right to go to your wife. Is she feeling better?"

"She's lying down. I don't want to take any chances. I'll probably have the doctor look at her, too."

George flipped his notebook closed. "Mind if I look around, see the damage?"

"Help yourself." Don sat down heavily in front of the whiskey bottle and poured another shot. George gave him a worried look and went through to the foyer.

Cuyler hadn't exaggerated; the place was wrecked. While the living room looked untouched, the dining room and kitchen were chaotic. Chairs had been overturned, a couple smashed completely, dishes shattered on the floor, newspapers tossed around. The silverware drawers of the kitchen had been pulled out, sugar and flour were dumped out on the linoleum, the table knocked over. The five delicate china cups in the sink—a different pattern than the smashed china—appeared to be the only things of value left whole. Obviously the vandal hadn't noticed them.

While he was contemplating the mess in front of him, there was a soft footfall behind him. He turned around. A young woman in a crisp skirt and pink blouse nodded shyly at him. George found himself wishing he could shield her from the sight of her ruined kitchen. Instead, he took out his leather billfold and held it toward her, feeling apologetic. "Special Agent George Staub, ma'am," he said. "FBI."

She nodded without looking at the billfold. He put it in his pocket, unable to look away from the nasty bruise on her left cheekbone. She had tried to cover it with makeup, but it drew his eye and his sympathy.

"Your husband's been telling me what happened here," he said quietly. "I won't need to ask you many questions."

She nodded again, tremulously. She seemed frightened, but that was a normal reaction. Most people didn't realize that FBI agents could be gentle and coaxing in getting information, and George was an expert.

He was about to direct her into the living room when Don Cuyler appeared. For a man who'd been drinking heavily, he must be naturally graceful, because George hadn't heard a sound until he came into the kitchen. "Now, Sandy," he said reprovingly, "I thought we agreed you were to stay upstairs."

She looked appealingly at George, then at her husband. "But—he might have questions I could answer."

"Of course, but your health comes first, and the health of our baby. I'm sure Agent Staub understands that." Cuyler had his arm around her and was guiding her toward the stairs before George could protest.

Over his shoulder, he threw back, "Whatever she can answer for you, I'll answer. If you need to talk to her later, you can come back when she's rested. Agreed?"

"Certainly," George said politely, but observations were crystallizing in his mind as he stood there. If Sandra had plainly told them her car wasn't there, why would Oswald and the Roberts girl, however vicious and frustrated they were, have taken the time to beat her up and destroy two rooms in the house, when they needed to get away quickly? They should simply have gotten out and looked for other means. Something didn't ring true here.

When Cuyler finally came downstairs, he apologized. "Sandy doesn't know when to stop. If she feels someone needs help, no matter how ill she is, she gets right up and goes."

"Is she often ill?" George asked politely, more to hear Cuyler's answer than because he believed it was true.

"Oh, not often. But she does all her own housework—she's so particular— and since we run the rooming house, she's always washing and ironing or scrubbing floors. It wears her out."

George had noticed Cuyler's expensive suit, and he knew that his title at ISI was Executive Vice-President. He wondered why a man of such obvious means lived in Oak Cliff, of all neighborhoods, and why his wife didn't have at least a part-time maid to help her.

The truth was, he didn't want to ask Cuyler any more questions, but he had a number of questions for his pretty wife. However, to appease the man, he would go through the motions. They sat down again in the living room, and George took out his notebook and fountain pen.

"How well did you know Catherine Roberts?"

"Not very well." Cuyler's voice was shaky and thickening from the liquor. "She was only here a few days. She was referred by friends of ours. That's why I took her in."

"Do these friends know her better than you do?"

"They've been on vacation, Mr. Staub. I haven't been able to reach them to check her out. She seemed okay when she showed up here, nicely dressed, well spoken."

"And you gave her a job at ISI as well, even though you'd never seen her before?"Cuyler shrugged, his eyes wide and innocent. "It's our busy season. We needed a temporary telephone operator, and like I said, she seemed okay."

George checked his notes. "The day she started working at your company, she signed out a 1962 Thunderbird to a guy who was killed in that car that night. The car was heavily loaded with military weapons."

Cuyler shook his head. "This is all news to me."

"You don't know anything about how those weapons got there?"

Cuyler looked at him, bewildered. "Why the hell should I? My company imports and exports liquor, not stolen guns. I don't know why that girl was trying to use our company for her shady connections."

"You think she's shady, then?"

"What else could she be? Do you know at six this morning, I got a call to open up the office and warehouse, so your guys could search it? Of course they didn't find anything. I run a respectable business. What was that all about?"

"I wouldn't know. It wasn't my call," George said smoothly. He hesitated. "If she had been using your company for some shady purpose, she would have had to move awfully fast."

Don looked at him. "What do you mean?" he asked, though George could swear he knew what he was about to say.

"I mean," George explained, "that you offered her the job out of the blue—right?—and yet all of a sudden, the next day she's able to engineer a shipment of military weapons in one of your cars." He deliberately snapped his notebook shut and put away the pen. "Oh, and Mr. Cuyler?"

"What?"

"How did you know those weapons were stolen?"

"Pardon?"

"I didn't say they were stolen." George looked at him steadily.

Don gave him a look through narrowed eyes. "You must have mentioned it."

George knew he had not, but he pretended to accept the explanation and shrugged. "Maybe. It's been a long day. Thanks for your time, Mr. Cuyler."

"What about my car? You think there's a chance I'll get it back?"

George shrugged. "They're on the run. Maybe they'll steal another one along the way and abandon yours. We're doing all we can. This case is the Bureau's top priority."

"I'm glad to hear it. I hope when you get hold of that little creep that you fry him. I'd volunteer to throw the switch myself."

George smiled. "You and everybody in Texas. But that's not my job. Right now I'm tracking down those weapons you so rightfully noted were stolen. Thanks again." He saw Cuyler flinch. *Good, he thought. I haven't liked you from Day One, and I like you less now. But I do feel much more… informed.*

Feeling well satisfied, George strolled out and headed for his car.

He drove purposefully away from the block, turned right, and continued driving half a mile down, then made another right. Slowly and deliberately, he drove around again to the other side of Rosebud Lane and parked a block from the Cuyler house in the opposite direction from the way he'd left, behind a Volkswagen bus. Then he took up his notebook, lit a cigarette, and waited.

It didn't take long. Twenty minutes later, a sleek red Pontiac drove up to the curb in front of the Cuyler house. The horn blared. In a minute, Cuyler came through his front door. The haggard, jittery demeanor of a tense, frightened and tipsy man was completely gone from his face, and the sickly pallor George had seen only a half hour ago had been replaced by a glow of health and sobriety. He looked calm, confident and in control. *It had all been an act,* George realized in a flash of clarity, and then he was angry: He had actually, for a moment, felt *sorry* for the son of a bitch!

With Cuyler were two burly men with dark hair and olive skin. George broke into a cold sweat—the two men had obviously been in the house while George conducted his interview with Cuyler. Cubans, yet!

When everyone had climbed in, the car pulled out smoothly and drove at a moderate pace down the street. Five minutes later by his watch, George crossed Rosebud Lane and tapped on the front door once, then twice.

Three minutes later, Sandra opened the door. Her eyes were wary as she recognized George. The bruise on her face looked livid on her creamy skin. "My husband just left," she murmured in barely audible tones.

"Yes, ma'am," George began softly, trying hard to make her feel comfortable. "Actually, I had a couple of questions for you. Perhaps you'd have a few minutes for me?"

"No, really," she began, "if my husband comes back soon—"

"Will he be back soon?"

"I don't know. I don't think so. He didn't really tell me."

She was still tense, gripping the front door tightly. George managed a chuckle, trying to relax her. "I know. I'm always forgetting to tell my wife when I'm going to be home. Drives her crazy." He smiled engagingly at her. He had no wife.

Sandra smiled back shyly, though she didn't open the door any wider. She seemed willing to talk with him, though, so he continued to press. "Your husband was very helpful. He seems awfully worried about you. He tells me you're expecting a baby. Your first?" She nodded, but he got the feeling the question made her nervous. So he switched subjects.

"I hope you weren't too frightened today having to deal with Lee Harvey Oswald. Mr. Cuyler tells me he was pretty brutal to you."

She looked down. There was just the faintest tremor of her head that George finally decided was a negative shake. "He didn't frighten me," she said in a low voice.

"Oh, I must be mistaken. Was it Miss Roberts who frightened you?"

"No!" Sandra cried, and he was stunned by her sudden vehemence. "No, I liked her! She never tried to frighten me. She was... kind... " Sandra began to cry in earnest, holding the door and leaning her head against it.

George felt genuinely sorry for her. He hunted for a handkerchief in his pocket and held it out to her. "Here. You should sit down and have something to drink." He remembered then that she was pregnant and amended, "Well, a glass of iced tea or something. I'm sorry I've upset you."

She pressed her face to the handkerchief and cried harder.

"Look," George coaxed her. "I can fix you some coffee or tea, if you'll let me in. And we can have a chat, just the two of us. No one will know. I get the feeling there's something you want to tell me. Is there?"

A tiny nod from Sandra, her face still hidden.

"Well, let me in, then. Come on. I'll help you clean up a little, too. You shouldn't be lifting anything heavy."

He almost had to shoulder his way past the door, but eventually he was with her inside her domain, the ruined kitchen. George immediately set about righting the table and chairs and picking up the shattered dishes. She showed him the garbage can, and he carefully dropped the shards and larger pieces into it. Without asking him, Sandra put the kettle on the stove.

When he had cleaned up as much as he could, Sandra began to bustle around, getting cups and saucers from a cupboard next to the sink. He noticed she was using a china set with pretty blue flowers on it, but nowhere near as striking as the dainty rose-patterned cups in her sink. Though he would have sworn she wanted to tell him something, there was silence except for the kettle as it began to boil on the stove.

On the pretense of helping her clear the table, George came up to the sink and pretended he was just noticing the cups there. "Very pretty," he remarked. "Your wedding china?"

Sandra nodded. Five cups, he noted again, with matching saucers. Sandra was carefully hand-washing them. He stood idly by and watched her, saying nothing. When she turned to throw a glance at him, he smiled easily at her. "You must have had special visitors, to bring those out. My wife is so particular about her wedding china, we never even use it when my parents visit. Only when hers do."

It was a lame little joke and he hadn't expected a laugh from her, but Sandra's eyes suddenly became bright and tense, and she nearly dropped the saucer she was washing. He caught it just in time, and reaching for a dry towel, wiped it off himself. As she washed the other cups and saucers, he wiped them carefully, finally setting all five cups and saucers on the clean counter.

Sandra didn't speak for several minutes. Finally, she said, "I had some neighborhood girls in today."

"And you used your best china? Girls you see all the time? I'm sorry, but I find that hard to believe. And five cups—did you give coffee to Catherine Roberts and Lee Oswald, Mrs. Cuyler?"

George waited. There was an endless silence. He probed harder. "She didn't hit you, did she?"

She shook her head, her eyes bleak and beginning to swim with tears again. "She was so sweet. She helped me carry the laundry up, and... she made me laugh... She was sure my baby would be a girl. I liked her."

George put three of the teacups into the hutch. "Lee Oswald, Catherine Roberts and yourself." He held up the last two cups. "Who else was here, Mrs. Cuyler?"

Sandra shook her head before him. "Cady said they could die if I told."

George thought 'they' meant Cady and Lee Oswald. "They could die if you don't tell me. You're the only one who can help her. Right now, everyone thinks Oswald is a murderer, and if she's with him, she's an accomplice. Is she? Who else was here?" She was still shaking her head. "Please, Mrs. Cuyler!"

Sandra's eyes filled with tears, but finally, she said tremulously, "Jackie was here, and the President."

George bit his lip in exasperation. Just when he'd thought he was getting somewhere! "Mrs. Cuyler, I know you've had a rough day, but really—"

Sandra wasn't listening to him. She went to turn off the heat under the kettle.

There was silence between them for a moment.

George heard the TV from the living room, but the broadcaster's voice was no longer flat and dreary; now it was charged with excitement. "... inside the St. Jude Catholic Church in downtown Dallas. I repeat, Mrs. Jacqueline Kennedy has been found alive and well at the St. Jude Catholic Church..."

George stood frozen to the spot.

Sandra turned to him, a Cheshire-cat smile illuminating her face. "I told you. They were here, and then they took Don's car. They must have gone to the church. They were both alive, even after the news people started saying they'd been killed... they came here while I was listening to the news, and Cady and Lee Oswald were taking care of them... they only left when my husband came home. And now I'm afraid..."

George didn't listen to any more. He ran to the television console in the living room. Network coverage showed live pictures of a rundown church, and of Jacqueline Kennedy, her eyes blank with shock, behind a Spanish priest who himself was waving away frantic questions from reporters. There were ten Dallas police officers battling to keep hundreds of onlookers back. Damn if that guy Tippit wasn't one of them, in there like the rest, pushing and shouting furiously, "Get back, get back!"

"Oh, my God!" He turned to Sandra. "Forgive me, Mrs. Cuyler. You told the truth, and I didn't believe you."

He was already thinking about how quickly he could get back to the office.

Traffic would be murder, and he had to reach J. Edgar Hoover privately before the Director left his office in Washington.

As he went out the door, she was saying defiantly, "I'm glad they took Don's car. They can keep it. I just hope they're safe…"

George hardly heard her as he hurtled down the front steps.

* * *

George made the four-mile drive in six and half minutes, his mind working furiously. Cady Roberts and Lee Oswald hadn't killed the President at Love Field *because they weren't there to assassinate or kidnap him.*

They were there to rescue him!

Cady Roberts had taken matters into her own hands. If this was true, it meant Don Cuyler had lied about Cady's involvement, and that could only have been to cover up his own. It also made Don Cuyler a very dangerous man with very dangerous friends, including those two Cuban thugs who'd driven off with him this afternoon.

It was the gunrunners who had planned to kill Kennedy.

He wasn't sure why at the moment, but he would find out. As soon as he finished talking with Hoover, he would get a warrant, go to ISI and search every inch of it. The answers were there. They had always been there, and he probably could have made some arrests by now, if he'd put the pieces together quicker and not concentrated so hard on Catherine Roberts, the girl from nowhere. It was his fault, because her background was so mysterious he naturally thought she had to be sinister.

Right now, it made no difference

Knowing his career and the President's life were on the line, George ran every red light and stop sign between the Cuyler house and the FBI office. He had one urgent thought as he ran up the steps to his office:

How could he prove it to J. Edgar Hoover?

* * *

Thirty-five minutes later, Air Force One landed at Andrews Air Force Base in Camp Springs, Maryland.

It was very dark when President Johnson, wearing his reading glasses and holding a typewritten paper, finally stepped to the microphones in a circle of bright artificial lights. Behind him, a dozen men scrambled to remove the heavy casket from the back of the airplane. While some reporters were focused on Johnson, many more were watching with troubled eyes as the men, sweating in the cool November air, grunted and pushed the casket into the ambulance that had drawn up close to the plane.

All eyes were on Johnson when he began to read in a stilted and wooden monotone: "This is a sad time for all people," he began. "We have suffered a loss that cannot be weighed. For me it is a deep personal tragedy. I know the world shares the sorrow that the Kennedy family bears. The Attorney General has asked for indefinite leave from his position to take care of his extended family, and in light of my sympathy for his situation, I have granted his request. Right now, his personal obligations, especially to the President's children, are of paramount importance. I will do my best to carry on

President's Kennedy's policies and programs. That is all I can do. I ask for your help, and God's."

He put the paper down and paused for a moment. When he spoke next, his voice had the steely ring of anger. Unlike his attempt at grief, it sounded genuine. "Those responsible are accountable for their actions. The guilty will be brought to justice. No effort will be spared to track them down, and when they are found, they will pay the ultimate price."

Johnson stepped away from the press pit without taking questions, as had been pre-arranged; nevertheless, the din was unbelievable: a hundred reporters shouted questions simultaneously, each of them drowned out by the others. A few somber handshakes and good wishes from members of Congress lined his approach to the H-21 helicopter destined for the White House. He would work through the night in the offices there.

As Johnson was thinking that he had acquitted himself well in front of the cameras and could begin to relax, J. Edgar Hoover stopped him, thirty feet from the helicopter. The Director's eyes had a malicious glitter in them.

"Mrs. Kennedy's been found alive," he said quietly. LBJ leaned lower, pulling the diminutive Hoover closer, to keep their conversation private. "In a church in Dallas. She's at Parkland Hospital now, getting treatment for shock."

"I know that," Johnson said irritably. "It was announced on board before we landed. You came out here personally to tell me that?"

"No," said Hoover smoothly. "I came out here to tell you that one of my men in Dallas has developed alarming information. It appears he has a very credible witness who says that President Kennedy is still alive."

"That's not possible!" Johnson's mind was racing, and he was starting to feel clammy and sick. A live Jack Kennedy was his worst nightmare. "You've got to shut up that witness! And get that agent out of there before he makes a real mess, shooting his mouth off!"

"I agree. The last thing we need is a constitutional crisis. I've recalled him to Washington for a personal briefing. He'll be here tomorrow afternoon."

"What about the witness?"

Hoover had hoped Johnson wouldn't ask about that. He fidgeted slightly as he answered, "He will of course turn over all that information to me as soon as we sit down tomorrow."

Johnson's eyes had a ferocity now that they had not had in front of the television cameras, and his mouth was drawn into a terrifying leer. He wanted to shake Hoover until the man's bureaucratic brain rattled in his skull, to scream at him: *Fix it, fix it, whatever it took!*

But his own Secret Service contingent was already surrounding him. Too many curious ears were close at hand. He dared not say anything explicit that could be overheard and, God forbid, repeated.

He merely gave Hoover a glare that made the tough old Director wary. "Get that information, Edgar," he said in low tones, and for the first time in his long relationship with Hoover, his voice was steely. "Get it and then find a way to bury it. If it turns out to be true, both our heads will roll."

Hoover, who was for once truly shaken, nodded quickly and stood frozen, watching as Johnson bent his long frame to climb into the helicopter and whirled away into the cold November night.

* * *

George, watching the black and white television set in the FBI office in Dallas along with every other agent and staff member, was still shocked himself. He had seen Hoover's unmistakable countenance at Andrews Air Force Base, had seen him apart from everyone else, talking softly to Johnson, though it was impossible for the camera to pick up his words.

Hoover's brusque order to be in Washington on Saturday to report to him directly, made George uneasy. Agents who reported directly to Hoover most often found themselves packing for a transfer to a highly undesirable new location. George wasn't anxious to be one of them.

He'd thrown himself into his office, kicked the door shut and dialed Washington frantically, and though it had taken 10 minutes to get to the Director personally, he hadn't recovered his breath or his composure by the time Hoover, highly displeased, had come on the line. George had blurted out everything he knew, from the gunrunning at ISI to his encounters with the mysterious Catherine Roberts to his latest discussions with both Don and Sandra Cuyler. Hoover had listened silently, and when George had finally gasped out the stunning news that Kennedy was almost certainly still alive, he had said nothing for a full minute.

George dragged air into his lungs and promised himself grimly that he would cut down on the cigarettes; they were shortening his wind. In his mind he reviewed a series of questions he was certain the Director would ask. The longer the silence, the longer, George figured, would be the list once the Director began to ask.

But Hoover surprised him. He said abruptly, "Agent Staub, I want you to meet with me in Washington tomorrow. If you take a flight in the morning, you can be here at the Bureau by 1:00."

"Yes, sir." George didn't know why he was beginning to feel apprehensive.

"And, Agent Staub, there's no need to brief anyone else. You and I have talked; that's enough. I'd like your word that you'll entrust this to me alone."

"Yes, sir." To say otherwise would be to invite instant dismissal and disgrace. This had to mean they weren't going to announce it. Why? *National security*, George decided. *Too dicey.*

"Good. Now, this witness of yours, the one who can positively put the President in her home after the plane exploded—her name again?"

George hesitated. "I'd rather not say, sir," he said finally.

There was a silence and an intake of breath on the other end of the phone. "I beg your pardon?"

George should have felt perfectly safe divulging Sandra's name to Hoover. But somehow he couldn't bring himself to do it. There was something about that frail, vulnerable girl that he wanted to protect. She had been viciously beaten, and George was sure it had been at the hands of her chameleon-like husband, not Lee Oswald. George felt a firm, if inexplicable, conviction that her name must remain his secret.

Now, watching Johnson's speech and seeing him huddle with Hoover, he was glad he'd stuck to his guns. He was afraid of what might happen to her if Hoover knew her name.

This thought in itself, the mind of an FBI special agent, was the rankest heresy. Reverence for the Director was a given among agents, even those who had been severely disciplined by him. But George was back to trusting his gut instinct. It was screaming at him now to keep his own counsel. Until someone gave him a good reason otherwise, he intended to obey his gut.

What disturbed him most in the television coverage was Johnson's brief mention of the Attorney General. Asking for a leave of absence, no matter how grave the circumstances, didn't seem to fit with what George knew of the Attorney General, a dedicated public servant in all seasons. George wondered if Bobby Kennedy really had asked for a leave of absence. What it meant in his eyes was that Kennedy, this morning the second most powerful man in the government, was now suddenly impotent. He wondered if the dark suspicions rising in his mind rose from the same gut instinct that told him Catherine Roberts was on the side of right.

He decided to go with his gut. He would go to Washington and answer Hoover's questions candidly. He, George, was tired and punchy from the non-stop activity of the day, and from his fiercely suppressed inner guilt that had he taken Catherine Roberts seriously on Thursday and persisted with the Secret Service, none of this might have happened.

He got up and made his way to his message box.

The fourth message almost made his heart stop.

Scrawled indifferently on a pink slip was "Catherine Roberts—Phoned, 4 p.m. Left no number. Will call back."

Will call back. George felt as though he'd been thrown a lifeline.

* * *

Night was closing in fast by the time the road sign came into sight, at the top of a gentle hill.

"San Antonio, 60 miles," Lee read aloud. "Houston, 140 miles. Where are we?"

I shook my head. I'd gone around Dallas in wide circles, trying to avoid roadblocks while still managing to turn south. I knew I had driven at least 50 miles west, past Fort Worth, before turning onto a small offshoot that I thought would take us in the right direction. Given the dangers, I thought it was wiser to keep meandering on small two-lane roads rather than risk a straight highway that would end in confrontation with the police, since they would probably kill Lee on sight. Even worse, the gas tank indicator on the Cadillac was well below empty. I was driving on fumes.

We had tried to stop, an hour ago, at a gas station. There were no cars around, and I thought I could try to call George. Maybe he could help us. In any case, he was the only law-enforcement agent I knew who might believe me, given what I'd told him yesterday.

But George wasn't in, and a curious gas-station attendant in starched white cap and clean white shirt was peering in the windows of the car. The President was lying in the back seat, covered by a coat, hat pulled over his face, but I wasn't taking any chances.

I'd taken off hurriedly, to avoid his questions. The tank had been over three-quarters empty at that point. Lee had said nothing; we both knew I couldn't risk the gas jockey seeing anything while he pumped gas and washed the windshield.

Now Lee glanced uneasily over his shoulder at the seat. The President, lying under Don's coat, hadn't stirred for some time. I hoped he was napping. With a sinking heart, I remembered that Kennedy was a man who lived with a bad back and a variety of illnesses. I wondered if he needed daily medication. If he did, and if he wasn't carrying it with him, we were in worse trouble than I thought.

It had seemed so simple at the church. Jackie, an actress I could take lessons from, had followed her husband's instructions perfectly: she had wandered, with a blank, staring face, into the sacristy as people were praying. It had taken only seconds before someone looked up, saw her and shouted, "Mrs. Kennedy!"

In a moment, she was surrounded by sobbing women and men whose eyes were suspiciously wet and who had trouble speaking. Miles Everett, the robust man who had sworn allegiance to the President in the priest's office, had appeared out of nowhere, thrown himself in front of her, clenched his fists and shouted to everyone to back away.

They did. In less than three minutes, though, the Dallas police poured into the church, to form a flying wedge around her. She was hidden from view, protected, and soothed. She was an extraordinary magnet for attention. It was precisely what the President had counted on.

Jackie played her part perfectly. When people asked her questions, she pretended not to understand. She was a woman who had just lived through a terrible ordeal and had somehow inexplicably survived. She answered nothing, and smiled vacantly at everyone. Sympathy showered down on her.

More surprising than the First Lady's acting ability was the scene I had inadvertently witnessed, just before she left the President to go downstairs.

Lee and I had left them alone to start struggling back into our disguises. I finished first and brought the President's coat and hat across the hall, tapping lightly at the door before opening it.

The First Couple hadn't heard me.

When I opened the door, they were facing each other, one of the President's hands clutched in both of Jackie's, her face turned up to his. He was talking softly to her, and she was nodding, heedless of the tears flowing out of her widened eyes. "You will be careful?" she whispered.

He smiled down at her.

Jackie dropped his hand and flung her arms around him, kissing him desperately, holding him very close.

The President kissed her mouth and the tears on her face, then gently loosened her grip and said quietly, "Take care of the children."

She nodded solemnly, her eyes never leaving his face, the tears still streaming.

In her face was the clear conviction that she would never see him alive again.

I closed the door hastily, embarrassed to have intruded, but fascinated at the depth of feeling between them. There was no mistaking her passion and fear for him. And though he might not reciprocate the passion, there could also be no doubting his very real concern for her.

Now Jackie was behind us in Dallas, the subject of countless news reports and speculations, which we'd listened to on the car radio for hours, and night was settling in fast.

Fortunately, the farm seemed quiet. No movements or lights in the house, no car or truck outside. There were several buildings behind. At least one, I thought, might contain something to eat and a place to rest. I weighed the options for a minute.

"Stay with the President," I said abruptly to Lee. "I'll scout around."

I walked toward the house. No lights flashed on suddenly, no alarms rang; for the first time since this morning, I could feel my taut nerves relaxing. The calm, measured quiet of the farm was a welcome antidote to the hours of driving, hot sun and the gritty feeling behind my eyelids. The air was cool and fresh. A rainfall was coming, maybe tomorrow.

I scanned the buildings behind the house. There was a barn, big and old and with what looked like rotted beams in the roof. There were smaller buildings, which I guessed were equipment storage spaces, and a pair of slatted doors set into a flat field ten yards away. Looking at them, I thought wildly of Uncle Henry's hurricane cellar in The *Wizard of Oz.*

Lee had come up behind me and was staring at the slatted doors. "Perfect," he said.

"What?"

"Cady, that's a bomb shelter!" He started to run toward it. "If we can open it, it'll have food, water, radio... everything we need!"

Twenty minutes later, we were ensconced underground in a cramped concrete room with thick walls and pillars, lit by a bare bulb overhead. Metal shelves and cabinets were bolted into two walls; four Army cots lined the others. To the side was another small concrete room with an old-fashioned claw-foot tub, toilet, sink and mirror. In the main room, we had what we needed: a cook stove with bottled gas. Folding chairs around a table. Blankets. Flashlights with boxes of fresh batteries, lanterns, candles and matches. A couple of transistor radios and a small television set. Bottled water and a well-stocked pantry. A first-aid kit and a few bottles of over-the-counter drugs. A month's supply of Lone Star beer as well as cartons of Coke.

"They sure are prepared," Lee said, eying a gas mask tossed in a corner.

The President looked at it too, and his mouth constricted. "I hope they never need it," he said quietly.

I raided the pantry, and within minutes, I'd opened boxes of pretzels, a tin of crackers, a jar of peanut butter, and a glass of strawberry jam. There were plenty of canned goods, but I wasn't sure I could manage the cook stove, so I opted for a cold meal. Kennedy made no complaint, but Lee whispered to me furiously that I couldn't serve peanut-butter sandwiches—on crackers, yet!—to the President of the United States!

I ignored him. I was hungry. Peanut butter and jam on crackers wasn't exactly gourmet food, but it would fill the hole in my stomach. Lee helped himself to the same. I noticed the President ate not only the peanut-butter cracker sandwiches, but also handfuls of peanuts and pretzels. When Lee poured water from a big bottle on the floor, splashing it into clean tin cups, the President drank several cups in a row.

Except for our brief, desperate meeting in the hotel last night, I'd had no chance to really study him. Now I peeked over between bites. His face, which I'd noticed the night before was unusually full and bronzed, was much paler now. He seemed very tired and kept putting down the crackers every few minutes and closing his eyes before opening them again with a jerk, as if he'd just remembered he was alone with two strangers and wanted to make a good impression.

Lee sat up straight at the table, his eyes darting to the President as often as mine did. Whenever the President looked his way, he smiled. When the President asked for more water, he hurried to pour more. It was obviously a thrill for him to be with an idol.

We were all silent for a while. This was the ultimate case of strange bedfellows: none of us belonged in the others' world. Our lives and experiences had all been so different. Now that we were temporarily safe, whatever would we talk about?

Perhaps it would be better not to talk.

My eye fell on the small radio on the shelf. At least we could listen to the news. I got up and turned it on.

All the news was about the President. There was more background information on crazed Communist Lee Harvey Oswald, his time in the Soviet Union, the street fight he got into in New Orleans last summer, his violent tendencies from childhood on. Lee scowled as he listened.

The President's eyes narrowed. Lee saw it. "It was my cover," he said defensively.

"So who are you really?" There was just the faintest skepticism in the President's voice.

Lee straightened proudly. "I'm a double agent," he said. "I've been working with a Dallas FBI agent whose specialty is ultra-right-wing groups. The FBI sent me to New Orleans this summer to penetrate one of them and send back information on their plans. The group—mostly CIA guys—started talking about killing you in August."

"And you didn't tell anyone then?"

Lee shook his head. "I'm lucky I kept my mouth shut. Turns out they did that to rout out the traitors in the group. One guy who did report the plot—he ended up in federal prison. He may do 10 years there."

The President looked him up and down. "You're awfully young," he said.

"I'm experienced," Lee insisted. "ONI sent me as a fake defector to the Soviet Union when I was just twenty. I lived there for almost two years."

"Alone?" Now there was a tinge of reluctant admiration in the Chief Executive's voice.

"I got married in Russia," Lee said. "And we had a baby. I brought them both back with me."

The President raised his eyebrows. "That's not easy," he said.

"I managed it. They gave me more assignments when I got back. I always worked other jobs, too, as cover. Right now I'm a stock boy at the Texas School Book

Depository. And I did warn the FBI about you, two weeks ago," Lee said, somewhat defensively. "I left a note at their office."

That must have been the famous note, I remembered, that had been destroyed on the orders of the Special Agent in Charge after the assassination. No one was ever sure what had been in the note Lee left at the FBI. If it was a warning about the assassination and it had been ignored, no wonder the Special Agent in Charge had ordered it destroyed!

The President was eyeing Lee frankly. "So you're supporting a wife and a baby doing odd jobs?"

"Two babies," Lee said proudly. "We had a second daughter last month."

I noticed suddenly that the radio station had taken a commercial break. A Salem cigarette commercial came on. The President began to sing along with it. He had a scratchy baritone that was so off-key it was painful.

When he broke off, I pretended to wince. "Don't quit your day job, Mr.President," I said, but I was smiling.

The President grinned back. Then his eyes narrowed. "You don't have to sing to be President. And I'm pretty good at giving speeches."

"In English, yes. In other languages…" I shook my head. I was getting a kick out of razzing him.

He bristled. "The Germans thought I did pretty well with 'Ich bin ein Berliner'."

"That's what I mean. It was a great speech, but your German was wrong."

"Impossible," he said dismissively. "It came from our State Department. I practiced it for a week."

"Then your State Department ought to be ashamed. You were supposed to say, 'The proudest boast of a free man today is… I am a Berliner.' Right? Do you know what you actually said?" It had been in one of George's books.

The President looked at me warily. "What?"

"You said, 'The proudest boast of a free man today is… I'm a little doughnut.'"

Lee snorted. In a moment, he had dissolved in laughter. Another minute and the tears were pouring down his face. He was gasping. He had to hold his stomach.

The President looked annoyed. "It's not that funny," he said.

Lee was now doubled over. His face was flushed, and his eyes were shining joyously.

I started to snicker myself. It *was* that funny.

The President looked at Lee. "I suppose you could do better?"

I managed, with difficulty, to halt my own laughter. Lee was too far gone to answer. "Remember, Lee's lived in the Soviet Union," I said. "He's fluent in Russian."

Lee finally brought himself under control, though his eyes were still dancing with glee. "I also speak some Spanish," he said to the President. "A buddy of mine in the Marines taught me."

"Can you sail a boat? Can you play golf?" the President challenged him.

Lee came right back at him. "Can you plot the flight path for a U-2 on a radar scope?"

I laughed at both of them. "Stop it, both of you!" I couldn't believe the President of the United States was trying to compete with a poor, much younger man whose range had always been limited by lack of education and lack of money.

Presidents, I supposed, were human too.

The President himself was the one who changed the subject. Looking at me quizzically, he said, "I'd really like to know about the year 2000—if you were telling me the truth last night, Miss Cuyler."

"I was telling the truth," I answered. "Life in the future is nothing like 1963."

"Well, what's it like? Flying cars and daily trips to the moon?"

I began with all the technology they could never have dreamed of. Desktop computers in millions of homes. Laptops that could be carried like briefcases. The miracle of the Internet.

I explained about the infinite information available at the touch of a button; that there was nothing you couldn't read about, research, or buy. Lee liked the idea of online discount bookstores like Amazon, while the President, hearing about auction sites like Ebay, said wryly he was glad his wife couldn't use them yet.

I told them about other household conveniences: cell phones, microwave ovens, ATM machines, fax machines, compact discs.

Both of them were fascinated at the idea of owning movies they could play at home. The President, of course, had the White House theater, but even he couldn't switch from one part of the film to another without a projectionist.

"Just imagine *Casablanca,*" he marveled. "You could touch a button and watch the flashback to Paris, and then move ahead and see the ending."

Amazing; if I didn't know better, I would swear it sounded like Jack Kennedy had a romantic side. But of course the books assured me his attitude toward women was casual, brisk and roughly akin to an invading army. Maybe he just liked Ingrid Bergman. Or Bogie.

"I'd want James Bond," Lee announced. "I liked *Dr. No.*"

"There are over a dozen James Bond films now," I told him. "And five different actors have played James Bond."

"There'll never be one better than Sean Connery," Lee said positively. He turned to the President. "*From Russia with Love* would make a great movie."

"It's one of my favorite novels," the President answered.

I started to say they *had made From Russia with Love*, but they weren't paying attention to me. Clearly, it was a male bonding moment.

I was struck by how much these two men had in common: Despite their social, economic and age differences, they were both readers and thinkers, more introverted than extroverted, deeply involved in politics and current events, both unhappily married but devoted fathers, both with older brothers they'd looked up to and a strong-willed, controlling parent, Kennedy's father and Lee's mother. They'd both grown up in dysfunctional families and struggled to make their own way, the President by his World War II service, Lee by joining the Marines and then going off to the Soviet Union. They might never be golfing buddies, but they were, I thought, surprisingly congenial.

"But why is it so important to the people in the year 2000 to rescue a one-term President from forty years ago?" the President asked. "What's happened in the world?"

Oh, God. How could I tell them?

But I had to, so I told them everything. Vietnam. Kent State. Attica. Student protests. Unending violence. They both began to look shocked and sick. When I got to 1968, I said, "In April Martin Luther King is assassinated in Memphis."

Both of them were stunned. "God!" Lee breathed. "King—what's happened to this country?"

JFK's mind was back on the Presidential race. "Wasn't there anyone who could stop this violence?"

"The country was torn apart. It was hard for any one man to hold people's attention. But for a while, somebody did."

"Who?"

I had come to the part I dreaded. "He ran for President in 1968. Started late but picked up momentum. And finally, he began to leave everyone behind."

They listened, saying nothing.

I looked back into the horror of that time, and went on, a little unsteadily.

"Then came the California primary. He won. Everybody knew he'd win the White House. The Republicans couldn't put up anyone who could beat him.

"And that night, he appeared before his supporters in a hotel ballroom in Los Angeles. He thanked everyone and said, 'And now it's on to Chicago, and let's win there.' Then he and his wife were taken out through the kitchen. He started to shake hands with the kitchen staff—and a man leaped out and shot him."

"Who was he?" Lee asked urgently. "What was his name?"

I looked directly at the President. "He was a Senator from New York. A Senator named... Robert Francis Kennedy."

JFK's eyes went wide in shock. "Bobby? They killed Bobby?" He had gone very pale. His mouth had opened. He shook his head. "Why? God, why?"

It took him some time to recover from that, though I tried to remind him that since all had not gone according to plan in Dealey Plaza today, there was still a chance to avert these catastrophes. The President was plainly shaken, and when he roused himself from his gloom, he asked another question. "What about Jackie? My children?"

Another tragedy. How could I tell him?

He was looking at me, though, and I knew I had to. I braced myself and said, "Your wife remarried in 1968. After Bobby's death."

"Who?"

I took a deep breath. "Aristotle Onassis."

The President all but soared out of his chair. "Onassis? That old Greek pirate! She married *him?*"

"She was terrified. First you and then Bobby... She was afraid someone would try to kill your children, and she wanted to get out of America. And he did protect her. But he died only a few years later."

"Thank God," the President said frankly. "Did she marry again, after that?"

"No. She became a book editor and lived in New York until she died, in 1994. Hodgkin's disease."

He digested this. Lee was sitting very still, his troubled eyes fastened on the President. Then Kennedy said quietly, "I hope she didn't suffer."

"She died at home. It's what she wanted. She was 64."

"That's not old," the President murmured. Then his face brightened. "What about my children?"

"Well," I said carefully, "Caroline graduated from law school and then started writing books. She got married and had three children, including a son she calls Jack."

Kennedy's tender gaze into the distance seemed to take in the little girl he knew and the grown-up woman he had never known. "My girl," he said softly. Then he focused on me again, his smile expectant. "And John?"

Oh, God.

"He went to law school too," I said, hoping somehow to stretch out the story and postpone the inevitable. "He worked for the District Attorney's office in Manhattan, but then decided to start his own political magazine, called George, after George Washington. He was the editor."

The President still looked expectant. He knew I hadn't finished.

He had just weathered the death of one son, only three months ago. How could I hurt him like this? But his eyes were waiting for me to go on.

Finally, I did. "He married a beautiful blonde girl named Carolyn and took up flying. Eventually, he bought his own plane."

The President's eyes were intent on me. He knew I was saying all this for a reason.

I forced myself to go on. "In July of 1999, he and his wife and her sister were flying from New York to Hyannisport. His cousin—one of Bobby's daughters; I forget which—was getting married. They flew up on a Friday night, and it was foggy. He didn't have an instrument rating… " I stopped. My throat had tightened.

The President's voice had become dangerously quiet. He swallowed convulsively. "Go on, Miss Cuyler." I looked at him appealingly, but he was implacable. "What happened?"

I swallowed hard. "The plane—disappeared from the radar scopes and crashed into the ocean." The President's face had gone white. I hurried to finish. "Everyone on board was killed. I'm so sorry, Mr. President."

The President put his head in his hands. Lee and I looked at each other. Neither of us knew what to do.

There was a long silence.

The President, head still down, reached into his pocket and came up with a handkerchief. He blew his nose and blinked several times. When he raised his head, his eyes were wet but steady.

I had no idea what to say.

He didn't want pity; that was clear. He wanted information. Abruptly, he asked, "What about Teddy? Did he ever run?"

"Once," I said, trying to sound matter of fact. "It didn't go very well."

"Why not?" asked the President, puzzled.

I wasn't going to tell him about Chappaquiddick; I'd told him enough about his family's tragedies.

Instead, I tried to tell them the happier things: Neil Armstrong's walk on the moon in July 1969, effectively ending the space race with the Soviet Union ("We *won!*" the President said jubilantly, "we won!"), the Woodstock rock festival in upstate New

York, the 1969 New York Mets' miracle World Series win. ("The Mets?" the President repeated in disbelief. "The *Mets?*") The destruction of the Berlin Wall in 1989. The end of Communism almost worldwide.

"Cuba?" the President said when I finished. "What happened to Cuba?"

I hesitated. "It's not very important anymore. Its economy is ruined. It's still Communist, one of the few countries left that still is."

The President was shocked. "Cuba's still communist? After 37 years? Who's running the damn country, anyway?"

" Fidel Castro," I said quietly. "A few years ago, Castro came to New York for a meeting at the United Nations. When they saw him in the streets, New Yorkers... they cheered."

Lee's face had gone gray. "It's not possible," he murmured. "How could they forget?"

JFK had closed his eyes. He pressed his fingers against his temples. "This is a nightmare. What did we accomplish, anyway? What good was any of it, if this is the outcome?"

I glanced into the future that was so real to me, and that was becoming more and more real to them, every second. "*That's* why you still matter, Mr. President. For a lot of us, what went wrong with America started when you died."

The President sighed. "This isn't the future I wanted for this country."

"I know," I said steadily. "A lot of people believed that with you in the White House, we would have a better future."

The President looked at me. "If I have anything to say about, we will," he said abruptly.

He rose slowly and walked toward the bathroom.

I saw that his face looked ashen, and beads of sweat ringed his forehead. When I walked over to look closer, he shut the door in my face.

He just needs a good night's rest, I told myself. God knows, we all did.

Saving Kennedy was critical. I would do everything I could to make that happen. I prayed that tomorrow would be better.

Stan's candy-apple red Pontiac Star Chief was parked at the front doors of ISI. Anyone passing by would have seen lights in the reception area, even this late on Friday night.

Don and Stan sat there, getting quietly drunk together on a bottle of the best Scotch from the warehouse. Things had turned out differently than they had expected, but all in all, it was a day to celebrate.

The President was dead. Even better, he was dead in an ambush that idiot Oswald had pulled off on his own, in front of hundreds of people, branding himself as the country's greatest enemy with no help from the original plan. He'd done it all by himself! *I couldn't have planned it better, Don told himself. It was beautiful.*

Of course, there were still a few minor issues. Oswald was still alive and on the loose. That hadn't been part of the plan.

The package of phony passports and Secret Service ID's that Jack Ruby had sworn he'd delivered on Thursday, as promised, had never arrived. The son of a bitch had even lied and said he'd given them to Hilda, who'd been sharply questioned, and for once was thoroughly cowed. She swore tearfully she had never seen them. They believed her. Not that they needed them now, but if Ruby for some reason really had delivered them, and they'd gone astray, Don didn't want to try to explain them away in another interview with that jerk from the FBI.

Debbie was dead. She'd been the woman originally identified as Jacqueline Kennedy at Redbird Airport; an understandable mistake, since she was about the same height and weight and even styled her hair like the First Lady.

He didn't waste time thinking about her. She'd been an enthusiastic and inventive bedmate, but he had other concerns now. God forbid Oswald should be captured alive. They had to send someone after him. But where the hell was he now?

"Great stuff," Stan said, pulling hard at the Scotch.

Don said nothing, but while he wouldn't admit it to Stan, tension was coiling tightly in him.

It *was that Roberts girl*, he told himself spitefully. When she'd turned up out of the blue on Sunday night, she'd looked so appealing, so fresh. She'd reminded him of someone, though he couldn't think of whom. He'd even toyed with the idea of trying her out as a replacement for Debbie in his bed. But the couple of times he'd made a move, she'd reacted with such revulsion that it had actually unnerved him.

Yet she had to know something, or be working for somebody. How else to explain what happened today? Damn Stan, too! As soon as she had warned Don about the dangers he was in—that was a laugh!—he'd sent Stan to kill her. Stan had reported that he had killed her. *How the hell had she escaped?*

He reached for the telephone and dialed swiftly. "Get me Jack." He paused. The familiar hoarse voice came on the line. Don spoke crisply. "Find Oswald and get rid of him."

Another pause. Stan leaned over and poured himself another shot of whiskey.

"How the hell do I know?" Don said irritably into the phone. "He's on the road somewhere with that girl. Get on the road yourself and keep your radio on."

He slammed down his whiskey glass. The little whiskey left in the bottom sloshed out. "You really think she's still with him?" Stan asked, his voice slurring.

There was grumbling at the other end of the phone, and a phrase that sounded like 'wild goose chase'.

"Get out there!" Don said sharply. "And be ready to take your shot when you get it. Call me from the road."

He slammed down the phone and reached for the whiskey bottle. A headache was beginning to pound behind his eyes. But damn it, now was the time for action, not self-pity. He would salvage this if he had to do it all himself!

The phone rang unexpectedly in the still room. They both started.

Don waved a hand at it. "You pick up. Tell him for me, no excuses. Get going tonight."

Stan lazily reached for the phone. "Yeah? Oh? Oh." His voice changed. "You better take this one. It's Tippit."

Don picked up the receiver. "Yeah?"

Tippit's deep voice in its soft southern tones came back at him. "Just thought you oughtta know… I talked to a woman out at that church, St. Jude's, where Mrs. Kennedy turned up. She does secretarial work for the priests."

"And?" Would this jerk never get to the point?

"And—she says Mrs. Kennedy wasn't alone. She was with Oswald and some girl, and also—" He stopped.

"Jesus, just spit it out!" Don snapped. "Who?"

"And the President himself. Kennedy. This secretary says *both* Kennedys were alive as late as 1:30 today."

Don's heart actually stopped beating for a minute. He worked his mouth but couldn't get any sound to come out.

"What do you want me to do?" Tippit asked.

Don couldn't think. Stan looked over at him curiously. He saw the shock in Don's face and started to get up. "You okay, chief?"

Don shook him off and tried to regroup. *Think! Make a decision!* He took a deep breath, then said to Tippit, "Stay there. Do your job. You hear anything, you let me know." He paused. The pounding in his chest was lessening; a few more deep breaths and he would be all right.

"Okay." Tippit paused. "You think Johnson's really President, if Kennedy's still alive?"

"How the hell should I know?" Don snapped. "Just go do your job."

He hung up. Stan was staring at him. In a few words, he told Stan what Tippit had relayed to him.

"Christ Almighty!" Stan said, thunderstruck. "How much more could go wrong today?"

Don was inclined to agree with him. "We'll leave at daybreak. Might as well get some sleep. There might even be more to go on by then. We'll take your car."

"My car!" Stan said, a little stung.

"We sure as hell can't take mine. They stole it, remember?"

* * *

When I glanced at the bathroom door at midnight, the light was still on underneath. Something was wrong.

I tapped gently on the door. "Mr. President? Are you all right?"

He called back, "Come in."

I did. He was lying on the concrete floor, the blankets scattered around him. His tie was off, his shirt badly crumpled. His mouth was drawn in a tight line, but when he saw me he tried to smile. "Couldn't sleep," he said.

I looked at him. "Does your back hurt? Do you need medication?" If he did, I had no idea what to do.

He shook his head and said lightly, "I always have trouble sleeping when I'm kidnapped." He pointed to the toilet. "Please, pull up a chair."

I knew he was lying. That white, pinched look around his mouth told me he was hurting. But if he wouldn't talk about it, what could I do?

I sat down casually, as though I conversed every day with a fully-clothed President lying on a floor in the bathroom of a bomb shelter. But I couldn't think of a thing to say. I didn't know why he'd asked me in.

"You risked your life for me today. I should thank you." He managed a smile, while I stared at his face, which was now pasty. "You two were right and I was wrong. I'm sorry you're in danger because of me."

I was a little taken aback, both by his soft tone and by his perception. I could see why people found him charismatic. When he decided to turn on the charm, you didn't stand a chance.

"Never mind," I said. "You're still our best hope. We've got to get you back to Washington safely."

He smiled again, but I could see it was an effort; instead of the famous toothy Kennedy grin, this was just a quick grimace. Whatever was wrong was getting worse.

I couldn't think about that now. I just couldn't focus on one more problem tonight. I was too tired myself.

I had no idea what to say, so I took the tie he'd discarded and smoothed it down, to keep it from wrinkling.

It was soaked with sweat. So was the expensive pinstriped shirt.

"Miss Cuyler?" he said abruptly, as though to distract me from his clothes. "How did you get into this mess, from the safe confines of the year 2000? I mean, why did you agree to do it?"

I thought about it. "I guess—because I idealized my father all my life, and kept doing it even when I got here, until I couldn't kid myself anymore." I told him rapidly how John had lassoed me into the project, holding out the carrot of changing my mother's life. "Now, though," I concluded, "I'm trying to see people for what they are, not what I want them to be. I think that's really the lesson I've learned here."

He nodded. "I'm an idealist too." He saw the skepticism on my face. "It's true. But unlike you, I have no illusions. I'd like to believe the best about people, but long hard experience tells me not to."

I remembered some of my reading, and said, "But you believe what your father told you. 'It doesn't matter what you are, it matters what people *think* you are.' Right?"

He hesitated. "Without his help, I never would have been President. But I don't believe everything he says."

"You believe that, don't you?" Idealizing him would be dangerous, I knew. I needed to see him as he was, not the glamorized version that had been fed to the press. Saving his life and his presidency didn't mean falling for his image. That would be just as dangerous as the lies I'd believed all my life about Don Cuyler.

"I do believe one thing he taught me," the President answered. "He said if you want something badly enough and you're willing to pay the price, you can have it. You just better be damn sure you don't regret it later."

"What price did you pay?" I couldn't imagine it. He had millions of dollars, a loyal bevy of friends, hundreds of willing women and a luxurious lifestyle. His health problems and his infant son's death would have happened regardless of his presidency. What could he possibly have given up?

He said nothing for a moment, looking past me to something only he could see, and it must have been something happy: his eyes, which had been gray, turned a vivid blue, the blue of the ocean under a summer sun. "What do the books say about me?" he asked in turn. "That I'm—what?—a spoiled rich kid who got everything in life easy, including the presidency?"

"And lied about your health problems and cheated on your wife and valued image over character. Yeah, that's pretty much it."

He jerked his head up, and there was a flare of anger in his eyes. "Then they hate me."

"No," I said reluctantly. "The truth is, they love you. They remember the—the hope you gave people, and that seems to outweigh everything. You're one of the best-loved Presidents we've ever had."

"Because I was shot down in the street."

I couldn't answer that.

Suddenly, he began to speak, not looking at me. "In the summer of 1953, Jackie was planning our wedding. We were getting married in September. I went off for a last bachelor trip on the Riviera. Everything was closing in on me—my father's expectations, Jackie's—I knew she was the right wife, the suitable one, but I just—I didn't really want to get married. I knew it would be a huge step toward the presidency, and it was necessary, but— "

I waited, and after a moment, he went on. "I met a Swedish girl in the south of France. She was just 21, and she'd been hitchhiking with her friend that afternoon. A friend of mine picked them up and when he saw me a little later, he invited me to dinner with them. I took one look at her, and—I'd have done anything to be there."

I was riveted. The man talking was looking back at something very precious to him— his eyes were liquid, his face serious.

"We talked half the night, and danced, and sat at the top of a cliff, looking at the ocean. God, she was wonderful, sweet and warm and *real*. I've never been so drawn to anyone. I told her I was getting married. I didn't have to, but I wanted to be honest with her. She sent me away. So I went home and married Jackie, in the wedding of the year." He smiled, bemused.

"So you met a girl for one night that you didn't sleep with—right?" He nodded. "This was your big sacrifice?"

His glance at me wasn't friendly. After a moment, he went on. "I couldn't stop thinking about her. I wrote her letters and called her from my office in the Senate. I was planning to go back and see her the following summer—but I needed surgery, and it took a long time to recover." This was the back surgery, if I remembered correctly, where he'd almost died. Yet his feelings for this girl, after spending just one platonic night with her, had survived not only a year-long separation, but all the harsh realities of his health and his new marriage?

He paused. I was fascinated. "Don't stop. Go *on*."

He laughed a little and did. "I did go to Sweden the following year, and we spent a week together. I met her family and friends and we drove around, seeing all the castles and historic sites and going to the beaches." His eyes were far away again. "That week with her, and those three days I spent in Ireland last summer, were the best moments of my life."

I was still trying to recover from my surprise that Jack Kennedy, the cool, unflappable, womanizing skeptic, had a romantic side after all. No wonder he liked *Casablanca*. "But you were still married to Jackie."

He hesitated. "Yes. But I thought of her constantly. We wrote each other, and I called. I was going to come back the following summer. I even wanted her to come here, so I could see her more often."

"Here—to America?"

He nodded. "Then I found out Jackie was pregnant. And I was being pushed for the Vice-Presidential spot with Stevenson in '56. Everything was happening so fast…"

"What happened?"

He shrugged, but the mantle of unconcern was visibly false. "She wanted a full life with a man who would marry her. She wanted children. I couldn't blame her. She said goodbye."

"Do you still think about her?" I knew the answer, but I wanted him to say it, if he could.

He glanced at me, and his eyes were once more gray, and, I thought, a little bleak. "I try not to," he said quietly.

In those four words, he'd said everything.

"Jackie loves you," I said helplessly. "I know—I mean, I'm sure she does."

He nodded. "I know," he said. "She's tried very hard with me. I don't make it easy for her. It's not her fault I felt so—trapped—in the beginning. And since Patrick died, well… it seems like we're a lot better together. I wouldn't leave her now."

"But you'd give her all kinds of reasons to leave you," I guessed. "All the women, all the partying—it's so blatant and so humiliating. You're giving her lots of excuses."

He gave me another Kennedy grin, as though saying silently that I had guessed right. Then I realized something. "All those women—it's not really about sex, is it? It's because you felt trapped. It was sort of a—a way to break out. Between your father and your wife, you couldn't live the life you would have chosen, so you found a way to break out."

He grimaced. "I hate all that couch stuff. Don't analyze me."

I stood up and looked down at him for a minute. "I'm sorry," I said at length.

"Don't feel sorry for me," he said sharply. "I have something few men ever get, the chance to really move this country onto a new course and affect our history. It's extraordinary. And besides, I have my children. They're worth everything."

Somewhat subdued now, I asked if I could get him anything. When he shook his head no, I said good night.

As I closed the door quietly behind me, I wished he hadn't told me that story. He was a man who wanted no pity for himself, and the truth was, I pitied him from the bottom of my heart.

* * *

George had spent the evening in the FBI office, going through volumes of notes and files. He had been right: the gunrunning *did* involve ISI and *did* tie in with the kidnapping of JFK and Mrs. Kennedy.

He had told no one except Hoover that President Kennedy was still alive.

Tomorrow afternoon he would tell Hoover about the entire operation—the pipeline through Dallas and New Orleans to Miami, the military bases being stolen blind, the works—and ask for coordinated help from the other Bureau offices in shutting it all down in one massive operation. It was like those creatures with several heads: you had to cut them all off at once, or the one you cut off would grow back, and the creature would stay strong.

At the same time, George felt uneasy that there had been no announcement that JFK was alive. Why had nothing come from the White House? Why were they not scouring the country for him?

He'd hoped to hear from Cady Roberts and had sat by his phone waiting, but she hadn't called. Right now his sympathies were wholly with Oswald and Cady Roberts—given the other players, they were the good guys. He had already asked to bring in Don Cuyler for further questioning, but Gordon, the Special Agent in Charge, had shrugged him off. "The investigation into the President's death is more important; concentrate on that," George was told.

The more time that passed without an official announcement from the White House that JFK was alive, the more uneasy George became. He finally admitted to himself, as he crumpled up the empty cigarette package and tossed it at the garbage can, that he was worried about the information he'd dug out of Sandra Cuyler. What would Hoover do with it? That was why he'd refused to give her name. He didn't want her intimidated into changing her story; she would be vitally important later on, as a witness, if Oswald was captured alive and went to trial.

Where was President Kennedy right now? Was he still alive? Did the Attorney General know? Did he know his brother had escaped the fire at Redbird Airport? And if he didn't know, shouldn't someone tell him?

He would sleep on it. He still planned to show up in Washington tomorrow afternoon.

If he didn't show up at all, he knew he faced dismissal, and George loved being an FBI agent as he'd never loved anything else.

But if he woke up in the morning and there had still been no announcement that President Kennedy was still alive, or if Cady Roberts called in the meantime, he would know what to do.

* * *

I couldn't get to sleep. My mind wouldn't quiet down. I hadn't seen this much death and destruction in my life, and I knew I was personally responsible for some of it. I twisted and turned, unable to get comfortable on the hard cot.

"Cady?" Lee came hesitantly into the room.

I gave up trying to sleep and sat up, brushing at my hair. My watch read 2:30.

"I checked around outside. Everything's quiet," he said. "How's the President?"

"Asleep. It's been a long day for all of us."

Lee clicked on the small radio, but when we heard the staccato voice of a newscaster, he twisted the dial. "I'm sick of the news," he said unexpectedly. He kept turning the dial until, to my surprise, a moment later he found a station playing soft orchestral music. "That's nicer," he said.

It was dance music, lush and romantic. Songs that had been sung by Sinatra, Tony Martin, and Frankie Laine were now arranged solely for instruments, with the accent on syrupy strings. We sat listening in silence, but it was a comfortable silence. For the first time all day I could feel my nerves relaxing.

It felt wonderful. Even if our shelter was temporary, it was shelter for tonight.

I got up and faced him.

"I never thanked you," I said, "for saving my life. Wednesday night, when we met— Stan would have hit me with that car for sure, if not for you."

He just smiled a little and said nothing.

"And at Love Field today—it was you who saved the President, not me. I was trying to get the attention of the Secret Service, but as soon as the guy saw I didn't have a gun, he didn't listen to a word I said. You were the one who took action."

He was quiet for a minute. Then he said, "I thought about what you said last night. They told me something... very different. They said I'd be... a hero. Then you told me they were setting me up. I didn't want to believe it. But I thought about this summer in New Orleans, all the things I did... it would be so easy to make people believe I was a Communist."

It was my turn to be quiet and let him work things out for himself.

"You don't know these people. Anyone they want to get rid of, they kill or ruin... they get away with everything... you saved me too, Cady. If they did set me up... no one would ever believe I was innocent. They'd make sure of it." He sat quietly for a moment, then added, "They told me I'd have a big role in getting rid of Castro, but I had to be at work on Friday... I'd have been the patsy when they killed Kennedy... poor crazy Lee Oswald, killing the President because he was a Communist..."

His face was so sad.

I looked at him searchingly. I hadn't noticed before how thick his dark eyelashes were, or how soft his brown hair looked. He wasn't blindingly charismatic like the President. He was just a good man doing his best in a very dangerous world. I admired him for it.

In his own quiet way, I realized, Lee Oswald was a very appealing guy.

Wait, what was I thinking?

Why did I suddenly want to be closer to him? Why did I wonder what it would be like to stroke his hand, lying on the table? Why did I hope he wanted to be closer to me too?

He looked up and caught me staring at him.

He started to smile, then stopped. He gazed at me, and I could feel the glow all the way to the pit of my stomach. His eyes were the deepest blue I'd ever seen, and they were smiling at me. What he saw, he clearly liked very much.

In this little oasis of calm, among all the flight and fear of the day... something wonderful was happening.

We stared at each other, unable to move, unable to speak. I wondered if I dared reach for his hand.

Then the music changed. I heard the soft string introduction to Henry Mancini's *"Moon River"*.

Without breaking his gaze, Lee reached out his hand to me. His warm skin made electric contact with my fingers. I couldn't believe how marvelous his hand felt. "Let's dance," he said.

We came together in the middle of the floor, and Lee brought me close to him, very gently. I leaned my head against his shoulder, and we picked up the waltz rhythm of the song and began to move together, slowly and sensually.

I felt happier than I'd felt in years. I felt like I was floating.

Then I realized with surprise that I *was* floating. Lee was a marvelous dancer. It wasn't just the joy of feeling him close to me, moving to the music: he had grace and strength in his slender body, and he knew how to signal his every move to me.

He was signaling all kinds of things to me…

I looked up at him. His eyes were very close to mine. His lips were even closer.

I don't know who moved first. Suddenly, we were kissing deeply, our bodies fused together, arms wrapped around each other, the soft music still enveloping us. He was as hungry as I was, and I couldn't get enough of him. When he drew his lips away from my mouth and kissed my neck and my jaw and then my collarbone, the fire inside me rose hotter.

The music ended, and we were still kissing fiercely. My hands roamed over his soft hair, over his face and arms and neck. His skin felt so warm and smooth and strong under my fingers.

Then a sound intruded, a sound outside the reality of the two of us.

It was… snoring. The President was snoring.

I suddenly remembered where I was, and why.

I also remembered, belatedly, that Lee was married. That his marriage was unhappy and probably destined to end was beside the point. For right now, at least, this was not in the realm of possibility.

With difficulty, I pushed myself away. Lee continued to kiss my throat, my chin, my cheek. I shook my head and pushed back my disarranged hair. With one hand, I held him away from me. "No, Lee. You're married, remember? We can't do this."

We were both panting, our eyes glazed, the rise of passion still so close to the surface. It was a few minutes before our breathing slowed down to normal. He said nothing, made no protest. He made no attempt to touch me. A moment later, he stepped back and headed for the other cot in the room, where he lay down. The sudden emptiness between us, when there had been so much joy and promise, made me feel so bleak.

I couldn't let him think I was rejecting him.

I went over to him, and put a hand lightly on his shoulder. He turned to look at me, the blue eyes sweetly hopeful.

"It's the wrong time, that's all," I said, as steadily as I could. "There'll be another time for us." I stroked his cheek for a moment, as his face grew brighter.

He reached his arms up to me. I leaned down to kiss him. His arms tightened around me. The throbbing deep within me had begun again.It took everything I had to break away.

Chapter Fourteen
SATURDAY, NOVEMBER 23, 1963

My watch read 7:55. With all our troubles and the distraction of having Lee nearby, I'd hardly slept. I woke feeling weary and hoped Bobby Kennedy would somehow rescue us today.

Lee was already sitting at the table. He looked as though he'd been awake for hours. When he saw me raise my head, he smiled at me. I could feel the glow from last night still between us. I smiled back. I wanted desperately to go to him for a kiss but held back.

"Is the President awake?"

Lee shook his head. I went to the bathroom door and tapped on it. "Mr. President?" There was no answer, but I thought I heard a faint groan inside. I tapped again. "Mr. President? Are you all right?"

Still no answer. Lee looked at me, tapped again and gently opened the door.

The President lay stretched out on the floor, eyes closed, his face the color of milk. He was moving convulsively from side to side, his forehead and shirt soaked in sweat. His hands trembled, and he was shivering.

I remembered my reading about President Kennedy's health problems: in addition to allergies, ulcers, asthma and debilitating back pain…

"He's got the flu or something," Lee said, frowning.

"He's got Addison's disease," I said in despair. Addison's was a failing of the adrenal glands, which made patients vulnerable to every kind of infection. Without proper care and medication, the President might die right here.

Oh, God.

I had forgotten that he depended on a plethora of daily medications. I had not asked about it, except briefly last night, and he had deflected the question so deftly and changed the subject so neatly that I had forgotten it.

Lee looked at me worriedly. "We have to get him to a hospital."

"No hospital," came a rasp from the floor. "No hospital." The body on the floor began to move, haltingly. The President tried valiantly to sit up, his mouth clamped tight with the effort. But soon he slid back to the floor and lay there, moaning.

He looked terrible.

The glowing, handsome, vigorous President of yesterday had given way to a haggard, shivering mess. His skin was clammy. His forehead was burning hot.

"Get me a dry blanket and some cold cloths," I told Lee.

"Where's your medication?" I asked the President, as Lee went out for the supplies.

The President shook his head. "Don't keep it—on me. A staffer always— carries a medical—bag."

I was appalled. "You mean someone else always has it, and they just give it to you?"

He nodded.

"What do you take?"

"Injections—cortisone—pain pills—haven't got any with me." His voice was weaker.

Lee came back with the blanket. Then he soaked the washcloths in the cold tap water. I wrung out and folded the first one and applied it to the President's forehead and sponged off his face, neck, throat and arms. Lee watched, fascinated. "You're an actress?" he said skeptically. "You seem like a nurse."

"Paramedic, actually. I used to play one on TV." Lee gaped at me. I tried to clarify. "Look, I learned a few things that are helpful now. The problem is, I don't have much to make him comfortable."

"Salt and water," from the inert figure on the floor.

I looked at him. "What?"

"My doctors said, in an emergency," he sounded so weak, "salt and water will— help." That's why he'd eaten all those salty snacks last night.

I nodded. "All right. We'll get you something." Lee left to raid the pantry.

The President was breathing hard and trying to sit up. I wrapped the blanket around him, rubbing his arms up and down with my hands to warm him up. He fought his way to a sitting position, one hand on his back, his handsome features twisted in a grimace. "I've got to get that truck stopped," he said quietly, and it was my turn to gape: he sounded more normal than he had since he woke up.

"You have to have your meds. You can't function without them. Lee's right. We have to take you to a hospital."

"And if you do?" He pulled the blanket closer around his shoulders. "You and Lee will be—arrested—who knows whether you'll be—protected? Who knows if they won't just—shoot you down in public and claim self-defense? I can't—let that happen."

Lee came in with boxes of pretzels and a tin cup filled with water. His hands, as he handed the cup carefully to the President, were unsteady. *Why, he's frightened, I thought. Not for himself, but for the President. And the President is frightened for us.*

It was a strange kind of bonding.

The President drank deeply and then began to eat the pretzels. He kept eating and drinking steadily, and in ten or fifteen minutes, color began to come into his face. He still looked nothing like the blindingly handsome statesman of the day before, but at least now he didn't look like he was going to die in the next few minutes.

I still needed to check on the car. "I'll be back," I said.

I came out of the bomb shelter to a cool overcast morning, a battered brown truck parked in the driveway, and flashing red lights down by the road. As I eased closer, crouching as low as possible, I saw that three sheriff's deputies surrounded the black Cadillac.

It was just past 8:00 a.m., and already it wasn't my day.

They'd found the car. They were probably only minutes away from searching the farms in the immediate area. When they did, they'd find us.

I saw no way out.

I returned to the bomb shelter as stealthily as I could. The President had cleaned up a little, with Lee's help, and was sitting at the table, drinking water and munching peanuts. He looked only marginally better. Lee was pouring more water and opening more boxes of snacks.

I gave them the bad news.

The President listened impatiently. He wasn't interested in obstacles: his mind was on the truck he had to intercept. "I need to talk to Bobby," he said. "This time I think we should do things directly."

* * *

I knocked lightly on the kitchen door to the farmhouse with my knuckles, a nervous knot growing in the pit of my stomach. This was the boldest move we'd made yet. I hoped the President's assessment of the situation was accurate.

I heard heavy footsteps, and then the door was opened by a woman in her early '40s wearing well-worn coveralls, rubber boots and a light plaid work shirt.

"Yes?" she said. She was neither friendly nor unfriendly. I was a stranger.

"I'm sorry to bother you, ma'am, but my car broke down..."

"The Cadillac down the road?" she asked, her voice going cold. "The sheriff wants to talk to you."

"Please, could I use your phone first? I have someone with me who's—not well." I wasn't sure how far I could trust her.

An eight-year-old boy with a mop of dirty blond hair called out behind her. "Mama! There's two men outside! And one of them is—"

"Please! It's an emergency," I begged, cutting him off. For the moment, I didn't want anyone to know who was with me.

"We'll let the sheriff decide that." She turned toward the phone on the wall. My hand shot out, forestalling her.

"Mama, look! I told you! It's him! That guy on TV!" the boy shouted. He was behind her, jumping up and down and pointing out the kitchen window.

"Oh, Billy, stop it." But she peered past me out the door. I followed her eyes as Lee stepped around the corner into full view.

"It's him!" she breathed. "That murderer!" She tried to back into the house, but I still had hold of her sleeve. "Billy!" she screamed to her son. "Go get your father! Run!"

Billy, alarmed at the shrill fear in her voice, took off like a cannonball into the house, screaming, "Daddy! Daddy!"

The woman reeled back into her kitchen, trying to slam the door in my face.

Lee's foot stopped her. We stepped into the kitchen together.

"We won't hurt you, ma'am," Lee said softly. He held his hands up, moving slowly, smiling reassuringly at her.

The farmer's wife would not be comforted. She had her eyes locked on the revolver in his waistband. She seized a long kitchen knife from her drain board, holding it in front of her.

"I'll kill you if you come near me!" She backed away, holding the long blade menacingly in front of her, until a voice behind Lee spoke up.

"Perhaps I can explain."

The voice was very distinctive: Eastern, very cultured, very... familiar. She stopped wielding the knife and squinted past Lee to the tall, hunched figure in the doorway, her eyes widening as she recognized him. "But you're dead!" she whispered.

"Someone told you I was dead?" The President feigned surprise. "Must've been a Republican." His face turned serious. "And I do need your help, ma'am. Could we possibly use your phone?"

I'm not sure she heard him. She sank down into a chair, dazed, but thank God, first gingerly set the knife down on the table. The President took that as a yes and went straight to the phone on the kitchen wall.

"Good Lord." Her husband, a husky six-footer in a plaid work shirt and Houston Colt .45's baseball cap, stood in the doorway, a double-barreled shotgun held casually in one hand. "Izzat President Kennedy?"

"Good morning." The President nodded graciously and continued to dial.

"Good Lord," said the husband, clicking the safety on the shotgun, a move that I saw relieved Lee as much as it did me. "They been sayin' you're dead. People been prayin' for you."

"I'm glad of that," the President replied, his ear to the receiver. "If ever I could use prayers, it's—hello, Bobby?"

* * *

Bobby Kennedy sat in his library at Hickory Hills in Virginia, clutching the phone to his ear. He had slept on the couch, the television set on all night, waiting for word. He had heard nothing.

Now it was just after 8:00 on Saturday morning, and Jack was calling again.

He sounded terrible.

"Jack, where are you?"

His brother told him, at a farmhouse south of Dallas. The owners gave him precise directions. Jack relayed them to Bobby. "And I need help, Bobby… " He was trying not to say too much in front of others. "Where's the closest—you know—stash?"

Bobby thought about it. His father, whom everyone still called the Ambassador, dating back to the late 1930's, when he had been Ambassador to the Court of St. James, had worried about his sickly second son. He'd been a monster, had Joe Kennedy, manipulating the stock market to make a fortune in the 1920's, manipulating his proud wife Rose with his insatiable demands for children that led to the births of nine Kennedy sons and daughters, ordering the frontal lobotomy of his retarded daughter Rosemary, flaunting his affairs with Gloria Swanson—and innumerable other beauties—before his family.

But he loved his children.

As terrible a man as he was, he loved them deeply.

He especially loved his sons, and most especially Jack, the frail, sickly one, the one who held his father's presidential dreams after his eldest son, Joe Jr., was killed during World War II. Despite his crushing expectations for Jack, Joe Sr. worried about him constantly. When Jack began using cortisone in the late 1940's to control his Addison's disease, it brought his health closer to normal than it had ever been. Joe knew his son depended completely on those medications and feared that someday he might run out of them unexpectedly while traveling. To counter this possibility, he had secretly stashed medications for Jack in hundreds of bank vaults in cities around the country and kept a meticulous record of where they were.

Those medications had never been needed before. Not once.

Now they were.

Bobby saw no possibility of getting Jack to a local hospital safely, but he could still arrange for them to pick up the meds at a bank. Bobby stretched the phone cord as far as it would go while he searched the drawers of his big corner desk for the loose-leaf notebook in which his father had kept the precious information.

He spotted it at last, brushing aside a crayon drawing done by one of his daughters. He scanned the pages as he talked. "Jack, how close are you to Houston?" He listened. "That's the plan, then. Here's the address." He read it out. "I'll phone ahead and make sure they're ready for you… And Jack, I'm coming down there myself… I'll meet you in Houston." He listened. His features, which had begun to relax, tightened in alarm. "What? No, I haven't talked to Jackie yet… she won't be back here until afternoon… Jack, no!"

But his brother's voice came over the line, trembling with weakness yet firm with resolve. Bobby heard about the truckload of stolen weapons and the planned invasion of Cuba. The grinding fear in his innards, which had eased when he heard his brother's voice again, was back.

He wasn't going to argue. He saw the same necessity Jack saw. He saw the impossibility of reaching anyone in the government to stop it. He also knew that Operation Mongoose had been a Kennedy Administration dirty secret; he had no desire to see it smeared around the halls of the Johnson Administration. He winced. Even the thought of that new Administration sickened him.

The Kennedys had started this thing. They would finish it.

* * *

Two sheriff's deputies were searching the black Cadillac. Another twenty men, in teams of four, were combing the woods along the road and knocking on the doors of the few small farms in the area. The gas gauge on the car read empty, which meant Oswald had probably abandoned it. No one had seen him on the road, so there was no telling when he had parked it here. *Do not attempt to apprehend Oswald*, the dispatcher radioed to the sheriff directing the manhunt in the area. The FBI was sending people from Dallas; they would take over the hunt. The Sheriff's Department was charged simply with keeping the car secure until the FBI arrived.

The sheriff, a maverick, decided he wasn't exactly disobeying orders to send his men to the various farmhouses in the area. He was simply being solicitous and neighborly in inquiring whether they were all right; with a killer loose in the area, it was the only thoughtful thing to do. Should they run into said killer and have to shoot him in self-defense, why, these things happen.

He himself was part of the contingent that knocked on the door of the Jones' farmhouse, a hundred yards down from where the Cadillac was.

A middle-aged woman opened the door. She flinched a little when she saw the group of armed men, but when they nodded courteously to her and tipped their hats, she listened without interrupting.

"'Morning, ma'am. We noticed you have a black Cadillac a little ways down the road."

After a tiny pause, she shook her head. "It's not mine."

"Would you have seen anyone around this morning? A stranger?"

She shook her head again. "Nope. Been gettin' breakfast on. I haven't seen anyone." The savory aroma of eggs and bacon wafted under their noses. She eyed them in a distinctly unfriendly way. "Now, if you don't mind, I got cookin' on the stove."

She closed the door in his face and went back to dishing up the food.

* * *

The eggs were runny, the biscuits were hard, and the bacon was cold.

Typical. George didn't really expect anything better.

He ate the greasy food resignedly, hunched over the counter at the airport luncheonette, his eyes pinned, as were everyone else's, to the little black and white TV the counterman had plugged in behind him. He concentrated to keep from thinking. They would call his flight in five minutes.

A man didn't throw away a promising career in law enforcement to fly off on a wild-goose chase fed by fantasies and silly theories, he told himself. He had reported the explosive information he knew but had still heard nothing on TV or radio to indicate that Hoover had passed it on.

He told himself that didn't necessarily mean anything; Hoover would only have given such explosive information directly to Lyndon Johnson. There had to be a good reason, an innocent reason, for Johnson's keeping it under wraps himself.

George could see only one reason why they had said nothing about Kennedy's still being alive: Johnson intended to keep the presidency, no matter what. The only way to do that was to make sure that JFK remained dead, in the eyes of the public. And that meant, if Kennedy was still alive, that… George's mind refused to accept that eventuality. He wasn't a fool—but the thought of one Commander-in-Chief killing another to seize power in this country made him feel sick. He knew this went on in Europe all the time—but here in America?

George thought again what he had thought last night, that perhaps Bobby Kennedy was being forcibly removed from his job by Lyndon Johnson. Last night he'd dismissed the thought as paranoid. A few minutes into his runny eggs this morning, he wasn't so sure.

He looked up at the TV set again. Chet Huntley and David Brinkley had been on the air continuously for almost 24 hours; their shirts and jackets were wrinkled, the ashtrays in front of them ominously full. They repeated the news that Mrs. Kennedy was leaving Dallas's Parkland Hospital and being flown to Washington today, to be met by her brother-in-law, Robert Kennedy. No one seemed to know what title to give him: Attorney General, former Attorney General. Most settled for just using his name. They also mentioned rumors—they were careful to label them as rumors—that Oswald's fondness for Fidel Castro went beyond admiration for a stranger and that there was a growing possibility that he had in fact visited Mexico City in September, just two months before, with the idea of getting a visa to visit Cuba.

Everyone in the airport luncheonette sat up and listened. Now it was getting serious: Fidel Castro was getting into it. "Somebody oughtta kill that son of a bitch Castro," muttered a guy at the other end of the counter. George looked around. A number of heads were nodding positively, and a couple more guys were mumbling, "Damn right" and similar sentiments.

George looked about him in wonder. He'd told himself he'd call the Attorney General if he heard nothing on the news in the morning, and he'd been stalling. He'd told himself that Bobby Kennedy didn't need him; he had brilliant, capable people around him, people who knew how to get things done. One schlubby agent in Dallas wasn't going to impress him.

"American Airlines Flight #23, to Washington, D.C., first boarding call. That flight is now boarding at gate 8," came the voice over the loudspeaker.

He hesitated. Another thought struck him, a thought that had not occurred to him last night. Hoover wanted him, George, out of Texas. George was to be the scapegoat. The Bureau's failure to identify the conspiracy to kill Kennedy would be blamed on him. His personal failure would be the spark used to ignite a war with Cuba. That thought made him feel sicker, but his gut was now broadcasting to him loud and clear. He dropped a dollar bill on his plate and instead of heading for the departure gate, he went to find a pay phone.

* * *

Bobby Kennedy was a man who had to believe in miracles—the fact that Jack was alive at all, after yesterday, was a miracle—but the stroke of luck that put him on a long-distance telephone line with Special Agent George Staub of the Dallas FBI office had to count as another.

After identifying himself, George told him briefly that he had reason to believe that President Kennedy was still alive, that he had a witness who had seen both Kennedys in her own home shortly after the Redbird explosion, that the Kennedys were both well at that time, and that since he had been investigating these gunrunning episodes from New Orleans to Dallas, he strongly suspected the two events were linked.

Bobby listened silently.

George stumbled a little over his words. He'd expected a reaction: shock, horror, denial, but Kennedy said nothing. George went on, hesitating a little. He'd given this vitally important information to Director Hoover personally last night but had heard nothing, not even rumors about it, afterward. Oswald was an FBI informant. George believed Oswald's actions yesterday were designed to protect President Kennedy, not harm him. It was also likely Oswald was traveling with a girl he himself had interviewed in connection with the gunrunning. He had just picked up a message at his office that that girl had phoned him. He was sure that wherever she was, Oswald and the President were, too.

George stopped speaking.

There was another silence.

Finally, Bobby spoke, his heart thumping so hard that he wondered if the agent could hear it. "What did the Director tell you to do, Agent Staub?"

"Sir, the Director has ordered me to come to Washington today and brief him."

"Does anyone else know about this?"

"No. He asked me not to say anything to anyone."

"Then why did you call me? I'm not in the Justice Department anymore."

"Yes, sir." George hesitated. "I felt—there seemed to be—well, differences between the Director's agenda and—" He didn't want to say 'The Kennedy Administration', but Bobby picked it up anyway. The understatement made him smile.

"Agent Staub, can you go back to your office now without arousing suspicion?"

George hesitated one final time. Over the loudspeaker came the voice. "Last call for American Airlines Flight #23 to Washington, D.C." George shut it out of his mind and committed himself. "Yes, I think so."

"Good. Whom do you trust in that office?"

George thought. He named Terence Miller and one other agent he'd gotten to know.

"Good," Bobby said again. "You get in there and get them, and then you get down to this address with those two guys as fast as you can." He read out an address, which George noted. "The President doesn't—the President isn't feeling well. He and the others are going on to a bank in Houston; you're to escort them there personally. I'll meet them in Houston. It's very important that he reach that bank safely, Agent Staub. I'm counting on you."

"Yes, sir," George answered, knowing his FBI career was finished. "Thank you, sir. I'll be on the road with those guys in less than an hour."

"Do it faster. And, Staub, that's my brother you're protecting. Be careful."

Bobby hung up and feeling relieved, called back the Jones farmhouse. When he reached his brother, he told him the plans had changed: have a good breakfast and stay put. Help was already on the way. He would be safe in the custody of people Bobby trusted within a couple of hours, and then they could all go on to the bank in Houston.

* * *

George was back at the FBI office in 24 minutes. Six minutes later, Terence Miller closed his office door and placed a call.

"Special Agent Miller from the Dallas office calling for the Director. It's an emergency." Terence Miller scrubbed out his cigarette in the ashtray. Hoover came on the line almost instantly.

"Miller?"

"Sir, Special Agent Staub has asked me and Special Agent Gamble to accompany him on an unspecified trip by car. I thought you ought to know."

"I ordered Staub to come to Washington!" There was fury in Hoover's voice.

"He didn't get on the plane, sir. He seems quite adamant that he wants us to go with him, but he won't tell us where or why."

"I'll tell you what he's up to, Agent Miller. He's on someone else's payroll."

"Staub?" Miller sounded startled. "No, sir. He's as straight as they come."

"I get paid to know a lot more than you do, Agent Miller. George Staub is no longer one of us. He hasn't been for a very long time. I had my suspicions; that's why I demoted him and sent him to Dallas, and now I've confirmed them. Staub is not to be trusted."

"Sir, honestly, I don't think that's true. I know Agent Staub."

"I've known better men than him to turn, Agent Miller," Hoover said in commanding tones. "The President has been murdered, and George Staub let his killer get away. He knows who killed President Kennedy *because he's associated with him.*"

Miller's voice weakened. "I—I had no idea, sir."

"None of us did. I can't tell you how I felt when I found out about it. Staub is using you to find Oswald, so he can eliminate Oswald rather than see him captured. That way, his own involvement will remain a secret forever. Stay with him, by all means, but I'm sending some men to follow you. They won't be noticeable. We've got to stop him now. And Miller, remember—" Hoover cleared his throat impressively. "Staub and his people are very dangerous. Protect yourself and your men. Don't hesitate to use deadly force. Shoot first if you have to."

"Yes sir," answered Miller gravely.

* * *

From the sheriff's radio in the dusty road outside Jewett to the sheriff's office in Jewett, to the offices of the Dallas Police and the Dallas FBI, flashed word of the discovery of the black Cadillac registered to Import Spirits International, Inc. The news was received with excitement by the sheriff, with resolve by the Dallas police, with satisfaction by a certain police officer 'on the take' in the department, who relayed it to a nightclub owner he'd long done business with, whose club was conspicuously closed 'out of respect for our beloved late President'. The nightclub owner, phoning in from the road, received the news with grim pleasure and conveyed it to some weary-eyed men in a cinder-block building out by Love Field.

The nightclub owner's own black Cadillac backtracked to a certain highway turnoff, and headed southwest.

A candy-apple-red Pontiac, gleaming in the morning light, loaded up in a matter of minutes. At the wheel was a big, hearty-looking young man in his twenties. Riding shotgun was a hard-eyed man in a wrinkled shirt that had been well starched yesterday. Behind them was a nondescript white van, manned by three heavily muscled Cubans, who smoked and said nothing, but kept pace with the furious speed of the Pontiac.

George Staub, unaware that his own handpicked companions were tracking him and reporting his moves to Hoover, turned south in the station wagon he'd signed out at FBI headquarters. He turned onto the same highway as the nightclub owner's black Cadillac and the red Pontiac. All knew the destination, though two of the three had no idea there were others on the trail. It would be a matter of sheer luck as to which one would arrive first.

* * *

George had wheeled the car to the entrance of the Jones farm, double-checking the address against the paper in his hand. Down the road, a pair of grim-looking sheriff's deputies still guarded the abandoned black Cadillac. George flipped open his pad and checked the license plate against the plate number Don Cuyler had given him last night: they matched. He had expected it. Obviously, they'd dumped the car here and backtracked to spend the night on the farm.

He got out to confer with the two deputies guarding the car, as Terence Miller and Nolan Gamble, a special agent who'd been in the Dallas FBI office a little over a year, conversed uneasily. "He doesn't seem to me like he's turned, Terence," Gamble said. "He seems the same as ever, even if he hasn't talked much."

Terence nodded, watching George through the windshield. "I know. But Hoover was absolutely sure."

"The old man's been wrong before," Gamble ventured after a silence.

Terence sighed. "I like George," he said. Slowly, he drew out his service revolver and deliberately and carefully checked the chambers.

George returned to the car and slid under the wheel. "They'll back us up. We're going in. There shouldn't be any problems."

"You're right, George," Terence said tightly, the barrel of his gun pointed straight at him. In an instant, Gamble was out the passenger side door and around the car, to hem George in on the other side.

George stopped dead and put his hands on the steering wheel, where both agents could see them. "You called Hoover, you son of a bitch. I thought I could trust you." Terence's finger tightened on the trigger. "You don't want to do that," George said quietly.

"You're right about that, too. Now we're going in to get Oswald, and unlike you,

I want him alive. This arrest is gonna be strictly legal. If he resists, well, we'll have to shoot, but not until then. We've got orders direct from Hoover."

George faced him down, his eyes like splinters of ice. "I've got my orders, too, and not from Hoover."

"That's what he said," Terence said, nodding. "He said you were in this with Oswald—that's why you were so hot to come out here and kill him, so no one would ever know... Jesus, George, how could you do it?"

George turned his head very slowly, so he didn't scare Terence into any sudden moves, and stared at his erstwhile friend. "Don't be an idiot. I'm not involved in any plot and I'm not on anyone's payroll. So you can just stick it, Terence. Hoover's lying to you."

Both Terence and Gamble drew in quick breaths of surprise. That wasn't said, not about J. Edgar Hoover, the staunchest crime fighter in the nation. George had committed a cardinal sin.

"Why don't you ask me?" George said evenly. "Ask me who I'm working for. I'll tell you."

Terence shook his head. "I don't want to hear it, George." He pointed the gun at him. "Let's just go up and ring the doorbell, nice and easy. And George, give me your gun. Just so you don't get any ideas."

George silently removed his gun and handed it, butt first, to Terence, who pocketed it and nodded. "Okay. Now drive up near that truck and park. Let's go get Oswald, nice and quiet. We can talk on the way back to Dallas."

* * *

The doorbell rang as I was toweling off my face upstairs. Water was running in the shower. I couldn't wait to hop in; clean hot water would feel so good after all the grime I'd acquired yesterday.

I heard the murmur at the front door and turned off the water; a ringing doorbell could only mean news for us. I hoped it would be good news.

I came out of the bedroom at the same time Lee came out of the kitchen, his revolver drawn.

Jared, his own shotgun cradled in his arm, opened the door.

George stood on the porch, two men in suits behind him.

Thank God. Thank God. We were saved. It was over.

"George!" I said, smiling and running down the stairs. "You got here after all!"

"Hi, Cady," he said, a grim smile on his face.

Jared, seeing the relief on my face, beckoned them in.

George came in first, his hands stiffly at his sides. The other two men followed.

Then I saw that they had a gun in his back.

Lee didn't know which way to look.

George's eyes caught his. "Where is he?" he said quietly.

The shorter agent pushed past George and the other man, his gun leveled at Lee's mid-section. "Lee Oswald, you're under arrest. Drop your gun; put your hands in the air."

Lee obeyed. The short agent spun him around and snapped shiny metal cuffs on his wrists. Then he let Lee turn around.

I felt hands on my wrists, too. In a moment, I was cuffed as well. A beige-uniformed sheriff's deputy emerged from behind me. He had obviously snapped the cuffs on me.

"Where is he?" George repeated to Lee, his voice becoming more urgent.

"Upstairs," Lee said, his eyes darting uneasily from one man to another.

"We're not going to hurt you, son," said the tall man. "We're FBI agents. I'm Special Agent Miller, this is Special Agent Gamble. Nothing will happen to you as long as you don't resist arrest."

"I'm not resisting arrest," Lee said.

Miller looked uneasy. "I guess you and George already know each other."

"I don't know him," Lee said positively.

Miller and Gamble exchanged looks. Then Miller said to Lee, "Who's upstairs, son?"

Lee eyed George and kept quiet.

"George, for God's sake, what are they doing? What's going on?" I asked him. My voice was becoming shrill; being handcuffed was a very unpleasant sensation.

George looked at me. "Cady, they think I'm part of some plot and that I'm here to kill Oswald to silence him. We need to show them."

George was right. It was time for some dramatic surprises.

The attic room was small enough with just one person in it; with five other people, it was crowded and stifling. They pushed in, looking over shoulders, down at the figure stretched out on the floor, shivering.

"Mr. President," Miller said in a hushed whisper.

Gamble had gone pale. George gave them both a look of smug satisfaction. "Now will you put that gun away and take off the damned cuffs? These people aren't dangerous."

Almost automatically, Miller holstered his gun, as Gamble freed my wrists. The President's face, I noted with alarm, had gone paler. We had to get him out of here fast, and get those meds. I had no idea how long he could hold out without them, but already he looked worse than he had at breakfast.

It took just a moment for George to regain his natural sense of command. "Let's get going now," he said quietly. "I talked to the Attorney General this morning, and my orders are to get you straight to Houston, Mr. President," he said to the man on the floor. "I promised him I'd get you there safely."

The President nodded weakly, his eyes closing involuntarily.

George gave his colleagues one good glare before bending down. *Next time, trust me,* said the glare. I hoped for our sake they would.

* * *

Downstairs, the sheriff's deputies released Lee at George's order and returned his gun, their eyes going wide at the sight of the President.

They took a small mattress from the attic and set it in the back of the station wagon, which was parked across the back of the truck. We were ready to go.

"Thank you," I said to Jared.

He nodded slightly. "Glad to have you." He nodded at the President, now being helped out of the house. "He's not so bad." He smiled one final time and closed the door behind us.

"Let's move." Gamble led the way. Miller and George, helping the President, were behind him, Lee and I behind them.

We were halfway between the house and the car when the first shot rang out.

Gamble dropped to his knees in the dirt driveway, a crimson stain blossoming across his chest. A second shot snapped his head backward, his lifeless body tumbling against the car. Another shot dropped the first sheriff's deputy beside Gamble. The fourth shot splattered the brains of the second deputy all over us.

"Get back!" George shouted. He and Miller dragged the President backward, into the grass behind Jared's truck, knocking into Lee and me, before snapping out their guns and firing back, toward the barn. Lee took out his revolver, and pushed in front of the President, to shield him with his body while he looked for a shot. I threw myself down flat next to Kennedy.

Miller fired toward the barn as he knelt, using the car to shield his body. Meanwhile, George crept around the side of the truck to the rear fender, poised for a moment, then dashed to the driver's side of the station wagon. A hail of bullets followed him, several striking the doorframe of the car, which George managed to pull open. He dove inside. An instant later, the ignition fired up.

Miller was firing steadily, stopping to reload, firing again. Even Lee was firing at the barn, though I doubt he hit anything. So far, none of us had seen anything except the stutter of light and smoke as shots were fired. We still had no idea who was shooting at us or precisely where they were.

George was at the wheel of the car now, crouching low, and pulling around the truck behind us. As far as I could tell, our assailants had hit only Gamble. The President and I were untouched, as were Lee and Miller. But we were being pinned down from what seemed like several directions.

As George swung the front of the car close to where we lay, his windshield shattered in a burst of gunfire. George slammed on the brakes and threw up his arms to protect his head, but glass was suddenly flying everywhere—I could see blood on Lee, on Miller, and when I raised my head cautiously, there were shards of glass all over me and the President.

Another shot sounded, and the right front tire of the station wagon exploded. The snipers seemed able to hit anything they wanted to. It would be just a matter of time, I was sure, before we were all gunned down. We had no idea which way to run. We had no backup. We had no real options.

George seeing what was coming, jumped out of the disabled station wagon and with quick movements, grabbed the President's limp body and yanked him away.

I felt like we'd been in this crossfire for hours, though it was probably less than a minute. Suddenly, though, I was startled by a squeal of tires across gravel, at the foot of the driveway. A white van was putting in, and as I watched, a window was rolled down while it still lurched toward us. Yet another gun appeared there, and I saw with horror that they were firing at us, too!

As he tumbled through the air toward the grass, Miller landed a shot right through the windshield and caught the driver in the eye. The van went crazily out of control. Miller tried to jump out of its way, but the van slammed into him just before it plowed into the truck, pinning Miller between the two vehicles. The driver of the van fell over the wheel, unconscious or dead, but the two swarthy men next to him began to push their way out of the passenger side.

Miller screamed as I stared in horror; his body was smashed between two hunks of metal which were ground together so tightly they could have been welded.

"Cady! Around this way!" George yelled, grabbing for my arm with one hand while he threw the President's body over his shoulder. He was looking at me instead of in front of him.

Trying to avoid the truck, he fell instead into the open door of the station wagon, which had been shoved violently aside when the van smashed into Jared's truck. The President fell, head first, into the grass behind him. George fell by the truck, groaned and lay still.

The two Cubans reached us as the barn door slid open. "Lee!" I shouted. Lee turned, both of us staring at Don Cuyler and Stan Marchand, rifles in their hands, smug satisfaction on their faces. Bloodlust filled Don's eyes, which shifted from Lee down to the helpless form of the President.

There was nowhere—and no way—left to run.

* * *

Don raised his rifle and aimed it directly at the limp figure of the President on the grass. "He won't look so handsome soon," he said.

The front door of the house opened, and Billy peeked out. He saw the smashed cars, the bodies of the dead men, the long rifle aimed and ready.

"Ohmigosh!" he squealed. "Daddy, look! Everybody's dead!"

Don and Stan, startled, swung their heads to look at him.

I saw my chance and without hesitation, took it. We had no other choice.

I snatched up Miller's pistol and clubbed Don over the head with it. He screamed, but far from crumpling into a heap, as I'd hoped, he merely staggered before regaining his balance.

Meanwhile, I felt something like iron close around my waist, pinning my arms. It was Stan, and he was restraining me from behind with one beefy arm that he squeezed across my chest until both my breasts and all my ribs were sore. I turned to him, to try to break free, and saw the cruel enjoyment on his face: he knew he was hurting me, and he was getting pleasure from knowing it.

Lee stepped in front of the President, blocking Don and Stan, but one of the Cubans backhanded him. Lee fell to his knees from the force of the blow.

The second Cuban had a pistol out, aimed at the President, still limp in the grass.

"No!" Don rasped. "Not your shot. It's my shot."

Reluctantly, the Cuban lowered his gun, though he kept it trained on the President. I struggled with Stan, trying to loosen his bruising grip. He only laughed and tightened his arm; I couldn't move and could hardly breathe. With no other weapon at hand, I finally sank my teeth into his arm.

Stan groaned, and his grip loosened for a split second. I started to dart away from him, and then heard the sweetest sound I think I've ever heard: the squeal of several police sirens in the distance. From the sound of them, I figured they'd be here in less than a minute. Don obviously figured the same thing.

"Let's get out of here!" Don shouted. Stan picked me up like I was a rag doll, threw me over his shoulder, though I struggled and pounded him, and flung me headlong into his car, which had been pulled up out of sight, on the other side of the barn. Sure enough, it was the red Pontiac Star Chief, and I landed unceremoniously in the back seat, picking up several more bruises as my head bounced off the door.

Lee was thrown in next, his face bleeding from the broken glass and a mark on his eye where the Cuban had hit him. The President was loaded next to him. Don jumped in next to the President, rubbing his head and glaring at me. Stan and the Cubans got in the front seat, and Stan drove without hesitation into the heart of the farm, emerging ten minutes later, after bumping through the back acres, onto a concrete road. Without slowing down, he turned north.

Instead of reading about or even witnessing the assassination of the President, I was now going to be part of it.

Chapter Fifteen
SATURDAY, NOVEMBER 23, 1963

The two FBI agents riding shotgun in the sheriff's cars were the first to jump out when the squad cars roared up the driveway of the now-violated Jones farm. They ran over to the white van and truck, with Miller's body smashed between them, his face drained white. Blood soaked the ground around him. A moment later, they saw the body of the Cuban slumped over the wheel of the van.

Gamble lay on his back in a pool of blood in the front of the truck. His eyes were open and staring at the sky.

"Jesus Christ," muttered one of the FBI men. "Jesus Christ!"

The sheriff was out of his car and running forward, his weapon drawn, but everything was peaceful. He looked at the men in suits lying on the ground. "Your guys?" he said quietly to the FBI man. The man nodded, sickened.

"The Cuban?" asked the sheriff.

The Special Agent shook his head. "One of Oswald's guys, maybe. Maybe they had an argument."

There was a sudden, faint groan from behind the truck. The sound was unexpected and startling.

"Sheriff! This guy's alive!"

Sheriff Bennett came on the run as his men waved frantically.

George Staub's eyes flickered. He was lying on his back, covered with cuts from flying glass. His suit had jagged holes in it, and there were grass and dirt stains all over him. He looked like hell.

The FBI guy dropped down next to him. "God, George," he said, "what happened?"

George gathered his strength. His head was pounding. His eyes weren't focusing clearly yet. There were no signs of Oswald or the President or Cady Roberts. He had to know where they were. Dimly, he also knew he couldn't say anything yet about President Kennedy. After his experience with Gamble and Miller, he knew not to trust even the guys at the FBI. "Oswald," he said slowly. He couldn't seem to manage more than that. "Oswald," he repeated.

"What's he saying?" asked Bennett, who had paused behind the FBI agent. "Oswald," the Special Agent repeated. "He's saying Oswald did this."

"God in heaven," the sheriff   mumbled. "The guy's a one-man wrecking crew!"

Word passed fast, from the men closest to Bennett down to those who had stayed in the sheriff's cars at the bottom of the driveway. "It was Oswald."

"Oswald killed these guys when they tried to arrest him."

"He drove a van right into Miller when Miller ordered him to drop his weapon."

The radio began to hum with activity and information.

By the time the press picked up the story, it had gotten better.

An hour later, when the first news reports were conveyed through broadcasters, television viewers were told that Lee Harvey Oswald, killer of President Kennedy, had cold-bloodedly murdered two FBI agents and two sheriff's deputies and severely wounded a third man in a shootout at a farm south of Dallas.

* * *

After a few minutes, the inside of Stan's car was stifling. The President remained limp on the seat. Lee was silent next to him. I felt paralyzed with fear.

This was the most dangerous situation we'd been in yet. We were cheek by jowl with the enemy, and he was going to kill us and make sure no one ever knew the truth about it. I figured when Stan stopped the car, Don would shoot me, the President and Lee, and claim later he had fired at the crazed Oswald in self-defense. Don would be hailed as a quick-thinking hero, and Lee would go down in the history books as the psychopathic monster who'd murdered a President and two FBI men.

It was just getting worse and worse.

Think, I told myself. *Think!*

I couldn't think of a thing.

"Stop here," Don called to Stan a moment later. Stan skidded to a halt. Don turned to us. "Out. All of you."

We were at the side of a road, adjacent to some kind of field. There were no houses or buildings, and lots of overhanging trees. It was a perfect spot for a murder. Several murders. My skin began to crawl.

Don held the gun on us until Lee and I pushed our way out of the car, Lee supporting the President, who was mumbling incoherently. The sweat was dripping down his forehead, and his skin was waxy. The three of us huddled together, facing Don, Stan and the two Cubans, whose eyes were alight with the thought of what was to come. Behind the President's back, I could feel Lee's fingers press mine for reassurance. Unfortunately, I was too frightened to be reassured.

"Jesus Christ," Don said in disgust, looking at Kennedy, "he looks like he's about to keel over right here. Some goddamned President!" He pushed me away and kicked Kennedy. Lee couldn't catch him fast enough, and the President fell over, striking his face on a jagged piece of rock in the field. Blood began to flow down his cheek. Stan, grinning viciously, kicked the President deliberately in his back. Even in his semi-conscious state, Kennedy obviously felt that: He groaned and tried to turn over. Lee locked his hands under the President's armpits to try to pull him out of Don's reach. Don kicked him in the ribs. Lee fell over.

"Stop it!" I shouted. I grabbed Don behind the neck and jumped on him, my fingers pressing on his windpipe. I could feel him choking as he tried to fight me off. Stan, several feet away, was slow to respond, but the two Cubans yanked me off him.

One of them, whom I had seen with the rifle in the Cuyler kitchen on Monday night, jerked a thumb at me and spoke a few words in Spanish to Don, who was still trying to breathe. Don jerked out a few words as well, also in Spanish. The two Cubans, responding to what was obviously an order, stood me up between them. Don, his breath still coming in heaves, came toward us. When he was an arm's length away from me, he slapped me across the face.

God! I felt as though he'd ripped my head loose from my neck. The entire left side of my face, from hairline to chin, felt aflame.

It hurt like hell.

And I'd be damned if I'd let him know it.

"Stupid bitch!" Stan had come up behind Don, and it was clear he was ready to punch me out, before shooting me dead. His face had turned almost purple.

I was truly frightened inside, but I would not show it. I would not. If I did, all was lost, and I had a dim, a very dim, idea that might yet buy us some time.

"Get that animal away from me," I told Don, my voice as icy as the look I was giving him.

He didn't. Stan whirled past him and slapped me on the right cheek.

It was like being broadsided by a two by four.

For a moment I almost lost my balance. I felt as though a flame had singed my face. Stan grinned as he saw my grimace of pain.

I managed to stay on my feet and addressed myself to Don as soon as I could speak. "This won't get you your invasion. Nothing can make it happen now."

He shrugged, but I could see just a glint of unease behind his nonchalance. "Nothing can stop it. Once that truck reaches Miami, the operation's a go."

"The truck isn't going to Miami," I told him, a little smugly. "I diverted it."

"Liar!" Stan shouted. "Those truckers had explicit orders. It can't be diverted!"

"You'd better find out," I said to Don. "That truck isn't going anywhere near Miami. And without all those guns, how are you going to invade Cuba next week?"

Don looked, for a moment, truly disconcerted. I'm sure he hadn't expected either my cockiness *or* my knowledge.

"She's bluffing!" Stan insisted. "She's just a telephone operator, for crying out loud. She doesn't know anything!"

"She knows something," Don said, looking hard at me. "And she wants to make a deal."

"You're right," I said, trying to match his cool tone, lifting my chin. The fiery pain from Stan's slap was receding on my skin. Maybe my head would stay attached after all.

Before I could go further, Don interrupted. "First I'll find out if you're telling the truth." He looked at Stan. "Let's get to a phone."

He paused for a moment. I could see his mind ticking over the possibilities. I hoped he would feel like a football team ahead by too many points: tossing a few to the other side would be meaningless. Lee was slowly recovering from the vicious kick in the ribs Don had given him. The President was lying still in the grass.

The sight of Kennedy seemed to revive Don's spirit. "All right," he said grimly. "If the shipment isn't where it's supposed to be, then we'll talk."

I dared not breathe a sigh of relief, though I could feel it inside. We were all more or less in one piece, and murder had been averted, for the moment. Maybe I was finally beginning to help, after all.

Ten minutes later, he wasn't laughing. We'd stopped at a small Texaco station surrounded by miles of farmland, with a tiny phone booth set off to one side. Don had leaped out and strode to the booth, while Stan prudently decided to fill up his tank, leaving the Cubans sitting in the front seat. He shoved our heads down in the back and grinned heartily at the man who came out to pump the gas for him. Stan got out and engaged him in conversation to keep him from noticing the three people crouched over in his back seat.

Don came back to the car incensed. He could barely contain himself while Stan paid the gas station attendant and waved off his offers to check the oil and tire pressure and wash the windows.

As soon as we were on the road, he directed Stan to find another secluded spot.

"Pick it, man," Stan said irritably. "You think we got an overcrowding problem here?"

When he finally stopped the car again, Don grabbed me. "All right, start talking!"

"Had trouble getting through?" I asked innocently. I thanked God fervently that I'd thought to put a password in place. Don didn't know the password, and he wasn't going to beat it or threaten it out of me. It was all I had, and it might, just possibly, keep the President alive until help, or a more opportune moment, arrived.

Don stared at me. "You're going to tell me about that shipment!"

This time, he yanked me out of the car and pulled Kennedy by his chestnut hair.

"Stop it!" Lee protested. "He's sick!"

"He's going to get a lot sicker," Don said grimly.

I decided to put a stop right now to any methods of persuasion he had in mind. "Let's look at this rationally," I said. "You need that shipment. You can't start your war without it; it's too late. You won't be able to find that many rifles in a week and get them to Miami; therefore, you've got to get that shipment."

Don looked at me with hatred. "Don't patronize me, you bitch. What do you want?"

"You can't have both, Cuyler," I said, hoping my voice wasn't shaking. "You can kill the President or you can have the war with Cuba. If you kill the President, I'll never tell you where the truck is. You'll never have your invasion. Or—I'll take you to the truck. You can have it and all the contents. Once you have it, the three of us go free. Until then, we get good treatment—food, water, medical help for the President."

"Cady!" Lee hissed at me. I knew he was thinking it was the stupidest bargain in the world. They would never let us go.

I hoped Don thought I was stupid enough to believe he'd keep his word, if he gave it.

Apparently, he did. "All right," he said warily. "Good treatment for you three, and you all go free once we get the truck back." He paused. "You're right, Cady—the war with Castro is more important even than getting rid of Kennedy."

"Thank you," I said, giving him a bright, relieved smile. I hoped he was thinking he'd just gulled this stupid girl into a fatal mistake. If he kept thinking that way, we might still have a chance.

"Where to, then?" he said.

"South," I said vaguely.

"South where?"

Lee spoke up quickly. "I'll direct you."

I hoped he remembered we had to detour to Houston. Then I caught the look in his eyes. He knew.

* * *

Lyndon Johnson had been busy on the telephone all night and most of the morning at the White House. The Oval Office was being stripped and refurbished for him.

Meanwhile, he was working in his old office, the Vice-President's office in the West Wing, the television set on in the background, while he quickly and decisively talked to Congressional leaders, foreign leaders, and of course, J. Edgar Hoover, who was to meet with him at 12:30.

Hoover was prompt.

As soon as the door closed behind them, Johnson said abruptly, "What's the news?"

"There's been a shootout," Hoover began.

Johnson waved that away. "It's all over the television. What else?"

"Two of my men are dead. The third, George Staub, was supposed to be in Washington today. In fact, he was supposed to be meeting with me in—" Hoover glanced at his gold watch, "—about an hour."

Johnson wanted to get to the point. He'd been President for less than 24 hours and could already feel the pressures weighing on him. Time had become more precious than ever. "So?"

Hoover paused. "Apparently the Attorney General—I mean former Attorney General—had a conversation with George Staub this morning, at his home in Virginia."

"This guy talked to Bobby?" Johnson said skeptically.

"We have it on tape. Staub's turned. He's thrown in his lot with the Kennedys."

"No!"

"Bobby Kennedy's been coordinating things from his home. He met Mrs. Kennedy at the airport in Washington and then left for Houston."

This was the first Johnson had heard about Houston. "What's in Houston?"

"Apparently the President—er—Mr. Kennedy, is ill," Hoover said. "They didn't say much about it."

So, he does have Addison's disease, Johnson thought. His own people had bandied about that rumor during the 1960 election, trying to prove that Kennedy wasn't healthy enough to hold the Presidency. Kennedy's camp had vigorously denied it (they did everything with vigor, it seemed). Johnson wondered how long it would be before Kennedy collapsed altogether. He wished he knew more about Addison's disease.

But what the hell was in Houston? A doctor? A hospital? Why not just stop off at a hospital somewhere else?

Because the dumb-ass bastard is trying to shield Oswald, he thought. There's no other possible explanation. Stupid. Potentially fatal.

"What have you done about it?" he asked Hoover irritably.

Hoover was embarrassed. "I had some men following Staub when he and the others drove out to the farm. They—er—they thought it was more important to stay far back, in case Staub—er—spotted them. Unfortunately, that meant they—"

"They lost 'em." Johnson slammed his massive fist down on the desk. "Dammit to hell!"

Hoover pursed his mouth primly. He didn't like being around men who cursed.

It was another reason he'd so disliked President Kennedy.

"Well, what the hell are you sitting here for?" Johnson asked, jolting Hoover out of his reverie. "Get some people following Bobby Kennedy, and God help you, Edgar, if you lose him."

"Yes, Mr. President."

* * *

All over America, particularly in Texas, television sets were turned on in diners, coffee shops, appliance stores, even beauty salons. They were turned on and eagerly watched in private homes and five and dime stores. And gas stations.

The black Cadillac fishtailed into place by a pump at a Humble gas station on the highway far south of the Jones farm. The driver was irritable from lack of sleep, frustrated from lack of information. He got out, leaving the boneless-looking dog lying sleepily on the front seat next to him, and shut himself into the phone booth outside the spotless white office.

The man dialed a number, identified himself, listened. The message was clear: *Oswald's heading to Houston. Get there before he does. Silence him.* They had paid to get a Texan in the White House, and it was his job to be sure the Texan stayed there.

He knew all that, and said so. But he hadn't heard the rest of the tale. Don Cuyler and his people were also on the trail, headed the same way. They might, possibly, even be together. This made things more complicated. Play it by ear, but be sure there was no one left who could tell the story.

He understood.

* * *

We reached Houston a couple of hours later, Stan driving deliberately slowly. The car was so flashy, in its freshly waxed red and white tones, that Don had debated stopping to borrow or steal another, more nondescript car. In the end he had decided it was more important to press on. That decision had also stopped Stan's whining about leaving his car somewhere. *He sure was attached to it,* I thought.

Even inside the car, with the sky growing steadily more overcast, I could see that the President was in terrible shape and getting worse. I'd tried to feed him a couple of the salty crackers I'd squirreled away in my purse, but he couldn't seem to bite down. Lee had helped, but in the end, we gave up. Kennedy was now dozing between us, Don watching him like a hawk.

"Houston," he said abruptly as we passed the city limits. "Where to now?"

I gave him the address of the Lone Star First National Bank. "This is where the truck is?"

"Just get there!" I snapped. I was still feeling edgy and frightened, but I'd long ago decided that cowering before these guys would be a terrible mistake: they were the kind who liked to see people whimper, and I'd be damned if I would be one of them.

Don gave Stan the address, and after a few false starts, Stan managed to turn onto the correct street. As we got closer and closer to the commercial end of the street, we saw fewer and fewer people. After twelve noon on Saturdays, no one did much business down here.

I pointed out the bank, the tallest building for three blocks, but Don had Stan pull over and turn into a side street. "Now what?" he said to me.

I had thought this out. "We have to take the President in there for a minute," I began, but he shook his head.

"Like hell you will. That's a bank. It's closed on Saturday afternoons. Where's the truck?"

I took a deep breath. "It's not here."

Don's eyes filled with fury. "You bitch!"

I gave him back a level look. "The President's sick. He needs medications, and they're in that bank. We've got to go in and get them, or he'll die. And if he dies, all bets are off."

The President was lying across Lee now, unable to keep his head up, moaning. Don looked at him with contempt. "Shit."

Stan leaned over the back seat and looked at me with unfriendly eyes. "Give me ten minutes with her. I'll get her to tell you where it is."

I looked back at him with the iciest eyes I could manage. He didn't seem impressed.

Don sat thinking for a minute. "All right," he said finally. "You can go in there." He pointed at me. "You have exactly ten minutes to get whatever you need. We wait here, especially the President. You delay or do anything to call attention to us, and he gets a bullet in the head. You got that?"

I nodded. I had wanted to get Kennedy inside the bank and shove him at whoever was there and beg for help, but I realized now I'd been thinking stupidly: Don would never let Kennedy out of his sight, or Lee either. They were his insurance. Only a fool would let his biggest prize slip through his fingers, and unfortunately, he was no fool.

"Oh, and Stan here is going with you."

My mouth went dry.

The double doors of the bank were thick glass, and behind them stood a middle-aged man in black-rimmed glasses and a suit, his solid navy tie stiffly knotted over an immaculate white shirt. He spotted us, unlocked the door quickly and ushered us inside, then locked the door quickly behind us and, taking a snow-white handkerchief from his pocket, carefully wiped the door handles where he'd held them.

Stan looked at him like he was nuts.

I was praying I could figure out a way to leave a clue for the people I hoped were still following us. *Improvise, Cady*, I told myself. Now, if ever, was the time.

"We're here—" I started.

"Yes, yes, I've been expecting you. I'm Alan Harcourt, President of Lone Star First National. You are *quite* late," he said disapprovingly. "This way, please."

He led us down a long carpeted hallway toward the vault at the back. I could hear Stan's heavy shoes slapping the carpet behind me at every step, and I was very aware that he had a gun inside his jacket. "The Attorney—that is, Mr. Robert Kennedy—asked me personally to stay and let you in. He said you'd be recovering some items belonging to the Kennedy family?" He looked at me questioningly. Houston, apparently, wasn't exactly Kennedy country either.

I nodded.

He opened a heavy metal door. "Right this way. You have your box key, I presume?" He looked at us like a principal eying a recalcitrant student.

I racked my brain to think of how to alert this man that we needed help, that the President was out there and that he had to notify the authorities. But I couldn't think of anything that would enlighten Harcourt without alarming Stan. Harcourt wasn't looking at me directly: he appeared to be looking over my head and past Stan, who wasn't bothering to hide his aggressiveness. But rather than seeming nervous, Harcourt appeared to be disdainful.

Out of the corner of my eye, on the empty desk in front of the vault, I caught sight of a faded brown ledger, but feeling Stan at my elbow, I looked away quickly.

"Key?" Harcourt repeated. It was obvious I hadn't been listening, and he was rather offended. I saw his eyes flicker over my dress, and I realized that the starched beige dress that had been so primly new a week ago was now covered in dirt and torn in several places. My stockings were in shreds. My shoes were filthy. I probably looked like someone at the end of a five-day bender, and this bank, it was clear, catered to a top-drawer clientele.

"Key?" Harcourt said again, and his tone was becoming weary.

I produced the heavy key ring I'd taken from the President's pocket. Harcourt's eyes dilated: the small gold ring must have contained fifty different keys.

"Good heavens," he said, somewhat faintly. "Which one is—er—ours?"

"I guess we'll just have to try them all," I said, looking straight at him, trying to send a silent signal. He stubbornly kept his eyes away from me, though his mouth quirked with annoyance.

"Oh, well, if we have to. This way. And please be careful!" he said sharply to Stan, who was rambling down the hall, bumping carelessly into the walls.

Stan glared at him but moved into the center of the hallway. Harcourt once more took out his handkerchief and carefully dusted it over the spots Stan had touched.

"This guy is a crackpot," Stan muttered to me. Harcourt must have really annoyed him, if Stan was making civilized comments to me.

Finally, we stopped by a nondescript row of boxes, no different from the dozens we'd already passed. "Here," Harcourt said shortly. "Box 324." It was a box about three quarters of the way up.

For once in my life I was glad I was under five feet four. This time, I had the perfect excuse. "Oh, I'll never be able to reach way up there," I said, trying to look innocent and helpless. "That's way too high for me. I guess St—my friend," I amended quickly, seeing the warning look on Stan's face, "he'll have to do it. He's so much bigger."

I had noticed the faint markings on the keys, some with initials, the other dots made by nail polish. I even had a pretty good idea which key was the right one. But I'd be damned if I told them. Every minute I could spend with Harcourt was more time to try to communicate with him.

"I don't wanna play with a bunch of keys," Stan said sullenly. "That's not why I'm here."

But when no one else made a move toward the boxes, Stan took the bundle of keys and grudgingly started to insert them, one after another, into the lock of box number 324. Even he had to stretch upward, and each time he tried a key and it didn't work, he rolled down onto his heels for a second.

At this rate, it would take a good long time.

Harcourt and I stood back, watching.

When Stan had established a sort of rhythm to his work—insert, push, push again, pull key out, try again—I moved cautiously closer to Harcourt. "Get me the ledger!" I said as softly as possible.

"I beg your pardon?" Harcourt said loudly.

I could have killed him.

Harcourt's voice, loud and sudden in the quiet room, broke Stan's rhythm. Stan swung around in the middle of trying a key. "Hey, what's up here?"

"Nothing," I said soothingly. "Mr. Harcourt was just telling me that bank policy is that we have to sign the safe-deposit ledger." I gave Harcourt a look, which he must have understood, thank goodness: He grunted something and headed for the ledger.

"We're not signing anything," Stan said. He advanced toward me, his eyes narrowing into slits.

Impulsively, I pulled him to one side and began talking to him softly and quietly. "Look," I said, "I know you've had a rough time. I'll bet Don Cuyler's never treated you with any real respect."

"He respects me!" Stan said, stung. "Of course he respects me!"

"Stan, come on—you're his driver! You and I know you're worth a whole lot more than that! Right here's where you can outsmart him."

Stan looked at me suspiciously, but he was listening, so I went on. "This safe-deposit box belongs to Joe Kennedy. You know how rich he is. It's filled with his stuff. All I'm picking up are some medical supplies, but I'll bet there's plenty more in here. You can have everything else—money, jewelry, you name it. Why should Don Cuyler get it all?"

He looked at me, and I held my breath, praying he'd fall for it.

Harcourt was coming down the long hall, holding the ledger.

"Yeah, why not?" Stan said slowly, and then with more conviction. "Why not! What the hell—to the victor go the spoils, right?"

"Absolutely," I said with relief.

"All right!" He turned back to the work with renewed enthusiasm.

He was so busy trying the different keys that he didn't notice when I opened the ledger to a blank page and scribbled in it, handing it back to Harcourt still opened. He closed it without looking at it.

I could have kicked him in sheer frustration.

Five minutes later, Stan found the right key on the key ring. Harcourt stood on tiptoe to fit his key into the second lock, then turned them both. The door opened, and Harcourt triumphantly lifted out a small box and took us into a private room to open it..

Inside, there was a single object: a small black box. I lifted the lid quickly. Two small medicine bottles, sealed. Some brand-new unused syringes. A sealed bottle of rubbing alcohol with saturated swabs in a separate box. A package of sterile cotton balls. New packages of unused bandages.

Joe Kennedy, thank God, had thought of everything.

I stuffed the box into my handbag.

Stan looked at the empty box in disappointment. "Shit."

He started for the front door, but I hung back. "Uh—Mr. Harcourt—I'm not sure I signed your ledger properly—"

"I'm sure it's fine, Miss."

"But if you'll check it—" I persisted in a whisper, "I'd feel better knowing I did it right."

"Come on!" Stan shouted back to me.

I gave Harcourt a look of despair, which he carefully managed not to see. He wasn't about to accept any messages from me, silent or otherwise.

There was nothing more I could do.

I had the precious medications for the President. But I'd failed in the rest of my mission.

I followed Stan toward the car, my heart sinking lower with every step.

* * *

Harcourt busily wiped the doorknobs as the young man and woman headed down the street. It took him a curiously long time. He watched them until they turned the corner, out of sight.

As Harcourt straightened up, five men in business suits slid out of their hiding places behind him.

"Why didn't we take 'em?" asked one agent, shifting his shoulder holster on his white shirt.

"Plate number?" another agent asked Harcourt. Harcourt shook his head.

"They must be parked around the corner. I didn't see the car."

Through all the chatter, George Staub's staccato voice now cut in impatiently.

"The ledger," he said.

George was cut and bruised, and his suit looked ragged; he hadn't changed clothes since he left the Jones farm and headed to Houston. He was lucky to be alive and he knew it, but he also knew the pressure was on now, more than ever.

When Harcourt didn't answer, George repeated, "The ledger."

Harcourt didn't even hear him. It was the fifth man who commanded his attention at the moment. Bobby Kennedy's hair was unkempt, as though he had run an impatient hand through it again and again. There were deep circles under his eyes, as though he hadn't slept in days, and his mouth was a thin straight line.

Harcourt stared at him, fascinated.

Bobby noticed. Abruptly, he said to Harcourt, "We need the ledger."

"The ledger?" Harcourt said.

"*The ledger*," George repeated forcefully. "She made a big point of signing it. She wanted you to *look* at it, or didn't you figure that out?"

He reached past Harcourt, and snatched at the unwieldy brown book, flipping through the pages urgently, until he came to a blur of ink on a clean page.

George's heart began to pound so hard it felt like it might burst through his chest. In a frantic scrawl on an otherwise clean page, he saw the words: "JFK is alive. 531 Lafayette Street, New Orleans."

Bobby pushed in next to him and read the words himself. When he addressed George, his tone was brisk. "You know this place?"

George nodded. "It's part of the gunrunning operation. An office building in Lafayette Square."

Bobby turned to Harcourt. "Mr. Harcourt, may I use your phone?" As Harcourt nodded and began to lead him to a desk, Bobby threw over his shoulder at George, "If that's where they're going, we're going to get there first."

* * *

"No problems," Stan reported to Don five minutes later. He had pulled into a deserted parking lot several blocks away, so I could administer the medication to the President.

"You weren't followed?"

"Nope."

I was thankful Don had moved into the front seat so he could talk in low tones with Stan, leaving me much more space to inject the President. While they talked and the Cubans smoked, I opened my handbag and slid the sterile wrap off the first syringe.

"Fill it up," the President whispered. I hadn't realized he was awake. He was watching me through half-opened eyes as I opened the bottle of cortisone compound and dipped the needle into it, carefully holding the plunger down until the syringe was full.

I was extraordinarily nervous.

In the first-aid classes I'd taken while preparing to play Sheila, the stakes had never been this high. If I made a mistake, the instructor simply had me do it again. If I broke a needle in the tough skin of an orange I was injecting for practice, the orange could be replaced.

If I made a mistake here, it would be fatal.

I started to roll up the President's left sleeve, trying to seem confident and experienced. His shirt was wrinkled, soaked with sweat, and filthy. He probably hadn't worn anything so dirty since World War II.

Kennedy looked at me, deliberately keeping his arm by his side, and I could swear a smile crossed his lips. "I take the shot in my thigh," he said. To Lee he said, "You'd better take down my pants."

I stared at him in astonishment. "Come on!" he said irritably. "Hurry up!"

Hesitantly, Lee reached over to undo his belt and unzip his expensive trousers. The President of the United States was exposed to me, and in front of an audience! I was so startled and nervous, I began to giggle, and once I began, I couldn't stop.

Lee pinched my elbow, hard. I turned to him. "Hey, that hurts!"

"Concentrate," he said quietly.

Don and Stan were looking curiously over the seat. "What the hell are you doing?" I didn't answer. Lee was right: I had to concentrate.

I also noticed that Kennedy's forehead was bathed in sweat and his hands were shaking. He was still very sick. I prayed the medication would really do the trick.

I picked out the alcohol swabs in the box. Lee held the syringe while I opened the swabs and rubbed one on the President's now-exposed thigh. His skin was the same bronzed color all over, I noted, trying to remain clinically detached. I also, when I looked closely, noticed the dozens of little pinprick marks under his body hair. He had obviously taken many injections there.

My hand was shaking as I took the syringe back from Lee. I wished the President could do this; but he was in no shape to administer a shot, even if he was far more experienced. It was me or nobody.

The pinpricks had told me something important, though: anywhere in the thigh would do. *Just get it in straight and push down the plunger, I told myself. You've done this before.*

Not on a human being. Never on a President.

I kept my eyes riveted on the exposed thigh and took a deep breath, then jabbed downward swiftly, feeling a slight resistance as the needle pierced the flesh, and pressed down on the plunger slowly and steadily with my thumb.

The President gasped. The medicine disappeared, little by little, from the syringe. When it was gone, I carefully removed the needle, took the President's handkerchief from his jacket pocket and pressed it over the site of the needle mark, to catch the blood.

"Okay, you're done," Don said abruptly. "Now where to?"

I looked up into his tight, angry face. I suddenly felt emotionally drained. It took an effort to continue this cat and mouse game with Don. I knew as soon as he got the truck, we were dead. I knew I had to stay alert, but the encounter with Harcourt at the bank and my attempt to warn him going unnoticed, and now having to jab the President's skin with a needle—I was just exhausted.

I thought. "Galveston," I said. "That's the city near the Gulf, isn't it?"

Clouds were still scudding across the sky. We were heading right into a nasty autumn thunderstorm. Once we got to Galveston, if I remembered right, we'd be stopped by a rousing storm across the Gulf from New Orleans. And while I figured I'd eventually have to lead them to the truck, I hoped that if we were delayed and couldn't get to New Orleans until Sunday, somehow, something or someone else would interfere first.

Don would not get that truck back without a fight.

* * *

Sitting at Harcourt's own desk at the bank, Bobby Kennedy finally reached the White House on his third try. When Johnson came on the line after six minutes, his voice sounded pleasant and full of sympathy. "Hello, Bob. Hope things are going as well as can be expected."

Bobby had no time to waste on small talk. "I won't take a lot of your time," he said in the icy tone he used with mobsters and steel executives. "I'm not in Virginia. I know this must disappoint Mr. Hoover, since he wants to keep such a close eye on me, even assigning FBI agents to shadow me full time. That's flattering, but it's not a very good use of the taxpayers' money, don't you agree, especially as this time I've managed to get away from them, and they have no idea where I am."

Johnson's voice altered. When Bobby Kennedy was on the warpath, it was wise to listen. Johnson also noticed he had not addressed him as 'Mr. President'.

"All right, Bob. What's on your mind?"

"The President of the United States—the *elected* President of the United States, John Fitzgerald Kennedy—is alive. I think this comes as no particular surprise to you."

Johnson's voice was cautious. "We've been hearing some—uh—wild rumors to that effect, but frankly, Bob, I couldn't believe it until it had been thoroughly checked out. It's much too inflammatory to release to the public. Hoover agrees with me."

"I have no doubt he does," Bobby said tightly. "But the President is alive, and I happen to know that for a fact because I've spoken to him, both yesterday afternoon and again early this morning."

"Then I'll assign people right away to investigate, and—"

"No," Bobby said, cutting him off. "I'm going to get the President and bring him back safely to Washington. What I was calling you about was your own part in this."

There was a long silence.

Then: "I don't think I want to understand what you're trying to say, Bob."

"I have a deal to offer you," Bobby said, and he sounded as sure of himself as though he still occupied the Attorney General's office. He wasn't begging: he was condescending. "Your dealings with people like Bobby Baker and Billie Sol Estes don't bear close scrutiny, and we both know it. If you'd remained Vice-President, you'd be facing almost certain prosecution. Right now, President Kennedy is dealing with enemies whose numbers we can't even really predict. We need him back in the White House. The country needs him. You and I both know your being there is a sham."

"Now, Bob," Johnson said reproachfully, "I'm trying to excuse all this, since I know this comes out of your grief, but—"

"Here's the deal," Bobby interrupted again. "You call out the federal marshals for tomorrow morning—I'll tell you exactly where. They'll be charged with rescuing the President and subduing and arresting anyone trying to stop us. In return—" He took a deep breath. He did not want to do this, but he had no choice, "—in return, once the Kennedy Administration is functioning again exactly as it was yesterday morning, there'll be no investigation of your past, no prosecution, and I give you my word you will be the Vice-Presidential nominee on the Democratic ticket in 1964."

There was silence on the other end for over a minute.

"I'm the President now," Johnson said, but his voice lacked conviction.

"You're a Vice-President who stepped in to do the right thing for the elected President and will graciously relinquish power as soon as he hears that President Kennedy has survived. I'm sure President Kennedy will commend you to the press; I suspect he also might have a much more active role for you in his second Administration."

The cards were on the table. Bobby waited. He knew, though he currently held no post in Washington, that he held the winning hand, and it was all aces.

Another two minutes went by. "Your word?" Johnson said finally. "I stay on the ticket in '64?"

"My word," Bobby confirmed.

"Where and when do you want the federal marshals?"

Bobby told him.

"They'll be there," Johnson said, and his voice had a ring of decisiveness once more.

There was a trace of resentment in Johnson's voice. "I'll see to it."

"Thank you." Bobby hung up. Always a pleasure doing business with you, he thought bitterly.

* * *

Forty minutes into the hour-long drive to Galveston, the President began to recover.

I saw with satisfaction that the clouds were becoming darker and denser and moving ominously nearer. Rain would be lashing down at any moment. By the time we arrived in Galveston and I had to name our final destination, the weather would be far too inclement to travel onward—especially, I hoped, because Don would want to take the quickest route Don would want to take the quickest route, text should read: to New Orleans—he'd want to fly. And flying tonight would be impossible.

I was right. Without asking me, Don directed Stan to a small private airfield that reminded me of Redbird. I found myself shuddering, remembering the fiery mess we'd left behind there—was it only yesterday? I felt like we'd been on the run for weeks.

All three of us looked awful. Kennedy was breathing easier and looked a lot better than he had. The bronzed color had returned, at least partially, to his face. But his hand-tailored suit was filthy, his cheeks were stubbly and one side of his face had a jagged cut.

Lee's stubble was even more noticeable on his thin white face. His shirt was torn, his face bloodied and bruised from the Jones farm shootout and then the encounters with Stan and Don. He kept cradling himself with one arm. I wondered whether Don had broken his rib with that kick.

I was the least banged-up of the three of us, and I didn't like to think what I looked like.

There was a small house at the far end of the runway. Stan pulled up beside it. Don, gun in hand, ushered us out. He held the gun on me as I emerged from the car. "The truck's in New Orleans, isn't it?" he said pleasantly, as though asking whether I'd enjoyed the trip.

Surprised, I just nodded.

He nodded back, pleased with himself. "Oswald said he'd direct us. The only place that twerp really knows is New Orleans. The truck has to be there. Or it will be soon," he amended, looking at his watch. "We'll be there to meet it bright and early tomorrow morning."

"You can't travel tonight," I began. "It's going to rain—"

Actually, it was already raining. The wind had whipped up to the east, off the water. Water was lashing down on us.

Don hurried us inside, Stan and the Cubans following.

The door was unlocked, which surprised me, until I saw that we were not alone.

A man of startling appearance emerged from a room at the back, holding a cup of black coffee. He nodded, clearly expecting us. "Ready?"

The President, leaning on Lee and me for support, frankly stared at him. The man was average size, about five foot ten, but he wore a strange-looking red wig, and black greasepaint eyebrows arched over his beady eyes and massive nose. He also wore a brightly colored Hawaiian shirt over rumpled trousers.

I knew this had to be the notorious David Ferrie, talented pilot, CIA operator, associated with mobsters, anti-Castro Cubans and the President's Operation Mongoose. His presence here in Galveston sent a chill down my spine.

I knew David Ferrie lived in New Orleans, where he had been Lee's group leader when Lee was a teenager in the Civil Air Patrol. Ferrie could only be here in Galveston because he was going to fly us over the Gulf tonight.

"Ready," Don confirmed.

"Let's haul ass then," Ferrie said shortly. "Weather won't hold forever." He put down his coffee cup and picked up a jacket slung carelessly over a chair.

Outside, the rain was getting worse. Ferrie directed Stan to one of the hangars farthest from the airport building. Inside was a small airplane, doors open. "I've already done the preflight check and gassed up. Get in," Ferrie said.

We did.

In a few minutes, Ferrie had taxied to the runway, and was requesting clearance on the radio. "Tower, this is Whiskey Delta Two One Two, requesting permission for take-off."

"Whiskey Delta Two One Two, hold your position. The pattern is full," the tower radioed back.

Three or four silent minutes passed. Ferrie radioed again. "Tower, this is Whiskey Delta Two One Two, requesting take-off. You boys forget about me?"

Finally, the controller radioed back. "Whiskey Delta Two One Two, please return to hangar. A tropical storm is coming in. The airport is closing."

Don stared at Ferrie. "What?"

Ferrie tried again. "Tower, we have an emergency."

The controller was firm. "Sorry, Whiskey Delta. A ground stop has been issued. Conditions are too hazardous. Return to hangar. You can fly out tomorrow morning if the weather clears."

Don was furious. "Damn it! Ferrie, take it up!"

Ferrie, who until a moment ago had been vibrating with nervous energy, now eased out his breath and shook his head. "Too dangerous. This is a light plane. We take it over the Gulf in a storm, and they'll be fishing us out."

For a moment Don glared at him. I could almost see the idea rising in his mind to pull his gun on Ferrie and force him up. But Ferrie, for all his jitters, was the man in the left-hand seat. He looked right back at Don, and his gaze was unyielding.

They stared at each other in a silence crackling with electricity.

Ferrie won. "Let's go back to the safe house." He began taxiing carefully back to the hangar.

As soon as we were inside the small house by the runway, Don snapped on the television set in the living room. "Damn news," Ferrie said. "The whole weekend, nothing but news. It's enough to make you nuts." He was fishing out more cigarettes from packs in his pockets, lighting one with nervous fingers.

The match still burning in his hand was forgotten when the staid studio shot of the anchor gave way unexpectedly to a shot of a young reporter in the field, his thin tie askew, his voice throbbing with excitement. "We're live in downtown Houston. An unconfirmed report now says that President Kennedy *may still be alive.*"

There were gasps all over the room. Don had turned chalky. Ferrie dropped the match; it had burned his fingers, and he stamped it out furiously. "Damn it!"

The reporter was going on, his voice vibrating, rapidly spilling a waterfall of words. His eyes, even on the black and white set, were luminous. "We have very few details because this report is unconfirmed—I repeat, unconfirmed—but a supposedly reliable witness has provided the FBI with information that President Kennedy is still alive."

It pleased me to see a newsman labeling rumor as rumor and not fact, and warning viewers not to accept anything until it was confirmed. I didn't remember the last time I'd seen that on a newscast in the year 2000.

Don turned off the television set. "We're going tonight," he said.

Ferrie, Stan and the Cubans stared at him. "How?" Ferrie said finally.

"The boat," Don said, as if that explained everything.

Outside, the wind had risen, and the rain slashed against the windows. It was dark, and wet, and terrifying.

"Let's go," Don said, and his tone was grim.

No one argued.

* * *

In a cheap motel on the outskirts of Galveston, a grimy black Cadillac was parked beneath one of the room windows. Behind the window, its curtains cautiously drawn, the man with the pouty mouth and hard eyes dialed a Dallas number and asked for instructions. A droopy-looking dog lay on the bed.

"Oswald isn't the only danger," he was told. "The others are on the road too, headed for New Orleans. Stop them. We can't afford any leaks."

The man said he understood and hung up.

The wind and rain were howling now. The man had half a corned beef sandwich in his pocket. He took it out, divided it carefully, and gave half to the droopy dog, munching on the other half himself. He'd better get to sleep early, he told himself.

Tomorrow would be a busy day.

* * *

Hours later, after a long drive in the darkness and rain, we spotted a 50-foot Bayliner yacht bobbing along a dock. Despite its luxurious appearance, it looked like a toy riding the five-foot waves. I couldn't imagine how Don thought we could cross the Gulf in this weather.

"Get on board," Don said, and his tone was not pleasant. To emphasize his point, he prodded me in the back with his gun.

The boat was splendid, with a fiberglass canopy atop the deck, keeping out at least part of the blinding rain, though the sides were open. The wheelhouse was above, a short climb up a ladder at the bow. It was completely enclosed.

"Take them below," Don instructed Stan. "Keep them there."

Stan nodded. "Right, boss."

He pushed me from behind so hard I almost lost my balance. "Get going,bitch."

Below, there was a large main cabin, with an oval table bolted to the floor, long wooden benches fastened to the walls, and stove and pantry behind it. Next to it was a small stateroom. It contained a bed, a couple of chairs, a desk and a night table. Another door led to what is colorfully described on a boat as the head.

Stan nodded us curtly into the main cabin.

I felt the ship veer to the left, pulling away from the dock with a surge of engine power. Someone had to be piloting it. Don? I supposed so.

"Sit," Stan said, pointing to the big captain's chairs in the main cabin.

Five hours passed in silence.

The storm outside grew worse.

The boat rolled from side to side. Stan began to make gurgling noises. He looked distinctly seasick. He sat down abruptly in a chair, his eyes half closed.

The President's pain had returned, worse than before. His forehead was dripping sweat, his teeth were clenched, and he rocked a little, back and forth, in the chair. No one offered to let him lie down in the stateroom next door.

Under the silent, malevolent gaze of Stan and the Cubans, I ransacked the cupboards in the galley, eventually finding a treasure trove of saltine crackers, peanuts, potato chips, and pickles. *Salt and water,* I told myself, that and another injection would keep him going through the night.

If we were lucky.

While I fed the President snacks through the night, Lee spent most of his time staring at the wooden floor under his feet. I wondered if he was trying, as I was, to formulate a plan. So far, my thoughts were largely unprofitable. I wondered why I couldn't think of something brilliant, to cleverly and easily rout the five armed men guarding us.

For some reason, no such idea came to me.

Suddenly, around four in the morning, the cabin lurched upward from the bow, then dropped sharply. Lee tumbled to the floor. The others were clutching the arms of their chairs for support. The President, without any support, had fallen sideways in his chair and was trying, vainly, to lift himself.

"He needs a shot," I shouted to Stan. "We have to move him into the stateroom so I can give it to him."

"He's not getting shit from me," Ferrie said. "I can't wait till he dies. The sooner the better."

"But Don Cuyler promised!" I said. "He promised us good treatment and food until we reached the truck in New Orleans."

Ferrie shrugged, and at his ominous glance, the Cubans and Stan edged back. "Cuyler's not here," he said curtly. "And I say the bastard doesn't get a damn thing." To Stan and the Cubans he added, "Don't move him."

They nodded.

Ferrie left. In a moment we heard his footsteps climbing up to the deck.

I couldn't leave the President like that. I got up from my own chair, with the floor still rolling under my feet, and slinging my handbag to my shoulder, used both hands to lift him back into the chair. I leaned his head against the cushioned back of the chair.

Lee had gotten up, too. He looked down at the President and spoke to me in soft tones, so the goons behind us couldn't hear. "Can you give him the shot here?"

I didn't know. The thought of doing it when the floor under my feet was swelling and dropping unexpectedly gave me the shivers.

Suddenly, Don Cuyler appeared in the doorway. As always, he seemed calm; the rolling floor under him didn't seem to bother him in the least. "What are you doing? Ferrie said you're not to move him."

"He needs another shot," I said. "I need to lay him down in the stateroom and give it to him."

Don sneered at me. "Tough shit." He advanced into the room and looked down at the President. "Feel comfortable now, Mr. President? Feel like a rich big shot on this yacht? You were in the Navy with me; this should be old hat to you. Great weather for sailing, isn't it?" His laugh rang through the room and chilled my heart.

With difficulty, the President lifted his head to look at Don. "Don," he said, "what the—hell—happened—to you?"

Don looked at him with undisguised hatred. "The Kennedys always get what they want, don't they? No matter who else gets hurt. You get it all. The rest of us get shit."

The President looked at him as though he couldn't believe it.

Don put his hands in his pockets. I could see them balling into fists as he spoke again, though his voice remained ominously quiet. "You got girls. Oh, you got girls, all right! Same rank as me, same job as me—but they lined up for you, didn't they? Even Maidie Belle Williams."

The President shook his head.

"Don't remember her? Well, why should you? One out of so many? I remember her. We dated for eight months; I was going to ask her to marry me. After she spent three nights with you, she wouldn't go out with me again." He smiled then, a cold ugly smile, and everyone in the room winced.

Don went on, his tone bitter. "That wasn't enough for you, was it? Getting my girl wasn't enough. There was a chance for a PT assignment, too. One spot open. I knew I could do it; I applied first thing, begged for it. But you got it, not me, while I stayed stuck in that stinking little room doing those asinine intelligence reports. Hell, you weren't qualified to run that boat, not the way I was. I'd been sailing since I was six; I could've handled one of them blindfolded. You—'Crash' Kennedy—couldn't even refuel without bumping the dock, huh?"

"Don—"

Don was past hearing him, lost in his own ugly thoughts. "They kept me in that lousy intelligence section with all those other miserable washed-up bastards for a year and a half. *A year and a half,* while you were sailing the Pacific! Don't you think we all knew how sick you were? Jesus, was there ever a day when there wasn't something wrong with you? Yet you didn't even have to take the physicals—who'd you screw to make *that* happen?—and next thing we knew, Lieutenant Kennedy got into combat! And I—I sat there typing reports no one ever read or cared about, while you were picking up medals.

"And then—" I'd thought Don's tone was bitter before; it dripped with venom now. "Then I got into trouble, because I was bored, do you hear me? Bored out of my mind! And jealous—you and other worthless rich-boy pieces of shit like you were doing the jobs I wanted. I thought I'd go crazy in Washington, while everyone was out in Europe or the Pacific *fighting!* So I broke up an officer's bar one night. You know what that means. Court-martial, and dishonorable discharge." His face twisted.

The handsome features were blurred with pain. "Know what that does? Ever think about what your *job prospects* are like when you can't show an honorable discharge?"

I stole a look at Lee. His honorable discharge from the Marines had been downgraded to dishonorable when he'd defected to the Soviet Union. There was no sympathy there for Don; Lee's face was grim.

"But I got a job finally," Don said, and now he was hissing, "helping those disenfranchised Cubans get their country back. Ever look at the list of CIA officers working on the Bay of Pigs, *Mr. President?* You'd have seen my name."

I could almost hear the silence. By now, the President's face looked as grim as Lee's.

Don went on. "I gave them my word that this operation would get rid of Castro. And then you didn't give us air cover when we begged you for it. When we knew it would make all the difference. And those poor guys—*my men!*—died on that beach, because they trusted us. And you."

I was horrified. The whole assassination plot had come down to a case of bitter personal envy going back 20 years. Others hated Kennedy for political reasons. My father, the planner of the whole thing, had political reasons too, but also deep personal reasons. He was the one who was most dangerous to Kennedy right now.

Don's eyes were glittering with malice as he came toward the President. I stepped in boldly. "Stop it!" I warned him. "If anything happens to him, you'll never find out where that truck is!"

Don swung his head over to me, and I could see him focusing once more on everyone in the room. His civilized facade closed over the layers of rage and frustration. In a moment, he was smiling pleasantly again. Seeing it chilled me.

"That's right," he said agreeably. "You haven't told me yet where the truck is." He was still smiling as he moved closer to me. "But you will," he said.

In one movement, he grabbed my wrist and yanked me toward him. I stumbled, and he pulled me up, almost tearing my arm out of its socket along the way. "Come with me," he said, and to Stan he said only, "Stay out."

Both Lee and the President yelled at him to stop. When Lee started to move toward him, Stan and the Cubans blocked his way.

Don dragged me next door to the stateroom and shut the door.

"Now, Cady, where is the truck?" he asked, and his tone was garden-party polite. I knew once he had that information, we were all dead.

I shook my head.

Again he asked pleasantly, "Where is the truck?"

"You promised us—"

He slapped me across the face; I felt like he'd torn my jaw loose. "Where is it?" he shouted, and the lightning-fast change in his tone frightened me. Under that civilized veneer was a man who lived by the instincts of the jungle.

"Go to hell!" I shouted back.

In what seemed like one movement, he picked me up and threw me on the bed, and then threw himself on top of me. "You will tell me, you little bitch!" he shouted back. "And I'm going to have a good time making you do it!"

In seconds he had ripped the jacket of my dress down my arms, trapping them. A moment later, he was shoving my skirt up my thighs.

I bucked furiously on the bed, trying to push him off, unbalance him, anything. He retaliated by wrapping a heavy leg over mine, trapping my legs underneath.

My mind refused to allow this horror to be unleashed on me. I was going to fight back or die trying.

My arms were almost immobile, but my hands still worked. I couldn't use my arms to batter him, but I could use my body for momentum. When he eased off me for a second to unzip his pants, I had my chance. In one movement I rolled over toward him and slammed my heavy handbag down on his head, using all the force of my body weight.

He let go, shouting in turn, and grabbed me again. The bag fell to the floor. He called me names I'd seldom ever heard. Then he pulled me close to him and kissed me, hard, on the mouth, his tongue probing, violating, even as I turned my head frantically in every direction to knock him off. I felt bruised and filthy when he pulled away. He slid his hands under my dress, up to my garters. I reached down between his legs, and he swung his leg over me again, blocking my hand from grabbing for his testicles. Though I fought and writhed furiously, he was too heavy, too strong. He was going to wear me down until I couldn't fight back. He bent down to trap my mouth again under his. I yanked my head away. It was going to happen; oh, God, it was going to happen, if I couldn't find a way to stop him.

"Stop it!" I finally cried. "You can't do this. I'm *your daughter!*"

He raised his head, and the look on his face scared me. His eyes were glittering, his lips peeled back, flecks of saliva in the corners. The pores of his skin, close up, looked enormous. His hair was mussed from the tussle with me. "My *daughter?*" he laughed softly. "My daughter?" If I'd thought this would stop him for a second, even out of curiosity, I was wrong. "Well, that's even better. Just the way I like it."

And he tore at me again.

He had lifted himself off me to look down into my face, and it gave me the momentary edge I needed. I drew up my legs and kicked at his chest with my high heels. An instant later, I had pushed myself desperately to the side of the bed. He fell on the other side of me.

I never thought I'd be grateful to be wearing those pumps.

I had a split-second reprieve. In one moment, he'd be trying again.

As Don gasped, I rolled away from him and fell off the bed, scarcely even feeling the bump of the floor or the pitching motion as the boat was tossed in the storm-whipped waves.

I landed next to my handbag. My blessed handbag, full of things to help me in 1963.

I scrabbled through it frantically, looking for the syringe I'd used on the President. I'd kept it, thinking I could use it again. Maybe I could give Don Cuyler a shot where it would hurt the most and then run like hell.

I couldn't find it. It was too small, and there was too much crowded into my bag.

My hand closed on something else, though—something that had fallen to the bottom of the bag, since I'd had no use for it. It was a small, smooth black tube, attached to a key ring. I'd last seen it when George gave it to me the day I started the experiment; I'd never even tested it.

It had better work now. All three of our lives depended on it.

As Don turned his head in my direction, snarling like an animal, I raised the pepper spray tube and aimed for his eyes. Just then, the boat jolted again—we'd hit another wave. My aim was off as the spray discharged.

It was enough, though. Don howled and grabbed his face, his nose and eyes reddening and tearing immediately. "You bitch! Stop her!" he shouted, loud enough for them to hear in the main cabin.

Keeping my bag tightly over my arm and clutching the tube of pepper spray, I ran out of the stateroom. Maybe I could raise the Coast Guard on the radio. Or maybe there was a flare gun on board—if I could get hold of that, I could signal. Even on a rotten night like this, maybe someone would see it and come to help us.

I got as far as the ladder leading to the deck.

"Grab her!" Stan shouted. The next second, his beefy fist caught my ankle. He yanked at me.

I held onto the ladder leading to the deck with one hand, held on like death, and swung around long enough to give Stan the pepper spray full in the face.

"Yah!" I heard him scream. "Christ!"

Two down. George had said the stuff would incapacitate for up to 30 minutes. I prayed he was right.

The Cubans came running. They grabbed for me, but Stan had fallen backward onto the floor, blocking them from reaching me. I tried to spray them, but they dodged and covered their eyes. Two shots of the pepper spray went useless into the air. Two more caught them on the ears and the back of the head. They showed no signs of slowing down.

I grabbed for the ladder with both hands and hauled myself up.

Ferrie leaned over me from the deck and gazed at me maliciously. "Going somewhere?" he asked.

Behind me were the two Cubans. Ahead of me, blocking my escape, was Ferrie. I swung the tube of pepper spray up and gave him a blast right between the eyes.

The container was empty.

* * *

Five minutes later, the Cubans, with spiteful glee, had brutally hauled the President and Lee up on deck beside me. Flashes of lightning in the clouds above us illuminated the deck briefly, every other minute or so. It was chilly and wet and frightening. Despite the fiberglass protection over our heads, the deck was drenched— the waves were so high now that they were splashing over the railings and soaking everything. Before we'd been on deck for one minute, they had soaked us all, head to foot.

Don and Stan were in the worst shape, thanks to the pepper spray. Stan's face was purplish-red and his eyes streamed tears. He was choking and coughing and mumbling dire threats against me. I had no doubt he intended to carry them out.

Don was in better shape: He hadn't gotten a direct hit of the spray, and he'd had more time to recover. Still, he was blinking and wiping his eyes every few moments, and I knew that he wouldn't regain full strength at least for a few more minutes.

Meanwhile, we were facing two armed Cubans. David Ferrie was piloting the boat. Despite his bizarre appearance, Ferrie was quick and smart—and he had a gun. Even if he had to stay at the helm, I knew he could cause us grief.

I huddled with the President and Lee, my arm under Kennedy's back, trying to hold him up. The Cubans refused to allow him to sit, even on the deck. They were shouting in Spanish, trying to make themselves heard above the sound of the crashing waves. It was chaos.

Don wiped his eyes one final time and straightened up. For all intents and purposes, he was back to normal.

He pointed at me. "One more time. Tell me where the truck is in New Orleans. Or your friends get it, right here in front of you."

On the other side of the President, I could feel Lee straighten up. He looked Don full in the face as he said clearly, "Don't do it, Cady. They don't want what you have as much as they want what I have."

Don began to laugh. Above him, at the helm, Ferrie laughed too.

Don stopped laughing and eyed Lee with bemusement. "And what's that? Last year's comic books?"

"I've got files," Lee said steadily. "Dozens of files. Copies of Guy Banister's files that I took last summer, when I was in his office. They've got your name all over them. And Ferrie's. And Clay Shaw's. Just think of it, Cuyler, hundreds of documents that tie you all to the assassination plot. And to the gunrunning. If I die, those files go to the Attorney General. And you guys will be executed."

Oh, Lord.

Even I saw Lee's ploy for what it was: a magician's trick, a desperate attempt to buy us time for another escape. I wished he had kept his mouth shut. It was undeniably brave of him to tweak these guys' noses, but nothing he said—especially not a pitifully transparent story like this—was going to stop them from getting what they wanted from me.

It didn't take them long.

After they finished laughing at Lee, Don pointed at me again. "Where's the truck?"

"Go to hell," I said.

Don rapped a sharp order in Spanish to the Cubans. They seized Lee and with incredible swiftness, clubbed him to his knees. One kicked him at the base of his spine; the other kicked him in the chest. This time, across the roaring wind and surging waves, I could hear his ribs crack.

Lee cried out.

"Where's the truck?" Don asked, and his voice was quiet, offhand, as though the vicious beating going on in front of him wasn't happening.

The big Cuban knocked his fist under Lee's chin, turning his face upward, and broke his nose with one quick chop of his huge hand.

"Don't...tell, Cady," Lee gasped, his voice sounding strange through the broken nose. Blood streamed down his face. "Don't... tell."

The Cubans kicked him again, in the stomach. He collapsed, bleeding, on the deck.

"Well?" Don said to me, almost gently. "Where is it?"

I was sickened by what I was seeing. The Cubans moved back so I could get an unobstructed view.

Rage and fear and a sense of helpless frustration were building in me. I couldn't do anything for Lee, nothing. They were going to kill him in front of me, and I couldn't stop them.

Don assessed me thoughtfully through reddened, teary eyes. I gave him back my steeliest expression.

He called over to the Cubans in Spanish. I understood only one word.

"Kennedy."

They left Lee lying on the deck. God knows how many bones they'd broken or how much internal damage they'd done.

I threw myself in front of the President, locking my arms behind him. They would have to go through me to get to him.

The big Cuban reached for my shoulder. He tore me off with one casual movement that knocked me to the deck. I slid about ten feet on the wet surface, back to where I'd been.

Now the Cubans grabbed the President, who was so frail, who needed my arm under him just to stay upright. They swung him around. One of them pinned his arms behind his back.

God, no.

Don called something in Spanish to them, and turned to me, smiling. "In case you don't speak Spanish, I told them to make it hurt," he said. "I'm sure they'll be glad to; they still haven't forgiven him for the Bay of Pigs."

The President looked at me grimly. "Don't tell them," he said.

Oh, my God.

Don turned to watch, as though this were an extra-special sporting event.

The wind and the rain lashed the fiberglass canopy.

The big Cuban swung his fist toward the President's face.

The other guy holding him let him go. The President took the blow in the cheek and fell to the deck.

Everyone was watching this, except Lee, who may have been conscious, but certainly wasn't moving. Stealthily, I pushed my hand into my handbag once more.

When it came out, it held the only weapon I could muster.

The big Cuban lifted Kennedy carelessly with one hand, the President as limp as a rag doll, but his eyes were open and still clear. As the Cuban drew back his fist, I ran straight past Don, the syringe high in my hand, and jabbed it into the side of his neck where, in his frenzy and blood lust, the veins were standing out.

I hit a vein. Jackpot.

My thumb plunged down on the plunger with all the pressure I could manage.

The Cuban reeled away from me, screaming in agony, his hands clutching the side of his neck. Blood fountained out of him, turning the deck scarlet. The boat rolled mightily to port as a wave washed over the deck, and he stumbled backward, his feet slipping in the bloody water.

Don fell straight down. I reached back and grabbed for the rope tied behind me. I didn't know what it was for, and I didn't care; it would keep me from losing my balance. Slowly, using the railing at the stern to support myself, I inched my way toward the Cuban, who was scrabbling for purchase as he slid nearer and nearer to the railing.

I edged toward the Cuban, who was still trying to wrest the syringe from the side of his neck. Rage rose up in me. I had never been more furious in all my life.

I understood now how a person could kill.

I planted my feet on the soggy deck, braced myself, and gave the Cuban a mighty shove.

He went straight over the side into the Gulf.

I could hear him screaming and thrashing in the water below, but paid no attention.

I heard Don shouting something in Spanish. He pointed at Lee and made gestures with his arms. I understood the intent, if not the words.

He wanted the other Cuban to throw Lee in the Gulf.

I grabbed hold of the second Cuban. He was much smaller, only an inch or two taller than me, and in holding Kennedy for the big Cuban to hit, he had stupidly put down his gun. My anger, along with the water under his feet, would take care of the rest.

I swung him around and shoved him toward the railing. He fought back, surprisingly hard. I had stopped thinking about getting hurt: I was thinking about my rage and my anguish, and the two men who had taken a beating and not given in. I bit him; I kicked him; I grabbed his balls without the slightest hesitation and squeezed harder than I've ever squeezed anything in my life. Behind me, I heard Stan and Don shouting, but the deck was sliding to and fro, and I knew they couldn't keep their balance long enough to get to me. Meanwhile, I had a death grip on the Cuban.

The Cuban still fought back, cursing, slapping the side of my head, as the boat pitched violently around us. I stumbled backwards, letting go of him finally, and banged my head painfully. For a moment my eyes wouldn't focus; then slowly, they began to clear. My head was throbbing; I was down on the deck on my hands and knees.

Don shouted again in Spanish. The smaller Cuban stumbled to Lee's inert body. Slowly, buffeted by the wind and the movement of the deck, he bent down and yanked at Lee's upper arms.

Lee tried to lean back and pull his arms away. The Cuban laughed at him, showing a row of broken teeth, and wrapped his hand in Lee's bloody shirt. He began to drag him toward the railing.

I had nothing left to fight with. I couldn't even stand up, let alone rush him. I struggled to my feet. If I could get close enough, I could throw myself on him, grab his ankles... I didn't know. I just knew I couldn't let him throw Lee overboard... I couldn't let him...

Something moved suddenly to my left in the dark. There was a thump and a grunt and a flash...

The Cuban screamed and dropped Lee on the deck.

The President, struggling to his knees, had thrown himself between Lee and the Cuban and brought his left fist up into the Cuban's ribs. When the Cuban snarled with rage and started to throw himself forward, Kennedy straightened up and brought up his right hand... which held the flare gun he'd wrested from its storage clips under the railing at the stern.

Without pause for thought or breath, he discharged the gun right into the Cuban's chest.

The Cuban screamed and tore at his chest, jumping up and down to get the burning flare off.

In one surging movement, the President staggered to his feet and threw his arms around the Cuban, using the momentum of the boat and his own weight to shove the other man toward the railing.

Kennedy braced his feet against the deck. In one quick, deft motion, he flung the Cuban over the side. There was a splash and a gurgling cry. Then silence.

Don had gotten precariously to his feet. He was coming toward me, his reddened eyes looking grotesque. He moved toward me slowly, buffeted by the strong winds, his arms held out for balance.

I grabbed for the railing but missed it and fell to the deck. What my groping hand found, though, was more precious than gold: The gun the smaller Cuban had dropped while struggling with me. It was loaded, and it was mine now.

I brought it up into Don's face.

He stopped moving and looked at me.

I had no reason to keep him alive. I had every justification to kill him.

All I had to do was squeeze the trigger... I could do it...

My finger closed on the trigger...... I couldn't do it.

I couldn't.

Wrestling the Cubans into the Gulf in the heat of battle and in self-defense was one thing. Shooting an unarmed man, even if he was a man who'd made my mother miserable and previously attacked me, was another.

Though I knew I should fire, I just couldn't look Don Cuyler in the face and coolly pull that trigger. It didn't matter that I knew, if the positions were reversed, that he could.

He must have seen my mental wavering in my face, because suddenly he smiled, leaned forward, and slapped the gun right out of my hand. It skittered along the deck and disappeared. "It would seem," he said, in the old pleasant, civilized tone, "that we're back where we started."

* * *

Not quite. Don and Stan pulled the President and Lee, both conscious but unable to walk or move, into the center of the deck, and tied them up with strong rope. While they did that, I fumbled in my handbag and found... nothing useful. I had hoped for a pen or something to jab at their eyes, to incapacitate them...

All I found was a Secret Service ID billfold that held one of the fake ID's I had intercepted at ISI on Thursday, a lifetime ago. I looked at it thoughtfully. It was small and inconspicuous. I pushed it under the belt of my dress and pulled the buckle firmly over it. In the dark, maybe they wouldn't notice it.

And if we ever got out of this alive, maybe the billfold could be used as evidence.

If we got out of it alive, which was looking more and more doubtful.

When Don and Stan finished tying Lee and the President, they grabbed for me. "Get rid of that bag," Don told Stan. "It's lethal."

The bag went sailing into the Gulf.

The blood flow from Lee's nose appeared to have slowed down; his face was a mess, but I had stopped worrying that he was going to die of internal injuries. If he hadn't collapsed into a coma by now, I guessed that even while kicking him, they hadn't hit any vital organs. Though most of the sounds he made were moans, his eyes were open and clear. I tore off my jacket and used part of the sleeve to wipe off the blood on his face; the rest I wrapped around his battered ribs. Don and Stan, grinning broadly, didn't try to stop me.

The President, after his mighty effort to save Lee from the smaller Cuban, seemed sapped of strength. He could hardly keep his eyes open, and the tight line around his mouth told me he was struggling against terrible pain. I couldn't imagine how he was still conscious.

Don told Stan to watch the others and pulled me to the other side of the deck.

"Storm's abating," he said, nodding out to the water. To my surprise, he was right: The wind had slackened, and the downpour was lightening. Maybe the boat wasn't going to capsize after all, and throw us all into the Gulf, to struggle until we drowned. Maybe we'd even live through this night, to face whatever happened in New Orleans.

The first gray of dawn was starting to dim the stars. Far in the distance, I thought I saw a dark speck that could be land.

"We're still an hour or so away," Don said, settling next to me against the railing. "No," he said quickly as I tried wildly to get away from him, "I won't hurt you." He looked at me thoughtfully. "Did you really mean it when you said you were my daughter?"

So he was curious. I wondered if I could keep him curious all the way to New Orleans. That might protect us, for a while.

I had no other weapons. I might as well use the truth—or at least, part of it.

"That's right," I said warily. "I'm the child who's going to be born to your wife in July of next year."

That startled him. "What? I thought you meant you were from some girl I was with long ago."

"No. I'm a time traveler. I live in New York, in the year 2000. I came back here to 1963 on a mission."

He smiled and shook his head. "Sure you did."

"I came here," I went on deliberately, "because I knew all about Operation Mongoose and about the plot to kill the President in Dealey Plaza."

His eyes narrowed. "And you came back here to stop him from riding into an ambush?"

It was a definite handicap that this guy was so smart. I shrugged.

"Maybe."

"Which means—if you're telling the truth—that Kennedy would have ridden into that ambush. We succeeded, didn't we?" He laughed. "Time traveler or not. And you know something? I'm almost tempted to believe you." He didn't seem to have any trouble making the leap in his mind to embrace an outlandish new reality. That must be why he was such an asset to the CIA.

He looked at me speculatively. "We must have succeeded. The only way you could have known about it in the year 2000 is if it actually happened." He shook his head in wonder. "Damn. We got the son of a bitch."

He got up and walked away.

A moment later, he relieved Ferrie at the helm of the boat. I felt the boat lunge forward as Don, standing at ease and perfectly confident, pressed the throttle, giving us a fresh surge of power.

I had a terrible sinking feeling that not killing him when I had the chance was going to come back to haunt me.

Chapter Sixteen
SUNDAY, NOVEMBER 24, 1963

Morning had broken long before we approached a narrow inlet. As we rounded a thicket of weeds, a trio of speedboats blocked our path. My sudden hope that they were Coast Guard or some kind of law enforcement plummeted when I got a clear view of the man in the lead boat. He wore faded army fatigues and cap over olive skin adorned by a thick, wiry beard.

"*Hola, Senor* Don!" he called.

Reinforcements. I should have known.

We docked half a mile up the inlet, at a rickety dock next to a crumbling swamp shanty. The new men were mostly Cubans, but there were two or three Americans, too, hair cropped short, eyes like flint, every one of them armed. I counted ten men. With Stan, Don and Ferrie, it was thirteen of them against the three of us—and two of us were barely conscious.

I saw no way out. I could try to stall them and send them all over New Orleans, but it was a city I didn't even know. In any case, it wouldn't work for long. They'd beat Lee again, not because they thought I would talk but out of sheer frustration, and this time they would kill him. They might well do the same to the President.

Sighing, I told them where to go.

To my surprise, Don let out a soft chuckle. "Clever. We send guns through that office all the time. I could have saved myself a lot of trouble."

It was nearly 9:30 when we arrived in Lafayette Square Park. The Square itself was deserted, the rays of sunshine splashing over splintered park benches scattered among the bare-leaved trees in the park. We drove around to the side of a squat two-story grayish cinderblock building that seemed deserted. To its occupants, it was known as the Newman Building. Its address was either 544 Camp Street or 531 Lafayette Street. Lee had used the Camp Street address on the "Hands Off Cuba" flyers he'd given out around the city this summer. Guy Banister's offices were listed at 531 Lafayette Street, and Lee had been a frequent visitor there, too. It was full of anti-Castro activity and people who lived on the fringes of society.

"There's the truck," Don called. The big white truck with "Taylor & Sons Trucking" printed in block letters on its side was parked by the Lafayette Street entrance.

Our car stopped next to it, and the Cuban who was driving jumped out.

Tension was now coiling its way through my entire body.

All they had to do was confirm that the boxes of weapons were in the truck.

Then they would kill us.

I had no ideas left, no weapons, and almost no strength.

Don, Stan and the Cuban approached the rear of the truck, though I saw no one there. Don unlocked the lift gate and pushed it upward, peering inside. A triumphant smile spread across his face. He turned to nod at Ferrie in the car beside me. "They're all here."

A gravelly booming voice over a bullhorn shattered Don's moment of victory. "*Federal agents. Drop your weapons and put your hands in the air.*"

At once, from every direction, the street was filled with men in blue windbreakers and gold badges, armed to the teeth. Unmarked sedans screamed into the street at either end, blocking off any escape.

Don Cuyler fired the first shot.

A volley of shots exploded around him.

Stan went over backwards in a heap, his right arm riddled and bleeding. The Cuban was hit in the chest. Don crouched for cover behind the truck and started to fire, but he was pinned down by a crossfire from three directions. A moment later, he squatted low and crawled beneath the truck, disappearing from sight.

Six of Don's men from the dock ran into buildings; twenty agents chased after them.

Ferrie slid into the driver's seat, throwing our car into gear. An agent nearby fired neatly at the front tire, exploding it with a single shot. Ferrie grabbed frantically for his own gun, but before he could dislodge it, four agents surrounded the driver's door, guns aimed directly at him. Ferrie froze.

I leaned toward them and screamed, "Don't shoot, don't shoot! The President's in here!"

"What?"

"President Kennedy, he's in here! Don't fire!"

The agents dragged Ferrie out, spread-eagling and handcuffing him in the street. His grotesque wig, knocked askew by their rough handling, slid forward, revealing the smooth, completely hairless back of his head.

The rear doors of the car were yanked open. "Jack! Jack?"

It was Bobby Kennedy, looking tense and gaunt. When he saw his brother lying, head back, eyes closed, on the seat, he grabbed for him. "Jack! Oh, God, Jack!"

His brother managed to open his eyes, just barely, and smile at him. "About damn time, Bobby. Thought you'd— never make it."

Bobby Kennedy's tense expression blossomed into a smile. "There's gratitude for you." He turned to yell behind him. "Over here!"

Immediately, half a dozen men crowded around the car, shielding the President with their bodies. I twisted around in the front seat, watching with astonishment as the agents separated the President from Lee, who lay limp next to him.

One of the men looked amazingly familiar to me. "George!" I breathed. "George, you're all right!"

George Staub gave me the nearest thing to a smile that he could manage.

A silver military helicopter, rotors spinning, hovered gently over Lafayette Square. It was waiting to land, I thought, until the gun battle was over.

Meanwhile, agents were cutting down Don's men, one by one. Some were led out handcuffed and bleeding. Others would be hauled out later in body bags. These were stubborn guys, and they weren't giving up their dream of a Cuban invasion without a fight.

Dust clouds whipped up and the sound of rotors became deafening as another helicopter descended out of the clouds and hovered over the square. As I watched, a police sniper, his rifle protruding from the chopper's open door, aimed at the building opposite. The rifle emitted a sharp *crack!*

"There's another one in the left-hand window." Another sharp *crack!* from the police chopper, followed by a voice on the radio. "Two down."

Then a different voice crackled over the channel. "A-team, we are in."

We heard two single shots, answered by bursts of five or six rounds each as the agents inside the building returned fire; then there was silence. Eight or nine seconds passed before the tense lull ended. "Point, this is A-team. Building is secure. Repeat, we are secure."

The radio began to buzz with requests for aid and orders to secure the square's perimeter. George turned down the volume.

"It's over, sir. We've got them all," said the agent who seemed to be in charge.

Bobby Kennedy nodded. "Get the chopper in here."

The men closest to the President began to ease him out of the car.

"Watch his back!" Bobby shouted to them. "Be careful!"

The President was out of the car, walking jerkily toward the chopper landing in the Square a hundred feet away. His face was pale and damp.

"Jack?" Bobby said quietly. "Can you make it?"

Behind me, Lee was being hauled out and spread across the hood of the car.

The agents frisked him roughly.

"He's not armed!" I shouted, emerging from the car myself. "For God's sake, leave him alone! He's been hurt enough!" The agents, satisfied Lee was unarmed, let him off the car. He pulled the jacket closer around his middle and winced.

A number of reporters suddenly ran toward us from the Newman Building. I have no idea how they got there. "Mr. President! Mr. President!" they called. They had cameras and pads and looked eager enough, and determined enough, to stampede the agents, if necessary.

"What the hell... ?" Bobby began.

The agents swung around to the front. Seeing the crowd, they pushed Bobby aside and advanced about ten feet in front of the President to cut off the mob. I moved with them. We had kept the President safe through all of this. I wasn't going to let news-hungry reporters get to him now. To my right, I saw more agents stuffing a bloodied Stan and David Ferrie, both of them handcuffed, into the backs of waiting cars.

From the corner of my eye I saw the President, swaying a little, standing alone and unprotected behind the car. All the agents with him had formed a line in front and were bunching together, facing the mob.

I saw a lone cameraman in a battered brown fedora, his big old-fashioned camera in his hand, approaching silently from behind. Something about him was familiar… but something about this whole setup was wrong…

The cameraman moved within a few feet and raised his camera with his left hand, his right dangling at his side. From the corner of my eye I saw Lee straighten up, his eyes narrowing on the cameraman.

Then I saw the gun coming up in the cameraman's right hand. I looked at the face under the fedora. It was Don Cuyler.

I started to scream a warning. But there was too much space around the President. The agents were in front of him, not behind, and they were too far away. Don had all the time he wanted; Kennedy could hardly move, even to jump out of the way. Nothing could come between the 35th President and his fate…… Except a stubbornly determined 24-year-old ex-Marine…

I saw a blur, a blur with something sandy around its middle. With cracked ribs, a broken nose and a terribly battered body, Lee had launched himself into the air between Don and the President.

The roar of the gun swung all the agents around. In an instant, half of them had surrounded and fallen on Cuyler, whose gun was still smoking from the shot he'd fired. One of the agents was banging his hand down on the grass, forcing him to release the gun.

The other half of the agents had surrounded and fallen on the President, who had already been knocked down by the force of Lee's leap across him. He lay in the grass.

Lee lay alone, a terrible stain spreading across his chest. I ran to him and fell down next to him, terrified. This couldn't be happening. It couldn't be. Not after all we've been through… not when it was almost over…

His eyes were open and clear, and when I took his hand, he knew it was me. "Cady," he said, and then he fell silent. He was gathering strength for what he wanted to say.

"Don't talk, Lee. We'll get you help."

"The President—?"

I looked hastily behind me. "He's okay. You saved him, Lee. You saved him." He smiled a little, but his face was going paler and paler. The stain was growing larger and larger. I looked frantically for something large to put on the wound. "Give me your jacket!" I said impulsively to the closest agent. Stunned, he took it off without a word.

I balled it up and stuffed it into the wound, pressing down as hard as I could. Immediately, my hands were soaked in his blood. "Don't move," I said to Lee again. Then I raised my head and screamed to the other agents. "Get an ambulance! Now!"

The President saw the paper-white pallor of Lee's face, and the stain spreading inexorably, no matter how hard I pressed on it. He knew what it meant. He leaned over Lee and took his hand. "Lee?"

Lee looked at him and nodded, a tiny nod of acknowledgement. He knew who was holding his hand.

"You saved my life. Thank you."

Lee tried to nod again, and suddenly coughed, and I saw blood at his mouth.

Oh, God. He was going so terribly fast.

His hand tightened on the President's. He wanted to say something. The President waited. "Files…"

He took a breath. It was shallow, so shallow. His lungs were filling with blood. Soon he'd be drowning in it. "Files… find them. They incriminate—everyone."

"We will. Don't worry."

"Hid… them." Lee seemed to be losing strength faster and faster. "My mechanic… Lou. Talk—to him. My daughter June—grows so fast. Needs new shoes…"

"We'll get them," I said, as steadily as I could, and thought I'd strangle from the lump in my throat.

"Lou… Junie… wish I'd—seen the new baby—more." He swallowed and looked into the President's grave face. "I was in the Soviet Union in '60… or I'd have voted for you…"

The President, too, was having difficulty keeping his composure. He took refuge in a quip. "All things considered, Lee, I sure could have used that vote."

"Next year…'64… I'll—vote—for you."

"Thanks, Lee." The President's eyes were glistening, though Lee didn't see it now.

"June… Lou… Cady?" He looked for me. I put a hand on his cheek. "You're a good… dancer…"

"So are you."

But Lee couldn't hear me. He had closed his eyes. We were all silent for a moment. Then the agent whose jacket I had borrowed put his fingers on Lee's wrist. He looked at his watch. Looked at us. Shook his head.

Lee was dead.

"What time is it?" I said suddenly.

The President, still holding Lee's hand, looked at me like I was crazy, but the agent glanced at his watch and said, "It's—10:20."

An hour earlier. He had died an hour earlier than the first time, when Jack Ruby shot him in the basement of the Dallas police station. I couldn't bear it. I'd promised him there would be another time for us…

I leaned down and kissed Lee on the cheek, then shook out the jacket and placed the unstained part of it over his face.

The shooting had stopped. The street was quiet. The sun was rising higher. The air was heavy and moist after the rain.

The President put down Lee's hand reluctantly and was helped to his feet. "Miss Cuyler," he said. "You come, too."

"No, Mr. President," I said. "Lee left his files here, and he wanted us to look for them. I think I should."

I paused as I saw the dark sedan where Don Cuyler sat handcuffed in the back seat. I'd had the chance to kill Don back in the Gulf and couldn't bring myself to do it. Now, because of my failure, Lee was dead. He had saved my life, saved the President's life. I hadn't saved him when I could have. That thought would haunt me forever, I knew.

I saw two agents approach the dark sedan, flashing ID's at the agents guarding him. The agents nodded and stepped away as the new pair climbed into the car, turned the key in the ignition and turned north out of Lafayette Square.

What was wrong with this picture?

The answer came to me in a flash: *the other agents weren't wearing business suits.*

The President and Attorney General were moving toward the helicopter.

"That's funny," said one of the agents. "They're supposed to be booking that guy. But they're driving away from the Justice Building."

"Seven team, who are those guys pulling out?" George asked into his radio.

"Federal marshals, sir. They're with the Attorney General's team out of Washington."

The Attorney General heard this exchange and turned to George urgently. "I didn't order any marshals out of Washington. Those guys are fakes!"

George was already moving toward his car. I was two steps ahead of him and moving faster. "Cady, get on the chopper!" he commanded, but I'd already climbed behind the wheel of his sedan and shut the door.

"Cady, get out of there!"

I didn't listen. I slammed the car into gear and sped off in pursuit, and behind me, I heard George swear vividly and saw him jump into another sedan nearby. Within half a minute I was two blocks away, but George, in the backup car, was sitting grimly on my tail. I glanced in the mirror and saw him hold the radio up to his mouth, calling, no doubt, for backup.

The car ahead zoomed to seventy miles per hour, keeping the half-block distance between us with no regard for stoplights.

Two New Orleans Police cruisers appeared behind George. The driver of the sedan ahead was an expert, weaving in and out of traffic smoothly to keep me at bay, though we were now almost on their bumper.

I felt waves of pain and rage. I'd let Don Cuyler live, and he'd taken a fatal shot at Lee. But he wouldn't get away with it. There had to be some justice in this world.

I matched the sedan's driver move for move, swerve for swerve, my eyes focused on him, yet still alert for obstructions ahead.

Mercifully, there were none. I waited impatiently for my chance, knowing that when it came, I would stop that car. The needle on my speedometer climbed to ninety, the police cruisers falling a hundred yards behind me. George stayed with me grimly, his front fender just yards behind my rear, and when I looked back, his eyes were blazing and he stuck his head out the window. As we went through an intersection, I thought I heard him shouting, "Get out of the way!"

I didn't even try to answer. I was thinking about a maneuver an old stunt driver had taught me, which was used all the time by police cars to stop vehicles they were pursuing. I'd never tried it at this speed before, but he said it always worked, and I had to assume that a car going this fast would be even easier to stop than one at a slower speed: Fast-moving cars are less stable, a condition I was counting on.

The sedan turned onto a wide, four-lane boulevard with big soft shoulders. There was no traffic in either direction. I closed to within three yards of the sedan. The driver nudged to his right, trying to force me onto the shoulder. It was exactly what I wanted him to do. He had to brake slightly, and when he did, I swerved back and left, ending up with the nose of my car just ahead of his rear bumper.

I focused on the left rear quarter panel of the sedan, about eight inches behind the tire well. I had no idea if this move would work with the heavier, more cumbersome vehicles of 1963, but I'd made it work before. If I missed the impact mark by so much as an inch, the resulting collision would be fatal to all of us.

I wasn't going to miss.

I gunned the accelerator until I pulled parallel with the impact mark on the rear quarter panel. I braked slightly as I started to turn into the sedan, letting the sedan move slightly ahead of me. The angle was perfect.

Suddenly, I cut the wheel hard and slammed into the left rear quarter panel. I hit the impact mark dead on. The sedan fishtailed slightly, then spun hard around into a 360-degree circle. Two loud blasts sent geysers of brown smoke skyward as the sedan's tires blew out.

I had seldom in my life ever seen anything so beautiful.

I braked the car hard, stopping across the lane of oncoming traffic to prevent other cars from getting close to the sedan.

It was over in a couple of minutes. George and the police cruisers sped up behind me. The officers jumped out and subdued the two shaken men in the front, handcuffing Don Cuyler to another officer and stuffing him in the back of the cruiser. This time he would not get away.

George jumped out of the car and ran to me. "Stupid, Cady! Really stupid!"

I felt infinitely relieved; at least I'd been able to do *something* to make sure they got the right guy this time.

George insisted on driving me back to the city, at a more moderate speed. As he drove, we began to hear shouts on the street.

"They found the President!"

"He's alive! Kennedy's alive!"

George turned on the car radio. "From New Orleans, Louisiana," began the voice of Walter Cronkite, "we have official word that President John F. Kennedy is alive. A morning gun battle in New Orleans' Lafayette Square has just ended with the rescue of the President, and the killing of eight kidnappers along with Lee Harvey Oswald, the alleged mastermind of the plot to kill President Kennedy."

I was shaken and horrified. Damn it! Lee was *still* being accused of crimes he had not committed! I listened to the rest, but there was no mention of Lee's heroics, nor of the reason why he had died.

When George, seeing my furious face, turned off the radio, I all but sputtered in my rage. "I'm staying here, George. I've got to find those files."

We drove through the gates of a military base.

"There's Air Force One," George said, pointing at the tarmac. He drove me right up to the ramp and shooed me up the steps.

I went up reluctantly, my feet dragging. I had left something important undone. I couldn't leave here till it was done.

The Attorney General himself met me at the top of the steps. "Let's go, Miss Cuyler," Kennedy said brusquely. "The President refuses to leave the city without you, but he needs medical attention right away. You had no right going off like that and participating in a high-speed chase."

He certainly was well informed.

"You had no right to let the press think Lee Oswald died because he was trying to kill the President," I shot back. "He died *protecting* the President! Why isn't that on the news?"

"Get on the plane," Kennedy repeated, and his voice took on a hard tone. "We'll get that taken care of later."

"No," I said. "I'm staying here in New Orleans to find those files." But I did look inside the plane.

The President himself was being tended by a doctor and two nurses, right in front of me. "Let's go, Miss Cuyler," he said.

"No, Mr. President," I said, going toward him. "We'll never clear Lee's name without those files."

"He was bluffing, Cady," said the President. "Those files didn't really exist. I thought you realized that. He made that up for Don and the Cubans, to buy us some time. And later on, he was delirious."

"No. I thought that too, but I was wrong. He's always told the truth about this whole plot. With his dying breath he told us to find them, and *you promised you would!"*

"Do you know where these files are?" asked Bobby Kennedy.

"They're here in New Orleans. I know I can find them." I was determined and implacable.

"We haven't got time for this," the Attorney General muttered.

I directed my gaze to the President. "Lee paid for your life with his own. I'm asking you to help me prove his innocence. Doesn't he deserve that? Or was everything you told me Friday night a lie?"

The President looked at me. The eyes were a stormy blue-gray now; conflicted. Weighing expedience against justice. I knew that every moment he spent in New Orleans was a moment of wrenching pain.

But he nodded to his brother. They conferred in whispers for a moment.

The Attorney General, resigned, took my arm and walked me down the ramp. He signaled to George, who came on the run. "Pick a team. Escort Miss Roberts anywhere in the city she wants to go." He looked at me. "You have until 2:00 to find these files. At 2:00 you return with us to Washington. With or without them." He looked at George. "We'll be waiting here—"

George nodded. "I'll have her back."

I glanced at my watch. It seemed like hours since Lee had died, and I had chased Don Cuyler into custody—but it had only been 45 minutes. It was 11:05.

I had less than three hours.

Think, I told myself. It has to be here in New Orleans. But where?

George watched me, waited for me. "Take me to Magazine Street," I said into the silence. "Lee had an apartment there this summer."

"Cady—"

"It's a place to start, damn it!"

We arrived at the Magazine Street apartment with a screech of brakes. George had enlisted three other FBI agents, their guns conspicuously close. We went into the apartment together.

It was small and we searched it swiftly, the new tenant, cowed and silent, not asking to see a search warrant. Nothing under the dingy carpet, in the baseboards, or in the plumbing. Nothing under the bathroom tiles or behind the stove.

We were finished in twenty minutes.

"Where to now?" George asked as the others piled into the car.

I thought quickly. "The Reily Coffee Company"

The Reily Coffee Company had briefly employed Lee in the spring and early summer of 1963 to grease their machines. He hadn't liked the job, apparently, as he spent most of his time around the corner at a nearby garage, talking guns with the garage owner. Reily had fired him after just a few months. Still, I thought it was worth a look.

As we drove the quiet streets, New Orleans began to come alive. Newspaper extras were already appearing, people piling out of churches and homes to snatch the fresh copies. "JFK ALIVE!" blared the headlines in the largest type I'd ever seen. "RESCUED IN NEW ORLEANS" was set in only slightly smaller type.

The car jerked to a halt in front of the Reily Coffee Company.

I also realized that my own belief had been hardening, minute by minute, through this tragic and terrible day. Lee had spoken his cryptic words with such desperation that he wouldn't find the breath, that I was sure somewhere close by, he really had stashed something of value. If I were right, the President would be safe, because we could prove the plotters' guilt.

I felt sick every time I thought of Don.

Lee was dead because Don was alive to fire at the President.

Lee was dead because I couldn't bring myself to kill Don.

Lee was dead because of *me.*

My thoughts were unbearable.

I looked at my watch. It was almost noon.

Less than half an hour later, we were back in the car. Another dead end.

"544 Camp Street," I said, feeling more and more dispirited. "Lee had an office there."

I had less than two hours to come up with these critical files, or—I finally faced it—Lee had died for nothing. People were already speaking his name with anger, with disdain; if I couldn't find what he'd left for posterity, he'd be just a crazy Communist who'd gone off the deep end and tried to kill the President, fortunately stopped by Don Cuyler, a patriot with a gun.

That thought was the most unbearable one yet.

The FBI driver stopped in front of the long cinderblock building at the end of the block. It was once again as quiet as it had been when we arrived early this morning.

The FBI man who had been driving sidled up to George. "Sir, the car needs gas—can I take it to the garage?"

George made a shooing gesture with his hand, and the man muttered, "Thanks," and ran off.

An upstairs office that could have been Lee's appeared unoccupied. George followed as I dashed up the steps.

The door was unlocked, because the little room behind it was completely bare. There was literally nothing in it at all, not a slip of paper or a stick of furniture.

We examined every inch of wall space, every step of wooden flooring. There was a small dark closet in one corner; I burrowed in, flashing a light everywhere, but saw nothing but what looked like a small heap of wood shavings in the furthest corner.

"It's got to be here," I muttered.

George looked at me sympathetically. "Maybe someone else found it first."

I looked at him dully. There was no mistaking his meaning: If they had, it would be destroyed by now. A cold cloud of misery settled in my chest.

George looked at his watch. "The guys need to check the car in, after it's gassed up. I should go over there now and make some calls." He hesitated. "I'm sorry."

I felt suddenly leaden, almost unable to move. George steered me out of the room. "Come on. You have to be on that plane in an hour."

I don't remember much of that walk on Camp Street; I didn't notice much of anything until George called, "You ready, Steve?"

I looked up. We were in a garage; I could smell the heavy-sweet odor of leaded gasoline, and saw rows of dark cars.

Talk to my mechanic, Lou.

What had Lee meant?

He'd been so insistent, so desperate…

This was a garage. And it was close to Oswald's best-known hangout in New Orleans.

"George… what is this place?" I asked.

He looked puzzled. "All the law-enforcement people in Lafayette Square get our cars serviced here. Good mechanics." A guy in Crescent City Garage overalls was walking toward us, the name "HANK" written on them in red thread letters.

"Does a guy named Lou work here?" I asked.

The guy in overalls nodded. "Yeah. You wanna talk to him?" I looked at my watch and nodded.

"Hey, Lou!" bellowed Hank. "Little lady out here wants a word with you!"

A guy in amazingly greasy overalls came out, his hands soaked almost black. The pocket on his overalls read "LOU". "Yeah?" he said to me, hardly glancing at me.

"Did you know Lee Oswald?" I asked Lou, not expecting much of a reply.

He shrugged. "The kid whose picture's been on TV all weekend? Yeah, I knew him."

"He—he said you were a great mechanic," I said foolishly, fumbling my words.

He shrugged again. "Don't know how he'd know. The kid didn't own a car."

"But—he mentioned you by name."

Another shrug. "He was here almost every day, last summer. Talking to Mr. Alba. Sitting in his little space."

"Oswald had space here?" George asked.

Lou pointed at a corner of the big office at the end of the garage. "Mr. Alba let him have that corner. I think Oswald even called it his 'office'."

George and I looked at the little corner, as hope began to rise in me once more. "Did he—keep anything here?"

Lou shook his head. "If he did, it's probably still here."

"That's it!" I said urgently to George. "It's been here all along!"

I flew over to the office area and into the space Lou had indicated. It was tiny, dark, with almost nothing there. But there was a loose board across a radiator...

George aimed his flashlight into the cold radiator as I reached into the dark space.

My hand touched something smooth, something cool and small. George held the flashlight as I pulled it out.

It looked like...

"... film?" George said. "Undeveloped film? I've never seen film rolls that looked like that."

I turned it over in my fingers. The small black canister was marked with pen in very faint letters—"LHO".

George got it before I did. "He *photographed* the files," he breathed. "He couldn't copy them; they'd be too bulky to hide. But he could photograph them and store the film anywhere! Son of a gun!"

My relief almost knocked me flat. I should have realized that a man as careful as Lee would find a way to get those incriminating documents. It was his only defense against the massive evil he had encountered at 531 Lafayette Street.

When we'd emptied the cache, there were twenty little canisters.

George found a plain brown paper bag, and we dropped the film in.

A commotion across the square distracted us. "What's that?" he asked, as shouts filled the air.

We walked outside. There were frantic male voices shouting out and popping flashbulbs as a hundred bodies crowded in front of the police station.

"They must be transferring Don Cuyler," George said, his face as stony as his voice.

The man I hadn't been able to bring myself to kill.

A man I knew would never tell anything significant about the plot.

"Let's take a look," I said to George.

We cut across the park swiftly and headed for the entrance of New Orleans Police headquarters, filled with thronging crowds, shouting reporters and TV cameras.

A single harassed police spokesman stood on the steps, saying, "He'll be out shortly, folks, you'll get your pictures, hold on..."

"Standard booking," George said, when he saw I was puzzled. "They get mug shots, fingerprints, then transfer him to the county jail. He'll need guards, with this mob."

I looked at him. Lee had been surrounded by guards in the basement of the Dallas County Jail... yet even with guards, a man had broken through...

It wasn't fair. There would be no justice for anyone whose life Don had touched. And the President would never really be safe as long as Don Cuyler breathed.

I looked at the mob, and saw a man standing at the edge, in a brown suit and hat... a man whose face I recognized... a man whose purpose I could guess.

I knew then he was my instrument of revenge...

I broke away from George and reached behind my belt buckle. Miraculously, the small Secret Service ID billfold I'd stuffed down there remained. I picked it out, approached the man in the brown hat and tapped him on the shoulder.

"Look," I said quickly, showing the billfold, "I'm a reporter for... uh—*The Wichita Star*—but I'll never get in there to talk to that Cuyler fellow. Maybe you—here—"

He looked at me with beady eyes. "Where'd you get this?"

I feigned puzzlement. "I found it—by the car where Cuyler was arrested—"

The man looked at me. "Don't I know you?" I shook my head. He snatched the billfold out of my hand and pushed his way through the crowd, calling out, "Secret Service! Secret Service! Coming through!"

I watched as the crowd swallowed up the man in the brown suit and brown hat. The man I knew as Jack Ruby...

George had fought his way through the crowd to reach me. "What was that about?" he asked me.

I shrugged. "He asked when the transfer would happen. I said I didn't know."

There was a shout, "Here he comes!", and I caught a quick glimpse of a haggard Don Cuyler in handcuffs. Then the crowd surged backward, as the reporters scrambled to give him room to walk and still keep him in their camera lenses...

And then the roar of a pistol, fired at close range, and a TV reporter's voice: "He's been shot! Don Cuyler has been shot! I don't believe it! Don Cuyler has been shot! It's—absolute—bedlam here!"

If I had bothered to look, I might have seen Jack Ruby wrestled to the ground, the gun torn from his grasp, the frantic working over Don's still body ...

But I didn't bother. I had a pretty good idea how things were going to turn out.

Feeling better than I had all morning, I climbed into the FBI car to ride to the airfield.

And arrived in time to climb aboard the gleaming government airplane and hear the pilot radio, "Air Force One to Castle, Air Force One to Castle. Mission accomplished. We have Lancer, and we're coming home."

* * *

I didn't see the President at all on the flight to Washington. He stayed in a closed bedroom on board and his physician stayed with him.

I sat quietly alone in a small alcove near the front. I wanted to adjust, to do my grieving for Lee and think through all that had occurred since I first was thrust into Dealey Plaza only a week ago.

I also wanted to prepare to go home to the year 2000—if I even could. Or had throwing away my cell phone doomed me to remain here?

I didn't glance at the tray of food the steward had brought me, until a very familiar voice with an unmistakable accent said, "Miss Cuyler?"

I looked up. The Attorney General stood in the aisle, his left hand clutching the precious brown paper bag we'd brought from the Crescent City Garage.

"I thought you'd be hungry," he said. "And we need to talk. Privately."

I started to say I wasn't hungry, but the smell of smoking bacon and eggs set my stomach roaring.

The Attorney General said nothing until I drank down an entire tumbler of orange juice and ate at least half the eggs and all the bacon before he spoke again. "Feeling better?" he asked pleasantly.

"How's your brother?" I asked instead.

"*The President*," he emphasized, "is much better. Of course, he'll need to rest until we get to Washington." Then he added soberly, "You and Lee Oswald saved his life."

"Lee saved his life."

Kennedy hesitated for a moment. When he spoke again, his voice was soft with compassion. "We're all grateful for your help. Both of you. You'll never know how much."

There didn't seem to be any answer to that. I waited for him to go on.

After a moment, he did. He hefted the paper bag and said, "This is the evidence he hid?"

"That's it," I said succinctly. "The microfilm he told us to find with his last breath." I fought back my anguish. "It'll get you lots of convictions."

"Yes," Kennedy agreed grimly, "it will." His eyes were so fierce that I was startled. He seemed to sense my thoughts. "We heard about Cuyler's death in custody," he said casually. "The New Orleans police ought to be ashamed. I'll be looking into how anyone could get to him so easily. I heard that Ruby fellow had a Secret Service badge in his hand when he fired."

I looked him squarely in the eye. "Leave it alone, Mr. Kennedy. Neither you nor the FBI needs to know that." Deliberately, I changed the subject. "Do you still have problems with J. Edgar Hoover?"

He looked startled. I grinned. "Come on, I know Hoover kept files on all public figures for blackmail purposes, and that he's got files on both you and the President." I paused. "And we know what's in it." I paused. "And I know what's in them." I saw Kennedy wince. "The year 2000, remember? There are things published in books and newspapers in my time that are labeled Top Secret today. I know you'd like to get rid of Hoover." I paused again. "And I even know how you can do it."

"Oh?" he said, leaning forward.I told him.

Robert Kennedy leaned his head back and roared with laughter. He was laughing so hard that for a moment, he couldn't speak. His eyes were still twinkling as he caught his breath and grinned at me. "It's perfect. We'll do it."

I smiled back at him. "What is it your family says? 'Don't get mad, get even'?"

"I don't think we ever said that," he answered, puzzled. "But—" his grin returned, "it's a damn good idea."

* * *

It was late afternoon by the time Air Force One began its descent through the clear blue skies over Washington. I had talked to Bobby Kennedy for over two hours, and he had listened, rapt. At the end, he asked some questions, and I did my best to answer them. He took copious notes in a small leather-bound notebook and said he'd give the information to his top investigators at once. He also promised that Lee's film would be processed by the most trusted lab people he had, under the tightest security in Washington, next to the President's.

I saw a commotion at the door to the President's private quarters; people were bustling in and out, with what looked like fresh clothes for the President. It seemed like a waste of time, though. I hoped he had recovered, at least a little, from the weekend ordeal, but I still seriously doubted he would be able to walk down the ramp.

I should have known better.

The plane touched down, light as a feather, on the runway at Andrews Air Force Base, and swung easily around to taxi to a halt, a few hundred yards from the shouting, pushing reporters and their equipment. We would be facing a storm of sound and light when we stepped off.

A Secret Service agent stopped by me. "Please, ma'am, you're to wait here. When the press has gone, we'll take you out. The President has requested that you stay at the White House."

I smiled. "And he wants to be sure no one sees me?"

The agent had the grace to look embarrassed. "Well, ma'am, he'd like to avoid any—"

"—misunderstanding," I finished. I looked at him innocently. "How is that possible?"

I peered out the window, as President Kennedy slowly descended the ramp. As he did, from the ranks of the newsmen and reporters rose such a roar of relief and approval that he hesitated momentarily, startled by the heartfelt reaction. They had their cameras aimed at him and were clicking away... but they were also letting him know they were thankful he was back.

The President reached the tarmac and dipped his head just once, smiling. He looked toward a limousine waiting a hundred yards away.

Then he wavered. The strength and will that had carried him through this catastrophic weekend had suddenly ebbed, leaving him shaky and disoriented. Secret Service agents, seeing his weakness, reached out to help, but he gave them a warning look, and they backed away. He took a deep breath, lifted his head and straightened his spine. The pain was clearly etched in his eyes and mouth.

Then all eyes swung toward the limousine. Someone was jostling through the Secret Service agents waiting there.

My mouth dropped open as I recognized Jackie Kennedy. Beautiful, cool, poised Jackie. Never a hair out of place, never an ungraceful gesture—that lovely, gracious woman was shoving her way through the VIPs, frantic to reach her husband, her own security detail, shocked and unprepared, lost far behind her.

Arms outstretched, cheeks streaming tears, she stumbled toward the motionless figure fighting to stand upright. His men parted for her without a word. At this moment there was no best-dressed, most-admired First Lady, or witty, intellectual and spirited young President. There was only a woman in an agony of fear and relief, and a man fighting crippling pain to project the dignity and strength he believed the world expected of him.

They came together in the shadow of Air Force One.

The President of the United States—the most powerful man on the face of the earth—took two hesitant, faltering steps... and literally fell into his wife's arms.

They sank to the tarmac together on their knees, camera bulbs popping, the press suddenly and strangely silent. At that moment, they were just like any couple who had survived tragedy and death and despair.

The photo of the two of them kneeling and gazing into each other's eyes on that lonely stretch of concrete is the single most famous and lasting image of the entire eight-year Kennedy Administration.

PART FOUR
FORWARD TO
CAMELOT

Chapter Seventeen
SATURDAY, NOVEMBER 30, 1963

A warm, unseasonable breeze blew as the guests arrived at the Rose Garden, though the branches of the trees here in Washington were almost bare. It was one of those rare late November days people call Indian summer. It gave you hope.

Five hundred government officials waited in the blazing sunshine. Senators, congressmen, ambassadors, had fought to get into this event: It was *the* prestige event of the season, though the guest of honor would be absent. At least a hundred reporters, print and television, were covering the event live.

What made it especially remarkable is the fact that it was the Saturday afternoon of Thanksgiving weekend. Throughout the country, football games were being played and celebrations continued. Yet these people waiting in the Washington sunlight had the hottest ticket.

I sat in an inconspicuous seat close to the platform, wearing my simple beige dress, minus its jacket, from the year 2000. It had been mended and cleaned so expertly by the White House staff that it looked brand-new. The President himself had directed that I sit in the third row of the audience, where I would have an unobstructed view but remain unnoticed by the press and the other dignitaries. Six Secret Service agents from the President's own detail sat around me. A seventh agent, in the customary dark glasses, thin tie and nondescript single-breasted suit, stood at the head of the row, seemingly keeping a watch on the guests and the President, but always with an eye turned my way.

The six days since the President had been rescued in New Orleans had seen more activity in the Administration than any single week since the missile crisis the year before. Robert Kennedy and his staff had devoured Lee's files and used them to implement the most focused clean-up campaign Washington had ever seen.

With the assistance of the New Orleans District Attorney, an imposing six-and-a-half-footer named Jim Garrison, Bobby Kennedy had quietly carried out the arrests of private investigator Guy Banister and Clay Shaw, the director of New Orleans' International Trade Mart. David Ferrie had been in custody since Sunday morning. All three men were charged with conspiracy to commit murder and treason and were being held without bail. Lee's files, the Attorney General had told the President privately, would make their indictments and convictions all but certain. As he had been in most other aspects of his life, Lee had been quiet and thorough about collecting the incriminating evidence. Robert Kennedy told me he was certain that he would be able to indict at least a dozen others within the next two weeks.

The previous week had also been notable for the frantic, though absolutely secret, efforts over the President's health. From the time he had been borne away from New Orleans on Sunday morning, he had not been seen in person, though he had addressed the nation on television Monday evening. During that address he had been well protected, seated behind a high desk, lighted and made up to look as hearty as ever, dressed impeccably as usual, and shot only from the shoulders up. In that address, he had spoken briefly but reassuringly to the nation, saying he was glad to be back, that he thanked Vice-President Johnson for his 'able and resourceful leadership in a time of crisis', and that the nation should go on about its business.

The President's press secretary glanced behind him, nodded at a signal from a Secret Service agent, and stepped forward to the silver microphone at the edge of the platform. "Ladies and gentlemen," he intoned, "the President of the United States."

A door opened behind him, and the President, garbed in a handsome navy suit, his chestnut hair shining, stepped into the November sunshine.

The crowd rose as one to its feet, and a roar such as I had never heard rose into the autumn sky. I looked around at the celebrated, educated, often-jaded crowd around me. Every single person was on his feet; everyone, Republican and Democrat, was shouting and applauding, feet stamping thunderously, faces glistening with tears. I saw former President Eisenhower, ahead of me and to the right, solemnly salute the President; nearby, Richard Nixon seemed to wink hard, his eyes suspiciously wet. The Cabinet, on the platform, had abandoned all reserve and were all but jumping up and down at the sight of their Commander-in-Chief; Robert Kennedy gave the largest grin anyone had ever seen, and blinked uncontrollably; Vice-President Johnson stood at attention, his face blank and still, and bowed his head as Kennedy strode to the microphone, a small velvet-covered box in his right hand.

The New York Times would record that the ovation lasted over 16 minutes before the President could speak, and noted wryly, "There isn't a ballplayer, astronaut or movie star on the face of the earth who wouldn't hope to evoke such a storm of affection in such a multitude, and there is no one we know who deserves it more." Kennedy himself, unable to quell the sound, finally shook his head as though helpless, and I could swear a tear rose to his eye before the thunderous stamping, screaming and cheering finally hushed. On the platform behind him, Mrs. Kennedy, cool and beautiful in a lovely red dress, bowed her head for a moment, as though the emotions released had touched hers as well. When she looked up, the smile on her face seemed fixed in place, and her dark eyes looked glassy.

When the lawn was finally quiet, the President glanced down at the notes in his hand, then lifted his eyes to the crowd. "Thank you," he said. "It's good to be employed again." The ribbon of laughter that spread through the crowd threatened to erupt into another uncontrollable ovation, but the President cut it off to speak again.

"My fellow citizens," Kennedy began, "we come together today to honor a genuine American hero. More than anyone here, I owe him my gratitude and admiration for his courage. Without him, I would not be here at all. For that—" he grinned the famous Kennedy grin, "—you may not all be grateful, but I certainly am."

There was another appreciative roar, and the President continued, more seriously. "As with many such heroes, he came from humble beginnings. He struggled to find his place in the world. But he dreamed of better times and a better world for his children, as we all do. The difference is, when he saw that future threatened, he deliberately put himself in harm's way to effect a change. Last Friday afternoon, in Dallas, I would have ridden into a fatal ambush in an open car, if not for the quick thinking, resourcefulness and courage of Lee Oswald. The plotters who planned to kill me and destroy my Administration had prepared for every eventuality except that. They hadn't foreseen that a hero would force himself into the center of their conflict, nor that he would carefully document their crimes and preserve those documents, to be retrieved by others who value justice over tyranny.

"The truth is, Lee Oswald was serving his country long before I encountered him on November 22nd. From his enlistment in the Marines at the age of seventeen right up to last weekend, when he gave his life to save mine, Lee Oswald has been a patriot, a man of ideals and a man who takes action in service of those ideals. He gave his life to protect them, and to protect his President. This President and his family will never forget that, and we will remain forever in his debt.

"And so—" He raised the small box and opened it, to reveal what looked like a blob of bronze on a bed of velvet. "I am awarding the Presidential Medal of Freedom, the highest honor that can be bestowed by this country on a civilian, to the late Lee Harvey Oswald, for exemplary service to his President, and to his country."

He held the box up, to a round of applause almost as thunderous as that which had greeted him. As it began to die away, he added, "The Medal will be accepted by Lee Oswald's mother, Marguerite Oswald."

A public-relations ploy, I diagnosed. It would not look good at all, 'exemplary service' or not, for Lee's Russian widow Marina to stand up on a platform with the President of the United States, not during the Cold War. But a humble southern woman working hard to raise her sons after her husband's untimely death, who then lost her youngest son to an early and undeserved death as well… that could evoke nothing but sympathy from everyone.

Marguerite Oswald slowly ascended the steps of the platform. Her steel-gray hair was rolled into a bun, and she wore what looked like a new dress, of some dark stuff that probably would not photograph well. Behind harlequin-shaped glasses, her eyes were red-rimmed but dry, and they were fixed steadily on President Kennedy

The President stood waiting for her, smiling. She walked very, very slowly across to him, and he leaned away from the microphone to speak to her privately. She nodded, blinking suddenly, and he opened the box to show her the Medal. Then he faced the microphone again, lifted out the Medal and squinted at it in the sunlight

It was a ploy: Kennedy needed reading glasses but would never wear them in public, and it was unlikely he'd be able to work out the inscription on the Medal without them. He'd figured out a way around that: He'd carefully memorized the inscription hours ago.

"The Medal's inscription reads: 'To Lee Harvey Oswald, for courage and resourcefulness beyond the call of duty'. Mrs. Oswald, I award this on behalf of a grateful nation."

He held up the Medal once more, this time to show the crowds and the press, and I heard a hundred camera clicks and a hundred soft pops as flashbulbs exploded in the Rose Garden, recording the moment. Then he handed the box to Marguerite Oswald. She tried to say something—he leaned forward to hear her—and just as suddenly, her face crumpled and she bent her head, tears gushing from her eyes.

The President whispered something to her, something which made her lift her head and blink away the rest of her tears. He spoke again; she spoke back, nodding, and the corners of her mouth began to lift into a smile. He smiled back at her and held out his hand to shake hers once more. Her back straight, eyes shining behind the harlequin glasses, clutching the small velvet-covered box so hard her knuckles were white, she made a final gracious, dignified nod to the President, and made her slow, laborious way across the platform and down the shallow steps.

The President returned to the podium, and what he said then has become his signature speech, the speech for which he has consistently been remembered, the speech that has been quoted all over the world and reprinted on drinking glasses, plaques, and souvenirs at the White House for two generations.

He did not look at his notes but fixed his eyes on his audience. "When we see such an example of ideals in one person as we have seen in Lee Oswald, we're tempted to believe that our world today may be better than it actually is, a kind of Camelot that people can look back on and point to with bittersweet regret in years to come. This time is not and should not be remembered as paradise; we have a long way to go before we've achieved the hope of an America we all can cherish. The enemy of progress is remembering too fondly that which should not be remembered with fondness at all. No one can say that life at this point in time is perfect—but let no one say, either, that the seeds of that vision of perfection were not planted here, today, nourished by our dreams and our sacrifices to make them reality. If we are someday to find Camelot, we will find it not by looking backward, but by marching forward, together, with unbending resolution."

He stepped away, and the roar that rose from the crowd was so palpable I thought the President might be physically knocked over. He dipped his head in acknowledgement and left the podium, disappearing once more inside the Oval Office.

"Re-election in a landslide," a man murmured to a woman beside me.

"I never thought of looking for Camelot in the future—" whined the woman, gathering her massive handbag and gloves.

I thought of all we'd been through, Lee, the President and me, during that fateful weekend.

"… If we are someday to find Camelot…"

If the Kennedy Administration was not called Camelot far into the future, it would not be for lack of trying.

* * *

It was late afternoon by the time I was ushered out to the portico, and a winter chill was settling over Washington. Standing just outside the Oval Office, watching the distant dark shapes of the trees and bushes that shielded the White House from constant view, I took a deep breath of the icy air. Unlike the words of the great Beatles song (which hadn't been written yet), this would not be a long cold lonely winter. Though I had failed in a most profound sense, I suppose that together with Lee, I had also succeeded. And though I missed him and ached for the opportunities lost, I was also, slowly, learning to accept.

The door behind me opened, and the President walked out. He was alone, for the first time since I'd seen him in Washington, and despite the fast-lowering temperature, wore no overcoat.

"Miss Cuyler," he said, and I could hear the smile in his voice, even as I saw it reflected in his eyes. "You've certainly earned my respect. I haven't thanked you properly for all you've done."

I smiled back at him, but the smile, I knew, was bleak. "I was just wishing I'd been able to do more."

He shook his head vigorously, his eyes grave. "Don't regret," he said quietly.

I shook my head. "I could have saved him," I said slowly, "if I'd shot Don before—"

"Stop it!" he said sharply. "Thinking like that gets you nowhere. If you'd killed Cuyler, so he never had a chance to shoot at me, you'd have regretted that, too. Believe me."

"I hope you're right," I said, more out of politeness than conviction.

The President heard it in my voice. "I am right," he said tightly. "People do what's in their nature to do. Lee could have shouted a warning. He could have let me take that bullet. But he didn't. And maybe, ultimately—" He drew a deep breath, "he died because—he'd done what he was here to do."

It was my turn to look at him sharply. I knew now that Jack Kennedy had an introverted, spiritual side, apart from his hard-headed Irish practicality, but it wasn't a side that surfaced often. I was surprised he had shown it to me here. He saw that in my face and smiled at me.

I smiled ruefully back, thinking of Lee: The quick, long stride, the soft southern speech defiant with purpose... standing up against prejudice in a Texas coffee shop... his tenderness and need to be loved... and so very, very young to die...

"We never really knew who he was." I didn't realize I had spoken my thought aloud.

I thought the President would say, "It doesn't matter," but he didn't. Instead, he said, "History is kind to some people that way. We endow them in our imaginations with better qualities than they might actually have."

"Do you think Lee was that kind of person?" I was curious to hear his answer.

He shook his head, this time in bafflement. "I don't know," he said. "I knew him less than you did. But his daughters will grow up to be proud of him. Isn't that enough?"

I shook my head. "I can't help it. I think I'll always have regret."

The President nodded. "The trick is not to let it stop you from going on."

"Do *you* regret anything?" I had to know his answer. Did this man who was everyone's hero look back on *anything* and wish it could be different?

"Well, sure," he said quietly. I thought he would mention the Swedish girl, but he didn't. He looked at the dark shapes I had been looking at, and without looking back at me, he said, "I regret that I'm not—more like the person people think I am. A good husband. A family man, like Bobby."

I said nothing, and he turned to look sharply at me. "I'm not—proud of myself. I know these things I do are—well, wrong. Sinful, even. And I do love Jackie, in my way. But we both are what we are." He shook his head and smiled. "I don't know if I can change, anymore. Still, Lee gave his life for mine. I owe him that, I suppose. To try to change." He hesitated. "I really want to make things different, in the years to come."

Then he lifted his head again and laughed. "That has a nice ring to it—'the years to come'." His eyes were as blue as the calm summer waters off Cape Cod.

I smiled with him. There *would* be years for him now: Years of accomplishment, of peace, of change. Not the violence and chaos of the late 1960s. Once again, there was hope for the future.

He looked at me, and once more his face was serious. "I'll remember what we talked about."

I would remember, too. Hesitantly, I said, "No one should have to give up love, not even for the presidency. Even Presidents deserve to find love with the right woman."

His eyes were still a deep blue as he asked gently, "And how do you find it?"

I looked at him and said firmly, "You *look* for it. You believe in it. And," I added wryly, "you accept no substitutes until it comes to you."

He was silent for a moment. "I can't swear that I won't—but between what I owe you and Lee, I will try. I really will."

"That's more than enough, Mr. President."

Then he truly surprised me. He said abruptly, "How about staying here? With me?"

At first I thought in confusion that he was making a pass at me, but his face was serious. "You could be an advisor to the President." He gave a grin. "You know what's going to happen, what I have to be wary of. You could help make my second Administration a great one."

He was serious. His eyes were intent on my face, and they were once more gray. He was back to business.

I didn't even need to think about it. "Thank you," I said quietly, "but I really want to go back to my own time." If I even could.

But if I were really stuck, here, being part of the Kennedy Administration didn't appeal to me. I had saved his life. I wasn't going to save his ass. That was his problem now.

"Anyway," I said, trying to be diplomatic, "we've already changed so much in 1963, what I know probably isn't even relevant anymore."

He gave me one last look, and in it I read a goodbye to the kind of intimacy we'd had over that fast-receding weekend only six days before. When he raised his eyes again to look over the White House grounds, he was once more the all-powerful, unknowable President who would wave carelessly and smile to someone like me from his sleek Lincoln convertible while traveling down roads I could never follow. I felt a sadness that he too was receding from me, like all my other memories.

"You know," the President said, breaking into my train of thought, "all this time, I've always called you Miss Cuyler. Don't you think it's time I called you Cady?"

I tipped my head back and smiled at him engagingly. "Only," I said, "if I can call you Jack."

He was genuinely startled. He was so accustomed to deference and power. Then the Jack Kennedy of the peanut-butter crackers and bathroom confidences broke through, and he grinned at me. "Well, sure," he said. "Bobby'll have a heart attack, but you can call me Jack."

I tried, but the words stuck in my throat. I shook my head.

"What's wrong?"

"I can't say it," I said slowly. "I thought it would be—funny—to call you by your first name. But you're the President—and it's wrong to pretend you're just like everyone else."

He smiled at me ruefully, and I suddenly remembered the story from early in his presidency, when he met with former First Lady Eleanor Roosevelt. He opened a door to let her precede him into a room and she refused, saying, "You're the President."

"I keep forgetting," he had laughed.

And she answered softly, "You must never forget…"

I could never forget, either. And looking at Kennedy, I understood that by this time, the majesty of his office was like the air he breathed.

A moment later, though, his eyes twinkled in a most informal way. "By the way, I just finished meeting with Bobby and Mr. Hoover. We—er—used your suggestion." He looked like he was trying hard to repress a laugh.

I'd suggested to Bobby Kennedy on the plane that they try a little blackmail on J. Edgar Hoover, who blackmailed everyone else but had himself once been photographed in a dress and full makeup. "So you actually got hold of the photo?"

"We got hold of several. Some were really racy. I thought he was going to faint when he saw them." Now the President did start to laugh. "He agreed to resign, all right. Right away. And when I told him I thought he looked real cute in fishnet stockings—" his laughter grew to a roar, "well—Bobby had to help him to the door."

I broke into laughter as well. In a minute, tears were pouring down our faces. The specter of Hoover holding a sword over the President's head was almost as grim as the thought of the conspirators. I was glad I could help end it—and in such an entertaining way.

When we finally stopped laughing, there was an awkward silence. Then he snapped his fingers. "I believe you came here for a certain keepsake."

It took me a minute to remember myself. "The Bible!" I exclaimed. "George'll kill me if I don't bring it back. That is, if I can find a way to get back."

The President nodded, but before he could speak, the door opened again, and his secretary stepped out. "Mr. President," she said, "this lady came to speak to Miss Cuyler. I hope it's all right that I brought her here."

The President's eyes widened as he saw the woman walking behind. "That's fine," he said.

I turned. Sandra, pale but composed, was walking toward us. "Excuse me, Mr. President," she began.

"Mrs. Cuyler," he said warmly.

She went still paler. "You remember me?"

He smiled at her. "How could I possibly forget your hospitality?"

She began to laugh, a trifle hysterically.

The President, however, was ready to withdraw. "I understand you wish to speak to—er—Cady." He nodded at her, smiled again. "You have my sincere condolences. Whatever happened to him afterward, Don Cuyler was a good man during the war, and a good friend."

"Thank you," she said faintly.

He smiled again at me. "I'll be right back." And he was gone.

Sandra and I stood alone on the steps outside the Oval Office.

She looked at the steps, at the wide lawn, at the trees off in the distance, everywhere but at me. I felt the familiar tightness in my chest. My mother, it seems, would remain my mother.

I waited for her to speak.

She looked up, a hint of tears in her voice. "I—came to—" She stopped, shook her head. Composed herself. Started again. "I wanted to thank you. For everything you told me. For your encouragement. For your... example."

I looked up, genuinely startled. I thought she'd somehow divined that I had been an integral part of Don's death. She'd come to *thank me?*

I dared not say a word. I just nodded, encouraging her to continue. Haltingly, she did. "He—was a terrible man. You knew that. You knew—how he treated me. I was afraid to—to tell my family, or to run away. And with the baby coming—"

She gestured futilely. I understood. The baby would have trapped her even further, in a dangerous and hostile marriage. Until now, it was a baby she couldn't have wholeheartedly welcomed.

"The President," she started again, "he's arranging for—some additional funds... to help tide me over... and he'll make sure I get Don's Navy pension... it will help, Cady."

"Yes, I'm sure," I said.

She shook her head again. Angrily now. "I'm not saying what I want to!" She heaved a huge sigh. "I wanted you to know that—being around you has—taught me a lot about standing up for myself. I think—my life will be better because of it. The baby's, too."

She hesitated. "I was thinking—if I have a girl—I'd like to call her Cady. After you."

Tears stung my eyes. At that moment, I forgave my mother everything, everything. Every slight, every neglect, every childish act and stinging word, went by the wayside.

If I searched my memory I don't think I could have found one unhappy moment between us. The years of misunderstanding had been washed clean.

I was so proud of her.

"I think," I said after a pause, "that's just about the nicest compliment I ever got."

Unwittingly, I reached out to pat her stomach, to touch the child inside, to touch me inside her. Because I knew now that I would be all right too.

She saw my hand and didn't move away. "I hope—" she started again, "I really hope—if it's a girl—that she'll be just like you."

I looked up, my hand hovering over her mid-section, and smiled. "I wouldn't be at all surprised," I said.

And touched the baby whose life would be so much different, now. So much better.

There was a strange flash of light, and in an instant I understood what I'd done. *Two versions of the same person can't co-exist*, John had said to me, explaining why George couldn't go back to 1963.

I had set the wheels in motion myself. One touch of the me to come, and like it or not, I was on my way back.

Chapter Eighteen

THURSDAY, NOVEMBER 30, 2000

My head was pounding. My eyes actually hurt from the fluorescent light overhead. My arms and legs ached as though I'd just finished a bout with pneumonia.

I was back in the year 2000.

I staggered to my feet, feeling dizzy and very sick. This time I hadn't had one of John's anti-matter cocktails, and I felt considerably worse than the first time I'd time-traveled. The scanner was right in front of me, but I wasn't sure I could walk all the way through. Just beyond, John and George, their faces anxious, were waiting for me.

"Come on, Cady!" I heard John call encouragingly, as though from a mile away instead of just a few feet.

I rested for one moment against the metal detector. Walk through it, I thought, and I leave it all behind... Lee, the President, Sandra, Don... all in the past.

Let the dead bury their dead, said a verse in the Bible. I had never understood it before.

I understood it now.

I glanced behind me and saw nothing but the white walls of John's studio. The past was already past. All I had to do was walk into the present.

I drew deep breaths into my lungs and let my eyes and head clear.

John and George stood there... waiting.

I smiled weakly and stepped through the metal detector.

The moment I did, John rushed over to me. "Cady! You did it! You did it!"

George was just behind him. "Where's the Bible?" he shouted. "Give it to me!"

I stopped, reaching for the wall, my skin feeling clammy, my stomach heaving.

"Give it to me!" George insisted again, and in his haste he grabbed my arm and jiggled me. "Give it to me!"

I did. I vomited all over him.

* * *

John was still laughing ten minutes later when I finally lifted my head out of the bucket he'd hastily snatched up and offered to me.

"Thanks a lot," I said weakly. "That sure makes me feel better."

He managed, with difficulty, to stop himself, and as a kind of peace offering, I guess, handed me a cloth wrung out with cold water. "Sorry," he said. "But you should have seen my dad. Wish I had a picture of that!"

I looked around as I wiped my face and felt the stinging cold on my skin. The studio was empty except for us. The walls were as bright-white as ever, the whole atmosphere as sterile. For the first time ever, I noticed that the computer screen in the corner was dark.

The cloth felt wonderful on my forehead. The nausea had stopped. The room had stopped spinning. I was already beginning to feel better. John handed me a glass of cold water and I gargled, rinsing away the taste of vomit.

"Better?" he asked.

I nodded.

Now that I felt myself again, I was horribly embarrassed about vomiting in front of two men.

John was more concerned with something else. "You got hurt back there," he said, reaching out to touch my arm. I looked down; there were faint bruises up and down my arms, and on my legs. Don and his men had been anything but gentle, and being knocked down on the ship had taken its toll as well. Even though I'd had a week in 1963 to heal, there were still signs of what I'd been through. "We didn't think you'd really get hurt."

"They'll be gone in a day or two. Anyway… it was worth it."

He looked at me and shook his head softly, his green eyes warm on my face. "You did it, Cady… you really *did it*."

"I didn't get the Bible," I said ruefully. "That was the mission, after all… I failed, John."

He threw his head back and laughed. "The Bible was Dad's obsession, not mine. And not even his greatest one. You succeeded all right, Cady."

His eyes danced as I digested his words. "You didn't really think my dad would take all this trouble and all this work… just to pick up a Bible… did you?"

I almost staggered again as the truth finally flooded through my mind. "He wanted this, didn't he?" I said slowly. "He intended me to try to save the President… that was really the point, wasn't it?"

John nodded. I stood still, rocked by the implications. If he'd told me at the beginning… I shook my head. I could never have imagined myself pulling off such a mission. George had *wanted* me to get caught up in it. That was why he'd drilled me and rehearsed me so long—that's why he'd planted me right in the hub of the action, at ISI, which had to have been a CIA front operation, after all…

John nodded as he saw I suddenly understood all the implications. "You didn't look any too confident walking in here the first time. But my dad told me you were the one he'd been waiting for. He was sure you could pull it off. That you had the guts and the smarts and the—the persistence—to get it done, when no one else could."

I understood, suddenly. George had made the mistake so many others had made. "He thought I was Sheila," I murmured, almost to myself.

"No," John corrected me. "He knew Sheila was you."

Impossible, I thought. *That's impossible.* Mel had said it to me too, so long ago, and I'd dismissed it as ridiculous. Now, after everything I'd been through, I was at least willing to consider the possibility that he was right.

"Didn't *you* really know that, deep down inside?" he asked.

I shook my head, even more ruefully, and quoted softly, "I've always had the power to go back to Kansas…"

"You had it when you walked in here," John said calmly. "Maybe you just needed to get caught up in something bigger than you."

"Well, it was that," I agreed, handing back the cloth. "I still say George made a mistake. I was just an actress playing a part."

John shook his head tolerantly. "My dad doesn't make mistakes like that. He knew no actress could play Sheila like that and not *be* that, really. Plus, he knew about your family. He knew Don Cuyler, and he suspected you were a lot like him. In the good ways," he said hastily, as my eyebrows lifted. "Smart, courageous, good at getting things done. He said it was a gut feeling, choosing you. And he always goes with his gut."

"Yes, I know," I said dryly.

We'd reached the conference room, which for once was unlocked.

John sat me down at the big conference table. It was loaded with newspapers and news magazines, dozens or hundreds of them, some dating back to 1964, some as recent as this morning.

"We've been monitoring the changes while you've been gone," he said casually, waving at the table.

"How long have I really been gone?" I asked.

John looked at the calendar on his watch. "Mm—fourteen days. We phoned your mother and Craig, of course, told them you were holing up in the mountains working on your part—not exactly a lie—and you'll be able to go to Thanksgiving dinner tomorrow at your mother's house, if you feel—re-oriented enough." I raised an eyebrow, and he added, "It's Thursday, November 30th, in the year 2000. And I know Thanksgiving is over, but she wanted to cook."

"My mother?" I began, but he interrupted.

"Life has changed, Cady. Change the past, you change the future. Or didn't you realize that?"

"She's alive?" I whispered. "Are you telling me my mother's alive?"

"And well," John confirmed. "In fact, more well than you've ever seen her. I think you'll be pleasantly sur—"

"I can't believe it!" I got up swiftly. "I want to see her. Right now."

"I thought you would," John said calmly. He produced a fistful of keys. "Come on, I'll drive you over."

* * *

My equilibrium was almost completely restored by the time John made the final turn into Larchmont. The shooting pains in my arms and legs had subsided considerably, and I was doing some breathing exercises to try to calm my excitement.

"What happened to George?" I finally asked, as John made the last turn before Rockland Avenue.

"Well, once he changed clothes—" John began. We both giggled. John sobered. "He's probably a little overcome. Neither of us had much sleep, especially since your cell phone gave out."

"I lost it." I wasn't up to explaining it all right now. My heart was pounding strangely.

"We guessed that. Or had it taken from you. As soon as we got past November 22nd, George started combing through archives while I monitored you at the studio. You may have put him out of business," John added as he turned smoothly down Rockland, "now that the major political assassinations of the 1960's are all—"

I wasn't listening. He'd pulled close enough to my mother's house for me to run. I threw open the door and jumped out.

"Cady!"

I ran up the bowl of lawn to the front door and rang the bell long and hard, then pounded on the door itself. It was all I could do to restrain myself from shouting.

The door opened, and I was staring into the face of a tall, friendly-looking older man.

For a second I just gaped.

"Cady! Hello! Still in costume, I see. Come on in, honey." He turned to call over his shoulder, "Cady's back!"

I looked up into his face, and knowledge flooded into my mind from some secret door I'd never opened before. *Of course, this is Steve. My mother's second husband. Retired international businessman and all-around good guy. He and my mother have been married for years.*

"Hi, Steve," I said with a smile, and walked in feeling lighter than I ever remember feeling in my life.

From the kitchen issued a bouquet of beautiful smells: turkey, stuffing, and perhaps the makings of my favorite lemon pie. My mother's kitchen had never sent forth such inviting scents in the life I'd left behind…

"Hello, darling," my mother beamed as I walked into the kitchen, with John following. She didn't look at me as she rolled pastry dough. "With you in a minute." She was wrapped in a massive flowered apron—*of course, it's her favorite; she wears it all the time*—and her hands were covered in flour. She looked pretty, homey and… motherly.

I'd never seen her like that before.

She finished rolling out the dough and set aside the wooden roller, looking up to smile at me. As she caught sight of me, in the costume I hadn't yet removed, my hair still in a '60s flip, her smile faded. For a moment, there were tears in her eyes.

"Mom? Mom, what is it?" I moved toward her anxiously.

She shook her head, forcing a smile, and reached over to kiss me, careful to keep her flour-smudged apron from me. "Nothing, darling. Is that your costume from that play you were doing? You look lovely."

"Mom, you were crying."

She shook her head again. "For a second you just—reminded me so much of someone I—once knew. Back in Dallas." Our eyes met, and there was the same connection between us that I'd felt with the young Sandra Cuyler on the portico of the White House, not so very long ago.

I think my mother felt it, too. She looked at me, puzzled, shook her head once more, as if to clear out the memory, and turned to John. "Hello. You must be John. Sorry I can't shake hands right now."

I put an arm around my mother—she leaned into me while I kissed her cheek—as familiar, and yet as unfamiliar, as any scenario I could imagine. My mother beaming at me and welcoming my kiss? It was miraculous, and yet she accepted it as normal, long-held tradition. Would George and John and I be the only ones who could remember a different path that the world had once taken?

Clearly, my mother's alternate path had been much happier, much more fulfilled. "Now don't tell me you're not hungry," she scolded me, "because I'm making those mashed potatoes with all the trimmings and three different pies, and you'd just better be able to manage seconds!"

"I'll do my best, Mom," I promised, relief and happiness pouring through all my veins. It seemed as if even the light was brighter, tinted with contentment and a sense of security.

"You'll join us, too, John, won't you?" asked my mother, turning a smile on him that I could swear was almost flirtatious.

He glanced at me. "I'd love to, ma'am," he said hesitantly, "but my father and I were planning—"

"Bring your father, too," my mother said to my surprise. "I've heard a lot about him. Runs a bookstore, I believe?"

"He used to," John said, to my shock. "Now he's writing a novel about the Cold War."

"Good subject," my mother agreed placidly. She lifted a spoon. "Here, darling, taste the gravy. What do you think?"

Obediently I tasted. "Mom, it's delicious," I said. "Really. I can't remember—your ever making it better."

My mother turned smilingly to John. "You see, John? You and your father will be missing a treat."

"Well, we can't do that, ma'am," John said, not taking his eyes off me. "We'll be here. You can count on it."

I was a little dazed. I was part of a life I hadn't known, yet somehow I did—and I understood that in order to integrate this new life with the one I remembered, all I needed to do was open my mind and let the knowledge seep in. I didn't want to. I wanted to remain, for a little while, apart from it all, to remember 1963 as a place I had left only an hour or so before. And paradoxically, I also wanted to be part of this new life, this life which so far seemed to promise so much more.

"You know," John was saying to my mother, "Cady's never told me how she got her name. Why don't you?"

My mother finished stirring the gravy and began pouring it into a glass cup. "Oh, Cady was named after someone I met long ago, just before she was born."

"Yes?" John prompted her. "Someone you knew well?"

"No," my mother said, her voice that faraway tone often reserved for recollections of the distant past, "not well at all. My first husband—Cady's father—and I ran a sort of—well, boardinghouse—in Dallas. This young woman came to stay with us, just before Mr. Cuyler—"

John nodded.

My mother faced him, her back straight and her eyes steady on his. "You know who he was."

"Yes," John said gently.

"Well, this young woman stayed with us for a few days and then just—left. She was very—different. Not like the women I knew. I admired her and wanted my daughter to be like her. So I named Cady after her, hoping she'd—pick up some of those same qualities."

John glanced at me. "I'd say Cady's turned out a lot like that."

"I agree," said my mother, to my surprise. Then she shooed us out. "Go, you two! I have plenty more cooking to do. You're crowding me!"

John and I edged into the hall. "She's so happy," I said in a low voice. "She's alive and happy. I feel as though I've seen a miracle."

"And you made it happen," John reminded me. The warmth in his eyes was growing more purposeful. He gazed at me with a new focus that I knew meant my own days of loneliness and confusion might be drawing to a close… if I myself said yes to this new world and this new world order.

If I said yes now, though, it would close the door on 1963, and I still wasn't quite ready to do that…

"Come on upstairs," I said impulsively, even as John started to lean toward me. "I have something to show you."

Before he could reply I'd turned and whirled up the stairs to my old bedroom.

The room was just as I remembered it—and as I'd never seen it: Decorated in frilly pinks and whites, appropriate to the little girl I'd been, and filled with a lavish canopy bed and a desk and chair. There was a mirror on the closet door…

I moved toward it, letting my mind guide me where it wanted to go. In a moment I was inside the closet, reaching to the top shelf for a package wrapped in newspaper. My fingers couldn't… quite… reach…

"Help me!" I called to John.

Obligingly, he came in, reached up for the package and brought it down.

I led him out of the closet and seized the package, looking at it lovingly. The paper was crinkled newspaper. My mother had wrapped it that way herself to preserve it.

"Seems I brought it back after all," I said.

John looked at the package and at me, and his eyes widened. "You don't mean—?"

I nodded and slowly unwrapped the dusty newspaper, dropping it on the white eyelet coverlet on my bed. Underneath the newspaper was a tattered box that had once contained fine stationery. Atop the box was a neatly-labeled card: "Mrs. Sandra Cuyler, 224 Rockland Avenue, Larchmont, New York".

John's hands trembled as he gazed down at the box. I smiled mysteriously. I knew from the knowledge behind the secret door what we would find.

Carefully I lifted the lid. Underneath was an envelope, addressed to my mother. Under that, a white box.

I opened the envelope and shook out a letter. I held the sheet so that John could read the engraving, which read simply, "The White House". It was dated a week after my birth in 1964.

The letter was short and typewritten, but the signature was unmistakable. John gasped when he looked at it.

The letter read:

Dear Mrs. Cuyler,

Please accept my continuing condolences on the loss of your husband last November.

I am also delighted to congratulate you on the birth of your daughter, Catherine Marie. Mrs. Kennedy and I wish you and her all the happiness in the world.

I hope you won't mind our sending this little gift which I believe your new baby may someday find useful.

With my very best wishes,

John F. Kennedy

I looked at John. His face had gone ashen. I suddenly realized that for all his excitement about his time-travel machine, and his belief in the mission his father entrusted to me, he'd never really believed he'd see this.

Gently, I refolded the letter, returned it to its envelope and reached for the white box. Carefully, I took off the lid. Inside was a black tooled-leather book, the edges hand-sewn.

It looked as fresh as it had when careful hands had first wrapped it for mailing, thirty-six years before. It had a cross in gold leaf on the cover. And on the inside cover, stitched in black—

"—'JFK'," John said reverently, his fingertips gently caressing the initials. "Cady, who do you think originally took the Bible from Sarah Hughes?"

I thought of the people I'd known in 1963, and the answer rose surely in my mind.

"Stan Marchand," I said positively. "He was Don's personal henchman. Don must have sent him out to Love Field just to make sure Kennedy was really dead." I thought about it and shivered. "Maybe he was the final back-up, if Kennedy escaped ambush during the motorcade. Maybe he was supposed to wait for him at Air Force One, and just… blast him."

"Maybe."

"Stan was a kleptomaniac," I went on. "He took all kinds of things, all the time. Little things—pens, rubber bands. Sarah Hughes with the Bible in her hand would have been irresistible to him, and she handed it over so willingly, since he was acting officious… He would have loved that."

I looked again at the Bible. It really was a thing of beauty.

"How did you know it was here?" John asked curiously.

"Because," I said simply, "I asked him for it, at the White House. I told him about the experiment. But I came back before he could give me the Bible." I thought about it. "I guess the President wanted to keep his promise, so he sent the Bible to me through my mother, whom he'd been helping after my father died. He knew if he sent a baby gift my mother would see it as a thoughtful gesture and keep the Bible for me—and I'd get it sooner or later."

John shook his head, smiling.

"If I'm not mistaken," I said, gently turning to the title page, "yes, I thought he might have written a message—"

We stared at the page. In black ink only slightly faded from the years, there was a short, bold message: "To Cady, with admiration, thanks and RESPECT—Jack".

"He wrote it inside, instead of on the flyleaf," I said softly, "so my mother wouldn't notice it right away... but I'd find it. Eventually." I thought of something, and turned to John, hope singing in my heart. "John, he isn't still—"

"No, Cady," John said quietly. "He isn't still alive."

"I see," I said, feeling heaviness in my chest. Another loss. In a way, it was like losing him twice, when I'd never had the chance to say goodbye...

John was looking at the inscription. "Jack?" he said dubiously. "Cady, when you were in 1963, did you and the President—?"

I looked at him. He was turning a nice shade of cherry.

He couldn't be serious. He thought that the President and I had—? I could feel myself beginning to blush as well.

"That," I said, "is absolutely none of your business."

"Well, I don't blame you...

I mean, if you did—"

I averted my eyes and busied myself repacking the Bible in its box and then in the careful, years-old padding. How could I tell him—how I could tell anybody— that the little flutter I felt when I thought back to 1963 was due to Lee, a poor, scantily educated, married man twelve years younger than me? And that despite my admiration for him, I felt no flutter at all for the handsome, powerful and charismatic man who had occupied the White House with such flair?

I finished wrapping the paper over the old box, folding it in long strokes so it would stay flat. Nothing I could say would explain it. Not to him, nor to any other living soul. There are some secrets, after all, that should stay locked in a woman's heart.

At length I just looked up and gave a little shrug. "I guess," I said, "there's just some historic data in every period that has to stay a mystery."

And that was all I would say.

* * *

John would not let me go home to rest until George had a chance to 'debrief' me, but I was so weary and overwhelmed with what I'd already seen that he did agree to let me nap briefly on the couch in the lounge.

When I woke up 45 minutes later, George was waiting for me.

He looked as cheerfully grungy as ever, having changed into faded jeans, dark sweatshirt, and blue windbreaker. He smiled at me and held out his hand. "Well done, Cady. Very, very well done."

"You set me up," I told him, smiling nonetheless. "How did you know, George… how could you think I could really pull it off?"

He just smiled. "Maybe I just knew more about you than you did about yourself."

John interrupted. "Hey, no editorial comments. Let Cady tell her story."

He sat me down at the conference table, aimed a tiny tape recorder at me, clicked it on, checked the batteries, and said, "Come on, Cady. Start from the first day. Tell us everything."

I did. It took me over four hours, stopping frequently for John to change batteries and tapes, for snacks and water breaks and to stretch and move around. But by the end, I'd told it all… including my discovery of the Bible, tucked snugly away in my old bedroom.

I had expected George to jump out of his chair and demand the Bible once I finished, but he simply sat there, eyes fixed on the table. Finally, I said, "Do you want me to bring you the Bible, or do you want to pick it up?"

George, eyes half-closed, said lightly, "Didn't the President sign it for you?" I nodded. "Well, keep it then. To remember him."

This sounded so unlike George the Acquisitive. "Don't you want anything out of this at all?" I asked.

George opened his eyes all the way. "I got what I wanted. Now I don't have to feel guilty every time I think of him."

I looked at him quickly; he gazed back at me without blinking. "Do you know what it felt like every November? Every time I remembered I'd had a tip about the assassination and didn't act on it?" He saw that I was startled. "Oh, yeah. More than one, in fact. And I… didn't believe it. Thought it was crazy. Impossible. And after it happened… God, I'd have done anything to change it. But how can you change what's already happened?"

The grim look left his face, and he smiled at me. "Well, now you have. You've taken my guilt away, Cady. You've changed everything. That was what I really wanted."

For a moment, there was complete silence. John's face had a half-smile; he had known it all along. I was the only one who'd believed I was just chasing an artifact.

I felt stupid. And thankful they hadn't told me. I would never have taken on such a mission. Sometimes, when you just stumble into things, though, the most amazing things can happen.

I cast about for something to say, hoping to conceal the way I really felt, not ready to let go of 1963 yet. "Has the world really changed, since I went back? What about all those papers I saw on the table? Do they tell what happened?"

"You've got plenty of time to read them," John said calmly. "You're still between worlds. Don't try to catch up yet. For now, just change your clothes."

He left.

I opened the closet where I'd stored my jeans, my running shoes, shirt and my favorite peach sweater.

But the clothes hanging in the closet, though clearly mine, were not the clothes I had left here. Instead, hanging neatly on padded hangers I didn't remember seeing before, were obviously expensive white wool slacks, a soft cream cashmere sweater, and a narrow gold belt that probably cost about what my stepfather paid for one of his suits. On the floor of the closet were a big Gucci handbag and a pair of good-looking beige flats. Even the underwear looked expensive.

I changed into the new/old clothes, hanging the beige dress carefully on a hanger and stacking the slip, bra and girdle and nylons I'd worn underneath neatly on the chair next to it. The slacks and sweater not only fit beautifully, but conformed to my body as though I'd worn them many times before. I stopped and let my mind, once more, know something I hadn't known… and yes, the knowledge suddenly flooded in, I'd bought these myself in a designer boutique I admired in Manhattan but had never dared walk into, in my previous life.

When I'd finished dressing and wetting and brushing out my hair to its original style, I looked at myself in the mirror. The truth was I looked better than ever. Why? Well, expensive clothes and a good haircut helped—but had something else changed?

I turned to the handbag. Yes, it was mine. I opened the top zipper and began to plow through. The driver's license looked almost the same. The wallet was much nicer and newer than I usually carried, but its contents were less familiar.

There was a membership card for the Academy of Motion Picture Arts & Sciences—*hello? I thought—I'm a voting member, no less, of the group that gave out the Oscars?*—frequent flier cards—a number of platinum Visas and Mastercards—

My careful, frugal lifestyle had clearly been supplanted with something else, which I devoutly hoped I could afford.

Most intriguing of all was my key ring. Instead of my old key chain, I saw a shiny new one that held a number of keys, starting with my house in Tarrytown, which I obviously still owned. I thought back to my house and knew in my mind that the big colored travel posters I'd framed and hung on the walls when I'd never traveled anywhere had been supplanted by large framed color photos of me with various friends, shooting the rapids in Colorado, on the beach in Hawaii, exploring caves, tasting wine in French vineyards, hot-air ballooning in a puff of clouds.

John had been right: I was Sheila. Or more accurately, I was the Cady I'd always wanted to be, the Cady I'd deserved to be. And I'd become that woman by changing the past.

I felt a sense of accomplishment that outstripped anything I'd ever felt in my life before.

I looked back at the key ring. There was another set of house keys dangling from the ring. Could those be my keys for… my mind supplied the answer… the house I rented in Beverly Hills when I was filming on the West Coast?

Hm.

The little black keyless device for my car was still the same, though not quite as worn, and I smiled: I might have a more expensive lifestyle, but I still drove my blue Beetle. Some things, I thought contentedly, *would never change.*

Curious, I turned on my cell phone. The clipped feminine voice told me, "You have 16 messages," and played them for me.

All were from Craig, whom, I was relieved to realize, I'd never been married to, though he was still my agent, and as my agent, seemed to be much busier these days.

The messages were almost all the same, ranging from a courteous "Please call me" to "Cady, I'd like to hear from you soon" to an agitated "For God's sake, call me quick! It's urgent!"

Oh, all right, I thought, and I dialed his office.

He came on at once. "Oh, thank God! Are you okay?"

"Just fine," I said, surprised that he sounded so much… well, pleasanter. Maybe it was just as well we hadn't been married. "You called?"

"God, yes! Oh, Cady, you got it. I've been trying to reach you for days… the shooting's going to start in just over three weeks and they need you for wardrobe fittings and makeup and hair tests—when can you meet with them?"

"That's great, Craig," I said automatically, because to an actress, time traveler or not, the news that she 'got' anything was always a cause for wild rejoicing. "Tell you what. I just got—out—of where I was. I'm on my way home. Let me get there and take a quick look at my mail and I'll call you back."

"Terrific, Cady. I'm so excited about this. This is a whole new level for you."

Before I hung up, I couldn't resist teasing him. "You know, Craig, I had the strangest dream while I was up there. I dreamed that—that you and I were… well, married."

There was a pause. An uncomfortable laugh. "Well, that'll be news to Denise," Craig said, trying to sound light. "Call me soon, okay?"

Right. Denise, the dental hygienist, whom Craig had married three years before. I sent a projection-screen TV as a wedding gift.

John didn't press me to talk on the way home. I was glad; I was suddenly overwhelmingly weary. I glanced idly out the window at the quiet streets I was so accustomed to. They were the same, but somehow—unaccountably different. Or was it just me who was different? Was I just reacting like any normal traveler returning home after a prolonged vacation, seeing anew the place I was used to?

And what was this mysterious job I'd just won? Why was Craig so excited about it?

John pulled into my driveway and turned off the ignition, then took my house key from me and opened the front door.

Home was the same… but different. The walls were crammed, not just with books, but with those photos I'd remembered, and as I looked at them I saw the joy of every adventure in my face. Oh, yes, life had changed.

I was so busy examining the walls that I bumped into a coffee table, accidentally knocking over a thick hardbound book. John bent to pick it up. Letters spelling *The Fire Storm* were outlined in swirling red, and beneath it were photos of—I gasped—President Kennedy and Lee Oswald. The inside cover indicated that it was "the complete story of the remarkable weekend of November 22nd through November 24th, 1963, when President Kennedy was rescued from certain assassination by the heroic actions of former Marine Lee Oswald, and their odyssey together, which ended in Oswald's tragic death in New Orleans, shielding Kennedy from gunfire, and the arrests and convictions of the team who had plotted to kill the president."

The book had been thickly paper-clipped, and I'd stuck in a letter as a bookmark. The letter was from Craig on his office stationery: "Cady, the book was a huge hit when it came out in 1966. Apparently, a few witnesses remember a young woman traveling with Oswald, and their descriptions fit you remarkably well. It's a great role—be ready to meet with them Tuesday."

"And did you meet with them?" John asked, accepting the strange duality that apparently allowed me to recall both the old and the new, reconstructed pasts together.

"Yes," I said slowly. "To play a role that's really—hm—myself."

I thought of the two men I'd left behind, one in New Orleans, one in Washington. I would learn, I was sure, what had happened to them—and to us all—in due time. Right now, I wanted to savor the changes I could feel in myself, that leap to the place where I had always secretly known what I wanted and deserved to be...

And I wanted to savor the knowledge that the man with me was, by virtue of his brilliance, his warmth and his kindness, the man I deserved to be with. Because I suddenly understood what Mel had said to me weeks ago, and John again today: That Sheila was me, that I'd always had the power to do what I did. It took an adventure in the past to make clear to me how much I deserved my future.

It was a future I no longer dreaded. In fact, I would actively welcome it. But I wondered if there could ever be a portal to the past again...

"John, will you keep the time machine?"

He smiled like a Cheshire cat. "Sure. You never know when we might need it. There are more priceless artifacts out there, and someone will need to retrieve them." He saw the wild hope on my face and promptly quenched it. "Cady, you can't go back to 1963 again. You've left your imprint there. The past has a memory, too."

I'm sure he saw my face fall, because he asked, "Do you really want to do more time travel? Do you really want to leave here again?"

He looked at me wistfully. *He really liked me*, I realized. He had always liked me. I'd been so busy constructing reasons why I wasn't the woman everyone thought I was that I hadn't seen it. Hadn't felt I deserved it.

This was the end of the road for me, I knew. It meant accepting my future, but also slamming the door on the past. I still didn't feel ready to do it. I understood now why my mother, in another life, had clutched so hard at the past. There was so much there that was so sweet, so poignant...

For the first time that I could remember in my life, tears began to pour down my face, heedlessly, faster and faster, as though cleansing me and releasing me of all that I had lived through in these last astonishing weeks. I stood there sobbing, unable even to reach for the handkerchief John whipped out, my grief for all of us—my father, JFK and Lee—seemingly bottomless.

It was so easy to cry, when someone was there to be strong for you.

John reached over and pulled me to him and rocked me while I cried out all the pain and regret and, yes, guilt. Knowing some things were probably inevitable didn't make it easier to face them. Wishing to change the outcome never helped; all it did was postpone and magnify the grief.

I knew, even through my tears, that I was going to release it all, release it now, and never look back.

Gradually, the crying lessened, until I had almost stopped. I looked up at John, whose face was very close. And suddenly, without thinking, I lifted my lips to his.

He was startled, but only for a moment, and in the next moment I could feel his arms tightening around me, sheltering and nurturing. For a guy who sat behind a computer all day, he turned out to be one terrific kisser.

I came up for air reluctantly a few minutes later.

"What are you thinking?" he asked, as I felt a ridiculous grin spread across my face.

"I'm thinking… that it's nice not to know what the future holds," I said, wrapping myself about him even closer.

He bent down to kiss me again and whispered words no one had ever spoken to me in my life.

"Welcome home," he said.

EPILOGUE

The 1960's will be remembered for remarkable technological and social progress and for the news stories that transfigured a nation:

LEE OSWALD became a national hero for his role in saving the President from assassination and helping to break the ring of assassination conspirators. His daring, dangerous work during the weekend of November 22–24, 1963 won him, posthumously, both the Presidential Medal of Freedom and *Time* Magazine's highest accolade, 1963 Man of the Year. In addition, during the week following his death, his Marine discharge, which had originally been honorable, then downgraded to dishonorable, was mysteriously restored to an honorable discharge.

President Kennedy himself insisted that Oswald be buried at Arlington National Cemetery, and quietly visited the site two weeks after the funeral to lay a wreath on the grave. Oswald's modest gravesite attracts thousands of visitors every year. They come to pray, and to view and photograph his headstone, which reads simply "LEE HARVEY OSWALD, 1939–1963, U.S. MARINE & PATRIOT".

GUY BANISTER, CLAY SHAW, and DAVID FERRIE were indicted as co-conspirators in the plot to kill the President. The three were tried and convicted in the spring of 1964. Among the key documents used by the prosecution to prove their guilt were 'The Oswald Papers', the ragged collection of photographic files secreted by Lee Oswald in his hideout in New Orleans and retrieved later at the cost of his life. The jury foreman said later that on the strength of that evidence alone, they were able to convict 'The New Orleans Three'. Banister, Shaw and Ferrie were sentenced to death and executed in New Orleans in July 1964.

A smaller, less conspicuous trial in 1964 was the trial of STAN MARCHAND, former top salesman for Dallas import/export company Import Spirits International, Inc. Marchand, one of the henchmen who took Oswald and Kennedy prisoner in Texas and forced them across the Gulf of Mexico to New Orleans, was convicted in less than an hour of conspiracy and attempted murder and sentenced to death. His attorneys asked for clemency, and his sentence was commuted by President Kennedy to life imprisonment. Three years later, Marchand was stabbed to death in his jail cell by a fellow prisoner for stealing the prisoner's cigarettes.

JACK RUBY, who murdered conspirator DON CUYLER in the New Orleans Police Department, pleaded guilty but offered to work with the Justice Department to escape execution. His contribution to their investigation helped secure the indictments of eight more conspirators in the plot to kill the President, including Miami and Dallas gunrunners and CIA paymasters with long histories of organizing assassination teams for Operation Mongoose. Ruby was given a two-year suspended sentence and was last seen in May 1965 in dark glasses, boarding a plane bound for Israel.

PRESIDENT JOHN F. KENNEDY won a landslide victory in the 1964 presidential election, in part because of the thwarted attempt on his life and the ensuing surge in his personal popularity. His overriding concern in office until 1965 was the removal of U.S. advisors from Vietnam, all of whom returned home by January 1966. One hundred and eight men were killed in their advisory capacities.

Relations with the Soviet Union and the worsening economy dominated Kennedy's second term. Despite the enormous strides Kennedy made in his foreign-relations policies, he could not avert the crash of certain large American companies, many of whom were dependent on government defense contracts for much of their profits. Kennedy tried to ease the way for these companies by using adaptations of their expensive technology in the burgeoning space program, which benefited enormously from the combined efforts of the Soviet Union and the United States.

The famous 1968 moon launch was the first completely cooperative effort for the two countries, which featured two Americans and two Russians planting flags from their two countries on the moon's surface. As the world watched, they repeated the now-famous phrase in both English and Russian: "In friendship... in harmony... in peace."

President Kennedy scored a particular triumph in his eventual detente with Fidel Castro. With U.S.-Soviet relations becoming easier and more open, Castro found himself on the opposite side of the fence from the two world super-powers. As Kennedy slowly persuaded Khrushchev that their respective countries belonged in cooperation, not contention, Castro began to panic. The Soviets withdrew their support for Castro's regime in early 1966. Shortly after, Castro asked for a conference in Montreal with Kennedy, who agreed to meet, but once there, dictated the terms: All Cuban political prisoners released and permitted to emigrate to the U.S. or any country they chose which agreed to accept them, political and personal freedoms restored to all citizens of Cuba, and most important, democratic rule, or the embargo of the U.S. would become the embargo of the world.

Castro, with no other choice, agreed. He still had enough support on the island, however, to be elected its first democratic President, a post he continues to hold today.

The world well remembers his presence at the 1968 Olympic Games in Mexico City. We also remember Kennedy's gracious bow to Castro when a young Cuban swimmer beat American MARK SPITZ in the 400-meter freestyle race.

Civil rights became the third important prong of Kennedy's second Administration. The Civil Rights Act he sent to Congress in December 1963 was passed and signed in mid-1964. The President traveled extensively in the South in support of the bill, speaking at rallies and lecture halls. Where once he would have been booed off the stage, he was now invariably greeted with applause and cheers. And largely due to his own personal commitment, the South allowed their black citizens to rise in stature, for the most part peacefully. In the rural South, this led to greater prosperity than has occurred since before the Civil War.

The former President became an international ambassador and spent the ensuing years traveling the globe as a United States emissary. He also weathered a storm of controversy in the early '70's, when women claiming to have been his lovers began to step forward to tell their stories. Papers such as *The Washington Post* , edited by his good friend BEN BRADLEE, never printed even hints of these stories, though other papers, less friendly to the Kennedys, did, in big splashy headlines. There have been rumors, however, that these 'true confessions', as other press people dubbed them, had been carefully held back from the public until Kennedy finished his second term and was politically invulnerable. The Kennedy family has consistently refused to comment.

Kennedy also wrote several nonfiction books about his White House years, all of which enhanced his popularity even more. There have been consistent rumors that the bulk of the writing was done, not by Kennedy, but by his prized political advisor, TED SORENSEN.

Surprisingly, no one seems to believe that Kennedy's one attempt at popular fiction required a ghostwriter. An alternative-history novel written in 1974, it was titled *Decade of Darkness*, and traced a scenario beginning with the assassination of a Kennedy-like President in 1963 and all of its imagined consequences, ranging from an unpopular, dragged-out war in Vietnam to the scandal of a break-in at the Watergate Hotel that eventually toppled his onetime political rival, who greatly resembled RICHARD NIXON, from the Presidency. The book detailed the divisiveness of opinions in the country that tore it apart, the rise of drug use and disillusion among young people, and the assassinations of a popular civil-rights leader who resembled DR. MARTIN LUTHER KING and the President's senator brother in 1968.

Despite Kennedy's continuing popularity, the book didn't sell well. Critics hailed it as well written and imaginative but called the subject matter "depressing beyond belief". One critic wrote, "Too bad a man of Kennedy's optimism and clear-headedness can even envision such a downward spiral for the country. Like Orwell's *1984*, it reminds us of how lucky we are to be what we are—and how easily we might have become something else." Unlike the other Kennedy books, *Decade of Darkness* quietly vanished from bookstores only a few months after publication. Today, copies of its first—and only—edition are collectors' items.

A minor story that was reported by *The Washington Post* involved the disappearance of President Kennedy's personal leather-bound Bible in July 1964. The President's staff was upset by the loss of the Bible; however, the President appeared curiously unconcerned. He advised reporters to forget about it. As of the year 2000, the Kennedy Library in Boston has not recovered the Bible.

JACKIE KENNEDY continued to be the country's most glamorous and most photographed woman and gave birth safely, in 1965, to a daughter, Elizabeth Victoria, whom they called Beth.

Despite their seemingly happy marriage, continuing tension over her husband's infidelities led to the First Lady's decision to seek a divorce, shortly after they left the White House in early 1969. Mrs. Kennedy moved with her children to Boston, within easy distance of the former President, who lived in the Kennedy family compound at Hyannisport during his infrequent hiatuses from Washington and his foreign travels.

In the late 1970's, Kennedy became re-acquainted with a Swedish woman he'd known briefly during his travels in Europe, before his marriage. She had been recently widowed. Now, divorced and available, he fell in love with her. His friends hailed the relationship as 'the real thing' and rejoiced in the couple's happiness together. They were to be married at the Kennedy compound in Hyannisport at the end of the summer of 1979.

A week before the wedding, Kennedy went sailing in the waters off Chappaquiddick Island. He had intended to take his fiancée with him, as he usually did, but she had last-minute wedding chores and could not spare the time. Knowing how he loved the ocean, she suggested that just this once, he go alone. He did. As he was coming back in the late afternoon, a storm blew up, and the boat capsized. Kennedy fell into the roiling waters, and the heavy mast of the boat came down on his head, knocking him unconscious. He drowned at the age of 62.

His untimely and tragic death shattered his family and brought tributes from the leaders of every country in the world. His Swedish fiancée never remarried.

Jackie Kennedy remarried in 1971. Her new husband, a wealthy but low-key designer and antique collector, built her a beautiful new house in the heart of the Virginia horse country. When asked what his greatest attraction was, Jackie—obviously mindful of her first husband's many siblings and the unusual influence of his family—answered crisply, "He's an orphan."

ROBERT KENNEDY continued to serve as Attorney General in his brother's second term. He refused his brother's offer to become Secretary of State, preferring instead to continue his war on organized crime. His efforts eventually broke the grip of four nationally known syndicate 'families' and virtually destroyed them.

An attempt on his life in 1966 was traced to JIMMY HOFFA, whom Kennedy successfully prosecuted again, this time winning both a guilty verdict and life imprisonment for the famous Teamster president. Hoffa was sent to a maximum-security prison in California, where in 1977 he claimed to have had a religious conversion and became a born-again Christian. He later took instruction for the ministry and led prayer groups and Bible classes among his fellow prisoners. He died peacefully in his sleep in April 1986.

ROBERT KENNEDY and his wife Ethel had two more children after his brother left office, for a total of thirteen altogether. Kennedy decided not to run for President in 1968, telling reporters with uncharacteristic wit that he didn't think the White House was large enough to accommodate his family. (This led to a terrific private scandal in the Kennedy family, where it was hinted he was letting down the side by refusing the role his father had envisioned for him.) He concentrated instead on the war against crime in his role as the new Director of the FBI.

His interest in civil rights, which had always run deeper than his brother's, surfaced with great passion after the 1972 election, when he joined Dr. Martin Luther King in the drive to wipe out the Ku Klux Klan. His Virginia home, Hickory Hill, was firebombed in 1973, and in rescuing his children from the debris, he was hit by a falling beam, which severed his spine and made him a paraplegic. Today, he is confined to a wheelchair, but continues to devote himself to civil rights and his children—eight of whom have followed in his footsteps and taken law degrees.

J. EDGAR HOOVER unexpectedly resigned from his position as Director of the FBI in late 1963. When he later attempted to win back his position, in what some insiders hint was an attempt to blackmail the Kennedys, he was indicted as an accessory in the assassination conspiracy. He was prosecuted by Robert Kennedy in some of the most riveting legal proceedings Washington insiders have ever seen. Millions cheered when Hoover—stripped of his heroic status, exposed with his ugly secret files—was sentenced to life imprisonment. He died in Leavenworth in 1975. The Justice Department took possession of his secret files. There have been rumors that since the Kennedys left the White House, many of those files relating to Jack and Bobby Kennedy are missing.

LYNDON JOHNSON was suspected by many Americans of being part of the assassination conspiracy, but he quietly resigned the office of Vice-President four months later, at which time he was replaced by Eugene McCarthy. While Johnson was never mentioned as a conspirator or indicted, several previous scandals in his political life came back to haunt him during the Congressional hearings. He never worked in public service again and eventually filed for bankruptcy. He died at his ranch in Texas in 1971.

The CIA was dissolved as an agency by 1964, and its primary functions were assigned to the military. Since that time, despite Kennedy's—and subsequent Presidents'—attempts to diffuse its influence, certain military personnel appear to be operating in the same covert manner.

CAROLINE KENNEDY graduated from Radcliffe College and earned her law degree at Harvard Law School. Following in the footsteps of her father and uncles, she became a United States Senator in 1988.

JOHN KENNEDY, JR. earned his law degree as well, but then opted for a career as a political journalist, working under editor Ben Bradlee, a longtime Kennedy family friend, on *The Washington Post*. Later he switched to broadcast journalism, where his stunning good looks and easygoing interview style helped him become one of the nation's best-known on-camera talents. He has reluctantly but graciously acceded to his father's inexplicable but implacable wish that he never set foot in an airplane.

BETH KENNEDY became a free-lance model and married and divorced twice before the age of 26. While she was often seen with her father at his home on Hyannisport, it is rumored that she is not on speaking terms with her mother.

In 1966, a young journalist named CARL BERNSTEIN published a book, *The Fire Storm,* about the 1963 plot to kill the President. It detailed for the first time Oswald's penetration of the plot, his secret alliances with the intelligence community and his work to defeat the plotters and their sponsors and save JFK. Though critics hailed the book as a much-deserved tribute to Oswald, they questioned the accuracy of a few minor details, including Bernstein's claim that during Oswald's flight from Dallas with JFK, he was seen traveling with a woman. No such woman has ever stepped forward to assert that she was Oswald's traveling companion during that weekend. Despite that, the book touched such a chord with the American people that it became a national non-fiction bestseller and won the 1967 Pulitzer Prize.

The 2001 movie version of *The Fire Storm* did even more to immortalize Oswald in the eyes of the public. Major movie stars fought to play Oswald, a part which went finally to English actor GARY OLDMAN, who despite being some years older than the real Oswald, scored a sensation in the role. The other surprise was CATHERINE CUYLER, an actress who had started in daytime drama but turned in a remarkable performance as the anonymous woman JFK and Oswald traveled with on their flight to New Orleans. When asked how she could so capture the essence of this virtually unknown woman, she answered demurely that she felt as though she'd lived through it herself. The film's publicity handouts noted that among other interesting coincidences, she had been born in New York City on the very day that the 'New Orleans Three' had been executed. The film's brilliant special effects were created by F/X genius JOHN STAUB. Oldman, Cuyler and director OLIVER STONE all earned Oscars for their work in the film, and it became a cornerstone of all of their careers.

The Oswald Papers, Lee Oswald's famous photographic copies of files from the New Orleans offices of Guy Banister, which he had hidden in a tiny cubbyhole in a local garage, were auctioned at Christie's in late 2001. Bidding was intense and elevated beyond anyone's expectations. When the gavel came down at last, a tall rumpled man in the corner, slouched in a leather aviator's jacket and shielding his eyes behind dark glasses, had agreed to pay $2.1-million for the collection. He told reporters later that he would have paid twice as much. When asked whether he would eventually donate them to the National Archives, he abruptly ended the questioning.

In 1965, in a public-spirited gesture to the people of Dallas, Dallas city officials decreed that part of Dealey Plaza be turned into a children's park. They tore down part of the parking lot in the freight yard, as well as the picket fence separating the lot from the grassy knoll in front. Children gather there often to play baseball. Railroad men complain it's dangerous on the knoll—at any moment, they could be hit by flying baseballs.

November 22, 1963 was the subject 30 years later of an evening-long news special on CNN. Reporters interviewed residents of Dallas and New Orleans and other parts of the country, about their reactions, their memories, and their feelings about that most pivotal day in American history.

One older man summed up the mood of the country succinctly. "It could have been a real terrible day, couldn't it?" he said to CNN reporter John F. Kennedy, Jr. "I mean, imagine if they'd really done what they was plannin' to do—shoot your father, take over the country, go to war with Cuba! We owe a lot to that Oswald boy. Terrible that he had to die, but at least he was there."

To which JFK, Jr., signing off, said simply, "Thank God."

A Final Word from the Authors:
TWENTY YEARS LATER...

In 2003, we published the first edition of *Forward to Camelot,* a novel we co-wrote about a young woman's adventures traveling through time to Dallas in 1963. The story opened in October of 2000, which at the time was the recent past for us, though we'd actually started developing the story in the late 1990's.

The original edition of *Forward to Camelot* ran almost 500 pages, and we self-published it after 50 (seriously, fifty) literary agents turned down the chance to represent it for traditional publishing.

By 2003, many people believed JFK had been killed as the result of a conspiracy, but most didn't go around talking about it, lest they be labeled 'conspiracy theorists'. Since so many of the files on the assassination were still sealed, we didn't know nearly as much then as we've learned since. So, it could be both lonely and intimidating to start trumpeting our beliefs in print.

We did it anyway.

Ten years later, on the 50th anniversary of the assassination, Drake Valley Press brought out a new edition of the book in a shorter, leaner form, as *Forward to Camelot: 50th Anniversary Edition.* For this edition, we corrected some minor historical errors from the first edition and cut some 25,000 extraneous words. The story and its message remained the same, but now it was tighter and more powerful.

At this point, 60 years after the assassination, with many of the sealed files now open to the public, we know positively that the CIA was involved—and likely instrumental—in the planning and execution of this monstrous crime. We had theorized in 2003, based on what we knew then, that David Atlee Phillips, a career CIA operative, had planned it and been deeply involved in carrying it out. At the time it was only a theory, but we believed it so strongly that we made one of our main characters, Don Cuyler, a ringer for Phillips in looks and personality—and the main villain behind the plot. What we learned later was that Phillips *did* spearhead the plans for the assassination and brought together some of the key players. Once again, we were proven right.

Many incidents in the novel are historically true and took place in the time and manner we describe in the novel, though we did make adjustments to fit them into the story. We believed then—and now know for certain—that Lee Harvey Oswald, far from being the 'lone assassin', was not only completely innocent of JFK's murder but also likely involved in a counterplot on November 22nd to try to save Kennedy's life. This is all documented fact, easily searchable in JFK assassination records.

What remains, after twenty years of involvement with this topic, is our passion for the story and for what we believe is the most accurate portrait of both JFK and Lee Harvey Oswald that's ever been attempted in a fictional setting. We're proud that our instincts have proven right and that the novel remains memorable to its fans and accessible now to a new generation of readers.

We hope you enjoy this latest edition, and we plan to continue 'talking Kennedy' for as long as anyone wants us to.

A Tip of the Hat

… to the people who made the journey with us on Forward to Camelot: Our heartfelt thanks to you all, for helping us reach a new generation of readers:

To sam_4321, my great Fiverr connection, for his beautiful formatting and typesetting of this new edition, and for his amazing work on the cover.

To Ross Matthei at the John F. Kennedy Library in Boston for photo images and clearances.

To the beta readers who wouldn't let us quit, no matter how much we wanted to, as times.

And especially to the readers since 2003 who have loved this story of what 'might have been'—this new, re-edited edition is for you.

ABOUT THE AUTHORS

SUSAN SLOATE is the author or co-author of 24 published books, including 2 previous editions of *Forward to Camelot,* the #2 Amazon bestseller and Hot New Release *Stealing Fire and Realizing You* (with Ron Doades), for which she invented a new genre: the self-help novel. The original 2003 edition of *Forward to Camelot* went to #6 on Amazon, was honored in 3 literary competitions and was optioned by a Hollywood company for film production.

Susan has also written 17 published books of young-adult fiction and non-fiction, including the children's biography *Ray Charles: Find Another Way,* which won the silver medal in the 2007 Children's Moonbeam Awards. *Mysteries Unwrapped:* The Secrets of Alcatraz led to her 2009 appearance on the TV series MysteryQuest for The History Channel. She has also been a sportswriter and a screenwriter, edited the popular *Kyle & Corey* young-adult book series, managed two political campaigns and founded an author's festival in her hometown outside Charleston, SC. Visit her at https://susansloate.com.

A Bronx native, KEVIN FINN began his professional writing career as a television news- and sportswriter just six months out of high school, moving on to produce & report for daily news shows, features, documentaries and live sports events. Over the past thirty years, he's established himself as a screenwriter and has mentored young writers for the American Film Institute's Writer's Workshop Program, as well as being a noted freelance script consultant and a novelist.

Equally adept as a cameraman and editor, he currently produces and films local media content in the Princeton, NJ, area, while continuing to mentor new and younger writers, including the heralded web series *The News Kids.* His first Young Adult novel, 200 METERS, will be published later in 2016, and the long-awaited novel BANNERS OVER BROOKLYN is scheduled for release early in 2017.

Follow Kevin on Twitter @finnkv.

Additional Titles by Susan Sloate

Realizing You (with Ron Doades) CreateSpace,2013

Stealing Fire Covfefe Press, 2018

Amelia Earhart: Challenging the Skies (Great Lives series) Fawcett, 2011

Abraham Lincoln: The Freedom President (Great Lives series) Fawcett, 2010

Ray Charles: Young Musician (Childhood of Famous Americans series) Simon & Schuster, 2008

Ray Charles: Find Another Way! Bearport Press, 2006

www.ingramcontent.com/pod-product-compliance
Lightning Source LLC
Chambersburg PA
CBHW022209010726
47493CB00002B/486